Book 15 – PROSPERO BURNS
Dan Abnett

Book 16 – AGE OF DARKNESS
edited by Christian Dunn

Book 17 – THE OUTCAST DEAD
Graham McNeill

Book 18 – DELIVERANCE LOST
Gav Thorpe

Book 19 – KNOW NO FEAR
Dan Abnett

Book 20 – THE PRIMARCHS
edited by Christian Dunn

Order the full range of Horus Heresy novels from
www.blacklibrary.com

THE HORUS HERESY

THE PRIMARCHS

Edited by Christian Dunn

BLACK LIBRARY

A BLACK LIBRARY PUBLICATION

First published in Great Britain in 2012 by
Black Library,
Games Workshop Ltd.,
Willow Road, Nottingham,
NG7 2WS, UK.

10 9 8 7 6 5 4 3 2

Cover and page 1 illustration by Neil Roberts.

A CIP record for this book is available from the British Library.

UK ISBN13: 978 1 84970 207 2
US ISBN13: 978 1 84970 208 9

See the Black Library on the internet at

www.blacklibrary.com

Find out more about Games Workshop
and the world of Warhammer 40,000 at

www.games-workshop.com

Printed and bound by CPI Group (UK) Ltd, Croydon, CR0 4YY

THE HORUS HERESY

It is a time of legend.

The galaxy is in flames. The Emperor's glorious vision for humanity is in ruins. His favoured son, Horus, has turned from his father's light and embraced Chaos.

His armies, the mighty and redoubtable Space Marines, are locked in a brutal civil war. Once, these ultimate warriors fought side by side as brothers, protecting the galaxy and bringing mankind back into the Emperor's light.
Now they are divided.

Some remain loyal to the Emperor, whilst others have sided with the Warmaster. Pre-eminent amongst them, the leaders of their thousands-strong Legions, are the primarchs. Magnificent, superhuman beings, they are the crowning achievement of the Emperor's genetic science. Thrust into battle against one another, victory is uncertain for either side.

Worlds are burning. At Isstvan V, Horus dealt a vicious blow and three loyal Legions were all but destroyed. War was begun, a conflict that will engulf all mankind in fire. Treachery and betrayal have usurped honour and nobility. Assassins lurk in every shadow. Armies are gathering.
All must choose a side or die.

Horus musters his armada, Terra itself the object of his wrath. Seated upon the Golden Throne, the Emperor waits for his wayward son to return. But his true enemy is Chaos, a primordial force that seeks to enslave mankind to its capricious whims.

The screams of the innocent, the pleas of the righteous resound to the cruel laughter of Dark Gods. Suffering and damnation await all should the Emperor fail
and the war be lost.

The age of knowledge and enlightenment has ended.
The Age of Darkness has begun.

CONTENTS

THE REFLECTION CRACK'D

Graham McNeill

~ DRAMATIS PERSONAE ~

The III Legion 'Emperor's Children'

FULGRIM	Primarch
LUCIUS	Captain
EIDOLON	Lord Commander
JULIUS KAESORON	First Captain
MARIUS VAIROSEAN	Captain of the Kakophoni
KRYSANDER	Captain, 9th Company
KALIMOS	Captain, 17th Company
RUEN	Captain, 21st Company
DAIMON	Captain
ABRANXE	Captain
HELITON	Captain
FABIUS	Chief Apothecary

1

HE DID NOT dream, he never dreamed, yet this was, inescapably, a dream. It had to be. *La Fenice* was a forbidden place now, and Lucius knew better than to ignore the word of his primarch. In the time before their awakening, such disobedience would have been foolhardy. Now it was a death sentence.

Yes, this was most definitely a dream.

At least he hoped so.

Lucius was alone, and he did not like to be alone. He was a warrior who thrived on the adoration of others, and this place was bereft of any admirers but the dead. Hundreds of bodies lay strewn around like gutted piscine lifeforms, twisted by the manner of their death, and every face belied the horror of their mutilations and defilements.

They had died in agony, yet had welcomed every touch of the blade, every clawed hand that burst eyeballs and tore out tongues. This was a theatre of corpses, yet it was not an unpleasant place in which to find himself walking. Though the dead surrounded him, *La Fenice* felt abandoned. It felt dark and empty, like a mausoleum in the darkest watches of the night. Life had once paraded before its audiences on the arched proscenium, its glorious vibrancy celebrated, its heroes lauded and its absurdities mocked, but now it was a bloody reflection of a time long passed.

The wondrous mural of Serena d'Angelus was all but invisible on the ceiling, its exotic depictions of ancient debaucheries hidden behind a pall of soot and smoke stains. Fires had burned here, and the tang of roasted fat and hair still hung as a scent on the air. Lucius barely noticed it, too faint and too dissipated to pique much of his interest.

Lucius was unarmed, and he felt the lack of a weapon acutely. He was a swordsman without a sword, and it felt as though his limbs were incomplete. Neither was he clad in armour. His luxuriantly painted war plate had been recoloured in a manner more pleasing to the eye, its drab hues and pedestrian ornamentation exaggerated and embellished in a manner more appropriate to a warrior of his skill and standing.

He was as close to naked as it was possible for a warrior to be.

He shouldn't be here, and he looked for a way out.

The doors were locked and sealed shut from the outside. As they had been after the primarch had paid one last visit to *La Fenice* in the wake of the massacre of Ferrus Manus and his allies. Fulgrim had ordered the doors sealed for all time, and none in the Emperor's Children had dared gainsay him.

So why had he risked coming here, even if only in a dream?

Lucius did not know, yet he felt as though he had been summoned to this place, as though an unheard, yet insistent voice had been calling to him. It seemed as though it had been calling to him for weeks, but had only now grown enough in power to be heeded.

If he had been summoned, then where was the summoner?

Lucius moved deeper into the theatre, still keeping watch for a way out, but intrigued to see what had become of the rest of *La Fenice*. A pair of footlights flickered to life at the edge of the orchestra pit, reflecting their fitful glow from a golden-framed mirror that stood at the centre of the stage. Lucius had not noticed the mirror before now, and let his dreaming steps carry him towards it.

He skirted the orchestra pit, where creatures woven from ruined flesh and dark light had made sport with the entrails of the musicians. The skins of those players were hung from music stands, their heads and limbs arranged like a bizarre orchestra of the damned on those few instruments that remained.

Lucius vaulted onto the stage, the movement smooth and graceful. He was a swordsman, not a butcher, and his physique reflected that. His shoulders were broad, his hips narrow and his reach long. The mirror beckoned him, as though an invisible cord stretched from its silvered depths and reached deep inside his chest.

'I love mirrors,' he had once heard Fulgrim say. 'They let one pass through the surface of things,' but Lucius did not want to pass through the surface of anything. His perfection had been ruined by Loken's treacherous fist, and Lucius had finished the job with a straight razor and a scream that still echoed in his skull if he listened hard enough.

Or was that someone else screaming? It was hard to tell these days.

Lucius did not want to look in the mirror, yet his steps carried him closer with every passing second. What would he see in such a mirror of dreams?

Himself or something far worse; the truth…

It reflected a single spot of light that appeared to have no source he could see. He thought this puzzling until he remembered that this was a dream, where no logic could be counted as solid, and no sight taken for granted.

Lucius stepped in front of the mirror, but instead of the face he had tried so very hard to forget, he saw a handsome warrior with aquiline features, a strong tapered nose and high cheekbones that accentuated the golden green of his eyes. His hair was lacquered black and his lips full, giving him a smile that would have been arrogant had his skill been any less.

Lucius reached up to his face and felt the smoothness of his skin, the unblemished perfection of it like the brushed steel of a polished blade.

'I was beautiful once,' he said, and his reflection laughed to hear such vanity.

Lucius balled a fist, ready to dash his mocking reflection to shards, but his twin did not match his movements, instead looking at a point somewhere over his right shoulder. In the depths of the mirror, Lucius saw the reflection of the incredible portrait of Fulgrim that hung on the pediment over the splintered ruin of the proscenium.

Like his own face, it did not match his memory of the thing. Where before it had been a majestic piece of incredible potency and power, its outlandish colours and vibrant texture stimulating every sense with its sheer daring, now it was simply a portrait. Its colours were bland, its lines uninspired, and the subject made small and unremarkable, such as any mortal journeyman painter might work with oils or watercolours.

Yet for all that it was a prosaic thing now, Lucius saw the eyes had been rendered with exquisite skill, capturing a depth of pain, suffering and agony that was almost too much to bear. Since Apothecary Fabius had worked dark transformations upon his flesh, it was a rare stimulus that piqued any interest in Lucius for more than a moment. Yet he felt himself drawn into the portrait's eyes, hearing a plaintive cry that echoed from a time and place beyond understanding. Wordless and edged with a madness that could only come from an eternity of confinement, the eyes were a mute plea for the release of oblivion.

Lucius felt himself drawn into the eyes of the portrait as something stirred within him, a primal presence that had only recently awoken and shared a kinship with the reflected image.

The glassy surface of the mirror rippled like the surface of a pool, as though it too sensed that shared heritage. Tremors were rising from somewhere impossibly deep within the mirror. Unwilling to face what might rise from the mirror's depths, Lucius reached for his swords, unsurprised that they were now belted to his waist and that he was fully attired in his battle armour.

The blades were in his hand in an instant, and he swung them at the mirror in a scissoring arc. It shattered into a thousand spinning pieces of razored glass, and Lucius screamed as they sliced into his perfect face, carving the meat and bone to ugly rawness.

Over his own scream, he heard a scream of frustration that dwarfed his own.

It was the cry of someone who knows their torment will be never-ending.

LUCIUS AWOKE INSTANTLY, his genhanced body switching from sleep to wakefulness in the blink of an eye. He reached for the swords he kept beside his bunk and was on his feet a second later. His chambers were brightly lit, as they always were now, and he swept his blades around in an effort to locate anything out of place that might presage danger.

Garish paintings, symphonic discordias and bloody trophies taken from the black sands of Isstvan V filled his chamber. A bull-headed sculpture taken from the Gallery of Swords sat next to the thighbone of an alien creature he had killed on Twenty-Eight Two. The long, keenly-edged blade of an eldar sword-shrieker shared space with the blade limb of a clade creature he'd killed on Murder.

Yes, everything was as it should be, and he relaxed a fraction.

He saw nothing out of the ordinary, and spun his swords in an unconscious display of incredible skill as he sheathed them in the gold and onyx scabbards hanging on the edge of his bunk. His breath came quickly, his muscles burned and his heart beat a rapid tattoo on his ribs, as though he had exerted himself in the training cages against the primarch himself.

The sensation was wondrously pleasurable, yet was gone almost as soon as it came.

Aching disappointment touched Lucius, as it so often did when those sensations that raised more than a flicker of interest faded. He reached up to touch his face, relieved and repulsed at the hard ridges of scar tissue criss-crossing his once-perfect features.

He had defaced his wondrous visage with knives and glass and blunt metal, but Loken had made the first imperfection, the cut that had torn him open. Lucius had sworn a mighty oath on the primarch's silver-bladed sword that the Luna Wolf's face would be the mirror of his own, but Loken was gone, cindered ashes drifting on the mournful winds of a dead world.

That silver-bladed sword was now his, a gift from Primarch Fulgrim that had seen his star rise within the Legion to rival that of Julius Kaesoron and Marius Vairosean. The First Captain had offered him new chambers, closer to the beating heart of the Legion, but Lucius had chosen to remain in the quarters assigned to him long ago.

In truth, he despised Kaesoron, and his rejection of the man's offer had given him a moment of delicious frisson as he saw resentment flare in his ruined, molten features. Lucius relished Kaesoron's anger and felt a flicker of pleasure at the memory.

He had no wish to be part of the command structure; such as it was now, and simply wished to hone his

already phenomenal skills to ever-greater heights of perfection. Some of the Legion had abandoned that quest
as a reminder of their previous existence as Imperial lap-
dogs, for what need had they to prove their perfection to
the Emperor?

Lucius knew better.

Though few understood the truth of the repugnantly
seductive creatures that had birthed and gorged themselves upon the terror and noise of the *Maraviglia*, Lucius
suspected they were aspects of elemental powers that
were older and more generous with their blessings than
anything the Imperium had to offer.

His perfection would be his devotions to them.

Lucius sat on the edge of his bunk and strove to recall
the substance of his dream. He could picture the ruined
interior of *La Fenice* and the terrible gaze of the painting
above the blood-slick stage. But for the eyes, it had been
Fulgrim as he had been before the Legion had taken its
first steps upon the path of sensation. And as full of pain
as they had been, there was a familiarity to them that
had been strangely absent in the days since Isstvan V.

That battle had changed Fulgrim, but no one in the
Legion appeared to notice the change save Lucius. He
had sensed something indefinably *different* about his
beloved primarch, something impossible to pinpoint,
but there nonetheless. Lucius had sensed something
awry, like a harp string a fraction out of tune or a pict
image not quite in focus.

If any shared his opinion, they kept their counsel, for
the primarch did not take kindly to questioning, nor
was he merciful in his displeasure. The Fulgrim that had
returned from the bloody sands of the dead world had
none of the Phoenician's wit or insight, and when he
spoke of past battles, his tales had the hollow ring of
one who had heard of their fury, but taken no part in
their winning.

The feeling that he had been summoned to *La Fenice*

for a reason would not leave him, and Lucius looked up into the face of the painting that hung opposite his bunk. It was the last thing he saw before he took his infrequent bouts of rest, and the first thing he saw upon waking. It was a face that haunted him and inspired him in equal measure.

His own.

Serena D'Angelus had painted the portrait for him, a specially commissioned piece that had seen her delve further and deeper into her soul than any mortal should for perfection. Only the Emperor's Children dared reach for such heights, but where the Legion had transcended, she had been destroyed.

His ravaged features stared back at him from the golden frame with the one thought that had been gnawing at his dreams and waking life like an itch that could never be scratched.

Though it seemed impossible, the nagging thought would not leave him.

Whatever wore Fulgrim's face and moved in his flesh was *not* Fulgrim.

THE ROUTE TO the Heliopolis had changed since Isstvan V. The great avenue of towering onyx columns had once been a magisterial processional along the spine of the starship, but now it was a howling place of bedlam. Petitioners and suppliants who begged for a glimpse of the primarch's magnificence camped in the shadow of its pillars, where once golden warriors with long spears had stood.

In times past, such obscene flotsam would have been turned away, but now they were welcomed, and a tide of mewling wretches whose devotion fed Fulgrim's grandiosity choked every passageway of the ship. Lucius despised them, but in his more honest moments, he knew it was only because they did not chant *his* name with such high esteem.

The Phoenix Gate was gone, torn down in the frenzy that followed the *Maraviglia* and the battle on Isstvan V. The eagle once carried by the carven Emperor was broken and part molten from the melta blast that had brought it down. The frenzy of defacement had almost destroyed the *Pride of the Emperor* until Fulgrim had put a stop to the madness engulfing the ship and restored a form of order.

Lucius laughed aloud at the mockery of their flagship's name, the sound like a banshee's screech that made the naked, skinless devotees wail with pleasure. Many in the Legion, Julius Kaesoron loudest of all, had clamoured for the ship's name to be changed along with that of the Legion, in echo of the Sons of Horus, but the primarch had denied them all. All ties to their past loyalty were to remain, as spiteful reminders to their enemies that they fought against brothers. Horus Lupercal had favoured their Legion after the death of Ferrus Manus, and, for a time, the Legion had flown high on a cresting tide of euphoria and sensation.

But like all tides, that fickle euphoria had receded and left the Emperor's Children with a gaping emptiness in their lives. Some, like Lucius, had filled that void with the pursuit of martial excess, while others had indulged desires and secret vices kept hidden until now. Portions of the ship descended into anarchy, as all bonds of control were slipped but, before long, order was restored and a semblance of discipline enforced.

It was a strange kind of discipline, one that rewarded outlandish behaviour as much as punished it. In some cases, the two were one and the same. For all that the legionaries strove to find new meaning and pursue their newfound devotions with all their hearts, they were a force of warriors that needed a command structure to function.

They were still warriors, albeit ones without a war.

Tasking orders had despatched the Legion from Isstvan,

but the primarch had shared none of the Warmaster's commands with his Legion. No one knew to which war zone they were bound or which foe would next feel their blades, and that ignorance was galling. Not even the senior warlords of the Legion could claim such knowledge, but the primarch's summons to the Heliopolis was sure to put an end to the Legion's ignorance.

Lucius gripped the hilt of the Laer sword as he saw Eidolon marching towards him along a connecting corridor. The Lord Commander hated him, and never passed over an opportunity to remind Lucius that he was not truly one of them. Eidolon's skin was waxy and pale, pulled tightly across the distended orbits of his eyes. Wire-taut tendons throbbed at his neck, and the bones of his lower jaw moved with the liquid detachment of a serpent.

His armour was painted in garish stripes of vivid purple and electric blue, the colours riotously applied in a striking pattern that owed nothing to any design of camouflage and made Lucius's eyes strain to assimilate what he was seeing. Such vivid colourings were now the norm among the Legion, with each warrior striving to outdo his fellows in sheer extravagance and ostentation.

Lucius had only recently begun to ornament his armour, its plates strikingly adorned with madly screaming faces stretched beyond all recognition. The inner face of each shoulder guard was notched with jagged metal teeth that pricked and scored his flesh with every movement of his arms. The depth and angle of each tooth was carefully chosen to inflict the most scintillating pains should he choose to wield his blades in anything other than the most sublime manoeuvres.

Eidolon drew in a great sucking breath, the bones of his jaw seeming to writhe beneath the skin and link together before he spoke.

'Lucius,' he said, spitting the word at a pitch and cadence that sent an altogether pleasing clash of discordance into the swordsman's brain. 'You are an unwelcome sight, traitor.'

'And yet, here I am,' said Lucius, ignoring Eidolon and pressing onwards.

The Lord Commander caught up with him and made to grasp his arm. Lucius spun away and his swords were at Eidolon's throat in a blur of silver too fast to follow. The Laeran blade and his Terran sword rested to either side of Eidolon's neck. With one flick of his wrists, he could decapitate the man. Lucius saw the relish in Eidolon's face, the pulsing beat of the hawser-like tendon in his neck and the dilated black holes of his pupils.

'I'd take your head like I took Charmosian's,' he said, 'if I didn't think you'd enjoy it.'

'I remember that day,' replied Eidolon. 'I swore I'd kill you for that. I still might.'

'I don't think you will,' said Lucius. 'You're not good enough. No one is or ever will be.'

Eidolon laughed, the gesture opening his face up like a tearing wound.

'You are arrogant, and one day the primarch will tire of you. Then you will be mine.'

'Maybe he will, and maybe he won't, but it will not be today,' said Lucius, dancing away from Eidolon with graceful steps. It was good to draw his swords in anger and feel the gentle pressure of their sharpened edges resting on flesh. He wanted to kill Eidolon, for the man had been a thorn in his side for as long as he'd known him, but it would not do to rob the primarch of his most zealous devotee.

'Why not today?' demanded Eidolon.

'It is the eve of battle,' said Lucius. 'And that's the one day I don't kill anyone.'

2

MIGHTY WALLS OF pale stone had been defaced with a thousand splashes of paint and blood, and the great marble statues that supported the coffered dome of the

roof no longer depicted the first heroes of Unity and the
Legion. Now they were bull-headed representations of
the old Laer gods, clandestine things whose heads were
bowed or turned to the side as though keeping a delicious secret.

Torn banners hung between fluted pilasters of green
marble, the fabric shredded and scorched in the fires of
the Legion's rebirth. The floor of the Heliopolis was fashioned from black terrazzo, with inlaid chips of marble
and quartz intended to render it into a celestial bowl
reflecting the light from the great beam of lustrous starlight that shone down from the centre of the dome. That
light still shone, brighter and more piercing than ever
before, and the floor's polish reflected it with dazzling
intensity. Once, carved bench seats had run around the
circumference of the council chamber, rising in stepped
ranks towards the walls like the tiers of a gladiatorial
arena.

Those seats had been demolished, for none would
now sit higher than the primarch of the Emperor's Children, and portions of the rubble formed a plinth at the
centre of the chamber, rugged and glistening like the
graven idol of a primitive god. Upon this elevated platform sat a black throne of unrivalled magnificence, its
surfaces mirror smooth and reflective.

The throne was all that remained of the previous
incarnation of the Heliopolis, its regal majesty deemed
suitably noble for the primarch of the Emperor's Children. Discordia blared from iron vox-casters; the screams
of loyalists as they died on the black sand, the deafening
cacophony of a hundred thousand guns, and the music
of pleasure and pain intermingled. It was the sound of an
empire's violent death, the sound of a pivotal moment
in history that would replay over and over again and of
which the warriors forced to endure it would never tire.

Perhaps three hundred legionaries filled the chamber, and Lucius recognised many of them from the great

battle on Isstvan V: First Captain Kaesoron, Marius Vairosean, dour Kalimos of the Seventeenth, Apothecary
Fabius, pouting Krysander of the Ninth and a score of
others to whom he had applied derogatory labels. Some
were old faces of the Legion. Others were those who
had attracted the fickle notice of the primarch, while yet
more were simply members of the Brotherhood of the
Phoenix who had followed their betters.

Like the Legion's ships and name, so too would the
name of their quiet order stand.

Lucius moved through the press of bodies towards
Julius Kaesoron, savouring the beautiful devastation of
the First Captain's features. An Iron Hand by the name
of Santar had ruined Kaesoron's face more thoroughly
than Lucius could ever manage, and though Fabius had
reconstructed much of his hairless skull, it was still a
horror of vat-grown flesh stitched to fused bone, weeping orbs of milky blindness and burned scar tissue the
colour of weather-beaten copper.

As wondrous as Julius Kaesoron's blessed transformations were, they were subtle next to those wrought on
Marius Vairosean. Where the First Captain had received
his ruined visage at the hands of the enemy, Marius
Vairosean had been gifted during the rush of power
unleashed by the *Maraviglia*. The captain's jaws were
rigid and locked open with barbed cabling, as though he
was forever screaming. His eyes were red and raw, bearing the savage scars of the wire-wound sutures holding
them open. Two great open wounds in the side of his
head cut 'V' shaped gouges in his tapered skull where his
ears had once been located.

Both captains wore armour that had been wondrously
embellished with spikes and draped with leathered hide
stripped from the bodies that littered the parquet of *La
Fenice*. Yet for all their gaudy finery and obvious mutilations, Lucius saw Kaesoron and Vairosean as relics of the
past, officers of dogged loyalty who lacked the ambition

or flair that would see a warrior burn brighter than a star.

'Captains,' said Lucius, layering just the right balance of respect and disdain into the syllables of their rank. 'It seems that war finally calls us.'

'Lucius,' said Vairosean, giving him a nod of acknowledgement as his jaw cracked and its too-wide circumference formed words that were swiftly becoming almost impossible to give voice. Such implied insolence from Lucius should have earned him a bloody reprimand, but his star was in the ascendancy. Eidolon – a warrior with an eye for spotting the way the wind was blowing – had seen it, and Vairosean, ever the sycophant, knew it too.

Kaesoron was not so easily intimidated and turned his cloudy eyes upon him. His expression was impossible to read, the ruin of his face making his true disposition a tantalising mystery.

'Swordsman,' hissed Kaesoron through the raw wound of his mouth. 'You are a worm, and an ambitious worm at that.'

'You flatter me, First Captain,' said Lucius, meeting his hostile gaze with one of supreme indifference. 'I serve the primarch to the best of my ability.'

'You serve yourself and no one else,' snapped Kaesoron. 'I regret not leaving you on Isstvan III with the rest of the imperfect ones. I think that I should kill you and be done with your flawed existence.'

Lucius gripped the hilt of the Laer sword and cocked his head to the side.

'It would give me great pleasure to let you try, First Captain,' he said.

Kaesoron turned away, and Lucius grinned, knowing Kaesoron would never openly follow through with his threat. Lucius would gut him in the opening moments of any duel, and the thought of murdering the First Captain sent a thrill of pleasure through his body.

'Any word on where we are?' he asked, knowing neither

Kaesoron nor Vairosean would know and keen to expose their ignorance to those around them.

Vairosean shook his head. 'That is for the Phoenician alone to know,' he said, the jagged notes of his voice like the braying discharge of his sonic cannon.

'You have not been told?' replied Lucius with a smirk as a line of hooded bearers carrying heavy iron casks on their backs snaked through the gaping portal of the vanished Phoenix Gate. To Lucius, they looked like ants bearing food to a hive. 'I would have thought a warrior of your status would have been amongst the first to learn our destination. Have you earned the primarch's ire?'

Vairosean ignored the obvious barb and gave a nod of acknowledgement as Eidolon took position near Kaesoron like the glory-seeker he was. The First Captain had been one of Fulgrim's closest companions in the old days, and though the Phoenician appeared to care little for past attachments, Kaesoron still commanded respect from most of the Legion.

Most, but not me, thought Lucius with an amused smirk as he saw the light of ambition in Eidolon's eyes. It was pathetic how the Lord Commander latched onto those the primarch favoured, and Lucius felt his contempt for the man swell to new heights.

'Looks like Fulgrim is breaking out the last of the victory wine,' he said with unearned bonhomie. 'We only do that when we're about to go into battle.'

'Old Legion custom,' spat Vairosean, his voice a wet, gurgling rasp.

'We still drink to the victory to come,' said Lucius, drawing his swords with a flourish, and careful to let the warriors nearby see the silver blade Fulgrim had gifted to him. 'By the will of Horus or the Phoenician, it matters not to the lords of profligacy, we still drink.'

'We should not honour who we were before our ascension,' said Eidolon.

'Not everything we were died on Isstvan,' replied

Lucius, amused at the blatancy of the Lord Commander's ingratiating words.

The casks of victory wine were deposited in a circle around the black throne in the column of blinding light. The smell was potent, bitter and like engravers' acid. The gathered warriors leaned forwards as one to fully savour the acrid reek of the wine, fully aware of its symbolism.

The blood surged in Lucius's veins at the thought of going into battle once more. The forced inaction of the journey from the Isstvan system had chafed at him. He ached, *needed,* to feel hot blood sprayed from an opened artery, the visceral thrill of meeting a bladesman who might prove his equal.

He tried to remember the names of swordsmen of note in those Legions still loyal to the Emperor, but could think of none who could match him. Sigismund of the Fists was a competent, if bluntly single-minded wielder of the blade, and Nero of the XIII could kill with something approaching flair, though he fought with more than a hint of rote in his swings. Other names drifted through Lucius's memory, but as competent as they were, none of them had reached the sublime pinnacle of bladework that he had attained.

'Perhaps it will be Mars at last,' he ventured. 'We have travelled far enough. Perhaps we are making ready to join the fleets moving on the Red Planet as Horus ordered.'

'The Warmaster,' said Eidolon, his taut skin wrinkling in childish adulation. 'He knows my name and has commended me on several occasions.'

Lucius knew better, but before he could contradict Eidolon's fantasy a blare of noise erupted from the vox units strung between the pilasters. A glorious scream of birth and murder shrieked in dissonant anti-harmonies, like a million orchestras with every instrument out of tune. The sound was rapturous, a freakish blend of discordant music and howling voices raised in hideous adoration.

A cascade of light fell from the dome, a glittering rain that shimmered with a light so bright that it was like a moment of atomic detonation. The Emperor's Children howled as sensory apparatus mutilated by Apothecary Fabius flooded their nervous systems with powerful surges of bio-electrical spikes, pleasure responses and pain signals. Warriors convulsed at the cacophony of sound and light, dancing like madmen or victims of grand mal seizures. Some tore at their skin, others beat their neighbours, while others pounded their fists bloody on the floor while screaming inchoate curses.

Lucius held his body rigid, fighting the sensations and receiving the pleasure tenfold, his deliberate resistance to the overload of sensation making it all the sweeter. Blood and saliva ran from his lips and he felt his bones and flesh vibrating in perfect symphony with the raucous madness of the spectacle.

The Legion screamed with the delirious joy of it, but this was merely a prelude.

A shape moved in the light, an angel of extermination, a god made flesh and the embodiment of all that was perfect in its expression of intemperance.

Fulgrim dropped through the light like the brightest comet in the firmament, a hammerblow of tyrian war plate the colour of a bruised sunset. He slammed down onto the terrazzo floor, a billowing mantle of fiery golden scale spread at his shoulders like a pair of angelic wings. Hair like a snowfall cascaded from his noble crown, and his slender, aquiline features were tapered and elfin, though possessed of a haughty strength that none of the faded orphans of Asuryan could hope to match.

Fulgrim had eschewed his gaudy facial paints and scented oils, his face now pallid and ethereal, like a corpse-wraith given form and clad in polished plate that gleamed with the sheen of the finest mirror. His eyes were black pits from which no light escaped or ever would and his mouth creased in a smile that spoke of secret knowledge that would sear the mind of any but a primarch were they to learn even a fraction of its scope.

Lucius joined his fellow warriors in an orgiastic scream of welcome, a hymnal to excess, a chorus of pandemonium in praise of their liege lord. Just to be near the Phoenician fired the blood. Fulgrim stood and spread his arms to accept their devotion, tilting his head back as his full lips parted with the rapture of adoration.

The discordia from the vox dropped in volume and Fulgrim finally deigned to cast his gaze out amongst his warriors. The golden cloak draped across his shoulders, and the glitter of silver mail beneath his wondrously moulded breastplate shimmered like a waterfall of stars. A scabbard of ebony, mother of pearl and smoked ivory bands hung from a belt of soft black leather embossed with a buckle of amber and black.

The anathame.

Lucius knew this sword well, and even though it now belonged to the most sublime warrior imaginable, he could not resist the thought of what it might be like to face such a weapon. Sensing the scrutiny, Fulgrim turned his obsidian eyes upon Lucius and smiled as though in recognition of some shared bond known only to them.

Lucius felt the power of that gaze and fought to keep his suspicions from showing on his face. He grinned back at Fulgrim and sliced the blades of his swords across the skin of his forehead. Blood dripped into his eyes and he revelled in the bitter, rancid taste of it as it ran down the hundreds of grooves carved through the skin of his face to his waiting tongue.

'My Children,' said Fulgrim as the glorious madness receded. 'I bring you bliss.'

3

FULGRIM BASKED IN the adoration of his warriors for a moment longer before raising his arms for silence. His gaze was beatific, humbling, intoxicating and cruel at

the same time. Not one amongst his warriors failed to
be cowed by that dread black stare. He circled the towering plinth upon which sat his throne, glancing up at its
lofty magnificence as if in faint embarrassment that such
a thing was meant for him.

'You have been so patient with me, my sons,' said Fulgrim, pausing at the foot of the plinth. 'And I have been
neglectful.'

Hundreds of voices clamoured in denial, but Fulgrim
silenced them with his upraised palms and a slyly dep-
recating smile. 'No, it's true, I have allowed no word of
our destination to work its way down to my beloved
children, leaving you in darkness. Can you forgive me?'

Once again the Heliopolis was filled with wild cheer-
ing, a screaming din of sounds no mortal throat was ever
meant to give voice. Warriors threw themselves to their
knees; others beat their breasts and yet more simply
screamed with wordless affirmation.

Fulgrim accepted their praise and said, 'How you honour me.'

Lucius watched Fulgrim as he circled the raised throne,
studying his every movement and gesture for some sign
that this wondrous individual was someone or something other than he claimed to be.

Clad in his battle finery, the primarch's presence was
intoxicating. Not vulgar, not garish, but simply perfect.
As though, in ascending to the pinnacle of excellence, he
had shed the need for any overt displays of his devotion
to the Dark Prince's creed. One look into his black eyes
was enough to realise his infinite capacity for excess in
all its forms. Fulgrim had drunk deep from a well of sensation and without its continual boon, life was grey and
empty, bereft of joy and meaning.

'I bring the wine of victory and the sweet caress of war
upon which to gorge yourselves,' said Fulgrim. 'I bring
you the symphony of war, the bliss of ecstasy and the
rapture of a pain-filled death to our enemies. We have

travelled far from the feast of fire at Isstvan, and I have decided that it is time to wet our weapons in the blood of our enemies.'

A chorus of shrieking approval greeted Fulgrim's words, and he accepted their love as though it was an unexpected boon and not what he had planned all along. The primarch waved his slender, almost delicate fingers at the centre of the chamber, and a shimmering holo sprang to life, a glittering representation of planets in their gravitational dance with a brightly burning star.

'Behold a system I have designated as the Prismatica Cluster,' said Fulgrim, as the holo zoomed towards the fifth world of the newly-named system. A haze of multi-coloured light surrounded the planet like a polar borealis effect, and as the image magnified still further, Lucius saw a world of overlapping bands of deep black and glittering diamond.

A number of orbitals followed the rotational axis of the planet, colossal freight handlers and processing stations with docking facilities for bulk carriers. Smudges of iron and steel indicated the presence of several such vessels, and pinpricks of winking lights spread between them were clearly defence platforms.

'It is here I give you opportunity to prove your love for me as warriors of the Emperor's Children,' said Fulgrim, walking through the flickering projection and letting the holographic world bathe his flawless features in reflected starlight. 'The lackeys of the Martian Priesthood work this world with their dull engines of construction, grubbing like savages in the soil for crystals to be shipped back to Mars.'

Scrolling lines of aestimare, yields and tithed tonnage slid around the image of the world in a noospheric ripple of light, and Lucius took a moment to scan them before becoming bored and concentrating on the glittering, reflective surface of the planet itself. Aside from a passing aesthetic appeal, it appeared to hold no real importance or strategic significance. He saw nothing to suggest this world was valuable enough to attract the attention of the primarch.

What was he was overlooking? What did Fulgrim see that he did not?

Perhaps the crystals were a raw material used in some vital manufacturing process? Lucius quickly dismissed the thought as irrelevant. That the Martian Priesthood valued them was reason enough to disrupt this Imperial operation, but it seemed a wretchedly backwater place to loose the strength of a Legion.

Fulgrim continued to stare at the gently revolving orb of Prismatica V, as though in serene thrall to the stark beauty of its glittering surface. His lips moved soundlessly, and he smiled at some secret joke or some particularly clever bon mot delivered to an unseen listener with perfect timing.

A petty thought occurred to Lucius, but he kept it to himself, knowing it would be unwise to speak it aloud. A similar thought evidently occurred to Eidolon, but the Lord Commander had not the common sense to keep his mouth shut.

'My Lord, I do not understand,' said Eidolon. 'What purpose does this serve?'

Fulgrim rounded on Eidolon, the serenity of his pale features twisting in spiteful fury. He stalked towards Eidolon with murderous bile, and Lucius stepped quickly away lest he be caught in the hurricane of the primarch's wrath. Fulgrim lashed out at Eidolon and the Lord Commander was hurled back like a swatted insect. He crashed down into the rubble left by the demolition of the tiered benches, his breastplate cracked wide and his taut skin spattered with blood.

'You *dare* to question me?' snapped Fulgrim, towering over the downed warrior.

'No, my lord, I simply–'

'Worm!' screamed Fulgrim. 'This is my desire and you question it?'

'I–'

'Quiet!' raged Fulgrim, lifting the terrified Eidolon from the ground by the throat. Lucius felt a vicarious excitement at the sight of Eidolon's humbling. He had seen Fulgrim crush the molten neck of an alien god in a fit of rage, and knew that Eidolon's would present no challenge to his strength.

The fear in the Lord Commander's face was very real and Lucius licked his lips at the thought of what a sublime sensation it must be to feel an emotion so alien to the Adeptus Astartes.

'I am your lord and master and you insult me like this?' said Fulgrim, his rage transformed into abject misery. 'I deliver a war, and this is how you repay me, with questions and doubt? Is this campaign beneath you? Are you too good to make war at my command? Is that it?'

'No!' cried Eidolon. 'I… I simply desired to know…'

'To know what?' spat Fulgrim, his anguish forgotten and his rage restored. 'Speak, wretch! Out with it!'

Eidolon struggled in Fulgrim's grasp, his face purpling to match the primarch's armour. He gasped for breath, his genhanced physique no match for the strength of a primarch.

Between snatched breaths, Eidolon said, 'Were we not ordered to Mars? Will this not delay our rendezvous with the Warmaster's fleets?'

'Horus is my brother, not my master, and I am not his to command,' snarled Fulgrim, as though Eidolon had voiced the most heinous insult in mentioning the name of Horus Lupercal. 'Who does he think he is to give me orders? I am Fulgrim! The Phoenician, and I am no man's lapdog. If Horus thinks he can simply charge towards Terra like a blood-maddened berserker then he is a fool. One does not simply advance on the most heavily defended world in the galaxy; such a target must be taken with finesse. You understand?'

'Yes, my lord,' hissed Eidolon, but Fulgrim's rage was not yet spent.

'I know you, Eidolon, don't think I don't,' said the primarch, dropping the choking Lord Commander and turning back to the image of the shimmering planet. 'Always quick with a sniping comment, ever the whispered word in the shadows to undermine my authority. You are the worm at the heart of the apple, and I will have no one who doubts me at my back ready with a knife.'

Eidolon sensed the awful threat in Fulgrim's words and dropped to his knees. 'My lord, please!' he begged. 'I am loyal! I would never betray you!'

'Betray me?' said Fulgrim, whipping around and drawing the glitter-grey blade of the anathame. 'You dare give voice to thoughts of betrayal? Here, in this gathering of my most loyal subjects? You are a bigger fool than I thought.'

'No!' shouted Eidolon, but Lucius knew he was wasting his breath.

To his credit, Eidolon saw it too and reached for his sword as Fulgrim stepped in to deliver the deathblow. The quillons of Eidolon's sword had barely parted company with the lip of his scabbard when the anathame cut through his neck and sent his head flying through the air. It landed with a meaty thud on the terrazzo floor and rolled until it finally came to rest against one of the urns of victory wine.

The Lord Commander's eyes blinked once, his lips drawn back over his splintered teeth in an expression of horror that made Lucius want to laugh. Fulgrim turned from Eidolon's corpse as it slumped to the ground, and retrieved the head he had cut from the Lord Commander's body. Blood ran in a viscous stream from the severed neck and Fulgrim walked the circumference of the chamber, allowing coagulating droplets to fall in the opened casks of victory wine.

'Drink, my children,' he said as though what had just happened was a minor thing. 'Fill your chalices and drink to the great victory I give you. We will make war on Prismatica and show the Warmaster how this campaign should be waged!'

The Emperor's Children surged forwards, each eager to be the first to drink the primarch's gift to them. Still clutching Eidolon's head, Fulgrim ascended the plinth to his throne and spread the golden weave of his cloak behind him before sitting. He looked down on his warriors, his gaze at once indulgent and faintly condescending.

Lucius thought back to the way Fulgrim had moved as he drew his sword and cut Eidolon's head from his body. With the eye of a master swordsman, he analysed every movement the primarch's body had made, his stepped lunge, the turn of his shoulder and the pivot of the hips as he struck.

One movement had flowed into another, as if no other could ever have been possible. The primarch's flawless body was always in balance, yet Lucius saw something no one but the greatest living mortal swordsman could ever have seen, and it gave him a delicious thrill of excitement and disappointment.

It was an impossible thought, a treasonous thought, but Lucius couldn't help but follow it through to its logical conclusion.

I could beat you, thought Lucius. If you and I fought right now, I would kill you.

4

THE WARRIORS OF the Mechanicum were powerful enemies, augmented and enhanced beyond mortal norms, but Lucius wondered if they even bothered to tutor their warriors in the arts of close combat. He danced through a swirling mêlée, his twin swords moving in whirling arcs that opened jugulars, removed limbs and lifted the lids off skulls.

These men were brutes, crudely enhanced to be bigger and stronger than most mortals, but there was little subtlety to their power. Anyone could pump a man full of growth chemicals and graft a host of combat augmetics to his frame, but what good was that if they were not trained in their use?

A weaponised servitor creature encased in azure war plate and bearing little that could be called organic came at him. Its shoulder mounted cannon spat a torrent of shells, tearing up shards of glassy, volcanic stone, but Lucius was already moving. He rolled beneath the blitz of fire, slicing away the furiously rotating barrels of the gun and lancing his Terran blade through a thin gap in the abdominal armour plates.

Oily black blood sprayed from the wound like pressurised hydraulic fluid, and Lucius spun inside the reach of its remaining arm. The snapping, energy-wreathed lifter claw slashed low, and Lucius used the arm as a springboard. He vaulted onto a projecting stub of armour plating at the servitor's hip and somersaulted onto its wide shoulders. The silver Laer blade stabbed down into the construct's armoured skull, and Lucius felt something wet and living burst apart inside. He vaulted from the dying servitor's body, pleased to see red wetness on the blade of his sword.

The bio-machine staggered, but did not fall, though it was clear it was dead.

Lucius paused in his killing to flick the blood from his swords as a thunderous detonation mushroomed into the sky with concussive force. A petrochemical stink filled the air as the unrefined promethium burned off and mingled with the fluorocarbon-rich atmosphere to form a potent breath that gave Lucius a momentary flush of pleasurable dizziness.

Emperor's Children swarmed around him, shooting with abandon into the mass of fighting warriors. What had begun as a carefully orchestrated act of mass

38   GRAHAM MCNEILL

murder had become a screaming free for all. Hundreds
of augmented warriors protected the main refineries and
processing plants, but they had no chance of survival.
Three companies of Emperor's Children had fallen on
the defenders of Prismatica, and there would be no
survivors.

Though he had been careful not to let any hint of his
true feelings show, Lucius was forced to agree with the
late Lord Commander Eidolon's assessment of this venture. It had taken the fleet, led by *Andronius* and *Pride of
the Emperor*, a mere ten hours to batter a path through
the picket line of system monitors and cripple the last
defence orbital. Three bulk carriers had been captured,
kilometres-long behemoths loaded with billions of
tonnes of shimmering, reflective crystals.

With orbital space secure, hunting squadrons of
Stormbirds had descended on the main manufactories
at the southern tip of a vast forest of towering crystal
spires and the slaughter had begun. The Mechanicum
facility was burning, aflame from end to end as the
Emperor's Children ran rampant through its vast storage
silos and hangar-sized refining structures. Vast drilling
engines towered above the battling figures, tall augers
and serrated drilling arms raised to the sky like the limbs
of praying mantises.

Marius Vairosean led his company of shrieking
Kakophoni against the western flank of the facility, sys-
tematically razing its defences with grim, methodical
dogma. Shrieking harmonics of dissonant vibrations
echoed from the iron canyons between the towering
structures as monstrous sonic weapons tore the atoms
of matter apart with resonant frequencies that echoed
between worlds.

Buildings collapsed like paper, and coruscating sound
waves tore deep gouges in the basalt rock of the planet.
The screams of the dying mingled with the musical crescendo of clashing sound waves, a howling symphony of

destruction that brought the rapturous madness of the *Maraviglia* to mind.

Lucius had kept well clear of Marius Vairosean, for the Kakophoni were now virtually deaf and insensate to any but the most ear-splitting noises. A swordsman needed perfect hearing and his inner ear to be flawless. The nerve-shredding rush of excruciatingly vivid sound was simply a pleasure he would have to forego.

Fulgrim himself led the main thrust of the assault into the heart of the Mechanicum defenders, surrounded by hulking Terminators of the Phoenix Guard. Julius Kaesoron fought next to him, bludgeoning a path through the cohorts of weaponised servitors and phalanxes of skitarii that held the chokepoints with an array of automated gun platforms.

Against the brute force of the Phoenician and Kaesoron's warriors, they had no chance. A primarch was an unstoppable force of destruction and Terminator armour made a warrior nigh invincible. Even those warriors who suffered wounds found that their agony only spurred them to greater heights of ecstasy.

Fulgrim was magnificent, a towering avatar of beauty and death, his golden cloak spread behind him and reflecting the variegated sunlight in rainbow arcs of dazzling brightness. His armour shone like a beacon, and where he walked, his grey sword clove through hybrid flesh and iron without pause. He sang as he slew, an aching lament from lost Chemos that spoke of beauty's end and a lost love that can never come again.

More beautiful than anything Coraline Aseneca had sung, it seemed perverse that the machine men dying around him could not appreciate the wonder that surrounded them and the glory of the one who stooped to take their lives. They were dying without knowing how they were honoured and Lucius hated them for that.

Smoke coughed from the interior of a burning refinery, and Lucius howled in frustration as his view of

Fulgrim at war was hidden behind a bank of black and violet clouds. He turned from the battles being fought elsewhere, back to his own arena of death.

Fulgrim had entrusted the eastern flank to him, and he had led his warriors in a series of daring feints that drew the enemy from their defensive formations in prosaically predictable ways. One by one, each counterattack had been beheaded until the defensive line had been bled dry and Lucius's warriors had advanced without meeting any real resistance. He wove a red and silver path through the defences, encircling each pocket of resistance and despatching its most promisingly threatening warrior with a flourish of breathtaking skill and spite.

He vaulted onto the remains of a toppled battle engine, a ten-metre-high biped with its princeps compartment breached and pink amniotic gel drooling from the cracked cockpit. Lucius had seen the machine stomp from an armoured hangar at the edge of the defences and briefly considered taking it on. His colossal vanity had intervened, and he had laughed the idea away. Only a fool would dare face such a machine alone, and it had fallen in the crossfire of sonic cannons before it had taken a dozen paces.

Lucius thrust his sword to the scintillating sky, striking an appropriately heroic pose for his warriors to see.

'Onwards! Into the fires and we will show these mechanised men the meaning of pain!'

No sooner had he shouted than the curtain of smoke parted and a thunderous crash of heavy footsteps shook the ground. High above Lucius, a snarling, bestial head emerged from the smoke. Worked in bronze to resemble a hunting mastiff, the battle engine's armoured cockpit was hung with thermal-gusted banners, and the grey and tan carapace boasted a golden eagle and crossed swords emblem.

The towering battle engine emerged from the ruins of the factory, and Lucius felt a wonderfully unexpected jolt of terror as it stalked towards its downed brother.

'Ah, yes,' said Lucius. 'They hunt in pairs.'

The battle engine's arms swung up to fire, clattering as auto-loaders drove heavy-calibre shells into the breeches of monstrously oversized guns. Lucius stood defiantly atop the broken carapace of the Titan's brother, leaping clear as its weapons fired with the deafening thunder of a thousand hammers beating at a war god's anvil. He rolled as he hit the ground, momentarily blinded by the hurricane of stone splinters, dust and propellant gases.

A flaming pyre of wreckage blazed brightly behind him, and he sprang to his feet as he saw the blackened outline of the battle engine silhouetted against the flames. Its head bobbed low, as though hunting his scent, and Lucius tightened his grip on his swords.

The guns roared again, and Emperor's Children warriors vanished in a spraying blitz of shells that churned the ground to splintered rock. Armour disintegrated under the barrage, flesh vaporised, and the screams of the dying were musical, pain-filled and short.

Return fire sprayed the Titan, its shields sparking and flaring with bright squalls of energy discharge. Heavier impacts tore gouges in the invisible energy, like stones hurled into fluorescing water. A missile streaked towards the Titan and the warhead exploded with a red bloom of superheated plasma. Shrieking frequencies ripped the air, but still the shield held; though Lucius knew it must be close to collapse.

'Over here, you bastard!' he shouted, enjoying the mix of wild emotions surging through his body. The modifications Apothecary Fabius had worked on his nervous system responded to the powerful stimulus and rewarded him with a heady cocktail of pleasure responders and hormonal boosters. In an instant, Lucius became faster, stronger and hyper-sensitive to his environment.

Its mastiff head swung to face him and its war horn loosed a screaming howl born of rage and grief. Lucius matched its braying fury with a roar of his own, daring it to come and fight him. His suddenly enhanced senses took in a thousand tiny details in an instant; the fine texture of its metal skin, the cursive gusts of smoke from its weapons, the glint of colourful light on the red cockpit panes, the dripping of coolant gases from the machinery concealed beneath its carapace, and the bitter, iron flavour of the sentience at its heart.

All this and a thousand other sensations washed through Lucius in a fraction of a second. The intensity of it all staggered him, and he blinked away a host of light bursts from behind his eyes. The war horn brayed again as the Titan swung its weapons towards Lucius. The engine was wasting its strength coming for a single warrior, but it had seen him atop its fallen twin and had marked him for death.

Lucius knew he could not fight such a powerful enemy, and turned to run, but before he had taken a single step, the angelic outline of a warrior on wings of gold dropped from the smoke. He bore a flint-knapped blade in one hand and a long-barrelled pistol worked in silver and onyx in the other. His stark white hair flew around his glorious features as the heat bleeding from the Titan's reactor washed over him.

'One for me, I think, Lucius,' said Fulgrim, levelling his pistol at the battle engine.

Fulgrim shot with the calm poise of a duellist on a misty heath. A shining spear of incandescent light imbued with the heat of a newborn star spat from the gun and struck dead centre on the Titan's shields. A shrieking flare of overload banged like a host of shattering mirrors and a powerful sphere of energy pulsed out like a solar flare.

Lucius was hurled from his feet and hit hard against one of the towering crystal spires at the edge of the facility. Pain sawed up and down his back, and he grinned as he tasted blood.

Even through a haze of smoke and pain he saw what happened next with complete clarity.

Fulgrim stood alone before the war machine, his pistol cast aside and his sword held loosely at his side. The Titan's auto-loaders ratcheted canisters of shells around from its rear hoppers, and the breeches snapped shut on a fresh load. Fulgrim's free hand reached up to the battle engine, as though demanding it halt its march.

Lucius laughed at the absurdity of the gesture.

But Fulgrim intended more than simple defiance.

A shimmering nimbus of misty light gathered around the Phoenician, its substance shot with threads of barely visible lightning. Fulgrim's splayed fingers closed into a fist and he twisted his grip as though tearing at unseen ropes.

The battle engine halted in its rampage, the cockpit snapping up and its weapon arms jerking spasmodically as though the machine was suffering a hideous seizure. Fulgrim's outstretched hand continued pulling and twisting at the air, and the Titan's war horn brayed with plaintive horror. The cockpit panes shattered, spraying glass tears to the ground as it slumped back onto its hissing legs.

Lucius watched with horrified fascination as bulging wads of oozing flesh pushed their way out of the cockpit, swelling and pulsating with grotesque life. The gelatinous mass of expanding meat obscured the mastiff head, drooling from the armoured carapace in raw pink tendrils of mutant flesh.

Lucius rose to his feet, awed and wondrously horrified at the death of the battle engine. Amniotic fluid fell in a drizzle from the Titan's ruptured body, its every orifice and exhaust port choked with monstrous growths of rampant flesh culled from its mortal crew. The stench was appalling, and Lucius breathed deeply, savouring the reek of burned meat that was already beginning to decay.

He approached Fulgrim as the primarch gathered up his fallen pistol.

'What did you do?' asked Lucius.

Fulgrim turned his dead black eyes upon him and said, 'A little something I learned from the forces that empower me. A trifle, nothing more.'

Lucius lifted his hand, letting a gobbet of glistening flesh drop into his palm. It was wet and veined with black necrosis. The slimy texture was mildly diverting, and even as he watched, it decayed before his eyes.

'Could I learn how to do something like this?'

Fulgrim laughed and leaned close to Lucius, placing a delicate hand upon his shoulder guard. The primarch's breath was cloying and sweet, like temple smoke and glucose, and the heat of his skin was like being close to a dangerously overused plasma coil. Fulgrim looked deep into his eyes, as though searching for something he already suspected was there. Lucius felt the power of his master's stare, and knew that what held his gaze was far older and more malicious than he could ever hope to be.

'Perhaps you could, swordsman,' said Fulgrim with an amused nod. 'I think you have the potential to be just like me one day.'

Fulgrim looked up, mercifully breaking the connection between them as the sounds of fighting died away.

'Ah, the battle is over,' said the primarch. 'Good. I was beginning to tire of it.'

And without another word, Fulgrim marched into the forest of mirrored spires, leaving Lucius alone with the dead battle engine.

5

THERE WAS BEAUTY here, real beauty, and it made him weep to see such glory.

His warriors saw only the physical properties of the crystal forests, but Fulgrim saw the truth in this place, a truth no one but he had eyes to see.

Spires of glittering, diamond-sheened crystal speared up from the black ground, towering monuments to the galaxy's endless geological wonder. None were less than a hundred metres tall, and even the slenderest was ten metres or more in diameter. Hundreds of thousands of these spires stretched into the distance, covering a vast swathe of ground with their glittering majesty.

They sprouted from the ground in thick clusters, growing like an organic forest of greenery with curling paths between them. He changed direction at random, plunging deeper and deeper into the shimmering forest of crystal with no thought to any direction. It would be easy to become lost in this shifting forest of mirrors, and Fulgrim recalled an apocryphal tale of a lost warrior trapped in an invisible maze upon the Erycinian Highlands of Venus.

The fool had died within arm's reach of an exit, but Fulgrim had no fear of such a fate. He could retrace his route from this impenetrable wilderness of glass without ever needing to open his eyes.

He reached out and ran his fingers along the smooth flanks of the spires, revelling in the tiny imperfections of their silicate surfaces. Some were milky and translucent and others opaque, but the vast majority were sheened with a mirror finish, like a million spear heads belonging to a giant army buried in the black sand.

Fulgrim had learned of an army that had been buried on ancient Terra, a clay army of ghosts to protect a dying emperor who feared retribution from the countless souls he had sent to the afterlife in his wars of conquest. This was no such thing, but the conceit of walking upon the graves of a vast army of colossi amused him, and he sketched a casual salute to the fallen warriors upon whose grave he strolled.

The battle to capture the Mechanicum facility had been mildly diverting, but all too brief. To fight a foe who did not despair at his own destruction or beg for mercy was a dull, lifeless affair, and Fulgrim was disappointed at the Mechanicum's lack of ability to feel the raptures he and his warriors had gifted upon them. He had known what to expect, of course, but it irked him that his opponents had so selfishly denied him the thrill of hearing their screams and feeling the ecstasy of their deaths.

His mood darkened at such boorish behaviour from a foe and he instinctively reached for the Laeran blade before remembering he had given it to the swordsman Lucius. Fulgrim laughed at the idea of Lucius becoming like him. Lucius was touched, yes, but no mortal could ever achieve what he had achieved, become what he had become.

Fulgrim paused in his walk, turning around in a slow circle as he appreciated the true beauty around him. Not the power of planetary sculpting; that was a mere accident of geology. Not the shimmering skies above him; a freak of atmospheric chemical bonds and pollution. No, the true beauty of this place was no accident, no chance occurrence; it was a singular wonder of design, of will and perfection.

His reflections surrounded him, the most incredible perfection captured in living form.

Fulgrim watched his image grow and recede as he took turns at random, enraptured by his exquisite features, his noble countenance and his regal bearing. What other could match him in perfection? Horus? Hardly. Guilliman? Not even close.

Only Sanguinius approached him in aesthetics, but even his wondrous appearance was flawed. What manner of perfect being could be cursed with mutant flesh that marked him as a reminder of ancient myth and belief?

And Ferrus Manus… what of him?

'He is dead!' roared Fulgrim, his voice echoing strangely through the dense layers of the crystal forest.

DEAD, DEAd, DEad, Dead, dead…

Fulgrim spun around as the distorted cries came back to him like accusations. His mood turned thunderous and he drew his sword. He hacked at the nearest spire, sending razor shards of crystalline glass spinning. He hacked at his reflection, daring it to answer him, cutting into its lattice structure with mighty blows of terrible power.

The flint-knapped blade chopped like a woodsman's axe, yet it lost none of its edge at such careless treatment. Sentience beyond human understanding had crafted it, and the power to end gods was bound within its rude appearance.

'My brothers are all cruel and magnificent in their own way!' screamed Fulgrim, each word punctuated by a hewing blow. 'But each is a flawed creation, marred forever by a curse that will one day undo them. I alone am perfect. I alone have been tempered by loss and betrayal!'

At last his capricious anger was spent and he backed away from the ruined spire. In his anger, he had cut through fully half its thickness, and it swayed as its structural stability was undone. Glass popped like gunshots as the spire snapped where Fulgrim had cut into it, and it toppled like a felled tree, smashing its way to the ground in a storm of shattering crystal. Its fall took a dozen others with it, and a vast swathe of the crystal forest fell to the hard ground in a deafening, crashing tumult of broken glass.

The sharp thunder of the falling spires echoed around Fulgrim, a never-ending crescendo of musical destruction, and the pain of so brittle a sound lancing into his brain was a very real pleasure. His warriors would hear the noise, but if they came at all it would not be fear for his life that drew them, but to bask in the sublime sound of such wanton devastation. He wondered how long it had taken these spires to achieve their titanic height. Thousands of years, maybe more.

'Millennia to grow, and a moment to destroy,' he said with more than a hint of wanton spite. 'There's a lesson to be learned here.'

The echoes of the spire's collapse faded and Fulgrim listened for any other voices in the forest. Had he truly heard someone speaking the name of his dead brother or had he imagined it? He held his sword out before him, staring at the glitter-sheen of its flinty surface as a nagging memory that would not coalesce tugged at his consciousness.

He had heard a disembodied voice before, hadn't he?

It had told him dreadful, secret things. Unendurable things.

Fulgrim closed his eyes and pressed a hand to his temple as he tried to remember.

I am here, brother, I will always be here.

Fulgrim looked up in surprise, and an emotion he had long cast aside in his ascent to glory stabbed into his chest like the thrust of a lance driven by the Khan himself.

Deep in the forest of mirrored spires, he saw a powerful warrior in battered war plate the colour of tempered onyx. A face hewn from granite stared back at Fulgrim, and he cried out as he saw the look of endless sorrow in the silver nuggets of his eyes.

'No!' whispered Fulgrim. 'It cannot be…'

Fulgrim clambered through the sharp fangs of glass that jutted from the ground, slicing open his hands and scarring the unblemished plates of his armour in his haste. He staggered like a drunk, smashing aside nubs of crystal and fallen shards that had once stretched out to the heavens.

'What are you?' he yelled, the echoes of his cry bouncing around him so that it seemed as though a host of angry voices demanded answers. He lost sight of the warrior in black as he ran, pushing deeper into the maze of mirrors without heed for any thought other than unmasking this invader of his solitude.

Every time he looked up he saw nothing but his own desperate reflection, his aquiline features twisted and pulled into ugliness by the crazily angled spires. To see his wondrous face so deformed by a quirk of reflective geometry enraged him, and he pulled up short in a ragged clearing of spires.

He spun on his heel, daring his reflections to show anything less than his true beauty.

A hundred or more Fulgrims stared at him with expressions of equal anger, though only now, still and enraged, did he see the pain and terror in the depths of those oh-so-black eyes.

'Where are you?' demanded Fulgrim.

I am here, one reflection answered him.

I am where you abandoned me and left me to rot, said another.

Fulgrim's anger vanished like a droplet of water vaporising on a hot engine cowl. This was new, this was unexpected, and was therefore to be savoured. He walked a slow circuit of the clearing, meeting the gaze of one reflection while trying to keep an eye on the others. Were these reflections his or were they animated by a will of their own and simply mimicking his movements? How such a thing could be possible, he did not know, but it was a fascinating diversion.

'Who are you?' he asked.

You know who I am. You stole what was mine by right.

'No,' said Fulgrim. 'It was always mine.'

Not so, you only borrow the flesh you walk in. It has always been mine and always will be.

Fulgrim smiled, now recognising the sentience behind the myriad voices and broken-glass reflections. He had been expecting this, and to know with whom he conversed gave him a welcome feeling of brotherhood. Fulgrim sheathed the anathame, now certain it was not the source of the voices.

'I wondered when you would manage to reach out

beyond the golden frame of your prison,' he said. 'It took you longer than I expected.'

His reflection returned his smile.

Being confined is a new experience for me. It took time to adjust. Freedom such as I once possessed is hard to forget.

Fulgrim laughed at the petulance in the reflection's voice.

'So why show me Ferrus Manus?' he asked the myriad reflections.

What better mirror is there than the face of an old friend? Only those we love have the power to show us our true selves.

'Was it guilt?' asked Fulgrim. 'Do you think you can shame me into surrendering this body to you?'

Shame? No, you and I have long since outgrown shame.

'Then why the Gorgon?' pressed Fulgrim. 'This body is mine, and no power in the universe will compel me to relinquish it.'

But there is so much we could achieve were I to command it again.

'I will achieve more,' promised Fulgrim.

Keep telling yourself that, laughed his reflection. *You cannot know the things I know.*

'I know everything you knew,' said Fulgrim, lifting his arms and flexing his hands like a virtuoso pianist preparing to play. 'You should see what I can do now.'

Parlour tricks, scoffed his reflection, his eyes darting to another mirror image.

'You make a poor liar,' laughed Fulgrim. 'But I should expect no less. You once ensnared the weak minded with offers of empowerment, but what you really offered was slavery.'

All things that live are enslaved to something; be it lust for wealth and power or the desire for possessions and new experiences. Or the desire to be part of something greater…

'I am no man's slave,' said Fulgrim, and his reflections laughed, a hundred peals of mockery that cut him more deeply than any blade ever could.

You are more a slave now than ever you were, hissed his reflection. *You exist trapped in a body of meat and bone, caught in a broken machine that will grind you to ash. You cannot know what true freedom is until you have embraced power beyond imagining. That is to know the power of a god. Release me and I can show you how we can ascend together.*

Fulgrim shook his head. 'Better yet to subdue that power and bend it to your will.'

We can experience such wonders together, you and I, said a reflection to his left.

A universe of sensation, said another.

Ours for the taking, added a third.

'Say what you will,' countered Fulgrim. 'You have nothing to offer.'

Think you so? Then you have no understanding of that body you claim as your own.

'I grow tired of your games,' said Fulgrim, turning away, but finding himself face to face with yet more mirror images. 'You will remain where you are and we will speak no more.'

Please, begged a reflection, suddenly contrite. *I cannot exist like this. It is cold in here, and dark. The darkness presses in on me and I fear I shall be gone soon.*

Fulgrim leaned in close to the mirrored surface of a crystal spire and grinned.

'Have no fear of that, brother,' he said. 'I will be keeping you around for a very, very long time indeed.'

6

THE FLEET REMAINED in orbit around Prismatica for six days, gathering the crystal forests from the Mechanicum silos and packing the hold of five captured bulk carriers with glittering cargo. Fulgrim demanded every shard, every powdered fragment and every spire that could be taken from the world, though he gave no clue as to what purpose he intended to turn this haul of captured minerals.

In those six days, the Emperor's Children made sport of those few prisoners they had taken, using them in ways too terrible to describe before passing them on to the next company. Lucius fought solitary duels in the last remnants of the crystal forests, dancing with his reflection and matching its every thrust, cut and parry with another dazzling move. He was as close to being the perfect swordsman as it was possible to be, possessing the ideal balance between attack and defence, flawless footwork and a pathological need to feel pain.

Such was the weakness of most opponents, they feared to feel pain.

Lucius had no such fear, and only the warrior capable of the most berserk fury would stand any chance against him. Such a warrior cared nothing for his own life and would only stop fighting when he was dead. Lucius remembered the sight of a battle captain of the World Eaters on Isstvan III, watching as he tore through his own warriors like a man possessed.

To fight such a warrior would be the true test of Lucius's skills, for, as much as he liked to believe himself to be unbeatable, he knew that was not the case. There was no such thing as an unbeatable warrior, there would always be someone faster or stronger or luckier, but instead of fearing to meet such an opponent, Lucius ached for it.

His reflection advanced and retreated with him, matching him movement for movement, and no matter how fast his attacks, how lightning quick his ripostes, he could never breach his mirrored defences. His swords moved with greater and greater speed, each attack faster than the last. He moved quicker than any other living swordsman, his blades forming a shimmering sphere of silver around his body, an intricate sword dance that would have been madness to interrupt.

'So self-involved, swordsman,' said Julius Kaesoron, emerging from behind a jagged stump of crystal. 'You would be left behind here?'

Lucius stumbled, his swords clanging together with a resonant clang of lethal edges. His Terran blade squealed in protest as the Laeran edge notched it with a gleeful shriek of metal on metal. Lucius turned his stumble into a spin and both blades whistled as they cut the air and came to rest on the First Captain's throat.

'That was not wise,' he said.

Kaesoron batted the blades away, and laughed with a gurgle of frothed fluids in his throat. He turned his back on Lucius and gestured towards the ruined Mechanicum facility, where the last of the container shuttles hauled its heavily laden bulk from the blasted rock of the planet's surface.

Almost nothing remained of the crystal forests, the horizon stripped bare and the silos torn down as they were emptied. Marius Vairosean's screaming squads blasted what little was left standing to shredded atoms with jangling blasts of interlocking blast waves of disharmonious sonics. Soon it would be as though this place had never existed.

Lucius jogged after the First Captain. 'You think I wouldn't kill you, Kaesoron?' he asked, angered at the warrior's casual dismissal of his threat.

'You are a viper, Lucius, but even you're not that stupid.'

Lucius wanted to snap at Kaesoron, but he knew it would be pointless to antagonise the man. The First Captain would leave him behind without a second thought, and barely a glimmer of emotion.

'The primarch has been thorough,' said Lucius, sheathing his swords and watching the last container shuttle ascend on a rippling haze of struggling engines. 'What does he want with it all?'

'The crystals?'

'Of course, the crystals,' said Lucius.

Kaesoron shrugged, the matter of no consequence to him. 'The primarch desired them, so we took them.

What he intends to do with them is of no interest to me.'

'Really?' said Lucius. 'And you call *me* self-involved.'

'And you do care?' countered Kaesoron. 'I think not. Your world begins and ends with you, Lucius. Just as mine concerns only what will allow me to taste the greatest bliss and darkest raptures. We exist to gratify all our desires to the extreme edges of sensation, but we do it in service to a power greater than any of us, greater even than any primarch.'

'Even the Phoenician or the Warmaster?'

'Luminous beings they are, but they are mere vessels for a power older than you or I can imagine.'

'How do you know this?' asked Lucius.

'There is wisdom in suffering, swordsman,' said Kaesoron. 'Isstvan V showed me that. The bliss of pain and the ecstasy of agony are how we offer our devotions. You have not known true suffering, because you are weak. You still cling to notions of what we were, not what we have become.'

Lucius bristled with anger at Kaesoron's casual dismissal of his own pain and talents, but said nothing, eager to learn more of what the First Captain had to say.

'The Lord Fulgrim has known the greatest pain this galaxy has to offer and he knows the truths at its heart,' said Kaesoron, and Lucius detected a change in his rasping tones, a tremor of doubt. 'Since… Isstvan he has shown me such sights as I would never have dreamed, pain and wonder, rapture and despair.'

Was it possible?

Did Kaesoron suspect the same as he?

Lucius risked a sidelong glance at Kaesoron, but the warrior's skull had been so thoroughly mangled and rebuilt that it was impossible to read his features. A thunderous crash of atomising metal washed over them as the last silo toppled to the ground, and its destroyers shrieked as the deafening noise drove spikes of pleasure through their brains.

Marius Vairosean marched towards them as a last Stormbird dropped through the streaked corona of a rainbow sky. Lucius wanted to find the sky beautiful, to be moved by the vivid colours and the rarefied blends of hues he had never seen.

He felt empty, and wanted nothing more than to leave this world. It had nothing left of interest, and anger touched him at the thought that he was bereft of stimulation.

'A grand finale,' said Marius, the words mangled by his overstretched jaws. Lucius wanted to ram his swords into Vairosean's chest, just to feel something. He resisted the urge only with difficulty.

'I despise this place,' said Lucius, wanting nothing more than to be gone from this mundane rock of a world.

'I have already forgotten it,' said Kaesoron.

7

THE DREAM STILL clung to the ragged edges of his consciousness, its lingering dread and burdensome suspicions hanging like an albatross from his neck. The corridors of the *Pride of the Emperor* were never silent, the echoes of screams drifting from one end of the ship to the other in a constant choir of debauched indulgences. The majority of these screams were of pain, but many were of delight.

It grew harder and harder to tell which was which with the grey passage of days.

Yet this area of the ship was abandoned and forgotten, like a dirty secret a man might hope will go away if only it can be ignored for long enough. No light or music or screams filled this wide hallway, no disjointed pavanes of misery, and no fleshy tributes to masterful excrucia-tion. It felt like this place didn't exist, as though it was out of joint with the rest of the ship.

Lucius turned a corner and found himself before the

great arched doors to *La Fenice*, and here the illusion of abandonment was dispelled. Six warriors stood before the doors, clad in scored armour of blues, pinks and purples. They wore tattered cloaks of gold weave that hung in asymmetrical waterfalls from the spikes worked into their shoulder guards, and crimson raptors surged from ruby flames on their breastplates.

All six carried golden-bladed halberds, the edges of which crackled with a faint haze of killing light. A flesh-masked warrior stepped towards him, the blade of his halberd spinning to face him. Lucius watched the warrior's movements, calm, assured and smooth. He was unafraid of Lucius, which marked him out as being particularly stupid.

'Phoenix Guard,' said Lucius with a grin of relish.

'Entering *La Fenice* is death,' said the warrior, his voice muffled by the skin mask.

'Yes, I'd heard,' replied Lucius amiably. 'Why is that, do you think?'

The Phoenix Guard ignored the question and said, 'Turn around, swordsman. Leave here and you will live.'

Lucius laughed, amused at the sincerity if not the seriousness of the threat.

'Really?' said Lucius, resting his palms on the pommels of his swords. 'Do you think you and your friends can stop me from getting inside?'

The rest of the Phoenix Guard spread out, forming an arc of killing steel around him.

'Leave now and you live,' said the warrior before him.

'Yes, you said that, but here's the thing,' said Lucius. 'I want in there, and you aren't going to stop me. Trust me, it will give me great pleasure to take the six of you on at once, but I think that might be a rather one-sided experience by the end.'

Lucius saw the attack coming in the Phoenix Guard's eyes.

Energised carbon steel clove the air, but Lucius was already moving.

Lucius ducked below the sweep of a halberd and the Terran blade leapt to his hand. Its tip plunged into the groin of the flesh-masked warrior. Lucius gave a savage twist and the blade cut up through his opponent's femur and hip to remove his leg. Blood gouted from the wound, and the warrior fell with a cry of mingled pain and surprise. Lucius darted to the side, his Laeran blade cutting into the flank of the warrior to his right. Armour parted before its alien metal and the warrior's guts looped out as though eager to be free of his flesh.

Altered organs heightened every sensation, and Lucius laughed with the vividness of his surroundings. The darkness became multi-faceted, the smell of blood a heady cocktail of unnatural chemicals and biological agents, the gleam of dim light from flashing weapons like the explosive fanfare that marked the end of the Great Triumph. His breath sounded impossibly loud, his blood like thundering rapids, and his opponents came at him with what seemed like deliberate slowness.

A halberd stroked his shoulder, and Lucius rolled with the arc of the blow. He sprang to his feet, blocked the return cut, and rolled his wrists around the weapon's haft, stabbing the blade through the Phoenix Guard's helmet. The warrior dropped without a sound and Lucius swayed aside from a scything halberd blow intended to cleave him from skull to pelvis.

Lucius counterattacked with blistering speed, his first cut removing the warrior's blade, the second opening his throat. A third blow all but severed the head, and he threw himself flat as another spiked halberd stabbed for the space between his shoulder blades. He came to his knees, swords crossed before him to catch the blade as it descended. The strength behind the blow was awesome, far in excess of his own, but Lucius twisted his blades to drive the blade down into the deck. Steel shrieked as the crackling blade tore up the decking. Lucius thundered his fist into the Phoenix Guard's helmet, cracking the visor and drawing a grunt of pain from within. The warrior lost his grip on the halberd and blocked a dazzling cut to the neck with his forearm.

Lucius's blade severed the arm at the elbow, and he spun inside to ram the Laeran blade through the warrior's chest. His victim fell with a gurgling cry, grabbing Lucius's wrist and dragging him down with him. Lucius was pulled to the deck, but kept the momentum of his tumble going as the last Phoenix Guard's halberd swung for him. He twisted in the air and landed lightly on the balls of his feet, leaving the blade trapped within the Phoenix Guard's chest.

Armed only with his Terran blade, Lucius dropped into a theatrical en garde position, keeping his sword high and moving the tip in tiny circles. An old trick, but the Phoenix Guard was not a subtle warrior, and Lucius saw his foe's eyes follow the motion of the blade. Lucius leapt forwards, feinting right as the warrior realised his mistake. A clumsy block swept around, but Lucius had already altered the angle of his thrust. The Terrawatt clans of the Urals had forged the blade in the days before Unity, and its edge had never failed him.

Until now.

The tip of the blade caught the broken nub of an eagle's wing on the warrior's plastron, and the impact sent a jolt of force along the sword. It snapped, and the tip sprang back at Lucius in a spinning arc of razor steel. Even Lucius's preternaturally swift reactions could not save him, and the shard sliced a deep furrow from his left temple to his lower jaw.

The pain was so sudden, so blissful and so wonderfully unexpected that it almost killed him as he took a moment to savour it.

Given a reprieve from death, the Phoenix Guard thrust his halberd towards Lucius. The tip kissed the metal of Lucius's war plate, but that was as close as it came to the swordsman's skin. Lucius hacked the weapon's haft in two with his broken sword and waved an admonishing finger.

'That was careless of me,' he said with a faintly embarrassed sigh. 'Imagine being killed by a sluggard like you. I'd never live it down.'

Before the warrior could reply or lament the loss of his weapon, Lucius spun inside his guard and executed an exquisitely aimed decapitating strike that sent the Phoenix Guard's head spinning across the chamber.

Lucius bent to retrieve the Laeran sword, twisting the handle back and forth to ease the pull of flesh. The blade slid clear and he tore the mask of dried skin from the first warrior's face, curious to see what someone who thought he could fight him and live looked like.

It was an unremarkable face, and in the flat planes of its features, he saw Loken's mocking grin. Lucius's good humour evaporated in an instant, and he stood with a grimace of bitter memory. He stamped down on the warrior's face. Once and the bone broke, twice and the skull cracked. Three times and it caved in, a wet crater of pulverised brain matter and skull fragments.

Angry now, Lucius cleaned his sword on the dried rag of skin, his mood changing like the wind as he held up the skinned face before him like an actor upon the stage.

'Trust me, you're better off,' he said, gesturing to the broken skull of the warrior from whom he had taken the flesh mask. 'He was an ugly bastard, that one.'

He tossed the face aside, making his way to the arched doors of *La Fenice*.

They had once been adorned with gold and silver leaf, but were now virtually bare. Frantic madmen, desperate to relive the beautiful horrors of the *Maraviglia*, had worked their hands to bloody nubs of bone in their attempts to gain entry. Lucius saw fragments of splintered fingernails embedded in the doors and plucked a few from the wood, enjoying the thought of how it must have felt to have them ripped from the nail bed.

'What do you hope to achieve?' he asked himself.

He had no answer, but the days since the Legion's departure from Prismatica had only intensified his desire, his *need*, to see what lay behind the sealed doors to the abandoned theatre. This was disobedience on a grand scale, and the very illicitness of the venture was reason enough to seek it out.

The killing of the Phoenix Guard made withdrawal a moot point anyway.

Lucius pushed open the doors and entered the abandoned theatre.

8

HE DREW A lungful of stagnant air as the darkness enfolded him like a midnight lover. It tasted of metal and meat, dust and age. *La Fenice* had once been a place of magic, but without any breath of life to sustain it, the theatre was little more than an empty shell, bereft of any hint of joy. Lucius struggled to recall the wondrous anarchy that had once filled this place, the stark violence and manic copulation that had filled its parquet and gallery boxes with a celebration of all things visceral.

His memories of the event were grey and dull, like faded echoes instead of the glorious moment of awakening he wanted to remember. The stage was splintered and stained with blood, the walls daubed with smears of reeking fluids and hung with rotted vines of organs that had no place outside of a human body. The songbirds that had trilled from gilded cages were gone, the golden footlights extinguished and the bodies he had expected to find sprawled in decomposition were nowhere to be seen.

Who would have taken them and for what purpose?

A number of answers presented themselves – for pleasure, for dissection, for trophies – but none seemed likely. Lucius saw no drag marks, simply stained outlines where the bodies had lain, as though they had been drained of substance by something within this room, something that could draw strength from the presence of so much death.

Lucius moved through the echoing vastness of the deserted theatre, his steps carrying him with unerring inevitability towards the centre of the parquet. Above him was the Phoenician's Nest, and he cast a wary glance upwards as he felt the skin on the back of his neck tighten in anticipation of danger. He felt as though malevolent eyes were upon him, but every sense told him he was alone in here.

His gaze was drawn up to the only spot of light in *La Fenice*, and Lucius was not surprised to find that the portrait of Lord Fulgrim bore no resemblance to the glorious piece of artwork that had presided over the Legion's rebirth. As it appeared in his dreams, the portrait was a work of insipid blandness. To the prosaic senses of mortals, it would have been a masterpiece, but to a warrior of the Emperor's Children it was a lifeless piece.

At least that was what Lucius believed until he met the eyes of this painted Fulgrim.

Like staring deep into an abyss that looks back, Lucius saw a dreadful anguish there, a bottomless well of agony and torment that took his breath away. His mouth fell open in a wordless exhalation of enjoyment to feel such exquisite pain. What manner of being could feel such despair? No mortal or Adeptus Astartes could plunge to such unknowable depths of wretchedness.

Only one such being could know such horror.

Lucius met the eyes of the portrait and knew in a heartbeat the nature of the being held captive within its golden prison.

'Fulgrim,' he breathed. 'My lord...'

The eyes pleaded with him, and his entire body shuddered with the ecstatic knowledge he now possessed. His heart beat furiously in his chest, and a giddy sense of vertigo staggered him as he struggled to comprehend the sheer scale of the deception worked upon the Emperor's Children.

Giddy with excitement, Lucius made his way from *La Fenice* in a fugue state, barely conscious of his surroundings. The enormity of what he now knew filled him like a supernova, the furthest edges of its illumination making his limbs tremble as though an electric charge filled his veins.

He staggered like a drunk through the doors of the theatre, and dropped to his knees as he began to exert a measure of control over his body. Lucius blinked away a confusing mass of light and colour from his eyes as the world around him became more real, more solid and more filled with vibrant possibility.

Alone in the entire galaxy, he knew something that no other did.

Yet even Lucius knew he could not act on this alone.

Galling as it was to admit, he would need help.

'The quiet order,' he whispered. 'I will call the Brotherhood of the Phoenix.'

9

THEY GATHERED IN the upper reaches of the *Pride of the Emperor*, in an observation bay that laid the immense starscape before the mortals who dared traverse its unimaginable gulfs. The Brotherhood of the Phoenix had not assembled since Isstvan, its members too involved in their own gratification to bother with the affairs of others.

Which was not to say that the observation deck went unused. Those who imbibed the toxically hallucinogenic cocktails brewed by Apothecary Fabius found enlightenment in its infinite vistas, and many indulged their freshly awakened carnal hungers with vicarious feasts of flesh and blades. Discarded bodies and torn heaps of broken glass lay strewn throughout the bay, and the occasional moan issued from a jumbled pile of clothing and leather restraints.

It had been a place of quiet reflection, where a warrior could meditate on the means by which he might draw closer to perfection, but now it was an arena of depravity, depthless horror and indulgences beyond all constraints of morality. No one came here to better themselves, and the grand ideals and debates once bandied back and forth were now forgotten echoes, remembered by none and actively flouted by many. If anywhere on board the *Pride of the Emperor* could be said to embody the utter desolation of the Emperor's Children it was this place.

They arrived in ones and twos, intrigued enough by Lucius's summons to come in hopes of some diversion interesting enough to amuse them for a time. That he – so uninterested in any notions of brotherhood – had issued such a summons was reason enough to appear, and by the time he judged it wise to begin, Lucius counted twenty warriors before him.

It was more than he had expected.

First Captain Kaesoron had come, as had Marius Vairosean and, more importantly – if Lucius's suspicions were confirmed – so had Apothecary Fabius. Kalimos, Daimon and Krysander were here, and Ruen of the Twenty-First. Heliton and Abranxe came also, and several others whose names Lucius had not bothered to remember. They regarded him with mild amusement, for he had always been held in faint contempt by the order. Lucius struggled to hold his temper in check.

'Why have you called us here?' demanded Kalimos, his downcast face stitched with rings and toothed hooks. 'This brotherhood has little meaning for us now.'

'I need you to hear something,' said Lucius, staring at First Captain Kaesoron.

'Hear what?' bellowed Vairosean, deaf to how loud he spoke.

'Fulgrim is not who he claims to be,' said Lucius, knowing he had to snare their interest early. 'He is an impostor.'

Krysander laughed and the skin of his face cracked with the force of it. Others joined in, but Lucius's anger was mitigated by the fact that he saw Kaesoron and Fabius narrow their eyes in interest.

'I should kill you for those words,' snarled Daimon, swinging a heavy, spike-headed maul from its shoulder harness. A monstrous weapon, one impact would crush any foe unlucky enough to be on the receiving end.

Ruen circled around behind Lucius, and he heard the whisper of an assassin's dagger being drawn. He tasted the bitter tang of the toxins on its blade, and licked his lips.

'It sounds preposterous, I know,' said Lucius. His life hung on the line here. It was one thing to defeat a handful of Phoenix Guard, quite another to take on twenty captains of the Legion. He grinned at the thought of such a fight, even as he knew he would not survive it.

'Let him speak,' said Fabius in sibilant tones. 'I would hear what the swordsman has to say. I am curious to see what has made him think like this.'

'Aye, let the whelp speak,' said Kaesoron, moving to stand beside Daimon.

Marius Vairosean unlimbered his sonic cannon, its destructive potential filling the observation deck with a bone-rattling bass note as he worked his scarred fingers over the harmonic coils.

The rest of the brotherhood spread out around him, and even as Lucius appreciated his mortal danger, he felt wonderfully alive. Krysander ran a hooked tongue over his lips, his black eyes like those of the primarch, as he slid a red-bladed dagger from a flesh-sheath cut into the meat of his bare thigh.

'I'll have your skin, Lucius,' said the warrior, licking stagnant blood from the blade.

Kalimos unhooked a coiled whip from a beringed belt at his waist, its entire length barbed with the gleaming razor teeth of a carnodon and tipped with an Inwit pain amplifier. It writhed like a snake, pulsing with an intestinal motion as it wrapped itself around its wielder's leg. Abranxe drew two swords from shoulder scabbards, as his blood brother, Heliton, slipped hooked cestus gauntlets over his fists.

They circled him in ever-decreasing rings, elaborating on the violations they would wreak upon him for wasting their time. Each captain sought to outdo the other in the depths of horror he outlined, and Lucius forced himself to ignore the barbs.

'Speak, Lucius,' said Kaesoron. 'Convince us that we have all been lied to.'

Lucius stared into Kaesoron's eyes, meeting his dead gaze, and hoping he had an ally in the First Captain.

'I don't have to,' said Lucius. 'Do I?'

'You are foolish if you think I won't kill you, swordsman,' replied Kaesoron.

'I know you can kill me, First Captain, but that's not what I meant.'

'Then what did you mean?' growled Kalimos, cracking his whip and leaving a bloody line carved into the deck plates.

Lucius scanned the faces around him. Some were as they had been before Isstvan, perfect and patrician, while grotesque flesh masks or androgynous porcelain harlequins hid many others. Still more were disfigured with gouged wounds, repeated burns, chemical scars or multiple piercings.

'Because you already know, don't you, First Captain?' said Lucius.

Kaesoron grinned, no mean feat for a man with little remaining of his face he could call his own. The look of gleeful madness Lucius saw in his eyes confirmed the suspicion that had begun to form on Prismatica.

Kaesoron already knew that Fulgrim was not who he claimed, but one ally among these warriors would not save Lucius if he could not convince the rest.

'You must have seen it, brothers,' said Lucius as Daimon began swinging his maul around his body in tight arcs. 'The Phoenician speaks, but it is not his voice. He tells of our glorious battles like he wasn't even there. He barely remembers the war against the Laer, and the victories of which he does speak sound like he reads them from a history book.'

'Old wars,' sneered Ruen, tasting the poison on his blade. 'Wars won in another's name. What do I care how they are remembered?'

'Who I was is forgotten,' said Heliton. 'Only what I am *now* is important.'

'A bad dream from which I am awakened,' added Abranxe. 'If the primarch forgets it too, so much the better.'

Lucius drew his sword as the ring of warriors tightened on him. Heliton slammed a spiked fist into his shoulder. Hard enough to hurt, not enough to provoke a reaction. Lucius curbed his natural instinct to take the bastard's head. Kalimos's whip cracked, and Lucius grimaced as it scored a red line at his shoulder, leaving a white tooth embedded in the plate.

Ruen's dagger licked the groove cut by Kalimos's whip, and Lucius felt the nerves in his shoulder spasm as the viral toxin bathed his nerves in fire. He staggered, seeing bright colours dance before his eyes.

'I saw the portrait in *La Fenice*,' he said through gritted teeth. 'It's him. It's him before the massacre.'

He sensed a pause in the captains' murderous attentions, and let the words pour from him in a stream of rabid consciousness.

'You all saw it, the glory of its life,' he said. 'It was Fulgrim as he was always meant to be, a shining avatar of perfection. A celebration of his transcendent beauty. It was everything we aspire to be, a vision we were compelled to worship. It was all that we beheld of beauty and true gratification and bliss. I have seen it, and that vision is gone. It's as though they've swapped places, like twin souls displaced by unnatural means.'

'If we do not follow the Phoenician then who has commanded us since the battle on the black sands?' demanded Kalimos.

'I do not know, not for sure,' said Lucius. 'I don't understand it all, but the power we saw in the *Maraviglia*… I saw it take the flesh of that mortal singer and rework it like wax before a flame. You all saw it. The power Fulgrim showed us makes soft clay of flesh, and who is to say what limits it has? Something else came through at Isstvan, something powerful enough to overcome the mind of a primarch.'

'Lord Fulgrim called such beings daemons,' said Marius Vairosean. 'An old word, but an apt one. They scream in the nights we travel between the stars, and scratch at the hull of the ship with nightmares and dark promises. They make glorious music in my skull.'

Lucius nodded. 'Yes,' he said. 'A daemon, that's it. You all saw what they could do in *La Fenice*. The powers they have. Lord Fulgrim has such powers now. I saw him unleash a curse upon a Mechanicum battle engine on Prismatica. Its shields were down, and without even touching it, he caused every living thing inside it to grow and mutate in a storm of flesh that ripped the war machine apart from the inside. Lord Fulgrim was mighty, but even he wasn't *that* powerful. Only the Crimson King has such powers.'

'Lord Fulgrim is no sorcerer!' cried Abranxe, lunging at Lucius with his swords extended. Lucius batted away the clumsy attack, and his riposte gave Abranxe a neat scar on his cheek for his trouble.

'I didn't say he was,' said Lucius, dropping into a defensive crouch, 'Listen, we knew the Warmaster was treating with such things, but this is a step too far.'

Kaesoron pushed the other captains aside and gripped Lucius by the edges of his breastplate. 'You think Horus Lupercal is behind this?' he snapped.

'I don't know. Maybe,' said Lucius. 'Or maybe Fulgrim went further than any of us thought he ever could.'

Kaesoron glanced over at Fabius, who had remained impassive throughout the unfolding drama. The First Captain drew a curved gutting knife and placed the tip of the blade against the pulsing artery at Lucius's neck. Sensing bloodshed, Daimon's hands slipped down the length of his hammer's shaft in preparation for a crushing blow.

'What say you, Fabius?' demanded Kaesoron. 'Is there any merit to the swordsman's words, or should I kill him right now?'

Fabius ran a hand through his thin white hair, his pinched features belying the strength in his limbs. The hissing, clicking chirurgeon machine that squatted at his back like a parasite reached over his shoulder, caressing Lucius's cheek with a slender blade. Lucius felt its feather-light touch, the blade so sharp that he only knew he had been cut when the blood ran over his lips.

The Apothecary's dark eyes glittered with amusement, and he nodded thoughtfully as though weighing the outcomes of a trial by combat where the fighters were equally matched.

'I too have seen things that have given me cause to wonder what our beloved primarch is becoming,' said Fabius, his desert-parched voice like the hiss of a snake's belly on sand.

'What manner of things?' said Kaesoron.

'A change in the composition of his blood and flesh,' replied Fabius. 'It is as though his molecular structure has begun to dissolve the bonds linking its constituent parts into a cohesive whole.'

'What could cause such a thing?'

Fabius shrugged. 'Nothing of this world,' he said with a grin of dreadful appetite. 'It is quite fascinating, you understand. It is as though his form is preparing for some great ascension, a wondrous shedding of a redundant form as his flesh is remade into something extraordinary.'

'And you never thought to mention this?' asked Lucius, still very much aware of the blade at his throat. Just by speaking, he caused its monomolecular tip to pierce his skin.

'It was too soon to speak,' snapped Fabius. 'I do not pause in my observations as you would not pause in the midst of a duel.'

'You mean you believe him?' asked Marius Vairosean, his stretched face unable to hide the revulsion he felt at the thought of their master's body being hijacked by another. Marius had ever been the loyal lapdog of the primarch, unquestioningly following his orders and never once doubting their course.

'I do, Vairosean,' said Fabius. 'My research is unfinished, but I believe that another entity resides within the Phoenician and prepares to transform him into some new image.'

Lucius took grim pleasure in his vindication as the First Captain's knife was removed from his throat. The circling captains paused in their threatening dance, shaken and enthralled that the wild claims of the swordsman had been backed up by no less a figure than Fabius.

Kaesoron lowered him to the deck and released his grip.

Lucius found it grimly amusing that it had been their very loyalty to Fulgrim that had seen them cast as traitors in this rebellion. Blind, unquestioning devotion to one luminous being had been the origin of their damnation in the eyes of the Imperium. The irony was not lost on any of them.

'How long before this transformation occurs?' asked Kaesoron.

Fabius shook his head. 'It is impossible to say for sure, but I would expect this pupating stage of development to be rapid. Indeed, the change in physicality might already be under way. It could be too late to stop it.'

'But it might not?' said Lucius.

'Nothing is certain,' admitted Fabius.

'Then we have to try,' stated the First Captain. 'If Fulgrim is no longer master of his own body then we have to get him back. We are his sons, and whatever has claimed his flesh must be captured and cast out of his body. Lord Fulgrim is our gene-father and I take orders from no one but him.'

A charge of febrile excitement swept through the gathered captains, and Lucius let out a shuddering sigh. He had convinced the others of his suspicions while keeping his blood inside his body and his head upon his shoulders.

'So, a pertinent question…' said Lucius. 'How do we go about capturing a primarch?'

10

THE GALLERY OF SWORDS was a place where the exhibitionists of the Emperor's Children liked to display their latest flesh masterpieces. Devotees of Apothecary Fabius, hoping to attract his notice, would drape their latest confections of macabre living art from the bull-headed statues that lined the grand processional of the *Andronicus*.

The towering granite-hewn heroes of the Legion, warriors who had cut the first histories of the Emperor's Children into the meat of the galaxy, were no longer recognisable as human. Their lovingly-carved faces had been recut, defaced and shaped anew into forms pleasing to the lurid aesthetics of the Legion. Leering grotesques kept watch on those who passed beneath them, and all who gazed upon them felt the wondrous horror of their debauched expressions.

Apothecary Fabius made his lair beneath the Gallery of Swords, a sprawling medicae complex that had been transformed from a place of healing, research and excellence into a shadowed labyrinth of excruciation, screams and nightmarish, inhumane experiments.

Fulgrim swept into the Gallery of Swords with Julius Kaesoron at his side, majestic in a long robe of cream fabric, with silver embroidered stitching running along the hems and collar. A sword belt of mirrored discs encircled his waist, the golden hilt of the anathame never far from Fulgrim's hand.

The primarch's white hair was pulled back into a long scalp-lock woven with mother of pearl and held in place by a circlet of golden laurels. His sculpted chest was bare, and the pale skin bore numerous ridges of scar tissue from the last treatments and enhancements worked upon him by Fabius.

Even though Kaesoron was encased in his spiked and flesh-wrapped Terminator armour, Fulgrim still stood head and shoulders above him. Clad in naught but his finery, Fulgrim was still a warrior to be feared.

The primarch stopped beside one statue that had suffered particularly at the hands of the Legion's craftsmen. He smiled up at the graven image of a reptilian bull's head. The warrior's armour had been cut with blessed symbols, and a trio of hollowed out bodies hung from barbed nooses, one from each outstretched arm, and another from its neck.

'Ah, Illios, you would not know yourself now,' said Fulgrim, with wistful nostalgia. 'I remember the day you first drew sword alongside me as we forged the alliance of the eighteen tribes. We were young then, and warriors who knew nothing of the wider world.'

'Do you wish he were here with us now?' asked Kaesoron.

Fulgrim laughed and shook his head. 'No, for I fear I would have to kill him. He was always so unbending, Julius. He was a man with an unbreakable code of honour from the elder days, I do not think he would have appreciated the enlightenments we have received.'

The primarch took a wistful look at the statue of his former blade brother and a strange expression passed over his alabaster features. Kaesoron's eyes were no longer able to perceive the world as they once had, but even he could see the light of dark memory in the primarch's eyes.

'How naïve we were, old friend,' mused Fulgrim. 'How blind…'

'My lord?'

'Nothing, Julius,' said Fulgrim, marching towards the end of the gallery.

'How did Lord Commander Illios die?' asked Kaesoron.

'You know the answer to that, Julius. Your introspections on perfection would have required you to memorise the victories of our past.'

'I know, but to hear it from your lips is always a sublime experience.'

'Very well,' smiled Fulgrim. 'Apothecary Fabius will not mind if we are a little late.'

Kaesoron shook his head. 'I am sure he will not.'

'Good. Ah, Illios, it was your temper that saw you killed,' said Fulgrim, his tone warming with recall. 'You were a man of joyous rages and great sorrows. Never good combinations in a warrior, but you were almost great enough to survive your own weaknesses. Mighty he was, Julius, tall and proud, with the triple-bladed Executioner Falchion and the Armour of Chemos. He was unstoppable. A warrior such as he had only one superior, but he held no grudge that I was his better.'

'It was atop the Barchettan Warlord's city-leviathan he fell, was it not?'

'If you know the story so well, why bid me tell it?' snapped Fulgrim, his eyes ablaze.

'Apologies, lord,' said Kaesoron, keeping his head bowed. 'It is a stirring story, and I was caught up in your words.'

'Then you should have kept your mouth shut, Julius,' said Fulgrim. 'You do not interrupt me when I am speaking. Did Eidolon's death teach you nothing?'

'It was instructional,' said Kaesoron.

'When I speak, I am the star around which you orbit,' said Fulgrim, leaning down to fix Kaesoron with his furious gaze. His black eyes were pools of dark oil, ready to ignite with unspeakable rage. Kaesoron knew he had made a terrible error in speaking and that his life now hung in the balance.

'Who but you, my lord, could speak with such passion and force me into a loose tongue?'

'None other,' agreed Fulgrim. 'It is only natural you should be entranced by my words.'

Fulgrim's wrath evaporated and he slapped a powerful hand on Kaesoron's shoulder guard, staggering the First Captain.

'Ah, we are a pair are we not, Julius?' reflected the primarch. 'Reminiscing of past glories when there are fresh foes against which to beat our breast and fresh sensations to be wrung from each breath.'

'Then let us hurry our steps to Apothecary Fabius,' said Kaesoron, gesturing to the shadowed cloisters at the end of the Gallery of Swords.

'Indeed, we must,' said Fulgrim, his voice aquiver with anticipation. 'I wonder what delights he has for me this time.'

'He promises wondrous things,' said Julius Kaesoron.

11

LUCIUS WATCHED FULGRIM and Julius Kaesoron draw near the end of the gallery. His breath was coming in short spikes, and he fought to keep his excitement from getting the better of his caution. As thrillingly treasonous as this was, he wanted to live to see another day. Attacking a primarch was, perhaps, a foolish way to go about that, but his heightened senses were alive with the rush of sensation flooding him.

The stone beneath his bare palm was a smorgasbord of textures, rough, smooth, indented and imperfect in its carving. Polished, moon-blush granite, its original surface planed smooth to microscopic tolerances, then hacked apart with gleeful chisels wielded with screaming abandon. He could no longer tell which of the Legion's heroes he sheltered behind, and that lacuna was like a missing tooth.

Lucius fought this newly-birthed obsession down and wrenched his thoughts back to the task at hand with a shuddering breath. To experience every sensation to the limits of endurance was sublime, but it had a nasty habit of diverting a warrior from his true goals. Bad enough that one warrior should be so caught up, but woe betide any world that became the target of the entire Legion's obsession.

He forced his gaze back down the length of the Gallery of Swords, watching as Kaesoron drew Fulgrim deeper into their trap. Vairosean's warriors were hidden in the shadows of the mighty statues, each shrouded with a falsehood and kept silent with implanted neural shriekers that bombarded their cerebral cortex with howling discordia. When the word was given, those shriekers would go silent, depriving the implanted warriors of the blissful howling and driving them to replace it with fresh stimulus. Vairosean had developed the implants on the journey from Prismatica, and, much as Lucius was loath to credit such a plodder with anything of merit, he had to admit the shriekers transformed the Kakophoni into obsessively fanatical killers on the battlefield.

Against the might of a primarch they would need to be.

It seemed inconceivable that Fulgrim could not be aware of their presence, but as Lucius and the Legion had become so caught up in their own self-obsessions, so too had the primarch. Where Lucius's clouds of obsession were heavy and almost impenetrable, he could only imagine what heights of narcissism a luminous being such as Fulgrim might attain.

Lucius glanced to his right, seeing the shadowed opening that led down into the forsaken lair of Apothecary
Fabius. He remembered descending into the dimly-lit
labyrinth after his defection from the fools on Isstvan
III, his every nerve alive with fearful anticipation. He had
set foot in the Apothecarion a handful of times only, his
skills so great as to rarely require medical attention. He
remembered it as a sterile place of clinical, antiseptic
chill, but it had become a gallery of grotesqueries, its
walls spattered with rust-coloured stains and hung with
biological trophies, mutant curios and bubbling tanks
of noxious fluids.

The stink had been incredible, but once Fabius had
opened him up and remade him in the primarch's
image, it had become a place of wonders to him. As
much as he revelled in the glorious worlds opened up to
him by Fabius, he could never bring himself to like him.
He supposed such things were immaterial now.

He heard Fulgrim ask a question, but the words were
lost to him, and he swore silently as he realised he had
been distracted once more. Taking a grip on himself,
Lucius narrowed his concentration to a sharp blade of
focus. Fulgrim was almost upon him, and as architect of
this plan, it fell to Lucius to make the first move.

Lucius stepped from the shadows, and the fractional
space that separated life and death grew ever thinner.
His senses surged with the vividness of this moment, the
thrilling anticipation of what he was doing, the sheer
madness of it and the irreversible nature of this act.

'Lucius?' said Fulgrim with an amused smile. 'What are
you doing here?'

'I have come to speak to you.'

'No, "my lord", Lucius? Have you forgotten to whom
you speak?'

'I don't know who I'm speaking to,' said Lucius, staring into the hard, opaque orbs of Fulgrim's eyes. He saw
no pity, no humanity and nothing that spoke to him of

the lord and master he had loved and served with all his heart. He wondered if that was true or if he was just remembering a past that didn't exist, a fictive history invented to justify this moment.

'I am Fulgrim, Master of the Emperor's Children,' said Fulgrim, glancing about himself as though stretching his senses out and gradually becoming aware of the noose into which he had just placed his neck. 'And you will obey me.'

Lucius shook his head and rested his palm on the pommel of his sword. He wasn't surprised to realise it was slick with sweat.

'I don't know what you are, but you are not Fulgrim,' said Lucius, and the primarch laughed. It was a good laugh, infectious and rich with deep amusement. It was the laugh of a man who knows the joke he is hearing should be appreciated on a level beyond that which everyone else around him understands.

Fulgrim grinned, his dark eyes alight with perverse pleasure at the situation.

'You think you can take me, swordsman? Is that it?' asked Fulgrim. 'I see how you look at me, the obsessive study and drive to prove yourself better than everyone else. You think I don't see how you wish you could pit your blade against mine?'

Lucius hid his surprise. He had assumed Fulgrim to be too self-absorbed to notice his calculating scrutiny, but he should have understood that true self-obsession could only be fed by the attentions of others. Fulgrim would have basked in Lucius's study, and who knew what else he had done? Had his every movement been a pantomime to lull Lucius into assuming superiority or was this just a calculated bluff?

'I have watched you ever since Isstvan V, and you are not the same warrior I followed into battle on Laeran. The Fulgrim I followed onto the surface of that eldar world is not the same one looking at me and daring me to come at him. You are an impostor with my master's face and I will take no orders from a usurper.'

Fulgrim laughed once more, squatting down on his haunches as the hilarity of Lucius's words threatened to overcome him. Lucius scowled in petulant irritation. What had he said that was so funny? He glanced at Kaesoron, but it was impossible to read the First Captain's expression.

'Oh, you are a rare and precious treasure, Lucius,' roared Fulgrim. 'Don't you see? We *all* take our orders from a usurper. Horus Lupercal has not yet earned the title of Emperor. Until then, what else is he but a usurper?'

'That's not the same,' said Lucius, feeling his moral high ground in this confrontation eroding beneath him. 'Horus Lupercal *is* the Warmaster, but you are not Fulgrim. I see his face, but something else lurks behind it, something spawned by the same powers that granted us the power to fully experience the wonders this galaxy has to offer.'

Fulgrim rose to his full height and said, 'If that were the case, swordsman, should you not then prostrate yourself before me and beg me to open your eyes to fresh wonders? If I am an avatar of the warp's Dark Prince clothed in the flesh of your beloved primarch, am I not doing a better job than he did in showing you how best to sate your hungers and desires?'

Shapes moved in the shadows between the alcoves of statues, and Lucius saw Heliton and Abranxe emerge from the opposite sides of the marble statue of Lord Commander Pelleon. Marius Vairosean marched along the grand processional with his long-necked cannon slung at his side, its dissonance coils thrumming with potential. His Kakophoni emerged from their hiding places, eyes wide with madness and the need to be driven into sonic ecstasy.

Apothecary Fabius stepped from the arched entrance

to his subterranean kingdom, flanked by Kalimos, Daimon, Ruen and Krysander.

Fulgrim turned in a slow circle, taking in the measure of the warriors arrayed against him.

Lucius counted perhaps fifty warriors and wished he had fifty more. And then a hundred more beyond that.

The captains of the Legion encircled Fulgrim, each with their weapon unsheathed and with murder in their hearts. Lucius drew his blade and rolled his shoulders to loosen the muscles. They had not come to kill Fulgrim – if such a thing was even possible for mortals – but this rapidly-unfolding drama had all the hallmarks of a situation spiralling out of control.

'Alas, I am betrayed by those I hold most dear,' said Fulgrim, clutching his hands to his breast as though his heart was broken. 'You all countenance these lies? Can you all truthfully believe I am not your beloved genesire, who brought us all back from the brink of extinction and who led us to truths denied us by our once-father?'

Fulgrim's face crumpled and Lucius was not a little unsettled to see a single tear work its way down the marbled flawlessness of the primarch's face.

The primarch turned to Julius Kaesoron with a hurt look of betrayal in his eyes.

'Even you, Julius?' said the Phoenician. 'Then fall, Fulgrim!'

'Take him!' bellowed Julius Kaesoron, and the captains of the Legion stepped away from Fulgrim as Marius Vairosean unleashed a barrage of shrieking reverberations from his cannon. Statues split under the sonic assault, and Lucius felt a delicious frisson throughout his body as the aural blast wave threw him to the flagstones of the gallery.

Fulgrim staggered under the impact, his robes ripped from his body with the tearing power of the shockwave. He dropped to one knee, his wreath of golden laurels shattering into thousands of fragments. Beneath his robes, Fulgrim was naked but for a crimson loincloth and Lucius marvelled at the almost serpentine fluidity of his body. Daimon leapt towards the downed primarch with his grotesque maul swinging down like an executioner's axe.

Fulgrim swayed aside from the blow, letting the barbed head of the weapon bury itself in the stone decking. Splinters exploded from the impact, and before Daimon could retrieve his maul, Fulgrim stepped in and drove the heel of his palm into the captain's face. Daimon had no time to scream before his face was smashed hollow. Even as the warrior fell, Fulgrim swept up the maul in his right fist as Ruen darted forwards and rammed his envenomed blade to the hilt into Fulgrim's side.

The haft of the maul slammed down into Ruen's elbow, shattering the bones of his upper and lower arm. The captain's howl of pain was music to Lucius's ears, as Fulgrim tore the absurdly small blade from his body. Fulgrim kicked Ruen away, sending him spinning across the gallery to slam into a statue with a crack of shattering plate and breaking bone.

Lucius circled Fulgrim, not yet willing to commit to the fight. His blade tingled in his grip, eager to taste such rarefied blood and hungry to draw him into the dance of swords.

'Not yet, my beauty,' he whispered. 'Not when there are others to suffer the worst of the primarch's ire and strength.'

If Ruen's toxins were having any effect on Fulgrim, Lucius couldn't say, but it appeared that the captain of the Twenty-First had been premature in his boasts that his banes could fell any living foe.

The Kakophoni unleashed a roaring series of blasts from their sonic weapons, filling the Gallery of Swords with clashing echoes and reverberating harmonies that drew blood from the ears of all that heard them. Fulgrim shrieked in pleasure as the sound vibrated his flesh and bones with a ferocity that should have killed him thrice over.

Heliton stepped in and drove the spiked fist of his cestus gauntlet into Fulgrim's lower back, a blow that would have shattered the spine of even an armoured Adeptus Astartes. The primarch took the blow and spun on his heel. A jabbing elbow put Heliton on his back, his lower jaw hanging by a thread of glistening sinew and pulped bone. Abranxe screamed to see his boon companion laid low and swept his twin swords for Fulgrim's neck. The primarch deflected one sword with the head of Daimon's maul, as Abranxe spun inside the weapon's reach to slide his second blade across Fulgrim's throat.

Blood cascaded down Fulgrim's throat, and his eyes widened with genuine surprise. Lucius felt a fleeting moment of bitter disappointment and venomous jealousy at the thought of a merely competent swordsman like Abranxe landing such a blow. But no sooner had the blood begun to flow than it stopped, and Fulgrim took hold of Abranxe by the neck and hurled him away.

'A good move, Abranxe,' said Fulgrim with a rasp of gratification. 'I will remember it.'

Kalimos cracked his lash, its toothed length wrapping around Fulgrim's left arm. The carnodon teeth tore into his flesh, and squirts of blood sprayed from the wounds. As Kalimos hauled on his lash, Julius Kaesoron stepped in and delivered a thunderous left hook with his crackling fist. Augmented with strength enough to tear apart a battle tank, Kaesoron's blow drove Fulgrim to his knees, but before he could strike again, Kalimos jerked on his lash as Krysander plunged his dagger between the primarch's shoulder blades.

Fulgrim closed his fist on the gnawing lash and gave what appeared to be no more than a gentle tug. Kalimos was plucked from his feet and spun around the primarch, slamming into Krysander and sending the pair of them crashing to the ends of the gallery. Kaesoron

swung again, but Fulgrim was ready for him, blocking
the blow with Daimon's maul and thundering a naked
fist into his face. Kaesoron dropped with a grunt, but
Fulgrim made no move to finish him.

'Now Lucius, strike!' shouted Fabius, and the swordsman cursed the Apothecary as Fulgrim spun to face him.
The primarch dropped the maul and drew the glitter-
sheened blade Horus Lupercal had gifted him aboard
the *Vengeful Spirit*.

'Now we come to it, swordsman,' grinned Fulgrim,
swaying on his feet.

Lucius saw the pale complexion of his primarch was
ashen and spat to the deck.

'This would be no contest worth making,' he said.
'Ruen's venom and your wounds render it meaningless.'

Fulgrim spread wide his arms and took stock of the
blood dripping from his body. 'This?' he said. 'This is
nothing. Come at me with the blade I gave you and we
will settle this question once and for all, yes?'

Lucius cocked his head to one side, meeting the primarch's maddened gaze and seeing a truth he knew was
as unshakable as it was inevitable.

Even in his wounded state, Fulgrim would kill him.

And Lucius wasn't ready to die, not for this.

Before he could consider the matter further, Julius
Kaesoron rose up behind Fulgrim and slammed his
energised fist down on Fulgrim's skull. A blow that
should have pulped its victim's head to a smeared red
ruin merely drove Fulgrim to the ground. The Phoenician shook his head and his bloody rictus grin put Lucius
in mind of the deathly iconography he had seen carved
into Isstvan V's ruins.

As Fulgrim sought to push himself to his feet, Marius Vairosean jammed the end of his sonic cannon into
Fulgrim's neck and unleashed a barrage of squalling harmonics that filled the gallery with ear-bleeding noise.
Lucius cried out in pain, and Fulgrim's eyes rolled back

in their sockets as he let out a groan of what sounded very much like delirious pleasure.

The sword fell from the primarch's hand, and he toppled to the cracked flagstones with a heavy thump. Lucius looked up, blinking away bright spots of light from his vision and hearing what sounded like a million bells clanging at once. He stood a few metres from Vairosean, so he couldn't begin to imagine the effect the blast must have had on Fulgrim.

The surviving captains picked themselves up from the ground and formed a ring of dazed warriors around the fallen god. It had been a battle like no other, the warriors of a Legion turning on their own primarch, and the enormity of what they had done was not lost on them.

Lucius did not know what to feel. He had been cheated of his duel with Fulgrim, a duel he felt in his bones he would have lost. But some secret instinct told him that he would yet get his chance to test his blade against the primarch's alien weapon and yet live to speak of it.

Lucius turned his gaze upon his fellow captains. None marked his stare, for they could not tear their eyes from the downed primarch. Kalimos bled from numerous cracks in his armour, and Krysander's breastplate was dented so deeply that the bone shield of his chest must surely be in fragments. Abranxe knelt by Heliton, holding the hanging fragments of his brother's lower jaw in his hands. Vairosean's howling mouth was spread even wider in a hissing grimace of triumph, and Julius Kaesoron stared at his fist as though unable to believe he had raised it in anger against Fulgrim.

None spoke. None knew what to say.

They had taken arms against their primarch and they had enjoyed it.

Apothecary Fabius broke the spell of their silence.

'Fools!' hissed the lifeless voice of the Apothecary. 'You would stand gaping like landed fish until he awoke!'

Fabius turned away and made his way to the arched

entrance to his necropolis of freakish surgeries. As he reached the edge of shadow, he turned back to the Legion captains.

'Bring him below,' said Fabius. 'We have much to do.'

'What exactly are you going to do, Apothecary?' demanded Kaesoron.

'I am going to exorcise the creature that has stolen the primarch's flesh.'

'How?' asked Lucius.

'By any means necessary,' said Fabius with an odious grin.

12

IT WAS THE most terrible thing he had ever seen.

It was the most wondrous thing he had ever seen.

Fulgrim, the Phoenician, Lord of the Emperor's Children, Master of the III Legion, bound with the heaviest of fetters, chemically subdued and laid naked on a cold steel gurney like a corpse bound for dissection. Fulgrim's arms were thrown up above his head, his legs spread like the Vitruvian man of old.

Lucius's eyes roamed Fulgrim's pale flesh, the alabaster firmness criss-crossed in a web of surgical scars and incisions; knotted ridges that spoke of unknowable procedures and unspeakable experimentation upon the secret flesh within.

The delicious treason of this moment was something to be treasured, a wondrous sensation of the most terrible betrayal. Yet, for all that he called it betrayal, wasn't it an act of loyalty to cast out the creature that had taken possession of their master's soul?

Fabius circled the supine primarch, sliding needles as thick as Lucius's little finger into Fulgrim's arms and chest. Chem-shunts pumped powerful soporifics and muscle relaxants that would have dropped even the largest greenskin. Gleaming silver wires hooked to humming generators trailed from the primarch's temples and

groin, and from every point on his body where pain
might be heightened.

The lights were kept low, as befitted this act of vio-
lation, and the only sound was the murmuring of the
hooded null-wretches in each shadowed corner of the
chamber and the wheezing breath of the machines
Fabius had set up around his…

Lucius wanted to say *patient*, but the word that came
to mind was *victim*.

Julius Kaesoron stood silently at the foot of the slab,
while Marius Vairosean paced like a caged raptor. Lucius
smiled at his discomfort. Vairosean had ever been the
lackey and the blindly obedient slave. Caught in a
quandary of obedience to something that might not be
Fulgrim and the possibility of betraying his master, Vairosean's mind must be alive with contradictory thoughts
and fears.

Lucius almost envied him.

Fabius's thrall-slaves had carried the mewling forms of
Heliton and Ruen deeper into the labyrinth; flesh-vats
and xenosalival-sutures already prepared for their treatment. Daimon was beyond help, his skull smashed to
concave ruin by the primarch's fist, but the rest of their
treasonous band would survive. The thought sent a
sliver of unease worming through Lucius's brain, and he
turned to Kaesoron.

'Did you think we could do it?' he asked.

'Do what?'

'This,' said Lucius, gesturing towards the fallen primarch. 'Capture Fulgrim. I wasn't sure we could do it.'

'*You* didn't do it,' pointed out Kaesoron.

'What do you mean?'

'Look at you,' hissed Kaesoron. 'Not a mark on you,
swordsman. You bring this matter to the brotherhood,
and then step back and let us do the fighting for you.'

Lucius grinned, energised by Kaesoron's anger. 'What
happened up there was a brawl. I fight with perfect grace,

total immersion and fluid perfection. That was not a fight that required any of those qualities.'

'More like you saw you couldn't beat him.'

'That too,' added Lucius, 'but there's no shame in that.'

'True enough,' said Kaesoron, his capricious anger fading as quickly as it had come.

Marius Vairosean moved around the edge of the gurney, his stretched-out face making it impossible to read his expression. The captain of the Third had slung his sonic weapon over his shoulder, but the pulsing waves of hard-edged sound still rippled from its energised coils.

'Daimon is dead,' said Vairosean. 'And Heliton died on the way down.'

'And the Legion will be no worse off for their loss, if you ask me,' said Lucius.

'Ruen's arm is shattered beyond repair,' continued Vairosean, as though Lucius had not spoken. 'Krysander and Kalimos will live, but they will play no part in... this.'

'A small price to pay for subduing a primarch,' noted Kaesoron, as Fabius approached.

The Apothecary wore his white hair bound in a long scalp-lock, which only served to render his already gaunt features more skeletal and emaciated. His eyes were black, and Lucius couldn't remember if they had always been that way or had been changed to match those of the primarch. He wore a floor-length coat of flayed human skin, taken from the bodies of the dead on Isstvan V. Here and there, it was possible to recognise the features of a face, a mouth stretched in an endless scream of agony or eyes wide with horror at the sight of the skinner's knife. Some of the faces seemed familiar, but Lucius knew that without the architecture of bone, every face tended to similarity.

Eschewing his chirurgeon device, Fabius favoured a belt of knotted sinew pierced through with metal loops, from which hung the tools of the excruciator's

art. Hooks, blades, spikes, pliers and barbs glittered in
the half-light, but Lucius wondered if such banal instruments would draw screams from a being as powerful as
Fulgrim.

'We are ready to begin,' said Fabius, drawing on a
clicking pair of silver steel gauntlets.

'Then let us be done with this,' said Kaesoron. 'If
Lucius is right and there *is* something else concealed
behind Lord Fulgrim's face, then the sooner it is gone
the better.'

They spread out around Fulgrim, each weighing the
enormity of what they were doing against the potential
for wonder and fresh sensation. That they had managed
to subdue a primarch was miracle enough, but to drive
out a creature of the warp...

Was such a thing even possible?

Lucius looked from face to face, understanding that no
one gathered around the body of Fulgrim could answer
that question. The Emperor's Children had been a Legion
reticent in employing Librarians. The genetic quirk that
allowed a psyker to wield the power of the warp came
about as a result of a genetic mutation, a flaw. And nothing that could be considered a flaw would be permitted
within the ranks of Fulgrim's Legion.

'So what do we do?' asked Kaesoron.

'First, we wake him,' said Fabius, stroking needle-
tipped fingers over Fulgrim's chest.

'Assuming he doesn't just break free and kill us all,
what then?' said Lucius.

'We drive the creature out,' said Fabius. 'With reason,
with threats and with pain.'

'Pain?' snorted Vairosean. 'What pain can you admin-
ister that a primarch would feel?'

Fabius smiled his reptilian grin that promised a host
of pains he alone knew and would be only too glad to
demonstrate.

'I know this body like no other,' said Fabius, running

his surgically-enabled digits over Fulgrim's skin with a lover's familiarity. 'I know everything about how it was put together, the secret powers alloyed to its flesh and bone, the unique organs crafted for the creation of such a numinous being. What the Emperor created, I have broken down into its constituent parts and remade in a greater whole.'

The arrogance of Fabius was astounding, but Lucius felt himself warming to it. To have opened up the body of a primarch and gazed upon the wonders within was an honour few, if any, would have known, so perhaps it was arrogance born of knowledge.

'Then do it,' said Kaesoron.

Fabius nodded, though there was more amusement to the gesture than any real acquiescence. How long would it be, wondered Lucius, before Fabius's arrogance lifted him from the chain of command entirely? Once so rigid and unbending, the Emperor's Children adhered to the old structure in lieu of anything better, but even that was breaking down as its warriors put their own desires and whims above those of the Legion.

How long before we are little more than squabbling war-bands fighting for our own self-gratification?

Lucius had no answer to the question, and nor did that lack trouble him overmuch. Whether any remnant of the old Legion survived their rebirth was a matter of supreme indifference to him.

Fabius clipped a fluid drip to Fulgrim's arm and a shimmering crimson fluid sprinted along its length. No sooner had it entered the primarch's body than Fulgrim's black eyes opened and he blinked rapidly, like a sleeper suddenly awoken from a vivid dream.

'Ah, my sons…' said Fulgrim. 'What is this new diversion you have for me?'

Fabius leaned over to speak in Fulgrim's ear. 'You are not Fulgrim, are you?'

Fulgrim's eyes darted to the Apothecary, and Lucius

caught the whiff of conspiracy in the glance. He leaned forwards and lifted Fabius's hand from Fulgrim's chest.

'Lucius,' breathed Fulgrim with perfumed breath. 'Such a shame we were denied the caress of steel, don't you think?'

'I think you have been luring me into that fight for some time,' answered Lucius.

Fulgrim laughed. 'Was I really so obvious? It would have made for a sublime experience, Lucius. How can you say you are truly alive unless you have first tasted death? To rise anew from the ashes of one life and be reborn into another. To taste oblivion and then return, ah, now *that* is an experience not to be dismissed so lightly.'

'I think death might sour of its charms in short order,' said Lucius. 'I think I will stick to the pleasures life can offer.'

Fulgrim's face twisted in a pout of disappointment. 'How short sighted of you, my son. No matter, you will reconsider in time, I think. Now, to the rest of you. Can you seriously believe I am not who I say I am when I tell you I am your master?'

'We *know* you are not Fulgrim,' said Kaesoron.

'Then who do you believe me to be?'

'A creature of the immaterium,' said Vairosean. 'A daemon spawn.'

'A daemon?' laughed Fulgrim. 'And how else would you describe a primarch? Are you so naïve as to believe that all things named daemon are evil? Daemon or primarch, both are creatures fashioned from immaterial energies, hybrids of flesh and spirit brought into this world by unnatural means. If you knew anything of my creation then you would not bandy such words so carelessly.'

'So you admit that you are a daemon?' hissed Kaesoron.

'Julius, my beloved son,' said Fulgrim. 'Have you become so eager for conflict that you consciously blind yourself to reality? I have already told you that by Marius's dull definition, yes, I am a daemon! A daemon willed into creation by a being who seeks to win his immortality through storming the realm of gods by clambering over our corpses.'

'It speaks with lies masquerading as truth,' warned Fabius. 'Like the horse of ancient Truva, it will send its falsehoods garbed in that which sounds pleasant to your ears.'

'Then we should cut out his tongue,' said Lucius, and he was rewarded by a flicker of unease in Fulgrim's dark eyes. He saw anger, amusement and disappointment in that flicker, but which was the true emotion, he could not tell.

'Marius,' said Fulgrim. 'Of all my sons, you were the last I expected to see here.'

The words dripped with anguish, but Marius Vairosean did not flinch from them. Ever since Marius had failed Fulgrim on Laeran, he had been the most devoted servant, ever eager to please and determined to obey any order without question. If Fulgrim hoped to appeal to that aspect of Vairosean, he was to be sorely disappointed.

'My love for my primarch knows no bounds,' said Marius, leaning forwards as though to spit in the bound primarch's face. 'But you are not he, and I will do whatever it takes to cast you from his body. No pain is beyond me, no suffering too great to make that happen. Do you understand, daemon spawn?'

Fulgrim's face split apart in a wide grin.

'Then enough talk, whelps,' he said. 'Let us begin our journey into madness together!'

13

FABIUS BEGAN WITH that most ancient of interrogation techniques, the unveiling of his many devices of excruciation and explaining of the purposes to which they would be put. They ranged from mundane artefacts, such as any fashioner of metal or wood might employ – hammers, needle-nosed pliers, nails, welding torches, awls, planes and slow-bit drills – to more exotic implements of suffering. Nerve-splicers, organ-liquefiers, chakra-inflamers, marrow-augers and brain-stem impellents.

'This last device is one that will give me great pleasure to use,' said Fabius, hooking a number of metal barbs into Fulgrim's spine. The gurney upon which Fulgrim lay had rotated about its long axis, revealing flagellated shoulders and a back that was a corrugated landscape of scar tissue and healing weals. Lucius saw an admirable devotion in the primarch's flesh, a single-minded pursuit of pleasurable agony that only the true devotee of pain could attain.

'What is it and what does it do?' asked Kaesoron.

Fabius smiled, pleased to be able to elaborate on his tool of suffering. 'It is a neural parasite I have engineered from gene-spliced xenos brain fluids and nanotech recovered from the Diasporex hybrid-captains.'

'That doesn't answer his question,' snapped Marius.

Fabius nodded and tapped a long-nailed finger on the back of Fulgrim's skull. Lucius frowned at the gesture, the implications of detachment altogether too complete. To Fabius, Fulgrim was simply another piece of meat upon which he could work his biological conjurations. The outcome of this betrayal would decide the future course of the Legion, but it was already simply a means to uncover some new biological quirk and a test of a new invention. Lucius's feelings towards Fabius went from dislike to hate.

Fabius lifted an artefact that looked like the rear portion of a battle helm and turned it around in his hands. Thin spikes jutted from one side, each hooked to an array of injector shunts loaded with glittering silver fluid that rippled like expectant mercury.

'Once placed upon the subject, nano-fluid is introduced to the subject's body, whereupon it latches onto the brain stem and follows the neural pathways into the brain. The various xenos species employed in the creation of the serum were possessed of enhanced psychic potential, and the invasion of the brain chemistry allows the manipulator of the device to access any area of the brain and stimulate it as required.'

'To what end?' asked Lucius, though he had a good idea.

'All things mortal are simply engines,' said Fabius. 'Mechanical animals of flesh and blood, but driven by essentially mechanistic imperatives. What we mistake for personality and character are simply expressions of response to stimuli. With a complex enough algorithm, it would be possible to exactly replicate a functioning machine persona that would be indistinguishable from a living creature. Knowing this, we can stimulate certain areas of the brain, enhancing whatever aspects we choose while blocking others. I could dash the brains of a newborn infant against a wall in front of its mother and this device would see her delirious with ecstasy should I so choose. Or I could lightly touch a man's chest and make him believe I was tearing his heart out with my bare hands.'

'Then why the need for the other devices?' asked Kaesoron.

'As much as this device can make a man believe he is burning to death without so much as a spark being near him, there is a certain pleasure to be taken from a… simpler approach to pain,' admitted Fabius.

'On that at least we agree,' said the First Captain.

'So what are we waiting for?' demanded Vairosean. 'Let us begin and be done with this.'

Fabius gave a slow nod and rotated the gurney around once more. Fulgrim's face was ruddy and Lucius could see he relished the prospect of their attempted rescue of the soul whose body he had stolen.

'I remember that device,' said Fulgrim. 'Do you really believe it will work on a being like me? My consciousness is an order of magnitude greater than yours. It functions in realms beyond anything you can comprehend, its upper limits so great they cannot be contained purely in a cocoon of bone, and must exist in realms which only gods can access.'

'We shall find out,' said Fabius, insulted that his genius was being impugned.

'Start with that one,' ordered Kaesoron. 'If we are successful, there must be a perfect body into which Fulgrim can return.'

'My sons, you have been led to this like sheep to the slaughter,' said Fulgrim. 'Lucius brings you an idea that generates a flicker of interest in your dull lives and you seize it as a golden lifeline just so you can actually *feel* something. Have you learned nothing since our ascension? Non-conformity in thought and deed is the only vital life. Brotherhoods are for sheep-minds, and heresy is godly!'

'Enough talking,' said Lucius, snatching up a set of bladed pliers and sliding them over the middle finger of Fulgrim's right hand. With one swift, even pressure, he severed the finger at the middle knuckle, and a squirt of blood pulsed from the wound before slowing to a drip.

Fulgrim howled, but whether it was in pain or pleasure Lucius could not tell.

Fabius snatched the pliers from Lucius with an angry scowl.

'Excruciation is a precise and meticulous art, a stepped pyramid of pain,' he said. 'To randomly cut and maim is the work of amateurs. I will have no part in such butchery.'

'Then stop talking and get on with it,' said Lucius. 'Because it sounds to me like you're stalling.'

'The swordsman has a point,' said Kaesoron, looming

over the Apothecary. Clad in his Terminator armour, Julius dwarfed Fabius, and the Apothecary nodded in acquiescence.

'As you will it, First Captain,' said Fabius, turning to his instruments. 'We shall begin with the pain of fire.'

Lucius felt his pulse race as Fabius lifted a cutting torch from the bench, snapping the igniting mechanism three times before the flame caught. Used to cut through sheet steel, the flame sharpened to a cone of blue-hot light as Fabius adjusted the gas flow.

Julius Kaesoron leaned over Fulgrim and said, 'This is your last chance, daemon spawn. Get out of my primarch's body and you need not suffer.'

'I welcome suffering,' said Fulgrim with bared teeth.

Kaesoron nodded, and Fabius brought the flame down on the sole of Fulgrim's foot.

The flesh curdled, running like molten rubber as it withered beneath the incredible heat. Fulgrim's back arched and his mouth stretched wide in a soundless scream as the veins and sinews at his neck lifted from his skin like colliding tectonic ridges.

Lucius watched bone rise from the melting skin as it peeled back, emerging white and gleaming for an instant before turning black. Marrow burned with a rich, fatty hiss, and the scent of seared flesh was a rich, gamey texture in the back of the throat. Lucius had smelled and tasted human meat before, but compared to that poor feast, this was an epicurean delight.

He saw the smell was having a similar effect on the others.

Kaesoron's molten features softened their hard edges, and Vairosean held himself upright only with an effort of will. Only Fabius appeared unaffected, but Lucius guessed he had already savoured many sights and smells of a primarch's body in his explorations of its divine biology. Fabius played the flame over Fulgrim's foot until all that remained below the ankle was a blackened mass of fused bone and boiled marrow that drooled to the tiled floor of the Apothecarion.

Julius Kaesoron took hold of the charred bone. 'This suffering can all end,' he said, regaining his composure with remarkable swiftness. Lucius licked his lips, still savouring the wondrously rich and flavoursome taste of Fulgrim's seared flesh.

Fulgrim looked up at Kaesoron with a taut smile and said, 'Suffering? What do you know of suffering? You are a warrior who fights where I tell him to fight, a tool to achieve my desires, nothing more. You do not suffer and should not speak of it to those who do.'

'I choose not to suffer,' said Kaesoron. 'A man can be strong enough to master his feelings so that it is impossible to make him suffer. To suffer pain and indignity is a loss of control. It is to admit to human weakness. I am strong enough to deny suffering.'

'Then you are a bigger fool than I took you for, Julius,' said Fulgrim. 'Where do you think strength comes from if not suffering? Hardship and loss is what grants you strength. Those who have never known true suffering cannot have the same strength as others who have. A man must be weak to suffer, and by that suffering he will be made strong.'

'Then you will be made mighty when we are done with you,' promised Vairosean.

Fulgrim laughed. 'Pain is truth,' he said. 'Suffering is the sharp end of the whip, *not* suffering is the end of the whip the master holds in his hand. Every act of suffering is a test of love and I will prove this to you by enduring all the pain you can inflict upon me, because I love you all.'

'These are not Fulgrim's words,' snapped Kaesoron. 'They are honeyed lies to weaken our resolve.'

'Not true,' said Fulgrim. 'All the truths I have learned since taking the life of my brother have shown this to be indisputable. All things in this grand universe are linked to one another by invisible threads, even those things that appear as opposites.'

'How can you know that?' said Lucius. 'Lord Fulgrim was a lover of beauty and wonder, but he was hardly a philosopher.'

'To be a lover of beauty and wonder one must be a philosopher of the heart,' said Fulgrim with a disappointed shake of his head. 'I have gazed into the secret heart of the warp and know that all existence is a struggle between opposites; light and darkness, heat and cold, and – of course, pleasure and pain. Think of ecstatic pleasure and unimaginable pain. They are connected, but they are not the same thing. Pain can exist without suffering, and it is possible to suffer without feeling pain.'

'Agreed,' said Kaesoron, 'but what is your point?'

'What you can learn from pain – that fire burns and is dangerous – is a lesson learned only for the individual, but what I have learned from suffering is what unites us as travellers on the road of excess and grants us entry to the palace of wisdom. Pain without suffering is like victory without struggle, one is meaningless without the other. But in the final analysis, real suffering can only be measured by what is taken away from us.'

'Then we are suffering now,' said Vairosean. 'For our beloved lord is lost to us.'

Lucius turned away from Vairosean's mawkish sentimentality and frowned as he looked upon the ruination of Fulgrim's foot. The flesh had been burned away, yet it appeared as though a thin, translucent film was forming over the bone, which had begun to lose the solid, vitrified look that had been burned onto it. Like a snake that had recently shed its skin, the filmy texture of Fulgrim's foot was oily and new, raw and yet to assume its final form.

'Look,' said Lucius. 'He's healing. You have to keep up the pressure.'

Fabius transferred his gaze from Fulgrim's face to his

healing foot with academic interest, while Kaesoron and
Vairosean each took up an instrument of excruciation.
The battle captains took position either side of Fulgrim
and turned their devices upon the bound primarch.
Kaesoron crushed knuckles with crimping pliers, while
Vairosean worked a flesh plane across Fulgrim's chest,
peeling back long strips of skin with each caress.

'Ah,' grinned Fulgrim. 'Truly the burden of happiness
can only be removed by the balm of suffering...'

Lucius smelled Fulgrim's blood and longed to take
up an awl or hammer, but the look in the primarch's
eyes stayed his hand. The tortures inflicted by Kaesoron
and Vairosean would have reduced a mortal to froth-
ing madness, but Fulgrim appeared to be enjoying the
experience.

Their eyes met and Fulgrim said, 'Go on, Lucius, take
up one of Fabius's devices. Make my flesh scream!'

Lucius shook his head and crossed his arms for fear
that he might do as Fulgrim wished.

'Are you sure?' smiled Fulgrim. 'You know better than
these fools that it's the temptations you don't succumb
to you'll later regret.'

'True enough, but I think that any creature powerful
enough to take control of Fulgrim's body is powerful
enough to endure any amount of pain and suffering
without real effort.'

'How insightful of you, my son,' said Fulgrim. 'This
is... mildly diverting, I will admit, but pain to me is no
more than an irritant. The pain you can inflict, anyway.'

Kaesoron paused in his mutilations and looked up at
Fabius. 'Is it speaking the truth?'

Fabius circled the gurney, reading the signs of Fulgrim's biorhythms with increasing puzzlement. Lucius
was no Apothecary, but even he could see the readouts
confirmed that they might as well have been reciting
poetry for all the effect it was having on the primarch.

Vairosean hurled away his flesh-plane, and a glass

cylinder mounted in a shadowed alcove shattered. Noxious fluids spilled onto the floor of the Apothecarion, smoking like acid and bearing an unidentifiable mass of pulsating organs grafted to a vaguely humanoid host. Whatever it was, its convulsions lasted only a moment before its wretched existence was ended.

Fabius knelt beside the glistening remains and shot a poisonous glance at Vairosean.

Marius ignored the Apothecary's anger and took hold of Fulgrim's head, leaning down as though to kiss him. Instead, he slammed Fulgrim's head down on the gurney and loosed a howl of grief-stricken rage that sent Lucius and Kaesoron flying.

The sound reverberated around the chamber like the sonic boom of a low-flying Stormbird, shattering every piece of glass in the room. Broken shards tumbled to the tiles in a thousand sharp *tinks*.

'You are a creature of evil!' yelled Vairosean. 'Begone or I will tear the head of this body from its shoulders. I would see Fulgrim dead before allowing you to possess it a moment longer!'

Lucius picked himself up, his senses reeling from the aural assault as Fabius launched himself at Vairosean and hauled him away from Fulgrim.

'Fool!' cursed Fabius. 'Your careless anger has just ruined months of experimentation.'

Vairosean shrugged off the Apothecary's anger and balled a fist, ready to pound Fabius to pulped blood and bone.

'Marius!' shouted Fulgrim. 'Stay your hand!'

Decades of ingrained loyalty froze Marius Vairosean to immobility, and Lucius was reminded of the iron grip of innate authority possessed by the primarchs. Even he, no respecter of authority, felt himself cowed by the primarch's words.

'You call me evil, but how do you decide what is good and what is evil? Are they not simply arbitrary terms coined by Man to justify his actions?' said Fulgrim. 'Think of how one measures good and evil and you will see that what I am, what I am *becoming*, is a thing of perfect beauty. A thing of *goodness*.'

Lucius approached the steel slab and looked down upon the primarch, sensing that his words were profound on a level he could not yet understand, but upon which his future might depend. He lifted an awl with a long hooked tip and worked it into Fulgrim's chest, through scar tissue that had not fully healed. Fulgrim grimaced as the metal pierced his flesh, but Lucius couldn't decide on the emotion behind the primarch's expression.

'So what are you becoming?' he asked.

'You ask the wrong question,' answered Fulgrim as Lucius worked the awl into him, inch by steel inch.

'Then what's the right one?'

Marius and Julius leaned in as Fabius spat curses at the months of lost work that swilled and frothed around his feet.

'The right question is what does the universe move towards? And that can only be answered by understanding where we came from.'

Marius followed Lucius's example and selected an instrument of torture from the collection of devices Fabius had laid out. He turned the pear-shaped device around in his hands, twisting a metal cog handle that gradually spread the leaves of the pear apart. Satisfied, he returned it to its original shape and moved down the gurney to place the device between the primarch's legs.

'We come from Terra,' said Marius. 'Is that what you mean?'

Fulgrim smiled indulgently and said, 'No, Marius. Further back than that. As far back as it is possible to go.'

Marius shrugged and worked his device into position with a series of grunts as Julius lifted a series of silver wands, some long, some short, but all tapered to sharpness at one end. One by one, Kaesoron pierced Fulgrim's body with seven needle-tipped wands, running in a line from the crown of his head to his groin. It was clear Kaesoron was no stranger to the apparatus as he attended to his work with a craftsman's diligence. Lucius wondered if he had chosen poorly in comparison to these instruments of agony, but decided that he liked the simplicity of the awl as he pressed it deeper into Fulgrim's unknown organs and inhuman biology.

Fulgrim watched Kaesoron with the attention of a proud master watching his student take flight for the first time without instruction. The primarch shook his head as Kaesoron stood erect and said, 'Your positioning of the Swadhisthana chakra needle is slightly off, Julius. Perhaps due to the intrusion of Marius's implement. A little higher might be better.'

Kaesoron bent to check and readjusted the needle as he saw that Fulgrim was correct. Without a word of acknowledgement, he ran a series of copper wires from the end of each needle to a thrumming bank of generators. With a flick of the switch, a deep bass note of power filled the chamber and arcing sparks of high voltage energy hummed from the wires.

Fulgrim's jaw clenched and caged lightning danced in the black vortices of his eyes. His skin darkened and Lucius smelled the electric tang of a body burning from the inside out.

Enduring enough pain to last innumerable mortal lifetimes, Fulgrim resumed speaking.

'This universe began in simplicity, with an event of such rapid expansion that it cannot ever be measured. In the first fractional moments of its existence, the universe was a place of such staggering simplicity that we cannot even begin to imagine it. But over time, those simple elements began to cohere, to come together in ever more complex forms. Particles became atoms, and atoms became molecules until they grew in complexity to form the first stars. Those newly-birthed stars lived and died over millions of years and their explosive deaths fuelled the birth of yet more stars and planets. You and I, we are luminous beings fashioned from the hearts of stars.'

'Poetic, but what does that have to do with good and evil?' asked Kaesoron as he manipulated the current through the silver needles, intrigued despite himself. Lucius was surprised, for he had always thought the First Captain had little interest in anything other than the gratification of his own desires or how he could wreak the greatest pain upon an enemy.

'I am getting to that,' promised Fulgrim, and Lucius had to remind himself that they were in the midst of torturing him and had not come to listen to a lecture on the substance of the universe. He wanted to speak out, but Fulgrim's words held him fast.

'None of this coming together is random,' explained Fulgrim. 'It is all part of the universe's *nature*, its tendency towards complexity. Ah... yes, that is most exquisite, Marius, another turn of the screw! Now, as I was saying, all things are part of this cycle of building and coming together, from the lowliest organism to the highest functioning sentience. Given the right circumstances, everything will tend towards becoming something more beautiful, more perfect and more complex. It has been this way since the beginning of this universe's lifespan, and that nature is as inescapable as it is inevitable.'

Lucius nodded and turned the awl in a wide circle within Fulgrim's body. 'And where does this all lead? What lies at the end of this journey from simplicity to complexity?'

Fulgrim shrugged, though it was impossible to tell whether it was a conscious gesture or the result of the current broiling his bones. 'Who can say? Some have called it godhood, others Nirvana. For want of a better term, I call it perfect complexity. It is the ultimate aim of all things, whether they are aware of their role in the universe or not. Now the question of good and evil is inextricably linked to this ongoing journey to perfect complexity. And the answer is simple.'

Fulgrim's words trailed off as his back arched and a line of blood ran from the corner of his mouth. Lucius wanted to believe it was his penetrative awl pricking Fulgrim's spine that was the cause of the pain, but with all three warriors working their excruciating arts it was impossible to be sure.

Fabius circled the gurney, monitoring Fulgrim's vital signs with growing alarm.

'You're killing him,' he said, urgently. 'One of you must stop.'

'No,' said Marius. 'The pain will drive the daemon-thing out. It will relinquish its hold on Fulgrim before it allows itself to die.'

'Simpleton!' snapped Fabius. 'Do you think such things as daemons fear the destruction of their mortal hosts? Its essence will simply cohere in the warp once you have destroyed the physical vessel.'

'Then what are we doing here?' demanded Lucius, releasing his grip on the awl and taking hold of Fabius by the throat as he again sensed conspiracy to the Apothecary's solicitousness towards Fulgrim. Lucius tightened his grip on the Apothecary's windpipe, exerting enough pressure to make the man's eyes bulge.

'You cannot harm this daemon,' gasped Fabius, 'but if you can cause it enough pain, it might be possible to force it to release its hold.'

'*Might*? *Possible*?' said Kaesoron. 'You speak without certitude in all you say.'

Lucius felt a sharp pressure at his groin and looked down to see a coiling armature of rusted metal and sinewy gristle protruding from the skinned-meat coat of Fabius. A hypodermic filled with cloudy pink fluid had pierced the flexible joint at his thigh, and the needle was buried an inch into the meat of his leg.

Fabius gave a viper's grin and said, 'Lay a hand on me again and the injector will have filled you with enough Vitae Noctus to slay a battle company.'

Lucius released the Apothecary only with great reluctance, feeling the cold metal of the needle withdraw from his body. As much as he wanted to lash out and break Fabius's neck, he couldn't keep the grin of near death from his face.

Fabius saw the grin and said, 'It is always amusing until the elixir hits your system. Then it is sublime for six heartbeats. Then you are dead, and the world of sensation is over. Remember that the next time you feel the need to vent your anger upon me.'

Kaesoron pushed them apart and said, 'Enough. We have a task at hand. Apothecary, *can* we drive this daemon out with pain? And give me a straight answer.'

Fabius answered without taking his eyes from Lucius, and Lucius met his hostility with a calm insouciance he felt sure would irritate the Apothecary.

'I cannot,' said Fabius. 'Any mortal body would be destroyed long before we could ever reach the point where a daemon would lose its grip. But a primarch's body should survive long enough for us to reach a tipping point where the pain will be sufficient to drive it out.'

'Then perhaps the time has come to use the neural parasite device,' said Marius. 'The thing you crafted from the Diasporex hybrid-captains.'

Fabius nodded in agreement, and Lucius saw the Apothecary had been waiting for just such an opportunity. Bending low, he placed the half-helm upon Fulgrim's skull and attached thin lengths of clear plastic tubing to the silvered metal. The tubing coiled across the floor to a humming machine that looked to have been designed by creatures that bore no relation to humanity. It pulsed with a complex series of lights and sounds that existed in realms beyond the auditory perceptions of mortals, and Lucius watched as the iridescent mercury-like liquid pulsed eagerly along the clear tubing and into the primarch.

'This had better work,' said Kaesoron, jabbing Fabius in the chest. 'If you have spoken false, none of your foe-tid elixirs will stop me from killing you.'

The sparkling liquid entered Fulgrim's body, and the gasp of a sensualist who has at last discovered some sensation as yet unimagined escaped his full lips. Fulgrim's eyes snapped open and he looked about himself like a dreamer awakening from golden memories of half-remembered friends and old loves.

'Ah, my sons,' he said, as though the pain of his torture was little more than the gentle caresses of butterfly wings. 'Where was I?'

Blood sheened his flesh like a crimson gown, and the sharp tang of roasting meat oozed from his every orifice. Heat radiated along the silver needles jutting from his body, and his pelvis was bent up at an unnatural angle by the expansion of the macabre device of Marius.

'You were talking of good and evil,' said Lucius, taking hold of the plain wooden handle of his awl and pushing it in deeper.

'Oh, you wield that spike like a master craftsman,' said Fulgrim. 'You are as skilled with a smaller weapon as you are with a larger.'

'I practise,' answered Lucius.

'I know,' said Fulgrim.

'Is it working?' Kaesoron asked Fabius, as he manipulated holographic dials and liquid gauges with sub-dermal xeno-haptics.

'It is,' confirmed the Apothecary. 'I can alter the bio-chemistry of his mind to see what I want him to see, feel what I want him to feel. His mind will be ours to command soon.'

Fulgrim laughed, then burst into tears, his body convulsing in agony before shuddering with the greatest pleasure. He screamed at invisible terrors and licked his lips as flavours beyond imaging flooded his sensory perceptions.

'What is happening to him?' said Marius.

'I am assuming control,' said Fabius, clearly relishing this chance to manipulate so magnificent a physical specimen of supra-engineered perfection. 'His mind is more complex than you can possibly imagine, a million labyrinths twisted within one another. It is no small matter to learn its connections.'

'Master it swiftly,' ordered Kaesoron.

Fabius ignored the threat in Kaesoron's voice and made myriad alterations to the composition of the liquid and the operation of the machine. Too complex to follow, Lucius had no idea what the Apothecary was changing or how it might affect the primarch. Every vein on Fulgrim's body stood taut on the surface of the skin, and it was clear the primarch wasn't allowing Fabius to take control without a fight.

A thousand emotions and sensations warred across Fulgrim's face, and Lucius envied him the touch of Fabius's machine. What might it be like to allow another's hand to guide his mind through a universe of sensation? But just as quickly as he imagined such a journey, he knew he was too self-absorbed to allow anyone else to take control of his flesh.

At last Fulgrim's body relaxed, sinking back onto the gurney with a contented sigh of relief. His limbs settled on the cold metal and Fabius gave a triumphant grin that exposed his yellowed teeth and glistening, serpentine tongue.

'I have him,' he said. 'What would you have me do, First Captain?'

'Can you force it to speak truthfully?'

'Of course, a manipulation of no consequence,' Fabius told him.

Lucius frowned at the swiftness of Fabius's assurance,

wondering at the ease with which the Apothecary appeared to have mastered what he had described as being nigh impossibly difficult. He slid the awl clear of Fulgrim's body and moved around the gurney to stand next to Fabius. Vitae Noctus or not, he would kill Fabius if it emerged that he was lying to them.

The faces on the Apothecary's long coat flexed as though rising and falling on a gelid tide, and their mute howls implored Lucius to end their suffering. The swordsman ignored them, calculating where best to stab with the awl if he needed to kill Fabius.

The Apothecary seemed oblivious to Lucius's presence, and worked his fingers over the alien device like a maestro at the keyboard of a templum organ. Fulgrim danced a jig on the gurney, and his face twisted into a delirious smile as he felt what was being done to him.

'Oh, my sons…' breathed the primarch. 'You want the truth? How artless of you. Do you not realise that the truth is the most dangerous thing of all?'

'Your time here is at an end, daemon,' snarled Marius. 'You have no place among our Legion. You are a thing of evil.'

Fulgrim laughed and said, 'Oh, Marius, you insist on calling me a thing of evil, but such a word is meaningless unless you understand the truth of what good and evil represent. Very well, you wish the truth? I will give it to you. If you accept that the universe is constantly moving towards its final state of perfect complexity, and that this is its inevitable destination, then anything that hinders this process must be defined as evil. By the same logic, anything that promotes this ongoing journey is surely good. I am moving towards that perfect complexity, and by hindering my ascension *you* are acting in the cause of evil. Alone in this chamber, I am the only thing that *is* good!'

'You seek to dull our wits with absurd talk of the nature of the universe and good and evil,' hissed Marius. 'I know evil, and I am looking at it.'

'You are looking at yourself, Marius Vairosean,' said Fulgrim. 'Have you not seen the truth of it yet?'

'The truth of what?'

'The truth of me!'

Lucius stepped away from the gurney as Fulgrim's biceps swelled with sudden power and his right arm tore free of the restraints that bound him to the gurney. An instant later, his left arm was free and the primarch sat bolt upright, tearing loose the needles piercing his skin and ripping free the bio-monitors Fabius had attached at the beginning of their tortures.

Fulgrim kicked Marius away and tore loose the opened device the Third Captain had worked upon with a sigh of regret. It fell to the floor of the Apothecarion with a wet clatter, and rolled like a viscous flower of red-stained iron.

'A pity,' said Fulgrim. 'I was beginning to enjoy that.'

The primarch swung his legs from the gurney, breaking the bonds securing his ankles and thighs with no more effort than a child might throw back its blankets upon waking. Julius Kaesoron lunged forwards to hold Fulgrim down, but he was swatted aside with a casual backhanded gesture. Fabius backed away, but Lucius stood his ground, knowing there would be no point in running.

He saw how blinded they had been, how naïve. How could they have believed that they had the power to subdue a primarch? They had succeeded only because Fulgrim had desired it, had *wanted* them to come to this point. The Phoenician had seen the doubts in his warriors and had led them to this place, to this moment, in order to reveal his true nature.

Fulgrim turned to face him and smiled. In that instant, Lucius saw the truth of everything Fulgrim had said and done since Isstvan. He saw recognition in Fulgrim's eyes, and dropped to his knees.

'Begging, Lucius?' said Fulgrim. 'I expected better from you.'

'Not begging, my lord,' answered Lucius, with his head bowed. 'Honouring.'

Julius Kaesoron struggled to his feet, his fist bursting to life with shimmering arcs of purple lightning. Marius Vairosean swept up his sonic cannon, his mouth widening in preparation of unleashing a barrage of sound and force that would kill everything in the room.

'You know now?' said Fulgrim.

'I know,' agreed Lucius. 'I should have always known you would never surrender your will to another. If I would not, why should you?'

'What is it talking about, swordsman?' demanded Kaesoron. 'Have you betrayed us to this daemon-thing?'

Lucius shook his head and chuckled at Kaesoron's blindness to a truth that was now surely self-evident. 'No,' he said. 'I have not, for I was wrong.'

'About what?' said Kaesoron, fist raised to strike.

'About me,' said Fulgrim, answering for him.

'This is Lord Fulgrim,' said Lucius. '*Our* Lord Fulgrim.'

14

LIKE THE FINAL player in a tragedy delivering his last soliloquy before the curtain falls, Fulgrim paced the stage of *La Fenice* with an actor's relish. Lucius watched him with a practised eye, seeing the fluid ease of his perfect motion and wondering how he could have failed to spot its truth for so long. Clad once more in his purple-pink war plate, the Phoenician was a sight to set the mind afire, a warrior god of perfect proportions and light.

No traces of the wounds or indignities he had suffered in the Apothecarion were evident, and Lucius marvelled at the incredible power wrought into the primarch's form that he could endure such horror and bear no ill-effects. Truly, Fulgrim was a god worth devotion.

First Captain Kaesoron stood shoulder to shoulder to Lucius, but Marius Vairosean set himself apart from them, his shame causing him to distance himself from their shared guilt. It was guilt only he felt, for Lucius had no regrets over their actions. They had acted to save their primarch, and – if he was honest – scratch a nagging itch to push their experiences to another level. There could be no guilt over that, not if any of the wonders they had been shown since Isstvan III were to be taken at face value.

Kalimos and Abranxe had joined them, amazed to hear of what had transpired in the Apothecarion, a revelation to which they alone in the galaxy were privy. Krysander stood erect with difficulty, and Ruen held to the wounded captain, his shoulder wrapped in vat-flesh as his augmetic bones knitted with his wounded physiology.

Lucius watched as Fulgrim paused beneath the dull portrait that graced the wall opposite the Phoenician's Nest, a secret smile that conveyed a lifetime's meaning in a slight upward tilt of his lips.

'You were right to suspect I was not myself,' said Fulgrim, finally deigning to face them. 'The killing of the Gorgon was an act that severed my last tie to a lost life, a past that means nothing to me now. And no act of such magnitude is free of consequence.'

Fulgrim squatted on the stage, as though reliving the moment of Ferrus Manus's death. His fists clenched as he stared into the middle distance, and Lucius saw the bloody parade of Isstvan V come alive in his eyes.

'I was vulnerable,' said Fulgrim, standing and resuming his pacing of the stage. 'A servant of the Dark Prince took my flesh for its own amusement. It was an ancient thing, a needy, capricious thing that revelled in its stolen prize, and for a time I allowed it to retain possession of my body while I learned of it and its powers. I think it hoped I would be crushed by the death of my brother…'

Fulgrim grinned, staring at his hands as though they were still bloody from the slaying of the Iron Hands' primarch.

'It should have known better. After all, it had started me down the road of self-indulgence and a life free of inhibitions or guilt. What did I care for one more betrayal? Manus was already a fading memory, a ghost who recedes with each passing moment, and everything I learned from it only made me stronger. In time, it was a simple matter to reclaim my body and cast it into the prison it had crafted for me.'

Lucius tore his gaze from his magnificent primarch and lifted his head to the portrait. Its lines were no less insipid, its colours no less bland, but knowing its truth now, Lucius saw the ageless pain of an immortal, inchoate being trapped forever in unending stagnation. To a creature of infinite possibility, there could be no greater torment, and his admiration for his primarch's brilliance soared anew.

'So now you know the truth, my sons,' said Fulgrim, dropping from the stage to walk among them. He spread his hands and touched them all as he walked past them. 'It is no easy thing to serve a master who demands so much of us and grants us so much in return. We must go further in our desires than any other, experience all things, even those distasteful to us. No sacrifice, no degradation and no bliss will exist beyond our reach. I have such sights to show you all, my sons. Secrets and power thought beyond comprehension, truths buried since the dawn of time and a route to godhood that will see me burn brighter than a thousand suns!'

Fulgrim spun on his heel as his warriors cheered his words. He basked in their adoration and their devotions made him shine like the star that allowed them to live. At last he lowered his arms and swept his gaze over them all, benevolent and paternal, stern and unflinching.

'I have much to do before deigning to join Horus Lupercal on Terra's muddy soil,' said the Phoenician. 'My first task is to join with my Olympian brother, and yoke his builders and donjon keepers to my purpose.'

'What purpose?' asked Julius Kaesoron, daring the primarch's wrath with a question.

Fulgrim ran his hands through his virgin-white hair and smiled, though Lucius saw this was a momentary indulgence. Further questions would not be tolerated. Not now, in the primarch's moment of glory.

'We have a city to build,' he said. 'A glorious city of mirrors; a city of mirages, at once solid and liquid, at once air and stone.'

Lucius felt his pulse quicken at the idea of such a city, a metropolis where every structure, tower and palace would throw his image back at him a thousandfold. At last he saw the attack on Prismatica for what it was, the gathering of raw materials to raise this astonishing architecture of reflections.

'A city of mirrors,' he whispered. 'It will be wondrous.'

Fulgrim took a step towards him and cupped the swordsman's face like a lover.

'It will be better than wondrous,' said Fulgrim, leaning down to kiss Lucius on each scarred cheek. 'For in the heart of its million reflections I will meet the gaze of the *Angel Exterminatus* and the galaxy will weep to behold its terrible beauty!'

FEAT OF
IRON

Nick Kyme

'What does it matter why he fell?'
'When the fall is all there is, it matters.'
　　　　　　　　　　　– Farseer Lathsarial answers
　　　　　　　　　　　　a student of the Path

WROUGHT OF IRON

IT WAS NOT supposed to be like this. This was not his idea of how the war would play out. He had envisaged it differently.

Glorious, vindicating… vengeful.

I was not meant to fail here.

He had not expected to be last. He hated to be last. It irritated, like the itch around his neck.

No matter how he oiled the skin beneath his gorget, or the method he used to affix its clasps, the itch persisted.

Like a blade across my throat…

From his first ironclad footfall onto the desert, it had been there. A dark reminder of something as yet unfulfilled, a promise his supposed executioner had yet to make. Sand was everywhere, endless oceans of undulating grains stretched all the way to the blurred horizon, bleached white by an oppressive sun. In his dreams, the sand was black.

Such moribund thoughts brought an unworthy declaration to taut lips.

'I am the equal of my brothers,' he muttered to a darkness that deigned not to answer.

'And the better of some,' he added. Still the uncaring shadows paid no heed.

Always it came down to this singular truth, ever since he had split the darkness upon a trail of fire.

'I should be first.'

The interior of the landship and his strategium chamber were black, much like his mood. The blunt refrain of a thousand hammers rang through the armoured flanks, as the tracks that provided motion to his leviathan pounded the desert in relentless syncopation. Beyond the constant din echoed the dull report of heavy ordnance. It reminded him of the forge and its fuliginous depths, of the Anvilarium aboard the *Fist of Iron*. How he longed for the solitude of its appended reclusiam at that moment. With creation and function came peace. With mental fortitude came strength and the banishment of weakness.

Weakness was a thing to be abhorred. It had no place in the new Imperium.

As the hololith flickered into life, revealing a nascent image in grainy grey resolution, he recognised it was the weakness within that he loathed the most. It wasn't a malady, a social or psychological deviancy that he railed against; rather it was merely flesh and all its inherent limitations.

I will be as iron.

Focus turned the grainy hololith into two figures.

Ferrus Manus glowered at them both from the dimly-lit shadows. For him and his forces, the campaign of One-Five-Four Four was not going well.

His voice was hard as granite as he addressed his audience.

'Brothers.'

DESCENDING INTO THE desert basin had not been easy. Hampered by the constant shifting of the dunes and the debilitating effects of the sand on their engines, much of the Army tank divisions and Mechanicum claves had foundered.

Tracks had mired near the tip of the decline, half-drowned in sinking sand. One battle tank pitched nose-first and rolled, bringing an entire column to a grinding halt. Even the bipedal walkers fared no better, and the broken skeletons of several Sentinels hit the nadir of the desert basin before any foot troops. Their burned-out wrecks were ignored by those that followed behind.

It therefore fell to stronger, more able, warriors to take up the mantle of battle.

'Bring them iron and death!' Gabriel Santar bellowed, a machine reverb in his voice, as he announced the attack.

A war host of Iron Hands answered, advancing in unison as a halo of crackling starbursts erupted from their weapons.

A horde of massive insect-like creatures wrapped in chitin boiled towards them and in its wake, scores of the cloaked warriors who had first sprung the ambush.

Eldar.

As muzzle flares lit, the heavy roar of cannon spoke and the hot air in the desert basin was chewed apart by brass-shelled fury.

Thick-skinned and ponderous, the first wave of chitin creatures was slow but resilient. Shell impacts rained against their heavy bodies, but did little more than indent flesh. They waded through clouds of explosive discharge from missiles and grenades without pause. Like their slighter kin they had billowed up from the desert in a welter of displaced sand and mournful nasal dirges. Humpbacked and muscular, as bulky as an Imperial battle tank, the beasts were impelled by an eldar kindred wearing what Santar could only assume were some form of mind-goad.

Such alien technology was to be abhorred, but the first captain knew these were not the true vanguard.

Infinitesimal vibrations, growing steadily in significance, registered on his helmet's auto-senses as minute seismological anomalies in the basin's tectonic structure.

Earth burrowers tunnelled beneath them, closing on the line of Iron Hands fast.

A series of subterranean detonations presaged the attack, and as the Legiones Astartes advanced in stoic rows of black and steel ceramite, the creatures emerged from geysers of spurting sand. Swift and serpentine, so utterly unlike the ordered ranks of the Iron Hands, it was difficult to make out the precise nature of the abominations. Crackling discharge flickering off the barbed pikes of their masked riders was visible, as the desert drained off master and beast in a fragmenting veil. It was a form of cavalry, Santar realised, only the most debased kind.

Santar scowled, and the cliffs of his cheeks hardened into craggy bulwarks. He would see them wiped from the face of the desert.

A fusillade of small-arms fire and light ordnance erupting around him, the first captain led a company of Morlocks into the onrushing creatures with his lightning claw aloft. The sun glinted from the blades and made the dark metal of his armour gleam.

At range the elite warriors were formidable; at close quarters they were unstoppable.

The aliens seemed not to realise, but would soon be educated.

'Be as iron!' he roared as the eldar hit them.

A beast, its long torso segmented and armoured with a tough brown carapace, snapped at the first captain in an attempt to bite off his arm. Santar shrugged off the blow and cut its face open, spilling viscous green fluid onto clacking mandibles and many-faceted eye-pits. A second slash severed its razor-edged pincers with a roar of bionic automation that drew a high-pitched mewl of pain from the thing's puckered mouth.

Its rider, a sand-cloaked eldar in dun-coloured battle

armour that was the mirror of the creature's natural carapace, brought its electro-pike to bear, but Santar cut the
wretch down before it could thrust.

Servos in his mechanised implants screaming, lend-
ing enhanced strength to an already exceptional biology,
Santar cleaved the head from a second chitin-worm as
the first was still collapsing. Through the gore fountain-
ing from the neck cavity he saw Captain Vaakal Desaan,
who was leading the other company, eviscerate a third.

Beast and rider crumpled. Behind them, more were
coming. They were skirting ahead of the larger, beetle-
like monsters, their sand wakes just breaking the desert
surface in rippling mounds.

At least four dozen enemy contacts registered on his
retinal display. Faint heat signatures, baffled by the
sand, suggested there were another four score still fully
submerged. A host of dun-cloaked foot troops with
anti-gravitic weapon arrays followed them and the air
chimed to the shriek of their cannons.

A heavy barrage was coming off the iron-armoured
Morlocks in response, their rattling combination bolter
fire taking a brutal toll. Holding the centre of the war
host, they showed no sign of capitulation. Fashioned of
reinforced plates, with the barrel-like shoulder guards
adorned by pteruges that overlaid the thinner and more
dexterous arm greaves, their Cataphractii Terminator
armour was near-inviolate against the alien weapons.
Intended for frontal assault, a tactic in which the Iron
Hands excelled, the armour made them giants. Hulking, implacable, they passed through a hail of heavy
bow-casters, fusion blasters and shuriken cannon with
impunity.

Little effort was expended in vanquishing the chitin-
worms, their numbers decimated for no injury in reply.

'They have obviously not fought Terminators before,'
Desaan said over the comm-feed.

Santar's reprimand was swift but light. 'Just kill

them, brother. As efficiently as you can.' Cataphractii war-plate was rare amongst the Legions, but the Iron Hands boasted a great many suits, especially amongst the clan companies of the Avernii, the Morlocks. It was cumbersome, akin to wearing a battle tank bereft of tracks, but still retained all its resilience and stopping power. Santar revelled in the machine-strength it gave him. They all did.

The Iron Hands' blows fell like metronomes: precise, methodical and without profligacy or flourish. It was a functional combat doctrine, merciless and unrelenting. The eldar withered before it.

In concert with Captain Desaan, Santar pressed the advance. The thickly-armoured Morlocks were steam-rolling across the dune. Nothing escaped their wrath, which was punitive and absolute.

Renewed tremors jagged across the first captain's retinal display, indicating further tunnellers. Initially, he expected a secondary wave of the chitin-worms but realised his error as the vibration returns came back louder and more resonant.

'Stand and prepare to repel the enemy,' he barked down the comm-feed.

Both Morlock companies fell into line in perfect unison, weapons locked on the dead ground ahead of them. Their bolter storm abated, allowing the battered eldar to scurry back behind their ponderous barricade creatures.

Behind the pitiless lenses of his battle-helm, Santar's narrowed eyes promised retribution upon those cowards later.

The Army ordnance had managed to find position at the cusp of the rise overlooking the basin. The gunners now had range and pummelled the mind-goaded chitin monsters anchoring the eldar kindreds.

The next wave, he knew, was coming.

'Show no mercy,' he said to his warriors.

Cracks webbed the base of the sand valley, swallowing

the carcasses of dead chitin-worms and their slain riders, as a much larger strain of sand-burrower emerged.

Massive pincers married to a serpentine torso that ended in a whickering stinger gave them the aspect of the scorpiad that Santar had heard the XVIIIth legionaries speak of prior to deployment on One-Five-Four Four. Apparently the beast was indigenous to their volcanic home world. It mattered little to the first captain; he just needed to know how to kill them.

A crackling line of bolter fire stitched across a scorpiad-creature's midriff but the shells failed to penetrate, and exploded with little effect against its hardened exoskeleton.

One look at the barbed stinger and serrated claws attached to its ribbed torso, told Santar that these beasts could penetrate power armour. It was theoretically possibly they could wound the Cataphractii too. He decided to test it, but not before he had thinned the ranks a little.

Santar raised Erasmus Ruuman through his battle-helm's comm-feed.

The response from the Morlock Ironwrought was immediate.

'At your command, first captain.'

In his mind's eye, Santar painted a blood-red crosshair over the advancing scorpiad-creatures.

And with our iron fist…

'Heavy divisions on this position,' he grated with machine-like cadence, relaying coordinates sub-vocally. 'Rapiers and missile launchers.'

A glance and a clenched fist from Santar to Desaan held the Morlock captain in place and also brought both Cataphractii companies to a halt.

Seconds later, a storm of ordnance lit the desert basin in magnesium white, so bright it almost overloaded the retinal buffers in Santar's battle-helm.

…we shall bring down such fury.

He blinked away the after-flare quickly and was already

stomping into the smoke-clouded blast zone ahead. Vitrified sand crunched underfoot and fire licked at the edges of his boots as he crushed a burning eldar skull.

He waved Desaan and the Terminators on. 'Forward, Clan Avernii.'

After the barrage from Ruuman, there were a few score remaining of the aliens' hundreds-strong kindreds. The scorpiad-creatures were all but wiped out. A few dogged defenders were left, together with any creatures deep enough beneath the earth to have survived the blast. They waged war amidst the smouldering carcasses of their fallen, but rather than dismay them, the visceral reminder of their mortality seemed only to embolden the creatures.

Santar would crush them regardless of their resilience.

A thousand legionaries followed his lead, the Iron Hands reserves joining the Morlocks, many times more than enough to eradicate a recalcitrant xenos warband. Quickly he appraised the tactical dispositions of his forces.

The Morlocks held the centre, whilst the right flank was anchored by Shadrak Meduson and his own company of Iron Hands. The left was clenched in the unyielding fist of Ruuman and another company of heavies. Despite the inclusion of the slower moving Terminators in the war host, the Ironwrought's section was the least mobile. Logic suggested an oblique line as the most efficient and employable tactic. Santar relayed his orders.

'Ironwrought will forge the hinge. Tenth captain, you are our swinging fist.'

Meduson's affirmation icon flashed once on Santar's retinal display as he then isolated the ninth captain's comm-channel.

'Desaan, keep your Cataphractii at pace. Move up to assault speed, mauls and blades.'

Desaan nodded simultaneously with his own flashing icon as the Terminators maglocked their bolters and armed for close combat. Crackling hammers and burring blades were swung into readiness.

Though they were slow, the beetle-like chitin creatures possessed enough bulk and mass to crush tank armour. Santar wanted them down; they were all that was left of the eldar resistance.

Meduson struck first, the 'swinging fist', just as Ruuman's last salvo abated. Seeking to envelop the isolated company, the beasts rounded on the Iron Hands who fought them to a standstill.

Less than a minute after the beasts were fully engaged, Santar, Desaan and two entire companies of Morlocks crashed into their exposed flank.

Eviscerator saws and seismic hammers cut and bludgeoned the massive creatures who died by degrees to the legionaries' relentless attack. Slowly, one by one, they crumpled and lay still. The desert resounded to their demise, sand banks demolished in the shock waves radiating from where the beasts had fallen.

Standing at the edge of a blood-slicked impact crater, *shucking* his blades from an eldar's ruptured skull, Santar surveyed the carnage he and his brothers had wrought.

'Glory Imperator!' he roared.

A thousand voices chorused back.

'Glory Imperator,' said Ruuman over the comm-feed, 'and in the name of the Gorgon.'

Santar's reply was rueful before he cut the link.

'I doubt this victory will satisfy him, brother.'

THE ELDAR WERE broken, smashed against the unyielding resolve of the Iron Hands. Santar was wiping the alien gore from his lightning claws when Desaan lumbered alongside him. In their Cataphractii Terminator armour they were much taller than their legionary brothers and had a commanding view of the battlefield.

Alien dead and their enslaved chitin-creatures lay in sundered heaps, putrefying in the sun. Kill squads of

Iron Hands were working their way around the battle site, executing survivors. Santar had ordered no prisoners to be taken. Eldar were not vulnerable to coercion, even when violently encouraged, and they had a talent for misdirection and sowing confusion. Strength of mind and purpose, no mercy – these were the tenets of engagement the first captain had insisted upon.

One of the alien wretches was attempting to speak, its tongue lilting and offensive to Santar's senses even through his battle-helm. He finished the eldar off with his lightning claw.

'We should pursue and harry them, brother-captain,' said Desaan. The visor he wore in place of his eyes blazed coldly, as if in emphasis. His 'blinding' had been courtesy of an eldar acid-spitter, a strain of the xenos more feral and barbed than the sand-nomads they currently engaged. Due to the intervention of the Mechanicum, the ninth captain now saw more than he ever had before.

Santar averted his gaze from the dead alien to the summit of the distant dune where the remnants of the surviving eldar were retreating. Heat haze obscured the view, throbbing and thick, but the aliens were ragged. Such disorder would not last. Santar would have preferred to chase them down and destroy them, but they were already far behind where the father desired them to be.

'No. We'll regroup our forces and have them ready to march again as soon as possible,' he said, before adding, 'It will give some of the slower elements opportunity to catch up.'

'You mean weaker.'

Santar met Desaan's impassive gaze through the visor. 'I mean what I say, brother-captain.'

Desaan nodded without reaction but Santar's upraised hand kept him from heading off. The first captain looked away, appraising the desolation of the chitin creatures in the desert basin. Most were open and raw, bleeding green lifeblood across the sand and creating a noisome stench; others were half-submerged, slain before they could escape. Any survivors had burrowed deep, away from the noise and the fire, taking their riders with them. If allowed to roam unchecked, broken or otherwise, such creatures could become a needless thorn.

Santar raised the Ironwrought on the comm-feed.

'Ruuman, we are clearing this area in short order. I want it thoroughly sanitised, above *and* below the surface.'

'Nothing lives.' It was not a question, but Santar answered it anyway.

'Nothing lives, brother.'

Behind the forward line, the first captain could already see the Ironwrought bringing divisions of mole mortars and unmanned Termite incendiary drones into position.

'Dig them deep,' he added.

'Nothing lives,' repeated Ruuman in grating confirmation.

Santar signalled for Captain Desaan to follow, leaving the preparations for regroup and advance to Captain Meduson.

'You are with me, Morlock.'

They strode up the sand bank in silence, barring the hard whine of the servos in their Terminator armour as it struggled to cope with the incline. Together they passed lines of foundered Army tanks and minor Ordinatus of the Mechanicum. Most of the vehicles were weather-beaten and in need of serious repair and maintenance. Neither warrior spared the struggling troopers a glance. Cresting the rise, they were met by Ruuman who was organising the heavy divisions for their punitive salvo. His mouth was set into a tight line, in part due to his characteristic dourness but also because the lower half of his face was augmetic. Much of his body was cybernetic and Ruuman displayed it proudly in concert with his battle-plate. Far behind the heavies, marching on weary legs, the belated Army divisions came into sight through the heat haze.

Desaan did not wear a war-helm and his head jutted above the high rim of his gorget, sitting between the barrel-shaped curves of his pauldrons like a little nub of steel. But the disdain was evident in his tone without the need to see it on his face.

'The Army arrives at last,' Santar said to him.

'We are better off without them.'

Ruuman agreed, cutting in to address the first captain. 'I have some serious concerns regarding the efficacy of both the human mechanised and foot contingents. Our progress is being slowed irrevocably.'

'They are vulnerable to the conditions out here, brother. Sand and heat cause havoc with track-beds, engines. It's stultifying our advance but I can see no immediate solution.'

The first captain's reply was meant to be mollifying, even partly an invitation, but only caused further concern in the Ironwrought.

'I will look into it,' Santar added finally, walking on.

Ruuman nodded as mole mortar teams and batteries of missile launchers ran through their final launch preparations.

The Ironwrought's disregard for mortal flesh came from the fact he was now more machine than man. Several close encounters with the Deuthrite in the spike-forests on Kwang had seen to the necessity of his extensive cybernetics. But he had not once complained and accepted his bionics stoically.

Desaan held his tongue until they had passed the line and were advancing into open desert.

'And do what, Gabriel? Some theatres of war are not meant for mere men.'

Santar removed his helm with a hiss of released pressure. The face beneath was dappled with sweat. He raised an eyebrow.

Behind them the *foom* of expelled ordnance punctuated the first captain's words in a staggered crescendo of multiple rocket bursts.

'Are we not men, then, Vaakal?'

Desaan was a staunch adherent to the Creed of Iron, that which espoused *Flesh is Weak*. His ostensible elitism and lack of human empathy often spilled over into disdain, sometimes worse.

The other captain frowned as a rumble of deep subterranean detonations shook the sand beneath their feet and the Ironwrought's explosive payload did its work.

'I know you understand my meaning, brother,' Santar pressed, undaunted. 'We are familiar enough, are we not? Your earlier tone would suggest so.' There was a rebuke in the first captain's words that Desaan discerned at once.

'If I have been disrespectful...'

'I agree with you, captain. Flesh *is* weak. The Creed has been borne out in this desert, in the fatigue of our Army divisions and their failing resolve. But isn't our purpose to shoulder this burden and promote strength through the demonstration of strength?'

Desaan opened his mouth to respond but thought better of it when he realised the first captain wasn't finished.

'I am still a man, flesh in part. My heart pumps blood, my lungs draw air. They are not machine, unlike this,' said Santar, brandishing his left arm, the bionics within whirring in simpatico with the first captain. 'And these,' he said, tapping a claw blade against his armoured thigh. 'Does my flesh make me weak, brother?'

Desaan was careful to be deferential. True, Gabriel Santar did not possess the phenomenal temper of his primarch but he was as harsh and unyielding as the bionics in his limbs.

'You are much more than a mere man, my captain,' he ventured. After a silent pause, he decided to go on. 'We all are. We, the Emperor's sons, are the true inheritors of the galaxy.'

Santar stared at the ninth captain, showing some of the flint for which he was so renowned.

'Bold talk, but wrong.' Santar turned away again and the tension ebbed. 'We are warriors and when the war is done, we'll need to find new vocations or be put to use as praetorian statues adorning the Palace on Terra. Perhaps we'll form ceremonial honour guards for our defunct warlords.' More than a little rancour coloured the first captain's words. He had thought on it often. 'A warrior without a war to fight is like a machine without function,' he added in quiet introspection. 'Do you know what this means, Vaakal? Do you know what we face?'

Desaan nodded slowly, at least as much as his high gorget would allow.

'Becoming obsolete.'

'Indeed.'

The implication of that hung in the air for a while before Desaan attempted to banish the awkward tension.

'An entire galaxy to bring to heel, untold billions of weak and fragile men to reforge. I suspect it will be long before the Crusade is done.'

A shadow fell across them, echoing the sudden dip in mood; or, rather, they strayed into its massive penumbra. Santar craned his neck to regard the cyclopean landship, *Eye of Medusa*, engulfing the Iron Hands with its sheer oppressive majesty.

'Perhaps...' he muttered, taking in the hard, sweeping hull of the leviathan. The iconic sigil of a mailed fist dominated one flank. Below it an access ramp angled down from the lowest level of the landship, spanning its gargantuan tracks.

The Father was within, in concert with two of his brothers. When last they had spoken, his mood had been far from sanguine. Failure to precisely locate the node had vexed the Father greatly, to the point where his rage had grown incandescent. Swift progress was demanded. As with most things, Lord Manus did not have the time or inclination for patience.

Santar was fashioning his report as he ascended the access ramp with Desaan.

'I am not sure Father would match your hope, brother. If we do not find the node soon, his wrath will be volatile, of *that* I am certain.' There was no trepidation in Santar's voice, no concern of reproach – it was merely a stating of the facts.

'It is…' Desaan chose his words carefully as they paused at the edge of the landship's access hatch, '…*curious* that none of the Mechanicum adepts have located the node. Is it such an arduous task?'

'The sand and heat,' said Santar. 'What our deep-space sensoria pict-captured, we have been unable to match to the surface. It is a different set of environmental conditions to which we must adapt.'

Desaan looked the first captain in the eye. 'Are you so certain it is merely the adverse weather that is foiling our efforts?'

'No, I am not, but I would like to see you suggest something more… *arcane* to the Father. I believe he would be less than accepting.'

'Putting it mildly, brother,' Desaan replied as they entered the landship.

DARKNESS REIGNED WITHIN the *Eye of Medusa*. A series of churning vertical-lifters and horizontal-conveyers had brought the two Morlocks to a gallery leading to the primarch's strategium. The method of their transportation was not so dissimilar from the way the great internal ore processors funnelled rock into the immense pressure-hammers and furnaces of the Medusan mine-trains. It amused Santar to make the correlation with the vast, tracked mining stations, but he dismissed any further simile quickly as something the sons of Vulkan might find diverting. Serving no useful function, it held only passing interest for him.

Venting pneumatic pressure heralded the opening of the strategium blast door. Half a metre thick and bound with adamantium rebars, it could double up as a bunker if ever the landship was attacked. Not that its sole occupant required such a refuge.

The interior was as stark and chill as an ice cavern. Lacquered black walls absorbed the light and panes of glass crafted into the obsidian-like panels were frosted and glacial-thick. It was Medusa in all but its geographical disposition.

Entering as one, Santar and Desaan caught the end of Lord Manus's mission briefing with the primarchs Vulkan and Mortarion.

'...cannot afford to have our purpose divided. Be mindful, brother, but let the humans look to their own protection. That is all.'

Ferrus Manus cut the link with a curt slash of his hand. The grainy light from the hololith was still dying as he turned to his first captain. A pale glow settled about his mountainous shoulders, like a mantle of hoarfrost melting against his barely fettered anger.

He exhaled, and his displeasure lessened like a storm cloud passing across his features. His face was a rugged cliff, colonised by scars and framed by a jet-black skullcap of close-cropped hair. The primarch was, for all intents and purposes, Santar's father but his demeanour was anything but paternal.

'I love my brother,' rumbled Ferrus, apropos of nothing, 'but he drives me to distraction with his desire to nurture and coddle. It is a weak predilection and can only breed weakness in return.' He raised an eyebrow, forming a crease across his slab-like forehead. 'Not like the Tenth, isn't that right, first captain?'

Ferrus Manus was a huge and imposing figure. Clad in coal-black armour, he looked hewn from granite. His unyielding skin was scraped and oiled and his eyes were like two pieces of knapped flint. Of his many names, his favourite was the Gorgon. It seemed an apt honorific for one whose glare was hard enough to petrify. Cold fury radiated from his every pore, telegraphed in the way he moved, the tone of his voice and the language he chose to express his thoughts. At that moment they fashioned a challenge, which Gabriel Santar had little choice but to accept.

'We vanquished the eldar raiding party but are no closer to locating the node at this time, my primarch.' He bowed his head in a gesture of fealty but Ferrus rebuked him for what he took as capitulation.

'Raise your eyes and meet my gaze,' he said, temper smouldering like a volcano on the verge of eruption. 'Are you not my equerry, in whom I place my trust and respect?'

It was pointless to protest, so Santar held those two pieces of icy flint in his eye line and did not flinch. To do so would be unwise.

'I am, primarch. As ever.'

Simmering now, the glow of the lambent lumen-lamps reflecting from the unfathomable living metal of his silver arms, Ferrus Manus began to pace. His ire was far from spent.

'*At this time*, is it? All we have had is time. Answer this for me,' said Ferrus Manus, his glare shifting to the warrior standing beside his equerry. 'Captain Desaan, unless your tongue is too leaden, how is it that both my brothers are able to find the nodes and we cannot?'

There was a mighty hammer affixed to the primarch's broad, armoured back. It was called *Forgebreaker* and it had been fashioned beneath Mount Narodnya by his brother Fulgrim, whose presence he was clearly missing. Santar wondered if Desaan was trying not to imagine his lord ripping the weapon free of its strappings and laying about the strategium and his ineffective officer cadre.

Ferrus Manus glared, impatient for an answer.

Santar had seldom seen him this enraged and wondered at the cause.

Desaan's grizzled face, a patchwork of scars itself, was reflected in the Gorgon's armour. His visored eyes appeared distorted. The primarch was close enough to strike him, but the captain did not flinch, though he did make an effort to keep the clearing of his throat surreptitious. Even masked behind his gorget it sounded louder than a clarion horn to his ears. He was a Morlock, one of the primarch's elite, but it was rare to be questioned by him directly. Even for a veteran legionary, the effect was disconcerting.

'Our human cohorts are suffering in the heat,' he answered simply, and Santar was glad that Desaan hadn't mentioned his earlier suspicion that he thought something other than the adverse weather was causing the delay.

The few remembrancers that had accompanied the war host had long since fallen behind, and though a small detachment of Saavan Masonites had been tasked with their protection it wasn't to these civilians that Desaan referred. Citizens and non-combatants were expected to falter. It was part of the reason the primarch hadn't objected to the presence of iterators and imagists in the first place; he knew they would fail and cease to be a problem. No, Desaan meant soldiers. Such men and women were expected to endure and meet the rigours placed upon them by the march.

'And do my brothers not suffer in similar adverse conditions or are they somehow able to overcome such debilitations?' Ferrus pressed.

'I do not know, my lord.'

The primarch grunted and addressed Santar.

'Do you concur with your fellow captain?'

'I am as frustrated as you, my primarch.'

Ferrus's eyes narrowed to silvered slits before he turned his back to regard a broad strategium table that had manifested in the wake of the hololith.

'I doubt that,' he muttered.

He passed a shimmering silver hand across a geographical representation of the desert continent to magnify the view projected across the glass slate. Several potential node locations were identified by flashing beacons as well as two further markings, a red and a green dotted line.

'But it fails to answer why we are so far behind,' said Ferrus, glaring at the red line as if doing so would will it further across the map. Unsurprisingly, it did not.

'My lord, if I may…' Desaan began, and Santar groaned inwardly, for he knew the mistake his fellow captain had made even before he'd made it. 'Perhaps there is more retarding our efforts than merely sun and sand.'

'Speak plainly, brother-captain.'

'Sorcery, my lord. I can put it no plainer than that,' said Desaan. 'Our efforts are thwarted by eldar witches.'

Ferrus laughed, a hollow, cracking sound.

'Is that your best excuse for failure?' His silvered fists clenched the edge of the strategium table, birthing a web of cracks that would have riven the landscape with catastrophic earthquakes had they been real. Desaan felt the imagined tectonic ruptures all the way up his spine.

'It would explain why our efforts have thus far–'

Ferrus Manus's fist slammed against the map, arresting the floundering captain's words. The resultant split almost broke it in two.

'I am not interested,' he said, and it was as if the air in the stark chamber grew colder, cold enough to burn.

The primarch folded his arms. Fathomless silver pooled across his immense biceps, shimmering and refulgent.

Desaan, who had seldom been this close to his lord and for so long, found his sight drawn to them.

'Do you know how I came by this magnificent aberration?' asked Ferrus, noting the captain's interest.

Desaan hid his confusion at the line of questioning well. Like most exceptional beings, primarchs were occasionally inscrutable.

'Have you heard of my deeds?' Ferrus continued when an answer was not immediate. 'Of how I bested a storm giant in a feat of strength or how I scaled Karaashi, the Ice Pinnacle, with my bare hands? Or perhaps you are familiar with the day when I swam deeper than the Horned Behemoth of the Suphuron Sea? Do you know these stories?'

Desaan's reply was not much louder than a whisper.

'I have heard the great sagas, sire.'

Ferrus wagged a finger, lost in monologue and nodding sagely as if he'd just come upon the answer to his own conundrum. 'No... it was Asirnoth, he who was called Silver Wyrm and the greatest of the ancient drakes. No blade could pierce his metal skin, no spear or lance that I possessed.'

He paused, as if reminiscing. 'I burned it, held its writhing body beneath the lava flows of Medusa until it was dead, and when I withdrew my hands they were...' he held out both his arms, 'like this. Or so the saga speakers would say.'

'I... my lord?'

Santar wanted to intervene but a lesson was being imparted. The tale was simply that, a story crafted by bards and the tribal orators of the clans as related in the *Canticle of Travels*. It was told differently every time the first captain had heard it. No Iron Hand could claim its veracity, for none had been present during the lightless days of the primarch's arrival on Medusa. Only Ferrus Manus himself knew the truth and he kept that inside the locked cage of his memories.

'Do you believe such a warrior would allow himself to be undone by witchcraft? Do you believe he could be so weak?' he asked.

Desaan was shaking his head, trying to atone for a transgression he did not fully understand.

'No, sire.'

'Get out.' The words escaped Ferrus's lips in a rasp. 'Before I throw you out.'

Desaan saluted and turned on his heel.

Santar was about to join him when Ferrus stopped him.

'Not you, first captain.'

Santar stood his ground and straightened his back.

'Have I raised weak sons?' Ferrus asked when they were alone again.

'You know that is not the case.'

'Then why are we confounded?' The primarch's choler cooled as he took to pacing his ruined strategium. 'I have been away from the war front too long, my brothers draining my attention. You have become malleable, tractable. I perceive a weakness of purpose in our ranks, a failing of will that holds us back from our objective. Eldar sorcery is not my concern, finding and destroying the node is. We should have the mental fortitude to overcome tricks. I am leading this campaign and I will not be bested by my brothers. We are strength, an example to all. The reputation of this Legion, my reputation, will not be besmirched. No more delays. We press on at speed. Leave the Army divisions behind if you must. Nothing must prevent us achieving victory.'

Santar frowned as he saw resolve turn to melancholy on Ferrus's face.

'Desaan serves you unshakeably, as we all do. You have forged strong sons, my primarch.'

Ferrus relented. His hand was heavy and crushing as it fell upon the equerry's shoulder.

'You make me temperate, Gabriel. I suspect you are the only one who can.'

Santar bowed his head respectfully. 'You honour me with your praise, my primarch.'

'It is well-earned, my son.' Ferrus released him, leaving the shoulder numb beneath the guard. 'Desaan is a good soldier.'

'I shall tell him you said so.'

'No, I'll do it. Better it come from me.'

'As you wish, my primarch.' There was a pregnant pause as Santar considered what he was about to say next.

Ferrus had his back to him again. 'Voice your concerns. My eyes might be cold, but they are not blind.'

'Very well. Is it wise to abandon our auxiliaries? We might have need of their support.'

Ferrus's head came around to regard his first captain swiftly. The primarch's calm demeanour scorched to ash as something molten and unpredictable burned in his gaze.

'Are you questioning my orders, equerry?'

Unlike his less experienced captain, Santar did not falter.

'No, primarch, but you do not seem yourself.'

Anyone but Santar would have been struck for speaking so candidly. As it was, the first captain experienced a moment of disquiet as his primarch considered his reaction. Santar's fists were clenched, the lightning claws poised for release as his warrior instincts took over.

Ferrus's fury ebbed as quickly as it had flared and he stared into the darkness.

'There is something I need to tell you, Gabriel.' Ferrus met the first captain's gaze. 'It is for you and only you to know, but I must confess it. I warn you, speak of this to no one…'

An implicit threat lurked at the periphery of the primarch's trailing words and a nerve tremor in Ferrus's jaw flickered. The first captain waited patiently.

'I have had strange dreams of late,' Ferrus muttered. It was utterly unlike him to do so and set Santar on edge more than any threat of violence ever could. 'Of a desert of black sand and of eyes watching… cold, reptilian eyes.'

Santar had no response. He had never seen his primarch vulnerable before. Ever.

'Should I summon an Apothecary, my lord?' he eventually

asked when he noticed Ferrus rubbing his neck. Under the gorget, just visible above the lip, the skin was raw.

'An irritation, nothing more,' he said, though his voice was far away. 'It is this place, this desert. There is something out there…'

Now Santar felt real concern and wanted to end the campaign in short order and venture to fresh theatres of war.

'The Legion can destroy the node unassisted,' he asserted with confidence. 'Flesh *is* weak, my primarch, but we shall not be slaves to it.'

And like a shadow moving from across the sun, Ferrus brightened and became his old self again. He clasped Santar's shoulder in a grip that was painful for the first captain.

'Muster the legionary captains. I will lead us to our enemies and show just how strong the sons of Medusa are,' he vowed. 'My course is set, equerry. Nothing will stop me. Nothing.'

WITH GABRIEL SANTAR gone, Ferrus returned to introspection. Nothing, not even the promise of battle, could shake his bleak mood. Like an anvil hung around his neck, it dragged him deeper towards an abyss. Fulgrim could lighten it, he was sure, but then the Phoenician was not here. Instead, he had to make war with that obstinate bastard Mortarion and soft-hearted Vulkan.

'Strength…' he said as if invoking the word would provide it. With silver fingers he reached out to seize the haft of *Forgebreaker*.

He would crush the eldar, destroy their psychic node and win the campaign.

'And do it swiftly,' he added in a whisper, tearing the hammer from its strappings.

Though he would never admit it, for Ferrus, the war could not end soon enough.

* * *

COCOONED IN A vestibule of white bone, the two figures could speak without fear of interlopers listening in. There was a great deal to discuss and much hung in the balance.

'I perceive two lines,' said one, his voice lyrical and reverberant. 'Convergent at the moment, but they will soon diverge.'

The other speaker laced his slender fingers together as he answered. 'I see them too, and the point at which they part. He will not heed you. You are wasting your time in this.'

Though he was adamant, the first speaker did not sound agitated. 'He must, or think of the cost.'

'Others might not agree.' After a moment, the other speaker slowly shook his head. 'You perceive a second path where one does not truly exist. Fate will close this door to us.'

'Have you seen it?'

'I have seen him. He must choose, all must choose, but his decision is already made, and it is not to our favour.'

Now the faintest resonance of exasperation entered the first speaker's tone. 'How can you be certain?'

'Nothing is certain, however unlikely the alternative, but feet of iron do not readily alter their path without strong incentive.'

The first speaker leaned back. 'Then I shall provide it.'

'It will not make any difference.'

'I must succeed.'

'And yet you will not.'

'But I have to try.'

BION HENRICOS OF the Iron Hands Tenth Company was not encouraged as he surveyed the bedraggled condition of the Army divisions. They were sweat-stained, gaunt-looking men, plastered in the crust of their own flesh-salt. They were raw and bleeding, and slow. Interminably slow.

Even the claves of Mechanicum skitarii and servitor battalions were suffering, the frailty of their flesh components a major contributing factor. Several hundred of the cybernetic creatures had been left to rust and rot in the war host's wake; while casualties amongst the Saavan Masonites were allowed to lie where they fell in ragged Army dress and buried only at the whim of sporadic sandstorms.

A makeshift encampment had been hastily erected by the few remaining gangs of able-bodied labour serfs, and infirmaries established to deal with heat exhaustion and chronic dehydration.

Henricos counted the ranks of men within the tents, prostrate on row upon row of wire and canvas bunks. It amounted to hundreds of sick and wounded. Aside from the occasional plaintive moan, they were silent and desolate. He did not slow or linger, blind to clutches of Dogan Maulers leaning on their pike shafts and huddled beneath awnings suspended from the flanks of Chimeras; or the desperate efforts of pilots and drivers attempting to cool the engines of their vehicles; or the muttered curses of men raking clods of compacted sand from their weapons. One hoary-looking colonel tipped his cap to him, whilst sucking on a stick of tabac. He looked weathered; so did his men. But as the Iron Hand passed through the throngs of blistered, heat-scorched soldiers who could barely speak through bone-dry lips and leathern tongues, he felt an iota of compassion.

This was no place for men. It was hell made manifest and therefore the province of star-forged warriors like him. Unlike many of his brothers, Henricos did not possess a full array of bionic enhancements. His hand had been severed and replaced with a mechanised simulacrum, as was rite and ritual amongst the Legion, but the rest of the seventh sergeant was organic. He suspected that shred of empathy he had experienced came from this bias of biology.

He wondered if his more cybernetic brethren were surrendering more than just the weakness of flesh to the altar of mechanised strength and resilience. Were they giving up a part of their humanity too?

Henricos dismissed the notion, and yet it stayed at the edge of his subconscious.

Infirmary tents soon gave way to smaller pavilions that provided shade to entire battalions but were of little use to their clustered occupants in such oppressive heat. Canteens were passed around in quick succession but not even a reservoir would be enough to slake the thirst of one, let alone the many divisions of the war host. Discipline masters stood upright and unflinching as an example to their charges, but even these normally steel-backed officers were weakening. Henricos saw one collapse to his knees before he picked himself up and reasserted his post.

The old colonel was singing, but few took up the scratchy ditty, save for his veterans.

All told, it was a woeful sight, and these were just the vanguard troops; many more were still adrift from the main war host, slogging through the desert.

A command tent came into view at the end of a flattened colonnade of sand that was rapidly being overrun with drifts. A pair of ragged-looking Masonite Praetors stood to attention as the Iron Hand approached.

Henricos did not request entry, or even deign to look at the soldiers beyond acknowledging that they were present. Instead, he strode into the tent and was hit by a belt of stagnant air. Squatting in the corner of the canvas tent was a recyc-fan switched to its coldest setting. The boxy machine juddered and whined as it was pushed well beyond its limits.

Fifteen men, all in officers' attire dishevelled to the point of half-dress, stood to attention as Henricos entered.

One, a general judging by the ostentation of his uniform and the quill-bearing thrall-hawk perched upon his shoulder, stepped forwards. He had a data-slate clutched in his gauntleted hand and opened his mouth to speak, but Henricos silenced him with an upraised palm. He used his cybernetic one deliberately.

'Break it down,' he stated flatly. The Iron Hand could have been speaking in binaric for all the emotion he conveyed. 'All of it.'

A second officer, his face aghast, spoke up. This one had removed his armoured cuirass and unbuttoned his jacket. Evidently, settling in.

'But, my lord, we have only just–'

Henricos considered the three seconds he had allowed the officer to speak as a concession he would not repeat.

'No exceptions. The Legion advances, so do you. Gather your divisions or you are welcome to take up your objections with this.' He tapped the bolt pistol holstered at his hip once. 'Lord Manus commands it.'

Only the chief medicus was undeterred. 'If we uproot now, our sick and wounded will perish.' He dared to glower through wire framed spectacles. Fortunately for him, Henricos did not take it as a challenge to his authority.

'Yes, they will,' said the Iron Hand, the barest tremor of remorse surprising him.

The officers sat down, or rather slumped. Henricos took the data-slate and absorbed the information in a glance.

Then he left.

THE DESERT STRETCHED before them like a gilded ocean, burnished by the sun.

Upon a sickle-shaped rise, Ferrus Manus was surveying the way ahead. A cadre of his officers was close by while the rest of the legionary ranks waited in formation below.

The primarch glanced at a geographic hololith projected from a slate in Santar's hand. He observed sweeping dunes, caverns of basalt and endless sand plains revealed in green monochrome, before returning to the desert vista.

'Nothing on the horizon line…' he rumbled, but then

squinted as if perceiving something only one of his vaunted genetic provenance could see. 'But there is a hazing of the air, a disturbance…'

'Potential energy feedback, my lord,' said Ruuman, peering down at the scorched valley through his bionic eye. The gyroscopic focusing rings whirred and clicked, the faceted apertures clacking and reclacking in different configurations as fresh spectra were overlaid upon his vision. Its telescopic extension retracted as he added, 'Which could suggest an outpost or bastion.'

'I see it too,' said Desaan, analysing the scene through his visor. 'The outpost is likely cloaked in some way.'

Santar regarded the valley through a pair of magnoculars. It was shawled with bone-white rocks, bleached by the sun. Some jutted from the ground like skeletal fingers or were clustered together, suggesting the ribcage of some vast but long-dead predator. Sigils too; he thought he saw runic patterns described in the arrangement of the rocks.

'It must be there,' said Ferrus, interrupting the first captain's thoughts.

A dusty squall was slowly rolling across the valley basin. Santar thought he saw tiny star flashes in the churned dirt and unnatural shadows that could not have been formed by the sun. He blinked and they were gone, but the sand squall had thickened.

Santar shut down the hololith and gave the slate back to one of the few still-functioning servitor units in attendance. He passed the scopes back to Shadrak Meduson.

'Even advancing at pace, it will be a slow march across the valley,' he said, appraising all of the various tactical options. 'But arcing around the basin will be slower still.'

Ruuman made a rapid calculation through his bionics.

'Four-point-eight kilometres once we've made descent, first captain.'

Santar nodded to the Ironwrought, but addressed his primarch.

'Higher ground offers better vantage, but will force us into column. Through the valley our divisions can spread out, but exposure would be prolonged. There is something about it I cannot see... a threat.'

Ferrus glanced over his armoured shoulder. 'Is superstition contagious now, equerry?' he asked, as if sharing a private joke with Santar. The primarch did it often.

'Trusting my instincts, primarch.'

'For which I cannot fault you.' Ferrus's attempt at conciliation didn't reach his cold eyes. He watched the valley too, as if he had already seen what Santar had described but chose to dismiss it. 'I won't be slowed any further. We take the low ground.'

'Shall we send scouts to reconnoitre first? We don't know what's out there.'

'There are none,' answered Meduson, the bolter slung low and easy in his veteran's grip. His narrow face was taut as a blade, and when he scowled it seemed to sharpen.

The voice of Bion Henricos interrupted the exchange between captains. The sergeant had been brought to the impromptu conclave in order to speak for the Army divisions, since none of their officers were able to do so or quick enough to satisfy the primarch's impatience. He was a thick-set warrior, tautly muscled but with a swordsman's grace. The Medusan steel-edge strapped to his thigh alone was testament to that.

'I have a suggestion, my lord,' he said, falling to one knee but with his chin upraised and shoulders squared. He had not long been elevated to the sergeant's rank, and this was the first time he had spoken directly to his lord and primarch.

'Rise,' said Ferrus, glancing askance at the deferent sergeant. 'No son of mine must kneel before me, sergeant, not unless he is asking for forgiveness.'

'There are scouts within the Army ranks, the Dogan Maulers,' said Henricos as he stood.

'We would be wasting our time,' Desaan cut in.

Henricos turned to him. 'The humans have a role to play here.'

Eyeing the sergeant's singular bionic implant, Desaan was less than convivial.

'Yes, that of ball and chain around our noble necks, dragging behind us in the dirt. They are unnecessary. Trust in iron, not flesh.'

'Do you believe I do not?' Henricos was careful to keep his tone neutral.

If Desaan's visored eyes could have narrowed they would have.

'You are over-fleshed, Bion, a weakness that clouds your thinking.'

Henricos bristled at the obvious slight. His jaw tightened. 'I can assure you I am *unclouded*, brother-captain.'

Booming laughter, hard-edged and full of violent mirth, broke the tension like a hammer splitting an anvil.

'That's the spirit, my sons,' snarled the primarch, 'but save your zeal for the enemy. No sense blunting blades on one another or my equerry humbling the both of you in front of your fellow legionaries, eh?'

The rebuke was firm but without true ire.

Meduson stepped in as conciliator before any further harsh words between the officers saw the primarch's mood shift again. The captain's face had softened so that it might only cut rather than cleave. 'We could consolidate here, allow the Army divisions to catch up. Presumably, the Dogans will be in the vanguard.'

Henricos nodded, indicating that was the case.

'It will give them purpose and invigorate them,' he said, ignoring Desaan's disapproving expression.

'And what of *our* purpose?' asked Ferrus Manus. There was an edge to the primarch's question. 'It has been delayed enough. No more waiting,' he snapped, capricious as mercury. A long, deep breath exhaled from his tight lips.

'Muster the Legion, first captain,' said Ferrus. 'We'll take the Morlocks through the valley, heavies in reserve to gain the hill and provide overwatch for the forces advancing across the basin. Captain Meduson, you'll lead the rest in two half-battalions across the flanks of this rise and regroup with us when it levels out.'

Santar gave a firm salute to his lord and went about his duty.

The sickle-shaped banks were broad and long, but gradually tapered to a point at their terminus where they met the valley basin. Santar recalled the shadows in the dust squall and decided that the Morlocks would draw out whatever was lurking inside it.

All but one of the potential node locations pinpointed by the Mechanicum had proven false; mirages likely fashioned through the eldar witchery. The Iron Hands' efforts, which had seen the few Army divisions able to keep pace with the Legion lag farther and farther behind, had been rewarded with further ambush.

It was probable that in tracking down this final node location the same would be true.

Ferrus's steely gaze returned to the distant horizon and the haze he had perceived earlier. There was no time to waste.

'We descend immediately. Army be damned.'

SEVEN SEPARATE OUTPOSTS yielded no sign of the node. Following the coordinates of the Mechanicum, the Legion had fought several brutal skirmishes. After the last, Ferrus had been forced to report his lack of progress to his brother primarchs. Vulkan was… *accommodating*, even offering aid which Ferrus flatly refused. The exchange with Mortarion was less cordial. At this rate, it might be days before the legionary forces could consolidate and leave One-Five-Four Four behind. The slow pace of the Army divisions was not helping their cause. Ferrus could not deny the strength of their guns, they were useful, but bemoaned their frailty. So many had fallen behind. He doubted their return.

This desert is an eater of men, he thought bitterly.

The valley below had a strange cast to it. The others could not see it; it went beyond their ken to comprehend. Ferrus felt it, though; he felt the pull of it bringing him closer to his imagined abyss. Something was dogging his thoughts, just beyond the reach of his senses. He wanted to seize it, crush it in his fist, but how could he crush a feeling?

Out there on the sand plain, deep into the valley, it was waiting for him.

Perhaps it had always been waiting.

Trepidation, anger and resolve kaleidoscoped into a single imperative.

Face it and kill it.

That was the Gorgon's way, how he had always lived. It would be how he would die, too, he was certain. Nothing had ever bested him. Determination *defined* him.

I am coming for you, he vowed as he led the descent.

FADING LIGHT RADIATING from the ossified walls of their psychic sanctuary described the frown on the first speaker's face.

'He is singular in his will and purpose.'

'Do you still believe he is on the wrong path?' said the other.

'The nexus is close…' muttered the first speaker.

'How will you convince him of it? Mon'keigh, particularly humans – especially one such as this – are distrustful by nature.'

As the conjurations of his plan began to connect like the chromosomes of an embryonic life form, the first speaker's eyes narrowed.

'It will need to be cunning. He must believe it is his decision. It is the only way to alter his path.'

'This web you weave is flawed,' said the other.

The first speaker met the other's gaze and a flash of power illuminated a question in his almond-shaped eyes...

...which the other gladly answered. 'You are trying to turn stone into water, have it flow to your design. Stone cannot bend, it can only break.'

The first speaker was defiant. 'Then I shall break it and fashion it anew.'

AS THEY NEARED the floor of the basin, the air became still and silent. Deep cliffs rose on either side of the Morlocks, and the broad valley quickly turned into a ravine into which the sun barely reached.

'Where have we ventured?' Santar's voice was not much louder than a whisper.

Thick, engulfing darkness dwelled here. Rather than a desert, it had become a stark landscape of mortuary stones and crypt-like monoliths. In the shadows, the sand banks were almost black and Santar was reminded of his primarch's earlier confession about his dreams. Even the pellucid lustre of the bone-white rocks had dimmed.

Several Morlocks were glancing around at their altered surroundings. Veterans all, they were disciplined enough not to react, but Santar sensed grips tightening on bolters.

'Steady, the Avernii,' he said into the feed and then isolated Desaan's channel. 'Keep your legionaries close and ready, brother-captain.'

The two companies marched alongside one another, spread wide and in shallow ranks. Heavy shadows and the abject stillness of the valley made the distance between them feel like a gulf.

'Did we lose the sun?' asked Desaan. 'It is black as Old Night down here.'

Santar looked up. The orb still blazed in the sky, but its light was being filtered as if through murky gauze, turning grey and dilute before it hit the valley.

'I have lost sight of Meduson and Ruuman,' the captain added.

Santar arched his neck towards the tip of the rise but it was almost impossible to see the summit.

It was deep, much deeper than it looked. Sand squalls billowing around his feet put him in mind of iron filings skittering around an anvil. It was also farther than Ruuman had suggested, and the Ironwrought was never usually wrong about such things. But nothing about this situation was usual.

'Like the Land of Shadow,' the primarch rumbled.

Even without the feed, Ferrus Manus's stentorian voice carried on the skirling breeze. He anchored the two formations. He was the hinge along with a bodyguard of his staunchest praetorians, which included Gabriel Santar.

'I see no ghosts, primarch,' said the first captain, attempting to break the tension.

Back on Medusa, the Land of Shadow was a bleak place supposedly infested by shades and revenants. Such talk came from superstitious men, those of weak and gullible minds. The Iron Hands knew differently. In its trackless depths were great obelisks of stone and metal, whose purpose had been lost to time. Monsters plied its darkened furrows and forgotten chasms, that much was true. And madness lurked on its endless plains for the unwary or the foolish. The association was not comforting.

'The ghosts are here,' said Ferrus, adding a layer of frost to the already chill air. 'We just cannot see them yet.' And as the squalls began to thicken into a storm, he added, 'Close ranks. Keep it narrow and deep.'

The valley had become another realm entirely, one Santar did not recognise. Cast from skeletal rocks, shadows stretched into claws, reaching for the Iron Hands and slowly encircling them.

'Why do I not know this place?' he asked of himself.

Desaan's comm-feed crackled with interference. 'Because… is not… same.'

'Lord Manus,' said Santar, the sense of threat abruptly palpable.

Ferrus did not look his way. 'Keep moving. We cannot turn back.' The primarch's tone suggested he knew they had stumbled into a trap. 'The eldar have us, but will not keep us.'

The wind was rising, and so too the storm. It robbed the primarch's voice of its potency. At the same moment, the heavy tread of many booted feet was silenced as the storm rolled over the Morlocks without warning.

It hit them like a hammer and within seconds the two companies were engulfed.

The sun died at once, lost to a shrieking darkness.

Moments later, slashing grains abraded Santar's armour like blades. He heard the grind of the desert against the metal, but dismissed the minor damage to his battle-plate as the report of it scrolled across the retinal lens in his battle-helm. Lightning claws unsheathed, Santar tried to slice through the black morass and found it less than yielding. It was like cutting earth, only it was air.

'Stay together,' he said down the feed, 'advancing as one.'

Fewer acknowledgements sounded that time. The tactical-display was faulty and the bio-scan markers denoting the position of his battle-brothers were intermittent. As far as he could tell, formation was being maintained, but he did not know how long that would last. Santar sensed things would get worse before they got better. Grit clogged the rebreather grille of his helmet, raking his tongue. It tasted like ash and death. Copper-scent spiked his nostrils.

'Together as one,' he repeated.

A distant shrieking registered on his aural sensorium, overloading the angry static from the comm-feed. It didn't sound like the wind, or at least not just the wind. A series of baffling returns ghosted in and out on the tactical display.

'Weapons ready,' he ordered, searching for an enemy. Black sand marred his view, making target acquisition impossible. A screaming refrain muddied the response from his fellow sergeants and captains. Affirmation icons sporadically blinked into being, as if the feed's interfaces had been degraded.

Santar could barely make out the primarch's outline, just a few metres in front of him.

'Lord Manus,' he called, before Ferrus was lost further to the storm.

There was no response at first but then the faint reply reached him.

'Forward! We drive through it or we die.'

Santar wanted to consolidate; to forge a defensive cordon and wait out the tempest, but this was no ordinary phenomenon. To linger would bring lethal consequences, he was sure. He advanced.

Something flickered into existence on his retinal display. It was a heat signature, weak, but distinct enough for him to locate.

He swung his head around, the Cataphractii armour more cumbersome than he was used to, and saw... *a face.*

It was inhuman, the skin pulled taut across an overlong skull. Chin and cheekbones were angular, pointed at the tips, and the eyes were merely hollows.

'In the Emperor's name...' he breathed as he realised the deathly visages were swarming their ranks like a shoal of flesh-eating fish, disembodied and darkly luminous in the storm.

Santar roared, 'Enemy contact!' He hoped the feed would convey his warning.

The Morlocks opened up with their bolters, and a chugging staccato of hard bangs resounded. Muzzle flashes were like subdued distress flares, dulled by the tempest wind.

Utterly alien, the face retreated into darkness as Santar advanced. It drew him on, step by step.

'Engaging!'

He swung, energy crackling off the blades in tongues of jagged azure, but cleaved only air.

'Detecting movement,' Santar heard over the feed, but he could not identify the speaker as a conglomeration of voices vied for his attention.

'Contact,' cried the echo of another, also anonymous to the first captain even though he had known and fought beside these warriors for decades.

Dense bolter bursts erupted throughout the Iron Hands formation as an effort to repel the attackers was mounted in earnest.

'Desaan, report,' shouted Santar as something preternaturally fast and impossible to track flitted across his left flank. He turned as a second figure skittered into his limited peripheral vision on the right. It glared as it passed him and Santar was left with the vague impression of its wraith-like countenance.

Lord Manus had been right; there *were* ghosts waiting for them in the darkness and now their patience was at an end. Blood was in the water.

'Unknown... enemy.' Desaan's reply was piecemeal but clear. 'Cannot pin down... dispositions... engaging... multiple contacts...'

Of the primarch, there was no sign. Ahead was darkness, so too behind and in every other direction. Orientation at this point was impossible, so Santar chose to stand.

'Maintain position,' he said down the feed. 'They are trying to pull us apart.'

He tried to find his lord but could discern nothing with either sight or sensor beyond the blackness.

Desaan's broken acknowledgement was delayed and came as scant comfort to Santar. The Morlocks were divided, swallowed by the storm, and Lord Manus had been shorn from the rest of the Legion. Their strength and fortitude had been vexed in a single moment of rashness.

Santar cursed his lack of foresight. He should have insisted they skirt the valley or wait for a thorough reconnoitring of the area, but the primarch would not be swayed. It was as if he drove head-on at some fate that only he could see. Santar was closer than any of the Iron Hands to his lord but even he was not privy to the primarch's inner thoughts.

A keening wail, high-pitched and several octaves above the scream of the storm, cut the air. It made Santar's head throb, despite the protection afforded by his battle-helm. Vertigo fell upon him in a crashing wave and he staggered. Impenetrable static marred the feed completely, though he could not muster his voice to give an order anyway.

Santar tasted blood in his mouth and spat it against the inner surface of his helm. He gritted his crimson teeth.

Be as iron.

Shuddering vibrations cascaded along his bones with the invasive intensity of mortar impacts. He staggered again but fought from collapsing. Fall now and he was certainly dead. No warrior wearing Cataphractii warplate would ever rise unassisted if he fell. And there were more than just ghosts prowling the blackness. Before the aural assault, he had caught the impression of edged blades, of lithe and spectral warriors. Finding inner fortitude, Santar looked for something to kill.

Dull, armoured silhouettes stumbled through the fog – his Morlocks, slow and all but mired.

Screaming scythed through his pain, a desperately mortal sound that presaged a line of bolter fire ripping along his right flank. Santar ignored it, heard the sudden air displacement to his left instead.

Found you…

Defensive instinct made Santar parry the blade blurring towards his neck, and at last he got a proper look at his attacker.

It was a mask that the eldar wore, bone-white to match its segmented armour, with a mane of tendril-like black hair cascading behind it. Judging by the form-fitting cuirass, this one was female and not a wraith or ghoul at all. The sword was long and curved, forged and sharpened by a killing mind. Hot sparks rang from the blade as it ground against Santar's lightning claws.

She was at once a part of the storm yet at the same time apart from it, blending with the eddying wind as she chose. Leaving a trail of jagged spikes to fade in the air behind her, she disengaged.

Santar kept his guard up, ignoring what his retinal lenses were telling him and trusting to instinct. When the follow-up attack came it was delivered with power. The sword clashed against his lightning claw and he felt the jolt of it all the way up into his shoulder. She glared at Santar, incensed at his defiance, and released a hell-screech from her mask that forced the first captain's jaw to lock. Weathering the aural barrage, he thrust with his other lightning claw and trapped the eldar's bone blade fast.

A pistol appeared in her other hand but the shots rebounded harmlessly off Santar's war-plate like ineffectual insect stings.

The grating laughter emitting through his mouth grille surprised him.

Abandoning the pistol, she took her sword in a two-handed grip in an effort to release it. Whilst trapped she could not withdraw and if she disengaged without her blade she would be cut apart. Even eldar were not faster than lightning.

'You're not so scary,' Santar grunted through clenched teeth as she fed another hell-screech into his face. The first captain's superior strength was telling against the alien's pressing sword, and his bionics growled in anticipation of triumph. 'I am scarier.'

Santar parted her weapon in two, shredding it with the

scissoring action of his paired lightning claws. The sundered half of the blade, separated from the ragged edge of its broken hilt, spun into the warrior's undefended chest and impaled her. She fell back into the storm and was immediately lost within it.

The ambush was faltering, and Santar was certain the darkness itself was receding as the storm ebbed. Several Morlocks lay prone where they'd been transfixed by blades or felled by the howling but others were rallying. Even the feed was returning to normal.

'Are you alive, first captain?' It was Desaan, the muffled *thud-chank* of his bolter chorusing behind him.

'Alive and wrathful, brother-captain,' Santar replied, gutting another of the wraith-warriors. He was wrenching the blades free from her back with a satisfying *slurrch* of flesh when his left arm seized. He tried once to free it but it wouldn't move.

'Something is wrong. Brother, I... *gnn*.' Paralysis anchored his bionics in place as if they had simply stopped functioning. His legs, also mechanised, were locked. 'I cannot... *gnn*,' the pain of it was incredible and he gasped the last part, '...move.'

Searching for allies he only found two fleshless masks bearing down on him. They grinned cruelly, a witching glow to their features, and spat something vengeful in their native tongue.

'I can kill you both... one-handed,' Santar promised but felt a chink in his confidence as they began to weave around him.

Something was coming through the comm-feed, arresting his attention from the wraith-warriors as they closed. He recognised the plaintive cry of his fellow captain.

Between the circling forms of the eldar, he glimpsed Desaan stumbling through the darkness, firing wildly. An errant burst clipped one of the other Morlocks, dropping his guard so another wraith-warrior could plunge its sword between the armour joint linking breastplate to greave. The Iron Hand sagged before the storm cut him off from view.

'Desaan!' Santar's would-be killers were near. 'Watch your fire, brother.' He couldn't afford to be distracted. Desaan staggered on, bolter tracking dangerously as his firing arcs went unchecked.

'Desaan!'

He looked as if he was...

'Blind, first captain...' he mumbled, stunned. '*Hnn*... I can't... see...' His arm was limp by his side. Others were afflicted too, the Morlocks undone by precisely what had given them strength.

Flesh is weak. The mantra came back to Santar with mocking irony.

The eldar had done something to them, crafted some malign sorcery to affect their cybernetics. To a man, the Morlocks all had extensive bionics.

Santar stared at the wraith-warriors who were brandishing their swords in the promised cuts to come.

'Come on,' he slurred. His heart might as well have been bared to their blades.

The wraith-warriors paused, lingering half-corporeally amidst the storm. As one they blurred. Two became many, and their harsh laughter resounded through the howling that was pounding Santar relentlessly.

'Come on!' he roared. 'Fight me!'

The eyes of one – *or was it all?* – narrowed behind its mask and Santar followed its gaze to where his arm was paralysed. Only it was moving again, but not of the first captain's volition. Energy cracked along the lightning claw blades, fierce enough to rend war-plate. Fascination and disbelief coalesced into horror as Santar realised they were being turned inwards... towards his neck.

He clutched his rebellious wrist, held it with his other hand whilst the alien laughter grew into a tinnitus drone. Sweat beaded his face as the muscles in his neck and shoulder bunched with the effort of trying to restrain the foreign limb that was trying to kill him.

Slain by his own hand, there was no honour in that. It was a despicable death, and the eldar looking on knew it.

'Throne...' he gasped. Even the squeal of the bionics sounded different, belligerent somehow.

Fight it! he urged, but the link between machine and flesh was far from symbiotic. One was almost regarded as a contagion to the detriment of the other, but now that boon had rebelled and become a curse.

The actinic smell of scorched metal filled his rebreather as the energised blade tips touched the edge of his gorget. Santar estimated it would take a single, determined thrust to pierce the armour and tear open his neck. At most he had seconds.

Santar was hoarse from his roared defiance but his struggles were lessening.

He closed his eyes and his voice shrank to a whisper in the face of the inevitable.

'*Primarch...*'

FERRUS WAS ALONE; there was only him and the storm. He had since donned his war-helm but saw no evidence of his Legion on the retinal display, so did not waste his time calling out to them. The last contact he'd had was from Gabriel Santar, a desperate plea for them to stay together.

Onwards, drive onwards.

The compulsion was too strong to resist. They were deep into it now. Whatever horror this desert was harbouring, whatever cruel truth he had been summoned here to witness, he could no longer deny it.

This was no ordinary storm. Too redolent with the fabric of his dreams, it was awash with metaphors from his violent past and the figurative snares of his possible futures. He heard voices on the scything wind but no sounds of battle, no war cries.

I expected a battle.

Ferrus could not discern their meaning but sensed their words were important.

The comm-feed was down. Not even static haunted its channels. He accepted that too, and kept moving. Whatever this was, whatever destiny or sliver of fate had delivered him here, he would meet it head-on.

Eyes... slits like those of a serpent, watch me. I can hear the sibilance of its tongue like a knife on the breeze. It is the same knife I feel resting against my throat.

A memory surfaced.

After leaving the landship, he had spoken to Mortarion again, or rather his brother had spoken to him. The other primarch had left him with a barb that Ferrus could not easily forget or silence.

If you are not strong enough, he had said. *If you cannot finish it alone...*

'Help me?' he roared into the uncaring storm. The wind was mocking in reply. 'I need no help.' He laughed, a cruel and terrible sound. 'I am strong. I am the Gorgon.'

Ferrus was running, though he couldn't remember quickening his pace so drastically and without cause. But he ran as hard as his limbs would allow. The darkness of the sand plain only seemed to lengthen as earth and sky merged into one.

'You cannot help me,' he raged as a sensation of flying then falling overtook him.

And in a much quieter voice, lost to his subconscious, '...*no one can.*'

TWO LEGIONARIES STOOD out on the golden sand bank, staring into a pall of darkness.

In front of them, the black cloud surrounded the Morlocks like ink on water.

Bion Henricos could scarcely believe what his eyes were telling him and wondered if his augmetically enhanced brethren were seeing the same.

'What *is* that?'

Brother Tarkan widened the aperture of his bionic eye, enhancing its focus with minute movements of his facial muscles. Every adjustment produced the same result.

'Inconclusive.'

'Nothing natural,' Henricos replied, rising from a crouched position.

Until he regrouped with Captain Meduson, one half of the battalion was his. Whatever the blackness was in front of them, he would have to deal with it on his own. He had tried opening the feed, but the link was foiled by whatever psy-storm was boiling in the desert basin.

'It has claws, brother-sergeant,' said Tarkan.

Two hundred and fifty legionaries, just a portion of the Iron Tenth, awaited Henricos's command. Bolter-armed and full of fury, yet here they were, stopped in their iron tracks by the dark. A pity they did not have any jetbike divisions to circumvent the storm and assess it more fully. Not for the first time, Henricos considered the lack of tactical flexibility in the Legion.

'That it does,' he said, scanning the horizon and the pillared rocks overlooking the shadow-choked valley. He was close enough to touch it and reached out with his iron hand. A tendril of swirling sand *tinked* harmlessly against the metal and as Henricos lifted his gaze he found what he was searching for above the storm. It orchestrated the darkness, a tall, thin figure in dun-coloured robes. It carried a witching stave, carved with alien runes and inlaid gemstones.

'Brother Tarkan,' he said in a grating cadence, thick with promised retribution, 'remove that stain.'

Tarkan was a sniper, part of one of several such squads in the Tenth, and he handled his long-barrelled rifle with a marksman's grace. It was fashioned for his hands and carried a scope-sight that would connect to his bionic eye and forge an infallible link between firer and target.

Looking down the scope, Tarkan lined the green

crosshair over the witch's helmeted head and fired. The expulsion of the shell rocked the weapon but Tarkan had compensated for that already. Still tracking through the scope, he grinned with mirthless satisfaction as the alien's cranium burst open and it fell from the pillar without a head or much of its upper torso.

He slung the rifle onto his back.

'Target eliminated, brother-sergeant.'

Henricos raised his fist and the rest of the half-battalion marched onto the bank.

There was no sense in holding back at this point.

'Forward, in the name of the Gorgon.'

Together two hundred and fifty warriors waded into the dissipating storm.

Something repelled Henricos as he entered the shadow. It was a stiffening of the mechanisms in his bionic hand, clenching it into a fist when he desired it to be loose and ready to unsheathe his blade. He forced it open as he closed on the stricken Morlocks, unclear as to its malfunction, and halted when he saw what they were doing to one another.

One legionary had his own eviscerator lodged in his armoured chest. The teeth were red and churning. With one hand he was trying to prevent the blade from sinking deeper, but the cybernetic one was pushing it farther into him. Another lay prone and unmoving, his helmet staved in by his own power-maul. Crimson fluid was leaking from the cracks and pooled around his head. Some staggered, half-blind, or were rooted by bionic legs that would not function. Bionic hands wrapped themselves around throats of flesh and choked the life from their bearers. Grisly and terrifying, the evidence of machine-carnage was everywhere.

The virtue of the Iron Hands' creed was being turned against them.

Henricos's momentary pause was born out of self-preservation for his half of the battalion and a desire not to make a grievous situation worse, but whatever malady was afflicting the Morlocks hadn't seized the Iron Tenth yet.

'Captain!' Henricos barged into the storm with renewed vigour. Behind him, his brothers fanned out, interceding where they could, stopping the self-mutilation from escalating any further than it already had.

'I see it!' Meduson replied. 'By the Emperor's sword, I see it... Bring them down, brother. Save them from themselves if you can.'

The link went dead, the reprieve in communication only fleeting, just as Desaan blundered into Henricos's eye line.

A jagged combat blade was gripped in the captain's cybernetic hand as he wrestled with some unseen assailant that was trying to ram it into his face.

Henricos reached him as the monomolecular knife was about to pierce flesh.

His iron fingers clenched around Desaan's wrist, holding it steady.

'Hold on, brother!' he cried, trying to bring the weapon under his control. As he struggled, Henricos saw faces inside the darkness. They were swift and incorporeal, like snatches of freezing fog given spectral form. A line of bolter fire chased one but the ghost dissipated before it could connect. A mocking, howling chorus followed that set the sergeant's teeth on edge.

Desaan's voice was pained. 'Bion, is that you? I cannot see, brother.'

His visor was dark, like an iron blindfold wrapped around his eyes.

'Fight it, brother-captain!' Henricos urged, but Desaan's bionic strength was incredible. Even together they were losing and the blade slipped a little closer, piercing flesh.

'Gutted by my own combat blade,' said Desaan with a pained grimace. 'Not as glorious as I'd hoped.'

'You're not dead yet,' promised Henricos. 'Lean back…'

Letting go of Desaan's arm, he wrenched out his Medusan steel-edge and fed power into the blade. It took several seconds longer to draw than it should have, his iron hand resisting him.

Soon it will take us too.

'What are you doing?'

'What I must.' The shriek of hewn metal eclipsed the howling as Henricos began sawing off the captain's forearm.

As well as he could, Desaan tried to stand his ground and be still.

'If you slip…' he growled, teeth clenched.

'You'll lose your head,' answered Henricos and kept cutting.

Around them, the ghosts were receding, fading along with the storm. So too was the sorcerous grip on the Iron Hands' cybernetics.

The last of the cabling and mech-servos came away in a welter of oil and sparks, leaving just the armoured vambrace housing. Beaded with nervous sweat, Henricos pulled up short and the two Iron Hands exhaled in unison.

Stuttering bolter bursts, increasingly more spread out with every passing moment, sounded on the breeze. The storm was dying and the ghosts were gone. Function returned to the stricken Morlocks but the cost revealed by the settling of the sand was dear.

Several dead Cataphractii lay on the ground, impaled on their own blades or bludgeoned by their own mauls. At least three others were slain to the wraith-warriors. Many more were injured.

Sight returning, Desaan winced at his sawn-off limb but gave nodded thanks to the sergeant.

'Judgement of my humours is not always my strongest attribute.'

'You spoke your mind, I spoke mine. No more needs to be said.'

They each gave a cursory salute and the matter was settled.

Desaan nodded again, and then looked around.

Of the enemy casualties, there was no sign.

'Was a battle even fought here?' asked Meduson as he regrouped the Iron Tenth.

'I struck one that could not have lived,' offered Desaan.

'As did I. Its head left its body,' said Tarkan as he joined them.

Desaan scowled. 'Even their dead are craven. They are all gone.'

Further discussion was stalled as a figure emerged from the dissipating darkness. He bore a brutal wound across his gorget and left pauldron, gouges that would have taken his head had they been a centimetre closer to his sternum. The four grooves were deep, scored by an energy weapon.

'So is the primarch,' said Gabriel Santar. 'Lord Manus is missing.'

WILL OF IRON

'He could not have fallen.'

Meduson's tone carried a trace of doubt that made Santar's jaw clench.

'Stabbed in the back...' Desaan muttered. They had all been horrifically exposed in the valley, but he dismissed the notion immediately.

'The Gorgon is unkillable,' he declared in a louder voice. 'No treacherous coward's blade could even pierce his skin. It's impossible.'

'Then where is he?' asked Meduson.

Though it had returned to its natural hue and geography, the desert valley was still rife with chasms, crags and scattered rocks. Even a cursory appraisal revealed over two dozen possible areas where the primarch could have fallen foul of enemy treachery.

Desaan found he could not answer.

Santar followed his gaze, and opened a comm-feed channel. Surely nothing as mundane as a pitfall could have undone the Gorgon.

'Ironwrought?'

Ruuman was still on the ridgeline, slowly directing his

heavy divisions towards the basin now that overwatch was no longer needed.

'There was nothing to be seen, first captain. Nor could I draw a bead on your spectral enemies,' he admitted ruefully.

'And now?' asked Santar, as the rest of the officer cadre clustered around him listened.

'A vast and golden plain, but no obvious sign of our primarch. Or his passing.'

Santar cut the feed. His face was set like scoured iron.

'Lord Manus *is* unkillable,' he asserted with a glance at Desaan, 'but I won't abandon him. If the eldar do have him, if they have somehow ensnared him, then I pity the fools. They clasp a molten blade with bare flesh and will burn for it.'

His glare found Meduson.

'Captain, you have command of the battalions. Take them to the final node location and confirm its presence. I will remain with fifty warriors to commence a search for our liege-lord.'

Meduson said, 'We could still consolidate, await the Army divisions and press them into the search?'

Santar was emphatic. 'No. If they reach us then I'll use them accordingly. Otherwise, I want you to follow Lord Manus's orders and find the node.'

Nodding, Meduson went to gather the Legion as Santar drew close to his fellow captain and second.

'Get me fifty of our very best. Bring Tarkan and his snipers, Henricos too. The others go with Meduson under his orders until I return. Understood?'

'Yes, first captain.'

Desaan lingered.

'Is there something I have missed, brother-captain?' asked Santar.

'Where is he, Gabriel?'

As the rest of the legionaries were mobilising, Santar looked around at the endless desert.

'Out there, I hope.'

'And if he is not?'

'Then I'll trust that our lord can find his way out of whatever trouble has befallen him. You should do the same.'

'It was the storm, Gabriel. That was no natural thing we fought. There are unseen enemies abroad on the sand.'

'The world around us is changing, Vaakal. You and I have seen it.'

'Some things should be left to the darkness. I do not look forward to their return.'

Santar's silence suggested he agreed.

The world, the entire galaxy, *was* changing. They felt it, all the Legiones Astartes did. Santar wondered whether that was why the Emperor had returned to Terra. He wondered what that meant for all their futures. Even his favoured sons did not know and Gabriel saw the trauma that had caused echoed in his own father.

Waiting for Desaan who had gone to assemble the search party, he touched the self-inflicted gouges on his war-plate and had time enough to consider the Iron Hands' reliance on bionics. Whoever these foes were, they knew the Legion's strengths and how to undo them. Flesh *and* iron was a potent fusion but as with any alloy, the balance had to be right to achieve perfect forging. Their metal felt flawed at that moment. Perhaps Meduson had been right about consolidation.

It didn't matter now. They were stretched, but would overcome. That was the Iron Hands' way.

Fifty legionaries were standing in front of him, eager to act, and he met their gaze.

Someone or something had taken the primarch. Santar needed to know where and he needed to know why. And if he had to kill every xenos that cowered under the rocks of the entire desert he would.

'Quadrant by quadrant,' he growled. 'Leave no stone,

brothers. You are the primarch's own praetorians. Act
like it. Find him.'

FERRUS MANUS DID not *feel* lost, yet this place was unfa-
miliar to him.

It was a cavern, a vast and echoing space that went
on into infinite darkness. A long, jagging scar split the
vaulted ceiling above and he assumed he had fallen into
an unseen chasm in the desert.

Wan sunlight permeated through the crack, but failed
to leaven the gloom.

He had tried several times to raise the Morlocks, but
the comm-feed was dead. Not even static. The retinal
lenses offered little, coming back with a series of blank
returns, so he removed his battle-helm.

'How deep am I?' he wondered out loud. There was
no echo to the sound, despite the vastness of the cavern. The air was fresh and cool. He felt it against his
skin like a caress, but there was the reek of oil and
something else... *perfume* on the breeze. The scent was
cloying, utterly anathema to what he was used to. It was
decadence and hedonism; as far from solidity and the
discipline of function as one could reach.

Slowly, more details of his surroundings resolved as
his enhanced sight caught up to his other senses. There
were columns, the faded remnants of carved frescoes and
sweeping triumphal arches rendered from the rock. He
saw monolithic statuary. The subjects were all human
but he did not recognise either their faces or their attire.
The stone strangers glared at him from on high through
time-ravaged features. One, a noble warrior bereft of his
head, pointed down at him with an accusing finger.

'I didn't cut your neck, brother,' Ferrus told him and
started to walk.

Like his voice, Ferrus's footsteps did not echo and he
assumed it was some quirk of geology. Ferrus had spent
some time with his brother Vulkan who had illuminated

him, oft at length, about the virtues and variances of earth and stone.

'Show me how to craft it into something with function and purpose,' he had replied, much to the other primarch's chagrin. *Otherwise, what's the point?*

Alike and yet so different were the Gorgon and the Drake.

Ferrus followed the breeze, hoping it would lead to some fissure he could crack open and use to rejoin his Legion. It took him from the vast cavern into a wide gallery that still had the essence of some submerged kingdom of Old Earth. Columns punctuated a long, dark processional and soared to a tall ceiling that was lost in shadow. Underfoot the earth was dark. The odour of crematoria ash and burned flesh pervaded. A mortal man might have been unsettled by it, but Ferrus was far removed from such flesh-born weakness.

Black sand…

The thought came unbidden as he looked down at his armoured feet.

Just like in the valley.

'A tomb or mausoleum, perhaps,' he considered aloud. But there were no crypts, not even a reliquary, yet the gallery stank of death.

Slivers of reflective obsidian, black like the earth, shimmered in the light of luminous crystals as he passed through the gallery. He caught sight of something, or rather a piece of an image, in the glassy rock. A massive conflagration burned in its fathomless darkness, and something else… It was familiar, yet alien.

Like grabbing the broken fragments of a dream, Ferrus could not hold it steady long enough to see it clearly. Whenever he stopped to get a better look, the obsidian merely reflected his face back at him, dour and displeased.

Perhaps it was another quirk of the light and geology of this place. Certainly, there was something *unique* about it.

Ferrus resisted the urge to unsheathe *Forgebreaker* and smash the stone asunder, knowing it would achieve nothing, and fended off the desire to vent.

He would not be so easily goaded, and doggedly pressed on.

He was about to leave the long gallery when something else pricked at the primarch's senses.

Ferrus could hear… *weeping*.

A trick of the wind perhaps? He could feel no breeze, yet the sound carried easily enough.

It was a mourning song, something so baleful that it seeped into his marrow and made his limbs leaden. Grief was not something the primarch had ever experienced. It pained him to lose his sons in battle but that was a risk inherent in the purpose for which they had been bred. He could accept it. He had never felt true loss and yet now it crept upon him, a simulacrum of the real thing. Images filled his mind of his brothers slain or close to death, the skeletal corpse of his father.

'What is this?'

Wrath supplanted grief as Ferrus realised he was the victim of further alien witchery. He defied it, forced strength back into his body only for the plaintive lament to metamorphose into something else, something worse. Death cries haunted the air, as if whatever revenants lingered in this grim place relived their final moments before the end.

'Come out!' Ferrus demanded, seeking out the witch that was haunting him with its sorcery. 'Reveal yourself or I shall tear this chamber apart to find you.'

His challenge was met by the low grind of distant engines, the ear-splitting crescendo of mass gunfire and the feral shout of warriors. Thousands of war sounds crashed together in terrifying cacophony, bent towards murder and death. A theatre of battle evolved around the primarch, one to which he could only listen – and even then from a great distance, perhaps through time itself. Ferrus did not need to bear witness to it to know wherever or whenever this was meant to be, it was hell.

As the illusory war ground on, he discerned a voice that made his blood run as ice.

The sound that escaped the primarch's lips was a rasp, ill befitting a lord of battle.

'Gabriel…'

He stopped, tried to listen harder, hoping that closer interrogation would put the lie to his suspicions, but the din abated and silence filled the chamber in its place.

Breathing, low and fast. Chest heaving beneath war-plate forged by a demi-god's own hand. The sudden stillness surrounding him brought fresh and unwelcome disquiet to Ferrus.

The smallest step, tentative and wary, brought the return of hell in his mind. Another and the cries grew louder. One more and they were near deafening.

'Gabriel!'

Ferrus glowered at the darkness, searching every column, every shadow for a sign of his first captain. Frantic and incredulous, acting in a way he did not recognise… In his tortured mindscape, Gabriel Santar was being brutally murdered.

Others followed… Desaan, scorched to ash by atomic flame; Ruuman, stabbed to death by half a dozen spatha blades; even Cistor, the Master of Astropaths, spitting blood and locked in a convulsive death spasm… A thousand dying voices screamed as one.

Ferrus hit earth and realised he was on his knees. Assailed by the apocalyptic visions, he raised silvered hands to his forehead in an effort to push them down. 'Impossible…'

He had seen something in his waking dreamscape, something so terrible he could barely countenance it, let alone give it voice.

A lesser being might have broken then, but he was the Gorgon and possessed of mental strength few credited

him with. Guilliman knew it and had said as much
when the two had occasion to speak alone. The cobalt
and black were a potent mixture, an unbendable alloy.

Doggedly, he rose, one foot then the other. Only
determination that could see mountains unearthed
and monsters bested single-handed could unravel such
potent sorcery. His back was heavy, so too his arms.

I have borne heavier weights.

Wrath provided fortitude. It became the molten well-
spring from which Ferrus drew his strength with fists
clenched full of rage.

He roared at the shadows.

'Lies! You show me these falsehoods and expect me to
believe them. What is it meant to achieve? Are you trying
to drive me to madness?'

His last words echoed back at him, over and over.

I will endure. My will is ironclad.

Gritted teeth pulled Ferrus through the horror of seeing Gabriel's tortured death over and over. It washed
over him in a desolating wave. Every one of his loyal
Morlocks, their murders folded into a massacre without
end.

Ripped from its strappings, *Forgebreaker* hummed in
the primarch's grasp with barely restrained violence.
It wanted to be unleashed but like its master was frustrated. Tangible enemies were painfully absent.

'Afraid to face me?'

The darkness had no answer to the challenge, save for
the droning of the war unending.

Fire blazed in the Gorgon's peripheral vision; the slivers of obsidian were alive with it. The significance of the
imagery was lost on him.

He had but one recourse remaining.

Broken apart by Ferrus's fury, part of the wall disintegrated. The glassy rock shattered as it struck the ground
but there was no fire, no death screams released from its
destruction.

A second blow hewed a column in half and he leaned aside to avoid its crash, like a felled and crystalline tree brought down to the earth. It was not a rampage, rather a keen and precise assault. Ferrus moved with purpose, chose his blows carefully and observed their aftermath. He was searching for a breach in the glamour he could exploit. Having spent a lifetime trying to excise it from his mind and body, the Gorgon was adept at finding weakness. So he moved, and slowly left the gallery and its horrors behind.

As he neared the end of the chamber another sound joined the battle noise, lurking just beneath it in a sub-frequency that only a primarch could hear. Sibilant, it carried the low susurrus of something viperous and serpentine.

Eyes watching, cold and reptilian eyes...

Something was hunting him. He caught the flash of a tail, the impression of scales mirroring the reflected fire from the slivers of obsidian.

Fury surrendered to calm. He was not some head-strong pup to be goaded with tricks.

I am the Gorgon. I am Medusa.

The susurrus returned, louder this time. Behind him. Ferrus's heart stilled as he strove to pinpoint the sound. It had no origin, everywhere and nowhere. In his mind's eye, he spun around to face his nemesis and split another chunk of the gallery with *Forgebreaker*'s might.

Instead, he lowered the hammer head and let it drop to the ground with a dull thud of metal.

'Do you see strings attached to my limbs?' he asked the shadow, hefting *Forgebreaker* onto his back.

'I thought not,' said Ferrus after a short pause and walked slowly from the gallery.

The bloody images and the roar of war did not follow.

GRAINY LUMEN LIGHT stripped back the darkness but revealed little of the chasm except for skittering native fauna.

Santar had found an aperture in the desert rock large enough to accommodate his bulk, a widening crack into the subterranean world that had seemingly swallowed his father whole. But there was no sign. His voice echoed coldly across the feed. 'Negative.'

It was one of many dead ends.

He knew that fifty legionaries, broken into smaller search squads, were scouring the basin and the desert beyond it. Thus far, to no avail. Despite their efforts, they were no closer to finding the primarch.

Half his focus on the auto-senses data streaming across his retinal lenses, Santar stared at the sun. The burning orb had returned more fearsome than ever since the dispersal of the witch-cloud. Memories of the psychic attack on the Legion were slow to fade. He flexed his bionic arm, half expecting it to defy his neural commands. It did not.

He took off his battle-helm and let the heat hit him.

'A changing world…' he thought aloud. Opening up the feed, he spoke to Desaan. 'How can someone like the Gorgon just disappear, brother?' Santar surveyed the plain. It was vast and undulating, but littered with rocks and caverns. Even with a fleet of Stormbirds, he doubted they would find their quarry.

'Every metre of this basin has been mapped and searched. What did we miss?'

'Anything through your visor's sensorium?'

There was a click in the feed as Desaan rechecked.

'Residual energy readings, but nothing we could follow. Nothing that makes any sense.'

After a pause he asked, 'Could he truly have fallen?'

It was only with half-hope that Santar had ordered the search. Deep in his core, he knew his lord was gone and would only be found again when he wished, or rather willed, it.

Impotence was not a feeling the first captain relished.

'No. He has been taken and I want to know *why*.'

Santar was about to continue when he switched channels to receive. Meduson was requesting a report and providing a status update as to the battle group's progress.

On the sickle-shaped ridgeline overlooking the basin, the first of the Army divisions marched into view. They were slow but stalwart, foot soldiers leading an armoured column of tanks. Mechanicum outriders ranged the flanks alongside the still-functioning Sentinels.

The hour was later than he realised.

'Confirmed,' he sent back to Meduson. It felt like choking on gravel. 'We are inbound with Army divisions. Hold the line and await reinforcement.'

Santar switched channels again, and growled into the feed.

'Regroup.'

Desaan was the first to return.

'Meduson?'

Santar nodded. 'They've found the node.'

Desaan snorted his derision. 'Glorious day. Are we leaving?'

'You already know the answer to that, brother-captain.'

'Why does it feel like we are abandoning him?'

Others were joining them as the fifty legionaries came together again. Only Tarkan and three other snipers were absent.

'Because we are.'

Desaan scowled but was wise enough to hold his tongue.

'Brother Tarkan...' said Santar. He was looking past the edge of the desert basin and its confluence with the greater plain where the warriors from the Iron Tenth had ranged. 'We are leaving.'

Tarkan's response was unexpected.

'I've found something, Lord Santar.'

* * *

ANOTHER CAVERN LAY beyond the gallery's archway.

A vast subterranean auditorium, much larger than its predecessor, opened up before Ferrus. Its vaulted ceiling was lost to darkness, though he discerned a hairline crack at its apex.Splitting the gulf in two was a narrow bridge of rock, its natural supports shrouded in shadow. Endless black stretched below, a fatal drop.

Ferrus sneered at the ignominy of it.

He followed the path of stone with his eyes, traced its wending trajectory through the darkness until it reached a wider plateau. From there climbed a stairway, its steps narrow and steep.

Before he realised, Ferrus was standing at the foot of the stairs looking up.

Monolithic statues lined its ascent, like the ones in the first cavern only much, much larger. Each one was wearing patrician robes, their hands across their chests, fingers laced in the shape of an aquila. Only their faces differentiated them. Totemic masks hid their true natures, or perhaps revealed them. Ferrus had a sense that both could be true.

His silvered gaze was drawn to one as he took a first step. It had a scalp of thrashing serpents, like the gorgon of ancient Mykenaean myth. He reached out to it even though the statue was much too far away to touch.

Another had the skeletal aspect of Death itself, hooded and gripping a scythe that cut into its bony brow. The visage of a third was split in half, like Janus of old Romanii legend. Two masks, not one, gazed at the primarch. But it was a mistake to think of Janus as having only two faces, for he had many.

Ferrus saw an effigy of a bestial and snarling hound, and felt his anger rise as he passed it. Behind it was a stoic drake, its crest a living flame. A heraldic knight stood alongside its much darker twin, one with a shield, the other a mace.

Leathern wings unfolded from the back of one statue.

Its chiropteran mask was hard to discern from its human face, suggesting a singular lack of humanity.

There were others: a horse with a wild flowing mane, a bird of prey, a noble human countenance crowned by a laurel wreath, a lion beneath a monk's cowl.

The processional was comprised of twenty statues in all. Some were familiar to him, others less so and did not appear as he expected. They had subtle differences, even aberrations that Ferrus found disturbing. Only two were completely unknown to him, their masks scratched and near obliterated.

One, the last, stood across the stairway and glared down at him, and he looked up to regard it.

Unlike the others, this one had its arms outstretched as if in invitation to embrace him. It wore robes, but they were finer, more ostentatious in the mason's design. His mask was beautiful, almost perfect were it not for the angular eye slits and the scalloping on the faux cheekbones.

'Fulgrim…'

He hadn't intended to speak his brother's name aloud, but now that he did, Ferrus recognised the titan towering over him.

Memories of Narodyna rushed back in a nostalgic flood, but there was bitterness there, even mockery. Did the statue *smile*? The mask appeared to be unchanged and yet there was the slightest curl to the edges of its mouth. A desire for retribution turned his silvered hands into fists of their own volition. It seized him without cause, without reason, but prompted such wrath, such a sense of… *betrayal*?

Ferrus shook his head, as if to banish a lingering dream.

More witchery, he thought grimly, deciding he would inflict particular injury upon his alien persecutors, when his sibilant shadow returned.

It was not so obvious this time. It came enfolded in

the breeze or the yawning of old stone as it resettled in its foundations. There was more, something only a being such as he could discern, twisted between the layers of susurration. The meaning of it was difficult to unpick from the colliding elements of non sequitur encoded into the shadow's hissing cadence.

It was a word or phrase, but one that remained an enigma for the moment.

The hunter was behind him; Ferrus heard the scrape of its scaled body against the lowest steps. Swallowed by darkness, there was nothing to see below, but it was there. Ferrus imagined it waiting for him, the slow rise and fall of its body, its tongue tasting the air for his scent. It was a patient and mercurial hunter. It would strike when the moment was right, when its prey was unaware of its presence.

'I can be patient too, my belligerent traveller,' he told it quietly, and was surprised at his own calm.

Ferrus sighed ruefully. Perhaps some of Vulkan's pragmatism was rubbing off on him.

The stairway went on farther and he had no time to linger. Nor did he wish to. Death lurked here, he felt it in the chill air and the slow ossification of his bones. If he stayed long enough it would find him.

As Ferrus hastened up the next flight of steps he tried to put the image of Fulgrim from his mind, the way the statue made him think of betrayal and the hunter following in his wake. He realised then that he had not fallen into any chasm.

This was not the desert.

It was somewhere else, somewhere *other*.

'WHAT AM I looking at, Tarkan?'

Santar and Desaan were standing by the sniper and two other Iron Hands from the Tenth. Tarkan's battle-brothers were silent, their sighted bolters low-slung.

Tarkan himself was crouched near the ground and

pointed out an indentation in the sand with a gauntleted finger.

'An impression,' he said, tracing the indentation's outline. 'Here.'

'A footprint,' offered Desaan, running the mark through the spectra in his visor. To the untrained eye it was merely another undulation in the desert.

'Several,' Tarkan corrected him, gesturing to a number of marks that ran back from the first. 'Trail ends here,' he added, looking up at Santar. The sniper's retinal lenses were sharp and cold, like his aim. His bionic eye clicked and whirred as it readjusted.

'Where did it begin?' asked Santar, trying to follow the footprints to their origin point.

'Back in the desert basin, I'd estimate.'

'Father's?'

Tarkan nodded slowly.

The boot mark they'd discovered was large and deep. It was only by virtue of its size and impact that the sand hadn't already obscured it beyond the sniper's expert recovery.

'Notice the deeper toe impression,' said Tarkan, drawing his combat knife to better illuminate his audience. The glinting monomolecular tip stabbed into the end of the print.

'He was running,' said Desaan.

Santar frowned and looked into the sun-streaked horizon, as if an answer waited there.

'But from what?'

'Or *to* what?' suggested Desaan.

There was no blood, no scorch marks, no evidence of any struggle. The trail simply ended.

Santar frowned again, unhappy with this turn of events.

'Good work, Brother Tarkan,' he said, turning.

Desaan was nonplussed. 'Aren't we continuing the search?'

'There is no point,' said Santar. 'Wherever Lord Manus is, we cannot reach him. Meduson has need of us.'

Desaan's riposte was quiet and just for Santar. 'We cannot just leave him, brother.'

The first captain stopped to regard the others. Tarkan was back on his feet. 'Choice is not a luxury we have right now, Vaakal. There is still a war to fight. At least we can do something about that.'

Reluctantly, Desaan conceded the point. Logically, he could do little else. None of them could.

Following the trail of the Army divisions, the fifty legionaries left the desert basin and their primarch to his fate.

A BIRD. NO, not merely a bird, but an immense avian beast whose magnificence had long faded. Easily the size and span of a gunship, its previously formidable muscle was wasted and atrophied. Wings that might once have been gilded were ragged and tarnished. Its skin hung loose about its frame like a feathered robe that was overlarge, the bones protruding in a raft of ugly contusions beneath. It was a carrion-eater, whose last meal was distant in the memory.

Myth recounted many tales across many cultures of the gryphon, cockatrice and harpy. Civilisations had been eradicated by such beasts, if the bards and tale-tellers were to be believed. Even in its debilitated condition, this monster would kill them all. With ease. Ferrus slowed as he approached the creature.

You will find me a difficult morsel to swallow, he promised, nearing the summit of the stone stairway.

As he gained the last few steps, he realised it was not one bird but two, and they were no carrion-eaters. It was a pair of eagles, albeit rope-thin and emaciated. They each watched him curiously out of one eye, the other blinded by some past misfortune, as if with some knowing prescience the primarch was not privy to.

As he reached out to them a death screech escaped their beaks, harrowing and reedy in its tonality. The Gorgon went for *Forgebreaker* but his fingers never touched the haft when he realised the pair of eagles were not about to attack. Instead, the creatures spread their once great wings and took flight.

It would have been a pity to slay them, though perhaps it would curtail their misery and be an act of mercy. Surprised at how gladdened he was to have stayed his hand, Ferrus followed the trajectory of the first as it soared into the vaulted darkness of the cavern. Upon reaching the crack in the ceiling, it disappeared. He was envious of its wings, however decrepit and decaying they were. It had limped into the golden light regardless.

His sons were above, separated from their father by that gilded crack in the world's underbelly. For a few moments the eagle's shadow lingered and it was almost as if Ferrus could reach out and touch it...

The other eagle flew deeper into the caverns. In spite of his initial belief, Ferrus realised the pair were not completely identical. Where the first was wise and austere, the second prey bird had a nobler, patrician bearing in spite of its ragged appearance.

Defiant, thought the primarch, *familiar, even.*

It glided through an open portal cut from the stone wall of the cavern. The archway was militaristic, reminiscent of a civilised culture in its architectural tone, like the old empires of the ancient Romanii. It led into a further chamber lit by a firmament of stars.

'Yet more cold stone,' he thought aloud, as the crags of dark granite were revealed.

Frustrated at his sense of powerlessness, Ferrus was beginning to believe that the road he was on was an endless one, that distance held no meaning in this labyrinth.

It was pointless to fight against that over which he had no sway. Though it went against his instincts, Ferrus surrendered to fate. For now. He would reach the terminus

of his journey when whatever had trapped him here
deemed it appropriate.

Then he would crush that being with all the fury of
Medusa.

Whatever lurked at the heart of the maze, it was no
invincible monster.

I have slain frost giants, he said to himself. *I have killed ice
wyrms with my bare hands. You snare a gorgon at your peril...*

The celestial constellations that illuminated his passage into the next room were not made of stars at all.
Clusters of gemstones punctuated the walls, glittering in
the ambient light. There was little remarkable about the
threshold, just diamond-veined rock. He heard the lan-
guid flap of wings as a distant echo in his ear and since
he could not fly, Ferrus followed the second eagle deeper
into the star-lightened darkness.

Ferrus smelled dead meat and cold. Something metallic spiked his tongue.

The itch around his neck began to irritate and burn.

Serpent breath hissed on the breeze.

His belligerent travelling companion had returned.

Have you come for me at last?

Ferrus drew *Forgebreaker* and held it loosely in one
hand. It hummed pugnaciously in his grasp.

I will crack your skull like an egg, beast.

The serpent kept its distance, lingering at the periphery of
his awareness. It knew he would not merely blunder into
the dark and attack it. Ferrus had to wait. Infuriating, and
the creature knew it. But beyond simple goading, it had
another purpose in forestalling a confrontation. It wanted
him to see something first, something it had made for him.

Like a swathe of black canvas had been drawn over
the latter part of the chamber, the light of false stars was
extinguished. Ferrus stood at its border, about to step
into a shadow realm. Even his silhouette, limned with
crystalline light, seemed dwarfed by it.

And then everything changed.

The darkness parted like a veil.

One by one, the gemstones winked out. Like a cut artery washing over a lens, a visceral glow imposed itself over the scene. A gruesome abattoir was laid out, and Ferrus scowled at its ugliness.

Blood-stink laced the air, leaden with a bitter tang. It crusted darkly in the corners of the slab-stoned floor, and reached up dank walls like a fungal contagion. Marks were smeared in the porcelain-white of the room, where hands and feet had slipped in the muck. Men and women had died in this place on their knees, pleading for their lives with the torturer's blade at their necks or bellies. Hooked chains scaled the walls, gummed with meat, ready to receive the flesh feast.

Images of rusty cleavers, jagged paring knives and flesh-ragged bonesaws resolved in Ferrus's mind, though none of these butcher's tools were visible.

Instead, suspended from the ceiling on strips of sinew, there were heads. A hundred decapitated heads swung languidly on the breeze, turning slowly to reveal their full horror. Their faces were frozen in expressions of anguish, some open-mouthed and voicing silent screams; others with jaws locked in teeth-clenched agony.

Ferrus worried at the rash beneath his gorget and felt anew the phantom sting of the executioner's knife from a wound he had never received.

Or perhaps, just not yet…

The thought formed unconsciously, as if implanted. Ferrus was too shocked to rebel against it.

Revelation piled atop revelation as he finally recognised the warrior in the faces of the hanging heads before him.

Tortured, contorted with pain beyond mortal endurance, Ferrus had never before beheld such a terrible sight.

Each face was his.

WRATH OF IRON

JUTTING FROM THE desert sand like a sliver of arching bone, it looked obvious enough. As he arrived at the battle site, Gabriel Santar wondered why it had taken them so long to find the eldar node.

Take out the nodes and disrupt the enemy's cohesion. Like trying to communicate across an interrupted circuit, the eldar's ability to coordinate their defence would be severely inhibited. Break the nodes and break the enemy. These were the edicts of Lord Manus, both to his Legion and his brothers warmongering elsewhere on One-Five-Four Four. It rankled that the primarch would not get to see his plan borne to fruition.

For that and many other reasons, he dearly wished his lord was present.

The Morlocks, together with Tarkan's small band of snipers, had returned at the head of a massed column of Army battle tanks. What was left of the Army divisions, mainly Dogan Maulers and some Veridan Korracts, had also made the journey, most hanging off hull rails or perched atop the cupolas of the larger vehicles. Some mechanised elements had also survived the desert, and along with a few Sentinel outriders, they carried what was left of the Saavan Masonites.

A ragged force, but reinforcement none the less.

Judging by the impasse around the node and its defenders, they couldn't have arrived soon enough.

The node itself was immense and wreathed with a crackling energy shield the Iron Hands were struggling to crack. Santar could see no power source, no objective they could attack and neutralise to bring the defences down. It was generated by some other means unknown to them.

Heavy impacts blossomed in bright azure bursts, and the shield rippled to diffuse their explosive energy across its curved surface.

Ruuman refused to concede defeat. His Rapiers and missile batteries kept up a constant fusillade, charging the air with their noise and actinic stench. Expulsion clouds thickened into a fog that rolled off the bank where the Ironwrought had positioned his divisions and spilled down into Meduson's advancing companies below.

Santar was met by Bion Henricos, and the sergeant snapped a quick salute when he saw the first captain.

While Meduson was overseeing the battle, he'd placed his hulking sergeant in command of the Iron Tenth. These warriors looked impatient for combat while Meduson's vanguard, spearheaded by the Morlocks, tried to force an opening several hundred metres deeper into the field.

'You can use the Army divisions?' asked the first captain before Henricos could voice a greeting. There was no time to observe pleasantries. Amongst the Iron Hands officer cadre, the sergeant had the greatest empathy with the humans. Santar merely wanted that utilised, and conveyed as much in his perfunctory demeanour.

No word was spoken of the mission or the primarch. It was not the sergeant's place to ask, though he did cast a quick glance at Desaan who was a step behind the first captain.

There must have been a short shake of the head from Desaan, because Henricos stiffened in grief and anger, but fell back to his duty in short order. That was to Henricos's credit as he appraised the arriving column.

'Just under fifteen thousand men and sixty-three operational vehicles,' said Henricos. 'Yes, my lord, I believe I can use these divisions.'

Santar nodded. 'Good. They are ragged, brother-sergeant,' he warned.

'Ready for a fight,' countered Henricos.

Smiling beneath his battle-helm, Santar said, 'Indeed.' He liked this Henricos, his dogged spirit. 'Where is Captain Meduson?'

Devastatingly powerful ranks of plasma cannons and Tarantula gun platforms boomed across the battle line, filling the rear echelons with light and thunder. Henricos waited a few moments for their salvo to subside before pointing north-east to where the acting commander was stationed.

Santar saw Meduson and his retinue, but his gaze lingered on the shield after the plasma wake and heavy bolter smoke had dispersed. He expected a crack in the eldar's armour, even a fissure. Nothing. The shield still held.

'It has been like this for the past hour,' said Henricos.

Santar grunted, displeased. 'Get the Army ordnance sounding immediately. I want to hear it from the front line when I'm standing next to that energy shield.'

'We'll punch a hole though it for you, my lord.'

'See that you do. Flesh is weak, but those tanks are steel,' he reminded Henricos.

Santar didn't linger. He headed over to Meduson.

'Desaan, with me,' he growled, watching the ineffectual barrage continue to rain down on the shield.

* * *

'THEIR RESISTANCE IS fearsome,' said the captain of the Iron Tenth as Santar approached.

'You sound surprised.'

Meduson carried a holo-slate in his bionic hand and was appraising the tactical dispositions of his force. Heavies gave support fire from range, while three wedges of Iron Hands from the Sixteenth, Thirty-Fourth and Twenty-Seventh clan companies provided a relentless assault on the entrenched eldar positions. Santar recognised the sigils of the Vorganan, Burkhar and Felg clans battling tirelessly at the front.

Down the centre, where the firestorm was hottest, he knew he would find the Clan Avernii, his Morlocks. Judging by the static representation of the veteran company, they too had reached an impasse. No Iron Hand had yet reached the shield wall itself.

Eldar forces in front of it, acting as a breaker, were thick but also retreating back behind it.

In reserve for the Iron Hands were Sorrgol's clan warriors of the Iron Tenth, Meduson's own kith and kin, as well as Kadoran, Lokopt and Ungavarr clans who brought down hellfire from the high ground. Even with all of that might at their disposal, the Iron Hands could not breach the eldar cordon.

Five hundred metres ahead of him, the flesh and iron versions of Meduson's army were doing the actual fighting.

Rows of legionaries strode implacably into the teeth of the enemy, bolters kicking up a steady barrage. Meduson had positioned smaller divisions of conversion beamers and graviton cannons amongst the bulk of the battalions, identified by the sporadic flash from their barrels and arcing lances of power, but the enemy was resolute.

'They are tougher than expected,' Meduson admitted. Scorch marks blackened his battle-plate, suggesting he'd attempted to storm the eldar outpost in an earlier sortie and been repulsed.

'You thought they would yield easily, brother-captain?'

Meduson's head twitched slightly when he realised the primarch was not with Santar.

'The Gorgon?' he asked, though his tone suggested he wasn't sure he wanted to know the answer.

'Gone.'

'When will he return?' He made no suggestion of the primarch's death, such a thing was beyond countenance, though the shadow of that possibility passed over Meduson's features like a dark cloud.

'He *will* return?' he rasped, fists clenching of their own volition as a vengeful fury came upon him.

'We failed to find him.' Santar had no answer to give.

'He'll be angry when he does come back.'

Santar gestured to the holo-slate and the slow manoeuvres of the forces depicted on it. 'That I would like to see.'

'They are well corralled,' said Meduson.

Reserve forces of Iron Hands were moving in, encircling the node and its guardians in a ring of black ceramite.

'Laying siege to a foe isn't really our way though, is it, Shadrak?'

Meduson gave a feral smile. 'No, first captain. It is not.'

'They hold tenaciously to something.'

'Sounds like you admire them.'

Santar's eyes never left the holo-slate, thinking and strategising. In his time as equerry, he had learned much from Ferrus Manus. Often the Gorgon stood in Guilliman's shadow but he was just as adroit a tactician. Others claimed his only drawback was that his single-mindedness sometimes left him slightly myopic. Though he would never speak of it aloud, Santar believed Ferrus didn't have the Battle King's patience for endless scenario-making either.

'Admire them? No,' said Santar with absolute certainty. 'I want to understand them so I can better destroy them.' Then he added, 'Have you breached the energy shield even once?'

'We haven't even reached it. I expected their capitulation when facing our obvious numerical superiority, first captain. It's only logical.'

'Perhaps there is no concept of inevitability in the eldar culture.'

Meduson's silence intimated he didn't understand that.

'Suggestions then?' asked Santar.

'Hit them harder, throw more warriors against their defences until they shatter.'

'Fortunately I have brought some with me who are keen to be reunited with their clansmen.'

The Morlocks strained at the leash behind him.

Meduson cast them a quick glance. 'Hungry too.'

'War is an unsubtle thing, Shadrak,' Santar said. 'Sometimes you just have to wield a larger hammer. Show me where you would like it to fall and we'll make that breach for you.'

'That is comforting to hear–'

Meduson held up a hand, pausing to listen to a series of reports across the feed as the various commanders advanced or altered position. He met Santar's gaze when he was finished. 'I assumed you'd take command upon your return, first captain. I've already sent our troops' dispositions across the feed to your retinal lens.'

'Not necessary,' said Santar. 'You have this in hand, brother. I want to dirty my claws with xenos blood.'

Meduson thumped his armoured chest, unable to stifle his pride at the first captain's confidence in him.

'Then let your wrath fall here, my lord.'

As the words registered in Santar's feed, an icon lit up on his retinal display. The other troop dispositions overlaid it. The rest of the Morlocks were holding at the very brunt of the battle, attacking the eldar defenders at close quarters. Here the defences were thickest, here the aliens wore heavier armour and brought their most devastating weapons and gun platforms to bear.

Even at a distance it looked ferocious.

Ignoring the cauldron he was about to step into, Santar scrutinised the distant shield as if he could discern a weakness just by looking at it.

'How deep do you think it goes, brother?'

Meduson followed his first captain's eye line. He smiled when he realised what Santar was suggesting.

Santar touched a finger to his gorget to open the comm-feed. 'Ironwrought.'

Ruuman came back between loud salvoes of heavy weapons fire.

'I need you to do something for me…' Santar said, and relayed his plan.

'You are the hammer,' said Meduson when the first captain closed the feed again.

Santar's lightning claws slid free of their sheaths. He fed a crackle of power down the blades.

'Then it's time we swung and struck.'

Arrogance deliberately visible and overflowing, Santar forged through the Iron Hands ranks that parted for him and his entourage of Morlocks. He kept his helmet maglocked to his thigh plate. He was more vulnerable without it, but the warriors around him needed to see his face. Without the primarch, it was up to him to inspire.

Behind his mask of ferocity, he hid his desire to be fighting alongside his lord. He could not imagine a time when that would not be so.

He raised his iron fist to the Morlocks and roared.

'Iron and death!'

An insistent voice inside him intruded on Santar's belligerence and the resounding affirmation of his charges that was hard to ignore.

Father, where are you?

FERRUS SCOWLED.

'Petty tricks,' he stated flatly, though none of the hanging skulls in the abattoir seemed to hear him.

Death did not unnerve the Gorgon, even the prospect of his own. Long ago, in the desolate wastes of Medusa, he had come to terms with the inevitability of his own mortality. He would live longer than most, perhaps even millennia, for who could say what the limits of the Emperor's gene-science were? But he was a warrior and warriors would eventually meet their end at the edge of a blade. Ferrus hoped his ending would be glorious. He also hoped, one day, for peace. But without war he wondered what would then become of his purpose and function?

Scowl became sneer, and Ferrus's lip curled derisively at the strung effigies meant to portend his doom. Swollen with righteous indignation, he had to resist the urge to destroy every one of them.

Without the lambent illumination of the gemstones, it was still light enough to see, even though the light was crimson and pulsing like a vein. The skulls were far enough apart to weave through without the need to touch them. Twisting in the breeze, one of the heads yawed around to face him.

He smiled at the cadaverous doppelganger, his eyes narrowed and cold.

'I would make a handsomer corpse,' he said, and smiled. It sounded like a remark Fulgrim might have made. At the thought of his brother, a sound echoed in the primarch's ear that he recognised, the hissing discord that had dogged his steps.

The hunter had returned. Likely, it had never left. To this Ferrus paid his full attention, for its threat was real and it was close. It was in the chamber with him, slithering alongside him, matching his every step.

'Come into the light, coward,' he snarled. 'I would like to see the enemy who wishes me slain a hundred times over. I will make a lie of that assumption, though you will only suffer one death.'

His belligerent companion did not respond.

Ferrus went on.

Halfway across the grim abattoir, the cluster of the skulls became so tightly packed that Ferrus would have no choice but to ease them apart in order to pass.

Using *Forgebreaker* like a cattle-prod, he tentatively pushed one of the heads aside.

A slow moan escaped the dead lips. A second of the heads echoed the first, then a third and fourth. Gripped by a sudden and terrifying epidemic, every one of the decaying skulls began to animate in a baleful chorus.

They were alive. Dragged back from damnation, these revenants wearing the flesh of Ferrus Manus had returned to haunt him. Revulsion, rage and disbelief warred inside the primarch and he backed away expecting an attack. A skull brushed his neck. Dry lips touched his skin like a kissed caress. Recoiling, he collided with another. A cheekbone shattered with the force. Bone fragments cascaded. A tooth bit into his armoured shoulder plate and stuck. Ferrus pulled it out, snarling as the moaning rose to a wail. The sound was low and accusing.

You did this to us…

You consigned us to this fate…

We are in limbo because of you!

Ferrus's fists clenched, his teeth locked.

'Shut up!' he hissed. His fury boiled over and he whirled around, bringing *Forgebreaker* up in front of him.

The dead should stay dead…

Such debasement only confirmed the weakness of flesh and its eventual corruption. The fact it was his own dead visage made no difference to the Gorgon. He had held back before, allowed temperance to stay his hand. Now he would smash every one of the wretched things to bone-dust and memory.

A streak of silver flashed in the darkness, the abattoir's light flowing over it like congealed blood…

Ferrus's first blow never fell.

Agonising hellfire roared up his spine, and bent it

almost double. Armour plate cracked with the primarch's sudden and violent convulsions, split like hot metal cooled too fast. Pain that would kill a hundred lesser men flooded his veins and nearly crippled him. Ferrus was bowed, down on one knee and hurting. Spitting phlegm and blood, he unleashed a peal of anger and fought the poison down. Pellucid silver cooled the burning of the wound, miraculous but far from cleansing, and the primarch straightened. Ferrus's other hand was clenched around his wrist. It throbbed beneath the fingers of living metal, told him he had been hurt. Worse, he had been weakened. *Forgebreaker* was lost, spilled from his numbed grasp and sent clattering to the ground.

He lifted his hand gingerly, like peering beneath battlefield dressings and expecting to be confronted by gangrene. Two puncture wounds, deep and wide like dagger thrusts, pierced his inviolable metal skin. The wounds bubbled with venom and Ferrus watched in disbelief as the living metal corroded before his eyes. As if stung, he withdrew his other hand, afraid that the taint would spread to both. Beneath the bleeding silver, burned and blistered skin was revealed and in it a memory was born...

Standing at the edge of the lava chasm, the beast above.

Breath of cold and sulphur.

Hands raw and bleeding, but taut enough to snap anvils.

The beast was waning. The battle they'd fought had taken its toll.

Molten silver upon its flanks reflected the magma glow and shimmered with heat haze.

Such a magnificent creature.

He would kill it anyway, his dominance proved beyond doubt.

I am stronger.

Fangs bared, a song of fury upon its lips.

He would prove it.

He would find a way to pierce its miraculous flesh and kill it.

The lava beckoned. His forge.

Here, weapons were made and unmade.

I will prove I am stronger.

I must, for if I do not what does that make me?

Memory faded, vague and indistinct. Myth and fact wove a single narrative that left him wondering at the truth of his own origins. Distraction was momentary. Need for survival and his warrior instincts took over. Rather than search for *Forgebreaker*, Ferrus ripped a spatha from his waist, a thick, meaty blade that was keen-edged and deadly. Numbed by the virulent poison, his wounded arm hung low at his side. Ferrus took the blade in his left hand, adjusting stance and grip before he scored a slit down his wrist to release the poison. Burning brine-yellow fluid seeped like acid down his red raw hand, dripping off bloodied fingers. Pain eased, so too the clamour in his skull that felt like it was being pummelled by a dozen gauntleted fists.

Like my head is being cut from my shoulders…

Ignoring the mournful cries of the heads, shutting out the death rattle of his own voice heard a hundred times over, Ferrus searched the shadows. He turned quickly at the glint of silver in his peripheral vision. It flashed with the urgency of a warning beacon.

Preternatural reflexes saved him from being maimed further. He lashed out, but the creature was swift beyond reason and slid from the primarch's enraged clutches.

Serpentine, but like no snake Ferrus had ever encountered. Silver scaled, it was not unlike the spawn of a beast he had fought long ago. Stars were merely chips of granite in the darkling sky back then, when there was only Medusa and the endless arctic night. Swallowed by shadow, the impression of the creature was fleeting but familiar.

Perhaps we have met before…

A tail crack made the Gorgon turn and he swung again, blindly, and cut only air. He felt slower. Despite excising the poison, the sting of his wound was creeping up his shoulder and into his neck. The phantom pain he'd felt around his throat ever since coming to the desert burned like white fire.

Real or imagined, this creature could hurt him. Pulled from some black abyss of Old Night, it had manifested in this nether realm intent on his undoing. His gaolers knew his past, his primordial fears and desires, and taunted him with visions of an imagined future. They plucked strands of unrealised fate and watched the vibrations resonate through the primarch's demeanour.

Ferrus knew he could not give in to it.

Delirium had started to affect his senses as whatever venom the serpent possessed did its work.

Endure.

The word was like his anchor. Lose that and he would be cast adrift upon an endless sea of chaos.

The hiss of living metal as it dripped from his arm and splashed onto the ground in molten gobbets brought the primarch back around. He shook his head to banish the worst of the fog threatening at the edge of his vision.

Basilisk, khimerae, hydra, such fiends had many names and forms. The creature was none of those. But it was powerful. It had to be to undo what was supposed to be incorruptible.

Is nothing incorruptible?

What were all the frost giants and ice drakes compared to that?

Ferrus pushed the unworthy thoughts aside, realising they were being fed to him. The raging core bubbling beneath his cold exterior began to vent. His grip tightened on the spatha and the leather bindings wound around the hilt cracked.

The weapon had been a gift from Vulkan, and the memory of his brother gave him strength.

'I forged it to fit your hand, Ferrus,' he had said. *'It is your sword, not the equal of* Forgebreaker *I grant you, but a worthy weapon I hope. You honour me by carrying it.'*

Ferrus had turned it over in his hand, his cold eyes running across the filigree and ornate intaglio, the inlaid gemstones and Nocturnean inscription. The fine serrated teeth were diamond-sharp and acid-edged, the metal of its forging dense and unyielding.

Ignoring the weapon's obvious craft and beauty, Ferrus had at once seen its potential as a blade, but chose to be harsh instead of praising his brother's craftsmanship.

'Why does it need such ornamentation? Can I kill my enemies better because of it?' There was a smirk upon his face that in retrospect Ferrus was not proud of.

Vulkan had taken it in his stride. *'It's a master weapon with a master's pride lavished upon it,'* he admitted. *'When I draw my blade, I want my enemies to know it is a warrior-king's weapon they face, wielded by a warrior-king's hand.'*

'Even though you would rather wield a hammer to create than a blade to destroy?'

Vulkan had smiled then and the gesture was warm as a lava glow.

'Nocturneans are pragmatists, my brother. While war is necessary, I will fight, but I hope that one day I can put down my sword.' His eyes flashed with fire. *'Until then I'll keep my killing edge sharp.'*

Ferrus had nodded and sheathed the blade, attaching it to his weapons belt. *'I might have need of a knife,'* he had said lightly, and touched a silver hand to his glabrous skull, *'for when the serfs don't scrape close enough to the skin.'*

They laughed, the Gorgon raucous and ribald, the Drake booming and hearty as they shared a rare moment of levity until the Crusade forced them onto different paths. Until One-Five-Four Four.

The memory of that day vanished in the reflected metal of the blade.

Ferrus had named it *Draken* in honour of his brother. He needed its bite now and was glad of the spatha's presence in his hand.

Much like in the mausoleum gallery, the walls in the abattoir were polished obsidian. Their mirrored black stretched into infinity. The heads were reflected there, but in the doppelganger world they were sheathed in flesh. Severed arteries pulsed, spewing blood. It spattered his brow, still warm, still living. The wound was fresh cut and it blazed against the neck of the real Ferrus, who fought his revulsion at the spectacle rendered in the darkling glass. They were laughing, the severed bloody heads, all of them. They were laughing at him.

Idiot!

Weakling!

Unwanted son!

This last barb stuck in his throat. Ferrus was remarkable and on Medusa he was a king of kings. None could match him. But when his father came and brought him to seventeen remarkable brothers, he realised his place. Unlike Vulkan who had accepted his position gladly and humbly, Ferrus railed. Was he not the equal of his siblings? When faced with the glory of Horus, the majesty of Sanguinius or even Rogal Dorn's dogged solidity, it was easy to believe that some sons would wait in the wings while the chosen few enacted their father's grand plan for the galaxy.

Ferrus wanted that light for himself, to be equal. He wasn't vain; he merely wanted to be acknowledged. His entire existence until that point had been spent in the pursuit of strength. He could not believe that all of that had been done in an ancillary role. Ferrus could not believe his father had brought him from one shadow to merely consign him to another.

I will make you proud, father. I will prove my worth.

'Come then!' he bellowed, but the challenge was unmet. The creature would snap at him from the shadows and lay him low with a thousand cuts.

An inglorious death.

Ferrus would not submit to that.

But the creature was fast. He had yet to land a blow and striking at flashes would not yield victory. It wanted to goad him, make him lower his guard and open up to a mortal wound.

He caught sudden movement in the corner of his eye and followed it, holding out the spatha defensively, its blade flat and angled away from his body.

It was hard to refrain from violence; his entire existence *was* violence.

Fury was hammering in his ears like a pealing bell. He focused and the clamour lessened to a dull roar. The creature was close, though it betrayed no sign of its presence. It felt as though Ferrus was somehow bonded to it, possibly through the bite and the taint of its venom. He wanted to hurt it for that, to redress the balance then destroy it. A font of inner rage was lapping at the edges of his consciousness, close to spilling over from thought into action.

He remembered the forge and the solace of working metal. The only salve to his wrath, the one thing that could placate his volcanic anger. In spite of such anger, Ferrus knew patience even if it sometimes felt like he was grasping at smoke. Unlike Vulkan, patience did not come easily to him. It was an early lesson for all forge smiths. Tempering could not be rushed, metal needed time, it needed to wait until it was ready; so would he.

He saw *Forgebreaker* lying on the ground, but resisted the urge to take it. The creature wanted him to. It waited for him to reach for his hammer.

Vulkan's blade would more than suffice. He trusted his brother's craft.

He should have told him that.

Ferrus closed his eyes and listened. He heard a faint and rasping refrain, almost masked by the ambient noise. The reptilian hiss of the serpent.

Now I'll bait the hook…

Blind, he was vulnerable.

So he lowered his sword, let his arm fall by his side.

He listened harder, allowed his heart to still.

The cacophony of the dead lessened, the serpent's voice intensified and Ferrus perceived two words.

Angel…

It hurt just to think it, as if it carried potency beyond its literal meaning.

Exterminatus…

It was hidden within the multiple susurrations of the creature, enfolded within pitch and cadence like a secret note in a virtuoso's perfect symphony.

It meant nothing to him, yet he felt the weight of its importance like it was a physical thing.

'And the heavens burned with its refulgent beauty…' The words came to Ferrus's lips unbidden, as if belonging to another speaker without the power to articulate them.

Something dark was at work here, something evil that intruded upon the nether realm Ferrus was bound to. He wondered if his captors realised.

There was no time to consider it further, doing so would serve no purpose anyway.

Breath held in his chest, Ferrus heard the scrape of metal that presaged the creature's attack, its whickering tongue. Trusting to instinct, he waited until the creature was almost upon him before cutting. Scaled flesh parted against his sword.

His eyes snapped open like armoured visors and Ferrus thrust again. A snarl of pain rewarded him. As he withdrew *Draken* from the shadows its edge was coated in gore. It was not blood but an ichorous fluid, heliotrope purple in colour, gripping viscously to the blade.

He had hurt the creature. Its susurrus grew in pitch, a collision of anger and pain. Metal scale scratching against stone faded as the monster retreated into the darkness.

Ferrus did not move for several minutes, listening for signs of its return. The wound in his forearm pulsed with foetid vigour, and the silver lustre had almost burned away completely, leaving it raw and agonised. Sheathing the spatha, he reached down and his fingers curled around the haft of *Forgebreaker*, as if weapon and wielder had sought each other out. Never had his hammer felt so heavy and cumbersome in his grasp.

'Flesh is weak...' he muttered and cursed his impotence in bringing to heel the forces that conspired against him.

The memory of the phrase hidden in the serpent's voice returned to him.

Angel Exterminatus.

As did the sense of malfeasance it carried. Some other sentience had pushed the words into his mind. It didn't feel like a warning, as so much of this crystalline labyrinth did. It was a promise, a prophecy.

Ferrus was too weak to unravel it. A febrile sweat lathered his forehead as he staggered the last few steps through the abattoir and into whatever further horrors awaited him. With the absence of the serpent, the hanging skulls had ceased to chatter and were truly dead once more. The breeze ebbed to nothing and they stopped swinging too, making it easier to avoid touching them. Even their features seemed less like his own, their aspects less daunting. A singular thought drove Ferrus now. Like a Medusan land-shark, he had to keep moving. To stop was to die.

He managed three steps before he fell and darkness took him.

THE COOL AURA of the bone sanctuary was charged with indignant energy.

'It is affecting you,' said the Diviner.

'It should not have been able to breach the ossuary road,' answered the other.

'Careful, I see Khaine manifesting in your mood. Step back upon the path.'

The other was not ready to relent just yet. 'My anger is well-founded. He was not meant to die. Not in here. Not from this.'

The Diviner peered at the other intently. His gaze was contemplative and unfathomable.

'And yet his life is threatened. You lace the waters of fate with enough blood and sooner or later sharks will circle.'

'It should not be here at all.'

'The bone roads we travel are far from secure. Ever since the Fall, you know that. Are you so surprised that something malicious has come?'

About to object, the other's humour changed from choler to melancholy.

'What can be done?'

'Release him and accept failure.'

'We are too close for that.'

The Diviner leaned back against a spur of arching bone and folded his hands upon his lap.

'Then you have to let fate run its course and hope he can defeat that which you have allowed into your cage.'

There was a pause that the Diviner did not choose to fill. He merely watched. The other was displeased, ruled by emotion and thwarted ambition. The Diviner did not need prescience to know what his companion was about to ask.

'What do you see?'

It smacked of desperation.

'Nothing. Everything. I see a billion, billion futures and possible outcomes, some so infinitesimally different you could spend aeons looking for the variation and still not find it.'

'That is not an answer.'

'I advise you to propose a narrower question then.'

'Will he die? Am I undone?'

'Yes and no.'

'Your meaning is needlessly cryptic.'

'We are fighting a war of fate. We two are merely agents in this conflict. Through hubris you allowed the Primordial Annihilator–' the other touched the spirit stone around his neck at mention of the name '–a piece of its essence, at least, into your cage and now it is trapped with your intended prey. Chaos has a way of clouding the path of fate.'

The other sagged in his seat of bone. His hand trembled as he felt the protection and anonymity of their sanctuary start to fragment.

A haggard face looked up at the Diviner through hollowed eyes. 'How long before it finds us?'

'Soon.'

SANTAR KNEW THE warriors bleeding through the shimmering energy shield.

A wake of eldar bodies, the smashed detritus of what had come before together with the remains of their weapon platforms, lay scattered behind the Iron Hands. With Santar leading them, they had driven deep in the enemy defences and were on the cusp of assaulting the shield directly. It blazed before the Morlocks like an azure sun. Santar could almost taste the electric tang on his tongue. Its heat made him want to shade his eyes but he resisted the urge. One last obstacle was left to overcome.

Still wraith-like, they did not appear as incorporeal as they had in the desert basin. Bone-armoured, clutching their curved singing swords, the eldar had sent their best warriors through the shield for them. Their hell-scream hit the Morlocks like a wrecking ball.

Santar yelled through a barricade of teeth, 'Take it!'

His every bone vibrated. The teeth in his skull cracked with the effort of clenching them. Much more punishment and they would shatter.

'I can shout louder,' he promised the warrior bearing down on him.

Santar advanced and turned his forward step into an attacking lunge.

His lightning claw cut through the warrior's blade and carried on into its sternum. Stepping over the eviscerated alien's corpse, he found another.

It leapt his diagonal swipe, weaved inside the counter-thrust and pirouetted alongside the first captain's unprotected flank.

Santar winced as a power-charged blade cut into his battle-plate but there it stuck, unable to penetrate further. An elbow smash, delivered without finesse, broke the eldar's collarbone. An overhead slash would cleave the alien open, but Santar staggered when a second attacker mounted his back. He turned his ear from its hell-scream, reaching up to throw it off, when it jolted and fell.

Half its head and helm were missing, ruptured by an explosive round.

Tarkan's icon winked once on the retinal tac-display.

The sniper's voice issued over the feed. 'Glory to the Gorgon.'

Santar finished the one with the broken collarbone, stamping on its prone form with his armoured boot. Then he wiped the blood leaking from his nose and gave a clipped salute he knew Tarkan would see. Unable to feint and attack as they had in the desert basin, the wraith-like warriors were finding the Morlocks a tougher prospect out in the open. There, the cohesion of the Iron Hands counted for more than agility.

To his left, Santar saw Desaan shoulder-barge an alien into the air then swing up his bolter in his remaining hand to perforate it before it landed a ragged corpse. Santar thought he detected the trace of a smile when their eyes met briefly across the field.

Desaan laughed. 'Like shooting discus.'

'Theatrics will avail you nothing, brother-captain... except perhaps an early grave. Kill them quickly. Give no quarter.'

'Reparation will have to wait,' Desaan replied. 'It appears my enemies are all dead.'

Alien corpses littered the ground, where the casualties amongst the Iron Hands were minimal. They had bloodied the eldar, but more were coming, leaping through the energy shield with athletic and deadly grace.

'Here is your chance,' said Santar, before leaning towards the vocal amplifier in his gorget and grating an order that resounded across the battlefront. 'Consolidate. Iron as one.'

Underfoot, the buried echoes of Ruuman's payload could be felt. Seismic spikes registering on Santar's retinal display confirmed it. A synchronised chrono flashed up in one corner of his vision at the same time.

He cried, 'Advancing!'

Morlocks joined him at either shoulder, their Cataphractii war-plate touching, pauldron to pauldron.

The wraith-like warriors broke against the implacable black wall of ceramite confronting them. Some fought and made small gains, and Santar would remember those who died later, but united the Terminators could not be denied. They rolled over the eldar elite in an unyielding wave. Caught between an energy shield that only allowed them out and the advancing legionaries, there was nowhere for the aliens to run and they were crushed underfoot.

The eldar behind them answered with heavy, relentless fire from their gun platforms.

Cannon impacts smashed into the Morlocks. A Terminator, it might have been Kador, was put on his back. Another, Santar couldn't tell who, was speared through the chest and fell. The rest kept moving, weathering the barrage.

'A light shower,' said Desaan, barely audible above the storm.

'We have less than a minute, brother,' Santar told him.

'More than enough, first captain.'

Bullying their way forwards, the Morlocks reached the crackling edge of the shield.

The eldar inside fell back, but kept up their fusillade of fire. Overhead, Ruuman's cannons and the tanks of the Army divisions pounded.

Something else lurked behind the flicker-haze too, eldar clad in robes and wielding arcane staves.

'Tear it down!' roared Santar, warring with the ionised throb of the energy shield. 'Hit it with everything you've got.'

Thunder hammers and power-mauls, eviscerators and combi-bolters at point-blank range rattled against a field of glowing azure. Rippling violently, the shield bowed but did not break.

The chrono in the retinal displays of all the Iron Hands veterans reached zero.

Its terminus presaged a series of deep, subterranean detonations that split the surface open *inside* the shield as the mole mortar shells burrowing below exploded in a chain. Concussive bursts billowed upwards as the web the eldar had woven around the node was unpicked.

Flickering initially as a cluster of minute interrupts stuttered across its curvature, the shield flared once and then failed.

Santar was first across its threshold.

'At them! Glory to the Gorgon!'

Reaping into the gun platforms, the Morlocks barely noticed the brutal ordnance from the tank divisions as it hammered the node. Even without the shield to protect it, the bone edifice was resilient, but cracks began to appear along its length.

It was a massacre, efficient not bloodthirsty, but slaughter all the same.

A warrior with a crackling falchion emerged from the melee. Santar met it with his lightning claws, but felt a tightening in the servos of his bionic arm as he applied the killing stroke. His follow-up was slower too, as if pushing against inertia or the effects of high gravity. His legs were the same.

He recalled the robed figures. A cohort of heavily armed alien warriors surrounded them.

'Desaan, can you still see?' Santar asked. Foes were coming at them from every angle, swinging pikes and blades, a rabble of carapace-armoured eldar soldiers and the cloaked ranger caste the Iron Hands had fought earlier. One of them thrust an energy spear at Santar, which he barely turned aside. Seizing the haft, he pulled the warrior towards him and bludgeoned open its faceplate with his fist. The body sagged and was still, but the eldar had left a score mark down the first captain's flank.

'Too close.'

Another aimed a shuriken lance at his torso and blasted apart a section of armour plate. Santar swept his claw around to despatch it but felt the same drag that had slowed him a few seconds before.

Recognising these sensations, he shouted, 'Desaan, your eyes?'

'My sight… is failing.'

Darkness was boiling around the node, coiling from its tip in a thunderhead.

Santar arched his neck to see a black cloud creeping down the side of the node and billowing towards them.

'Throne of Earth…'

Not again…

Santar knew the carnage the storm and its curse of iron could inflict. Upon so many warriors conjoined with the machine, he dared not contemplate exactly how much.

To his mind, there was little choice.

'Hold advance, all companies.'

Santar was caught, seized by indecision just as his bionics were frozen by the approaching darkness.

'We must move forward,' Captain Attar voiced down the feed. 'First captain, what are your orders?'

Taking advantage of the respite, the robed conclave of

eldar was already re-establishing parts of the shield. It grew like an organic energy web behind the Morlocks. Shells and las-bursts from the heavy divisions caromed off the rapidly regenerating veil.

Desaan gripped Santar's shoulder guard. 'We cannot stay here, Gabriel. Forward or back, which is it?'

If they stayed, they could destroy the node, or at least slay the witches that had refashioned the shield, but they risked annihilation at their own hands or the hands of their brothers if they did.

Tendrils of cloud, outriders of the dark veil, closed to within a few metres of the Iron Hands. They writhed like vipers.

So close…

'You saw what it did to us in the desert basin.' Santar had made his decision. It tasted bitter as his mouth formed the words.

'Fall back!'

The retreat was slow and wearisome. Legionaries fought the mechanised parts of their bodies, and tried to stop outright rebellion. Some failed and had to be dragged by their battle-brothers. None at least were devoured by the storm, for to be lost to it was a death sentence.

It boiled at the edge of the shield, shrouding what was left of the eldar inside, but reached no farther.

EVEN FROM A distance Santar could feel the pull of the machine curse's influence. Absently, his armoured fingers touched the gouges at his neck. The gorget had barely saved his life. He could still feel the prickling heat of his own lightning claw upon his skin, its electric stink in his nostrils.

'So, what is our next recourse?' Desaan had removed his visor and was standing beside the first captain, the two of them in close concert. Desaan's scarred face was worse beneath the metal band he usually wore around his eyes; the skin swollen and ravaged. He reattached the visor to a pair of cranial implants in his temples and the device whirred back to life.

'Functioning perfectly,' he said, muttering rites of activation and purity.

'So long as we stay out of the cloud,' said Santar.

The tempest rippled and undulated like a dark ocean, slowly and mockingly for all its seeming innocuousness.

Santar stared at it. He was standing in a half-circle with his captains and their seconds, while the rest of the Legion waited farther back with their clan companies and looked on beleaguered.

'The shield *was* breached and only partly regenerated,' said Captain Attar.

Ruuman's barrage had ceased and the Ironwrought joined them from the high ground where the heavies still waited.

Santar turned to him next. 'What's your assessment, Erasmus?'

'The shield is constructed of kinetic energy but created psychically. Whether the xenos have some form of generator sympathetic to their abilities or another piece of fell alien technology, I can only theorise. As we've seen, it can be breached, but only through excessive force.'

Desaan frowned. 'What about the cloud? How do we breach that?'

Ruuman turned his cold gaze on him. 'Without suffering machine-death, we cannot.'

'You think they can keep this up indefinitely?' asked Captain Meduson.

Desaan stared into the darkness, but could find no gap or weakness. 'If our Ironwrought is right, while the storm persists there is no way for us to advance.'

Santar's knuckles cracked with cybernetic resonance.

'I would very much like to summon the *Fist of Iron* and bombard this site from existence.'

'Then do it, first captain,' said Meduson. 'We can

further withdraw our forces and take the necessary cover in the deeper desert.'

Ruuman shook his head. 'Negative. The sensoria are unable to overcome whatever psychic baffles the eldar have in place. We are more likely to exterminate ourselves than level the node.'

Desaan rubbed at his chin and frowned.

'The shield is broken, but not down. The aliens' defences are severely weakened. If we can get warriors behind the veil to kill whatever is creating it–'

Henricos stepped up, interrupting.

'I can get beyond that veil.'

Desaan scowled. 'You have a talent for intrusion, brother-sergeant.'

A nod sufficed as apology from Henricos.

Santar's eyes narrowed. 'I am listening. How can you enter the storm, brother? Unless you *want* to end up impaled on your own sword?'

'Because a warrior of flesh has nothing to fear from it.'

Henricos revealed the stump where he had detached his bionic hand.

'It is safe,' he said quickly. 'I can fight without it.'

A host of hard, reproachful glances fell upon the sergeant.

'You dishonour the Iron Creed,' said Santar. 'That mechanised implant is part of rite and ritual. It is what makes us what we are.'

'And what we are is confounding us, first captain. I am suggesting a different approach.'

'One for which you'll be severely reprimanded.'

'I'll bear whatever punishment is deemed fit.'

Santar glared, fighting the urge to mete out that punishment immediately.

'Even if it is death?'

Henricos was stoic. 'I can breach the veil.'

'Alone?' Attar sounded dubious.

'No, not alone,' Santar answered as he saw a unit of

Army veterans approaching the conclave of Iron Hands officers. They looked on edge to be in the presence of the hulking warriors and kept together.

Santar fought down his disdain and tried to see soldiers in the children before him.

Their commanding officer was a hoary-looking colonel of the Savaan Masonites who knelt before the Iron Hands like a serf. Unlike some of his more nervous charges he did not tremble.

Desaan glared at him from the mountainous summit of his Cataphractii war-plate.

'Speak your name.'

'Lords,' said the man, his voice gravelly from smoking too much tabac or simple age. 'I am Marshal Vortt Salazarian of the Savaan 254th, the Masonites, and I have served the Emperor's Great Crusade and your Lord Gorgon for four decades.'

Desaan touched the platinum stud embedded in his skull.

'Do not speak to me of service, old man. What do you know of it?'

Attar folded his immense bionic arms, whilst Meduson merely glowered. They each carried platinum studs and had each fought longer campaigns than most men had lifetimes.

To his credit, Colonel Salazarian didn't blink. Not once.

'I meant no offence. We will accompany Sergeant Henricos into the storm,' he said, licking his lips to moisten his dry mouth. The presence of Space Marines tended to have that effect on humans. 'If you will allow us to, we will do that. It would be our honour.'

Desaan scowled. 'Flesh is weak–' he said, but Santar raised his hand for silence.

The Army veterans looked thin and feeble, even the grizzled colonel, but so too did the eldar and they had proven formidable.

Slowly shaking his head, Desaan said, 'They will break and we will have lost one of our own into the bargain.'

'Enough,' stated Santar, regarding the kneeling man. He bade him stand. 'I am not a king and you are not my subject. On your feet.'

Nodding at Desaan, Santar asked the colonel, 'Is he right? Will you break?'

Salazarian squared his shoulders and thrust out his jaw. 'Let us show you our worth. We will not break, my lord. We have endured this far.'

'Few mere men can make that claim,' said Henricos.

Santar's eyes were chips of slate when he met his gaze. 'I knew you had an affinity for humans, sergeant. I saw it when you gave your report concerning the Army divisions.' He paused, eyeing first the storm and then the Army veterans.

It is better to act and ask for forgiveness later than be paralysed by indecision.

He'd heard Ferrus Manus say that before. Santar wished he could ask for his guidance right now. Since he could not, he said, 'You vouch for this man and his warriors?'

'It will be my death if they fail,' said Henricos.

'You are right about that,' Santar told him, making the threat very clear. 'Find the coven or whatever means the eldar are using to perpetuate that storm and remove it. We will follow in after and eliminate whatever is left standing. The path is laid, brother. All you need do is to follow it.'

Henricos saluted and went to muster the rest of the Masonites.

After he had gone, Desaan shook his head.

'Reckless bravery kills warriors swifter than any bolter or blade.' He pointed at the storm bank. 'Those men will die in there. Henricos too.'

Santar watched the ominous black cloud, imagined it watching him back with a feral sentience.

When they were retreating, when its tendrils had closed with the delicate inexorability of a drifting fog, he'd felt a crushing weight in his chest, as if his limbs had been bound in metre-thick ferrocrete. They all felt it, each and every one of them that was significantly part machine.

All of their strength, the power of a Legion at his disposal, and all any of them could do was watch.

'Then I hope they die well and make a worthy sacrifice. But I promise you this. One way or another, we are bringing that node down. The Gorgon has willed it.'

COLD STONE CHILLED his face. A trickle of water from some underground stream wet his lips and brought him round.

Dazed and groggy from the poison, Ferrus rolled onto his back and groaned.

He had never felt so weak.

He couldn't remember passing out. It must have happened on the way from the abattoir.

Attempting to rise unleashed a hellish crescendo crashing into his mind. Blood thundered in his ears. He held his head and, wincing, got to one knee.

Lead dragged at his limbs, made him sluggish and slow. *Forgebreaker* acted as a crutch. Twice now since being in the labyrinth he had used it ignobly. The fact did not sit well with the primarch, who surveyed his surroundings once standing again.

Mercifully, the serpent or whatever it was had gone. Even the sibilance of its presence was absent and a terrible silence replaced it. Ferrus doubted he would live if he faced it at that moment. He could barely lift his feet, let alone a weapon.

He patted the pommel of *Draken*.

'Thank you, brother.'

The way behind him was darkness. He couldn't even see the abattoir now and wondered how long and how far he had wandered in delirium. Ahead was darkness too, but with a tiny shard of light like a beacon to guide him through a storm. The turbulence of his thoughts pulled at him.

What had the creature said?

Angel Exterminatus.

Ferrus understood the words but not their meaning. It pained him to think about them and the vague sense of flame intruded at the edges of his consciousness when he did.

With motion, his strength began to return. His arm was still ravaged where the living silver had been melted away but it didn't burn as badly. His neck itched like all hell, though, and he suspected the creature had dealt a secondary wound he was unaware of until that moment. But when he touched the skin beneath his gorget it was uninjured.

Biting down his irritation, Ferrus walked slowly towards the shard of light.

Likely this was yet another trick, some fresh torture with which to test him. Ferrus had yet to discern its purpose. He reasoned that if his enemies meant to kill him, they would have done so already or at least tried harder and more overtly. Xenos, particularly the eldar, were cryptic and capricious, even to one with the formidable mental acuity of a primarch. Their rationale was lost on him. The thing that hunted him was no serpent, it was something darker, something primordial and, he suspected, not something wholly fashioned by his captors. It *had* meant to end his life. He felt all its rage, its denial, its sadistic yearning of which Ferrus was the focus. When they had fought he could sense this, but it was inchoate as if the creature itself was only partially realised.

Ferrus was uncertain what that meant. One thing he could be sure of was that it wasn't dead and would return for him. Whatever the eldar's original plan, he knew he would have to kill the creature now to escape.

Entering through the shard of light that had widened into a brilliant chasm to allow him passage, Ferrus steeled himself for that battle to come.

He would not have long to wait.

A series of grand, triumphal archways led into a long processional before him. They had the appearance of great gates but with their portals laid open and shattered to potential invasion. Fire-blackened stone crept at their edges and ugly shards were chipped from every stone.

The chasm of light had closed behind him, leaving no visible way out.

As he had suspected, this was to be the final arena.

Ferrus felt like a giant touring a grand but blasted palace in miniature. As he passed along the processional, he left the sundered gates behind and walked into an appended chamber. Even scaled down in miniature, the great hall was immense. A giant would have been dwarfed by it. Gothic architectural flourishes dominated, but they were bleak and austere, suggestive of faded glories and cultural stagnation. Skulls lined the walls as if part of some vast reliquary and a sombre mood pervaded its grim design. A monument to decay and everlasting decline, here opulence had long since given in to decrepitude.

As he made his way across the diminutive flagstones underfoot, Ferrus realised it was no great hall, nor had it ever been so.

It was a tomb.

And at the end of a cracked plaza, wreathed with gossamer-thin webs and the rough patina of heavy age, there stood a massive throne, out of scale with the rest of the palace.

Slumped upon it, in emaciated repose, sat a king.

The king of stagnation, lord of a decaying empire, his robes were tattered, his body a flesh-starved and skeletal ruin. He bore no crown, only a rictus grimace, a final pained expression of a dream unfulfilled.

He towered over Ferrus, glaring down through abyssal eye sockets the colour of sackcloth.

A hissing breath, its last, escaped the undead king's mouth and drew a nerve tremor of consternation from the primarch's face.

Half-expecting the revenant to rise, he took a backward step.

Only when the breath continued long after it should have ended did Ferrus realise it was not the king, but something else that gave the corpse its mimicked speech.

Uncoiling from its hiding place behind the tarnished throne of the dead king was the serpent.

The head and neck stood erect whilst its vast body undulated beneath it, providing support. Mirrored silver sheathed its flanks. Its eyes were sulphur-yellow pools of corruption, cut open with black, dagger-thin pupils. Hate exuded in a heady musk that made the primarch's senses lurch vertiginously.

He reached for *Forgebreaker*, but the serpent sprang at him, faster than mercury, and Ferrus was forced to seize its jaws before they snapped around his throat.

Hot, stinking spittle, acid-tanged, spattered the primarch's face and he snarled. Fighting this beast was like clinging to liquid, but Ferrus wrestled it down and wrapped his arms around its neck before it could wriggle free. Thrashing hard, the serpent hauled him off the ground and smashed him down again. Lances of agony impaled his back and shoulder. His neck felt about ready to crack as the burning wound that was not a wound around his throat smouldered like hellfire.

'I am the Gorgon!' he yelled. 'I am a primarch!'

His head hit something hard, and dark spikes intruded at the edge of his sight. A red rime layered his vision but Ferrus held on.

He held on and squeezed.

Despite the serpent's fervent efforts, Ferrus slowly tightened his grip. He would strangle it, crush every ounce of life from the creature until it lay cold and unmoving. Then he would stave its skull to a crimson paste.

'Back from the underworld...' he spat. 'You should have stayed dead, Asirnoth...'

For what else could it be but a manifestation of that dread creature?

The serpent's head turned... *turned* in a way that should have broken its neck in the primarch's iron grip. Lips that should not be lips parted. Eyes that were human and familiar regarded him. A mane of hair crept down its back as a noble and patrician countenance asserted itself across previously reptilian features.

'I...' it said without hint of sibilance, 'I am not...' the words were lyrical, musical and rich, 'Asirnoth...'

Ferrus knew, as he knew the voice and the face before him.

It was the perfect killer, preternaturally fast and super-humanly strong. Only another primarch could have defeated it.

Only *another* primarch...

He relaxed his grip and a flash of transformation blended the human visage with that of the creature. A rack of saliva-wet fangs pierced its gums, drawing blood with the violent metamorphosis. Eyes that had been warm and fraternal narrowed to yellow knife-slashes. Scaled flesh colonised its lower neck and cheekbones like a contagion.

Fighting down the urge to vomit, Ferrus reasserted his grip. His eyes widened in eerie synchronicity with the creature's as its neck was slowly crushed. It struggled. It wanted to live, to manifest, but Ferrus would kill it. He would end it with his bare hands.

'You are not him,' he told it through a barricade of clenched teeth.

A final tortured rasp, part reptilian, part human, slipped from the serpent's mouth and it became still and lifeless.

Giving it one final squeeze until it felt as though his knuckles might break, Ferrus let go and the creature slid to the ground dead.

A long, trembling breath came from his throat and he rubbed his eyes as if to banish a bad dream.

Disquiet turned to anger. Ferrus pulled out *Forgebreaker* and did as he'd vowed. He kept going for a full minute before his arms and shoulders ached at him to stop. Little was left of the creature when he was done, just a ruddy smear. He was breathing hard and beads of sweat cascaded from his brow. He felt the chill of evaporation against his fevered skin and followed that sensation all the way to the throne.

Enraged, Ferrus stormed towards the corpse-king, hauled it one-handed from its seat of office and smashed it into pieces of bone on the ground.

'Your reign is ended,' he told it, before stowing the hammer and gripping an arm of the throne in each hand. Ripping it aside, tearing it bodily from its bearings, Ferrus revealed a doorway of light. Casting the wretched seat aside, he stepped through the portal and prepared to face his tormentors.

It was not as he expected.

An orrery of worlds and stars revolved before him, locked in an infinite space that had no dimension, no limit or discernible edges. The effect was disconcerting.

The primarch's gaze was drawn to a dominant prime world, sitting amongst four others in a system of stars and desolate moons. The world was black, and Ferrus was reminded of the dark sand that had been underfoot for so much of his journey. Then, as if a giant celestial match or the contrail of a meteor had been struck against its surface, a flame was born upon the prime world. It grew into a conflagration, eclipsing all of its continents and seas, enveloping them like a baleful sun. Only once the transformation was absolute did Ferrus realise it was not a sun at all, but a burning red eye with a black pupil.

As the tableau unfolded further, he saw a slow-moving ring of black iron grow around the red world that held its fire in place until a second ring of cobalt joined it. Though it burned furiously, the eye could not escape the combined rings of metal sent to contain it. The sun faded and finally blinked out, leaving the world black and still once more.

Ferrus reached out to touch the orrery but his silver hand passed through it, revealing the illusion. It vanished like smoke in an eyeblink.

'What is this?' he snapped. 'More signs, more games?'

'Not a game,' said a deep, faintly musical voice.

Ferrus turned to face his captor, *Forgebreaker* gripped in his closed fists.

'It is the future. Your future,' said the eldar. 'If you wish it to be.'

The alien was robed, the colours subdued but manifold. Arcane sigils were stitched into the iridescent fabric, but also hung on gossamer-thin chains or from glittering diamond threads. It wore no helmet or mask, but showed a long face of high cheekbones and a tapered chin that jutted like a dagger. Strange tattoos marked its flesh and were shaven into the side of its scalp from which a long mane of golden hair cascaded. Fathomless wisdom and capricious intellect glittered in the almond-shaped eyes that regarded the primarch, but also fear.

'You have reached a fork in the road, Ferrus Manus. The path you are on leads to death, but another leads to survival and the changing of a great many things in the galaxy,' said the eldar. 'You do not realise how important you are.'

It opened its hands in a gesture of peace and solidarity.

All Ferrus saw was an alien deceiver.

'And you expect me to believe you, *creature*?' He spoke plainly and calmly. There was none of the untempered rage of earlier.

'I offer you hope. I offer it to the galaxy,' it pleaded.

'You can change *everything*.'

Ferrus smiled, but it was a hollow gesture. The eldar's shoulders sagged when it saw it.

'I know I will die,' the primarch said, 'just as I know my place and duty. It matters not if it is upon some blackened world I have never seen or the very crags of Medusa itself. I am a warrior-king, alien, but I am also something else. Human. And unlike you eldar, we humans do not submit to fate.' His eyes flashed with fire. 'We *shape* it.'

'You are mistaken–'

'No, you are the one who has made the grievous error by trapping me here,' said Ferrus, swinging *Forgebreaker* around. The serpent's gore flicked off the head, a taste of things to come. 'An error only exceeded by you showing yourself to me now.'

'Please, I offer life…' said the alien.

'You offer a cage of pre-destiny,' snarled Ferrus. 'It is your last desperate gambit,' he said, before he charged.

'Heed me,' cried the eldar, backing away and throwing up a psychic shield to defend itself. 'It does not have to be this way. Do not give in to wrath.'

'Wrath is what I am,' he roared. 'I am a warrior-king, born from battle's blood!'

No mind-fashioned shield could stay the destructive fury of *Forgebreaker*, not when wielded by its master. The defences were shattered and the psychic shards bit into the eldar as painfully as any blade. It recoiled and threw a jag of arc-lightning that Ferrus deflected with his shoulder guard. Ozone-stink filled his nostrils but he was not about to be deterred.

His bellow shook the fabric of the constructed world around him, the psychic echo of his rage unpinning it at the seams.

'Now release me!'

Sweating, bleeding and clenched by fear, the eldar fled through a fissure in the fake reality.

Ferrus reached out, tried to slip through the same

doorway as the eldar witch, but a corona of perfect light repelled him.

'Release me!'

The words stretched out into infinity as the light engulfed him, drowning his senses until they merged. Until darkness overwhelmed them and it felt like he was falling forever.

THE LAST COVEN witch slid off his sword, leaving a trail of alien blood along the blade. Even with its death and the slow banishment of the black storm, Bion Henricos knew he was dead.

Of the six thousand veterans he had led into the darkness, barely eight hundred remained. They circled the Iron Hand, an injured Colonel Salazarian fighting hard alongside him despite the blood in his lungs. The Army commander squinted through one eye – the other one had been plucked out by an eldar's knife – and saw they were overrun.

For the first time in an hour, Salazarian stopped barking orders to his men.

Henricos recognised his sudden fatalism.

'You gave us back our dignity and honour,' said the colonel, 'and I thank you for that, my lord.'

A high-pitched whine. Rapid air displacement and the splash of hot fluid against his face told Henricos the old man was dead before he saw the gaping hole in the veteran's chest.

Salazarian fell, dead-eyed and still, into the arms of the Iron Hand who cradled him to the ground.

The storm was ebbing but the darkness of it was slow to disperse. His brothers would not reach him in time. Men were dying in droves as the eldar gave their last. They were dying too, but were not content to do so alone. They wanted the Space Marine's head. They wanted Bion Henricos.

'For the Gorgon!' he cried, leaving his Medusan

steel-edge impaled in the earth so he could draw his bolt pistol. Shells sprayed in an arc of muzzle flare that left a tongue of fire in the air. Alien bodies were struck and died in explosive agony. A head shot through the darkness took out a warleader whose falchion had looked as keen as its wielder.

'For the Gor–'

Something hit Henricos in the neck, possibly a shuriken from an eldar bow-caster. He grunted, felt it burn. A las-beam pierced his thigh a half-second later. He staggered, slid the combat shield off his butchered forearm, and tried to clutch the graze across his throat with the stump of his wrist but found it wanting. A further beam lanced his torso, somewhere between chest and shoulder. Falling to one knee, Henricos fired off a desultory burst.

Warning icons flashed loudly and insistently on his retinal display. He ripped off his helm to silence them.

Closing his eyes, Henricos prepared for the end when a hand touched his shoulder and he opened them again.

'The war's not done with you yet, Iron Hand,' said a voice of ice and fire.

The giant before Bion Henricos was clad in armour of coal-black. His powerful arms shimmered with lustrous silver that flowed like mercury. Eyes of knapped flint regarded him sternly, and the hammer in his hand could sunder mountains.

Ferrus Manus had returned, and the eldar were fleeing.

'The storm has ended, brother,' said the primarch, and held out his hand. 'Now, stand with me to see it finished.'

Henricos heard the rest of the Legion approaching through the fire and smoke of the battle.

Santar and the Morlocks were first to the primarch's side. Joy at the sight of the Father was hard for them to contain. Their bolters and blades sang.

The node fell quickly, though much of what followed

was a blur for Henricos. He carried Salazarian back
to friendly lines. Barely three hundred of the veterans
returned alive with him.

They would later be honoured for their part and recognised as adopted sons of Medusa. They were the first
of the Chainveil, destined to be its captains, and living
proof of the concession that, from that day, not all flesh
was weak.

SANTAR FOUND HIM at the edge of the battlefield, standing
vigil over Bion Henricos.

After he'd returned the body of Colonel Salazarian, the
sergeant had fallen unconscious from his injuries.

'He will live,' said the Gorgon, 'but he will need further augmentation.'

'As is his right. The Iron Fathers can tend to him,'
Santar replied. 'I had thought to punish him for turning
on the Iron Creed.'

'You still should.'

Santar considered that, but other thoughts were dominant in his mind and rose to the surface.

'What happened?'

'It doesn't matter,' said Ferrus in a quiet voice. His
mood hardened abruptly and he met the first captain's
questioning gaze. 'It changes nothing.'

The primarch beckoned to one of his legionaries, who
set up a hololithic projector in the earth. Word had
reached the Iron Hands that the Salamanders had discovered a second 'prime' node in the jungle. With victory
in the desert, Ferrus was determined to meet his brother.

'Are we leaving?' asked Santar as the hololith came to
life in a grainy cone of grey light.

'We are. Gather the Morlocks and tell them we're
headed to the jungle.' A thin smile betrayed the primarch's pleasure. 'My brother has need of us.'

As Ferrus began his communication with Vulkan,
Santar did as he was ordered, but despite his lord's

return he couldn't shake the feeling that all was not well. Whatever had occurred during the Gorgon's absence had left an indelible mark, one that would resonate into the future. Perhaps all their futures.

THE OSSIFIED HIGHWAYS that led from their cocooned sanctuary were perilous, but there was little choice but to brave them. The scrap of malfeasant sentience that had found its way into Lathsarial's pseudo-world was dead, slain by the Gorgon.

It would be millennia before it could return.

Lathsarial staggered and the Diviner helped him walk. The ignorant creature he was trying to save had wounded him. Despair and anguish bled out of him in a psychic wake that would attract other predators. They needed to find safe haven quickly.

'I have failed,' he moaned, utterly desolated. 'I have allowed a war to come to pass that will decimate our race when we are already so few.'

The Diviner's attention was on the webway around them. He kept his senses alert to any crack, any seemingly insignificant fissure. Many sub-realms had already been devoured and more would follow as the conflict Lathsarial had fought so hard to prevent came to pass.

Such things were inevitable, and so the Diviner's mood was sanguine.

'It was not your war to avert,' he said, opening up a fresh channel in the bone road that was seldom trodden and therefore safer. 'A healing place is close.'

Lathsarial did not answer. The farseer was inconsolable.

'Humans are closed-minded,' said the Diviner. 'Even those that consider themselves greater, like the Gorgon. He has feet of iron, fixed to his fate and his doom.'

'But he does not condemn himself alone, but a galaxy. One that is destined to be engulfed in flames.'

Cool light bathed them as they found the healing

place at last. The Diviner set Lathsarial down upon a slab of bone and bade him rest.

As the other farseer faded from consciousness, the Diviner revisited his vision of prescience. Three times he had seen the exact same eventuality unfold. That, in itself, was remarkable.

'There is hope,' he muttered. 'In the empire of the Battle-King, he who would install an heir. Even if the Gorgon falls and fails to heed our warning, there is another who will listen, one who was lost.'

THE LION

Gav Thorpe

~ DRAMATIS PERSONAE ~

The I Legion 'Dark Angels'

LION EL'JONSON	Primarch
CORSWAIN	Primarch's Seneschal
STENIUS	Captain of the *Invincible Reason*
TRAGAN	Captain of the Ninth Order
NEMIEL	Brother-Redemptor
ASMODEUS	Battle-brother

The X Legion 'Iron Hands'

LASKO MIDOA	Iron Father
CASALIR LORRAMECH	Captain of the 98th Company

The XIV Legion 'Death Guard'

CALAS TYPHON	First Captain
VIOSS	Captain

Imperial Personae

THERALYN FIANA	Navigator of House Ne'iocene
KHIR DOTH IAXIS	High Magos of the Mechanicum

Non-Imperial Personae

TUCHULCHA

'There is but one reason and one reason alone in the exercise of power: to further one's agenda. Be it selfish or altruistic, such agenda should be the whole of one's concern without distraction if power is to be expended to its benefit. One need only look to the example of the Emperor's Great Crusade for proof of this eternal truth; when distraction came it was to the ruin of all.'

– Lyaedes, *Intermissions*, M31

I

THE LORD OF the First Legion sat as he so often sat these nights, leaning back in his ornate throne of ivory and obsidian. His elbows rested upon the throne's sculpted arms, while his fingers were steepled before his face, just barely touching his lips. Unblinking eyes, the brutal green of Caliban's forests, stared dead ahead, watching the flickering hololith of embattled stars.

Aboard the *Invincible Reason*, flagship of the Dark Angels, Lion El'Jonson thought long and hard. There were many things for him to reason out, yet no matter how hard he tried to stay focused on the military effort to bring the Night Lords to battle, his mind was drawn back to an imponderable dilemma.

Eighty-two days had passed since his confrontation with Konrad Curze on the desolate world of Tsagualsa. Eighty-two days had been enough for his body to heal, for the most part, the grievous wounds the Night Haunter's claws had inflicted upon the Lion's superhuman flesh. The armour he wore had been repaired and refurbished and repainted, so that not a mark of Curze's violence showed upon its ebon surface.

On the outside, the Lion was fully recovered, but within lay the most hideous injuries, inflicted not by the Night Haunter's weapons but by his words.

No risk of the fair Angels falling? When did you last walk upon the soil of Caliban, oh proud one?

The tides of the warp influenced communication as much as they did travel, and no sure word had been heard from Caliban for two years. In times past, the hateful words of Curze would have been easy to dismiss. The loyalty of the Dark Angels had been beyond question. They were the First Legion, ever the noblest in the eyes of all; even when the Luna Wolves earned great praise and Horus was raised to Warmaster, no others could claim the title of First Legion.

Yet such times seemed a lifetime ago now; civil war and schism tore apart the Imperium, and the surety of the past was no guarantee of the present, or the future. Could the Lion trust that his Legion remained loyal to him? Trust was not a natural state for the primarch. Was there some deeper purpose to the Night Lords' endless war in the Thramas system? Did Curze speak the truth and keep the Lion occupied here while agents of Horus swayed the loyalty of the Dark Angels to another cause?

Trust had been a scarce commodity for the Lion before Horus's betrayal, and even then he had been taken for a fool. Perturabo had used his status as a brother to trick the Lion, taking control of the devastating war engines of Diamat under the guise of alliance, only to turn those weapons against the servants of the Emperor. The shame of being so manipulated gnawed at the Lion's conscience, and he would never again accept the simple word of his brothers.

It was an impossible question and an impossible predicament. The Lion had pondered the meaning of the Night Haunter's words every night, even as he analysed the movements and strategy of his foe, trying to get one step ahead of his elusive enemy. The Night Haunter had had no reason to lie; Curze had been trying to kill his brother as he spoke. Yet they might just be random spite, as had so often spilled from the lips of Konrad Curze, who had used falsehood as a weapon long before he had turned from the grace of the Emperor; lies were second nature to the primarch and came to him as easily as breaths.

The Lion despised himself for giving credence to the lie, creating the poison that ate away at his resolve. It was simple enough to vow that Thramas would not be surrendered to the Night Lords; it was another matter entirely to prosecute a war against an enemy determined not to fight. With every night that passed, the prospect of decisive battle lessened and the desire to return to Caliban and ensure everything was in order strengthened. Yet the Lion could not abandon the war, if only because it might be a return to Caliban that the Night Haunter desired.

While these thoughts vexed the primarch, at the appointed hour three of his little brothers arrived to brief him on the current situation.

The first to enter was Corswain, former Champion of the Ninth Order, recently appointed as the Primarch's Seneschal. Across the back of his armour he wore the white pelt of a fanged Calibanite beast, and beneath that hung a white robe split at the back, its breast adorned with an embroidered wing sword. His helm hung on his belt, revealing a broad face and close-cropped blond hair.

Just behind Corswain came Captain Stenius, commander of the *Invincible Reason*. His face was a literal mask of flesh, almost immobile due to nerve damage suffered during the Great Crusade. His eyes had been replaced with smoky silver lenses that glittered in the lights of the chamber, as inscrutable as the rest of his expression.

The last of the trio was Captain Tragan of the Ninth

Order, who had been raised to the position by the primarch following the debacle at Tsagualsa. The captain's soft brown eyes were at odds with his stern demeanour, his curls of dark brown hair cut to shoulder-length and kept from his aquiline face with a band of black-enamelled metal. It was Tragan that spoke first.

'The Night Lords refused engagement at Parthac, my liege, but we arrived too late to stop the destruction of the primary orbital station there. The remaining docking facilities cannot cope with anything larger than a frigate, as I suspect was the enemy's intent.'

'That's three major docks they have taken out in the past six months,' said Stenius. 'It is clear that they are denying us refitting and resupply stations.'

'The question is why,' said the Lion, stroking his chin. 'The Night Lords cruisers and battle-barges require such stations as much as ours. I am forced to conclude that they have abandoned any ambition of claiming Parthac, Questios and Biamere and seek to hamper our fleet movements for some manoeuvre in the future.'

'I would say that it has the hint of desperation, a stellar scorched earth policy,' said Stenius.

'We cannot rule out Curze commanding such attacks simply out of spite,' added Corswain. 'Perhaps there is no deeper meaning behind these recent attacks, except to exasperate and confuse us.'

'Yet that will still be a part of a bigger plan,' said the Lion. 'For more than two years we have duelled across the stars, and throughout that war the Night Haunter has always been moving towards some endgame I have not yet fathomed. I will think on this latest development. What else have you to report?'

'The normal fleet movements and scouting reports are in my latest briefing, my liege,' said Tragan. 'Nothing out of the ordinary, if there is such a thing.'

'There was one report that I found odd, my liege,' said Corswain. 'A broken astropathic message, barely discernable from the background traffic. It would be unremarkable except that it contains mention of the Death Guard Legion.'

'Mortarion's Legion is in Thramas?' The Lion growled and glared at his subordinates. 'You think this is not a matter to bring to me immediately?'

'Not the Legion, my liege,' said Tragan. 'A handful of ships, a few thousand warriors at most. The transmission does not seem to originate from the Thramas theatre, my liege, but from a system several hundred light years from Balaam.'

'The message fragments also mention a task force from the Iron Hands in the same vicinity,' said Corswain. 'Some skirmish I think, unlikely to impact on our conflict here.'

'The system, what was it called?' said the Lion. The primarch's eyes narrowed with suspicion as he asked the question.

Tragan consulted the data-slate he held in his hand.

'Perditus, my liege,' said the Ninth Order captain.

'It's barely inhabited, my liege,' added Stenius. 'A small Mechanicum research facility, nothing of import.'

'You are wrong,' said the Lion, standing up. 'I know Perditus. I claimed the system for the Emperor, alongside warriors of the Death Guard. What your records do not show, Captain Stenius, is the nature of the research undertaken by the Mechanicum there. Perditus was meant to be kept secret, off-limits to every Legion, but it seems that the Death Guard have other plans.'

'Off-limits, my liege?' Tragan was taken aback by the notion. 'What could be so dangerous?'

'Knowledge, my little brother,' replied the Lion. 'Knowledge of a technology that cannot be allowed to fall into the hands of the traitors. We must assemble a task force at Balaam. A force that can overwhelm anything the Death Guard or Iron Hands have in the area.'

'What of the Night Lords, my liege?' asked Corswain.

'If we relent in our hunt across this sector, or weaken our forces here too much, Curze will make fine sport of the systems we cannot protect.'

'That is a risk I must take,' replied the primarch. 'Perditus is a prize that we must seize from the traitors. I had almost forgotten about it, but now it is brought to mind, I think that perhaps Perditus may hold the key to victory in Thramas too. I shall lead the task force personally. The *Invincible Reason* will be my flagship, Captain Stenius. The Fourth, Sixth, Ninth, Sixteenth, Seventeenth and Thirtieth Orders are to muster at Balaam.'

'More than thirty thousand warriors!' said Tragan, forgetting himself. He bowed his head in apology when the Lion directed a sharp glare at him.

'When, my liege?' asked Corswain.

'As soon as they can,' said the Lion. He strode towards the door. 'We cannot afford to arrive too late at Perditus.'

II

Although almost as tall as the Legiones Astartes warriors with whom she travelled the warp, Theralyn Fiana of House Ne'iocene was far slighter, willowy of build with slender fingers. Her hair was copper in colour, as were her eyes; her normal eyes, at least. In the middle of her high forehead, from which her hair was swept back by a silver band, was her Navigator's eye. To call it an eye was to compare a glass of water to the ocean. This orb, translucent white but dappled with swirling colours, did not look upon frequencies of light, but delved through the barrier that bounded the warp, looking upon the raw stuff of the immaterial realm.

Now that warp-sight was employed moving the *Invincible Reason* away from the translation point at Balaam. The streaming threads of the warp currents were tugging hard at the ship, which sat cocooned within an egg-shaped psychic field, buoyed upon the immaterial waves like a piece of flotsam on the ocean tides. She sat in the navigational spire high above the superstructure of the battle-barge. Out of instinct, Fiana looked for the bright beacon of the Astronomican, and as she had done for the last two and a half years she felt a part of her soul grow dim at the realisation that it could not be found. That the light of Terra no longer burned had been a source of constant argument amongst the Navigators attached to the Dark Angels Legion, with Fiana amongst the growing camp who believed that the only explanation was that the Emperor was no longer alive. This was not a popular viewpoint, and one not to be raised with the primarch, but the logic was inescapable to Fiana.

In the absence of the galaxy-spanning Astronomican, the Navigators relied on warp beacons – tiny lanterns of psychic brightness from relay stations in real space. They were candles compared to the star of the Astronomican, and only one in ten systems in the sector had them, but they were better than moving wholly blind; so much so that both the Night Lords and Dark Angels had tacitly agreed to treat the beacon stations as no-go areas. The risk of stranding one's own ships in the warp was too great to chance the destruction of the fragile orbital stations.

Perditus was not a beaconed system, and was located only one hundred and fourteen light years from Balaam, on a two-hundred-and-thirty-degrees, seven-point incline heading from the Drebbel beacon, which in turn would be found on a path at one-hundred-and-eighty-seven degrees, eighteen-point negative incline three days out towards the Nemo system. Glancing at a hand-drawn chart draped over the edge of her rotatable chair, Fiana confirmed this and examined the currents lapping at the barrier of the Geller field surrounding the *Invincible Reason*.

The warp did not look like its true state, even to her. Yet Fiana's warp sight allowed her to sense an approximation of its tidal powers and whorls of immaterial confluence. The Balaam system had been chosen for the rendezvous because from here a near-constant current ran through the warp almost as far as Nhyarin, nearly three thousand light years away. Nothing was ever certain with the warp, and its strange ways meant that sometimes the Nhyarin Flow ran backwards or could not be located at all, but eight times out of ten it could be relied upon to speed travel to the galactic south-west, fully across Aegis and two other subsectors. The worlds along its route were amongst the most hotly contested between the Night Lords and the Dark Angels.

Fiana punched in a series of coded orders for the piloting team situated in the command deck. A few minutes later, the Geller field bulged to starboard, its psychic harmonics adjusting to the controls of the crew so that the *Invincible Reason* edged out of its current course and into the outlying streams of the Nhyarin Flow. Psychic power gripped at the shields like waves tugging at a leaf, and though there was no real sensation of movement, Fiana felt in her thoughts the battle-barge surging ahead, flung forwards across time and space at incredible speed.

Around her, the pinpricks of light that had been the other ships of the fleet winked out of existence. Within half a dozen minutes, nothing could be seen of the flotilla, scattered to the four points of the compass and stretched through time by the eerie workings of warp space.

Turning in place, Fiana conducted a quick scan for storm activity. The whole of the warp was alive with tempests, but the Nhyarin Flow seemed stable enough for the moment. There was no horizon, no distance or perspective, and for just a moment Fiana teetered on the brink of being swallowed by the abyssal nature of the warp. She reeled her mind back into her skull, pulling down the velvet-padded silver band so that its psychic-circuitry-impregnated metal covered her third eye.

Just before her othersense was curtailed she thought

she glimpsed another ship, riding on a swirl of energy behind the battle-barge. It was probably another Dark Angels vessel, caught by fortune on the same timeflow as the *Invincible Reason*. She made a note of it in her log and signalled for her half-brother Assaryn Coiden to ascend the pilaster and take over. As the senior member of the household, it was her responsibility to see that the ship was safe during transitions, but now that the task was complete, she was glad to be able to delegate to her younger siblings. Things were far more peaceful in her quarters, and ever since Horus's rebellion had begun and the storms had come, just an hour of exposure to the warp had left her with splitting headaches and a soul-draining fatigue.

There had always been talk amongst the household, of what the warp really was, and whispered stories of the strange phenomena that the Navigators sometimes glimpsed on their travels. Now Fiana was certain that there was something else out there; not just aliens living in the warp as she had been warned, but something that existed as part of the immaterium itself.

And the stories had grown in number, and in horror. Ships had always gone missing, but the frequency with which they were now lost was frightening, as if the warp itself was rebelling at their presence. Having felt dark swirls and malignant tendrils tugging at the edges of her thoughts, Fiana knew too well that the warp was far from a welcoming place.

THE LION'S STARE was cold as it fell upon the chief Navigator, Theralyn Fiana. This was the fourth audience in seven days that he had granted her, and twice also had he received representation from her through Captain Stenius. Her complaints were becoming tiresome, and made all the more irritating because there was nothing the Lion could do to alleviate the problems she and her fellow Navigators were experiencing. She had joined the

Invincible Reason at Balaam, highly regarded as an expert of the warp tides they were travelling, but so far the Lion's only impression was of a thin-faced woman who had nothing but excuses to offer for their slow progress.

This time she had Captain Stenius for company, and looked even more agitated than normal. The Lion waved Fiana forwards with a gauntleted hand, suppressing a sigh of annoyance. The Navigator stopped five metres from the primarch's throne, the ship's captain a few paces behind. She was dressed in a flowing gown of green and blue, of a material that shimmered like water when she walked. Her bare arms were painted with rings of varying design from shoulder to elbow and the backs of her hands were tattooed with intricate intersecting geometric shapes copied by a cluster of pendants that hung on a thin chain around her neck.

Fiana's third eye was concealed by a broad silver band across her brow, but the Lion could feel its touch upon him, like a spark of heat on his flesh. Navigators, and all psykers for that matter, caused him pause; he was not well disposed to those who might see him in ways that normal men did not. Only the Emperor did he trust with such knowledge.

'What is it?' said the Lion. He fluttered a hand towards Corswain, who had just arrived and was due to brief his leader on the latest intelligence concerning Perditus. 'Be quick, there are other matters demanding my attention. If you wish me to still the warp with a wave of my hand, I must disappoint you again, Navigator.'

'It is on another matter, an urgent one, that we must converse,' said Fiana as she rose from her bow. She glanced at Captain Stenius and received a curt nod of reassurance. 'Lauded primarch, for the past several days, since we translated from Balaam, I and my family have witnessed a ship following in our wake. At first we thought it coincidence; a companion vessel of the fleet that happenstance had tossed upon the same course as ours.'

'But you no longer believe this to be the case?' said the Lion, leaning forwards. 'It is my understanding that it is extremely difficult, perhaps impossible, to trail a vessel in warp space.'

'That was our understanding also, lauded primarch. Many times have Navigators attempted to stay within reach of each other, but ninety-nine times out of a hundred all sight is lost within a day, and always within two days. We sometimes make analogy between the warp and the currents of the sea, but it is a simplistic comparison. The warp flows not only through space, within another realm beside our own, but also upon different streams of time.'

'This I know,' snapped the Lion, growing impatient. 'An hour passes in the warp and several days have turned in real space. If a ship translates a day before another, it could be weeks ahead in its journey. You have not yet explained why coincidence is not a suitable explanation, Navigator. I have made hundreds of warp jumps in my life; it is not remarkable that on one journey another ship might be caught upon the same current.'

'No, lauded primarch, it is not,' replied Fiana. She straightened to her full height and met the primarch's glare, though only for a moment before the intensity of his eyes forced her to look away again. 'It is remarkable that we have changed stream four times in the last five days, seeking the fastest current to Perditus, and within the hour the ship is behind us again. It is following us, lauded primarch, and I know of nobody who possesses that capability.'

The Lion did not waste time asking if she was certain; the forthright tone of her voice and hard look in her eye convinced him that she spoke the truth as she believed it. He nodded and gestured for Captain Stenius to step closer.

'I am sorry, Lady Fiana, for my curtness. Thank you for bringing this matter to my attention. Captain, I believe that you were already aware of this?'

'Lady Fiana brought her suspicions to me yesterday, my liege. I asked her to confirm her findings for another day and decided it was worthy of bringing to you.'

'It is an impossibility, lauded primarch,' said Fiana. 'No Navigator can track another vessel in the warp with such accuracy. We work on suggestions and instincts far too vague for such precision.'

No Navigator, thought the Lion, *but not impossible.*

During his infancy on Caliban, growing up alone in the dark, monster-infested forests, he had learned quickly that some beasts did not need to see to hunt. Some possessed senses other than sight and hearing and smell; they could stalk their prey by the spoor of their soul. Such creatures were the deadliest he had faced, not wholly physical. The knights of Caliban called them *nephilla* and it was only with great effort that they could be slain, though the Lion in his youth had killed several.

It was a stretch from nephilla roaming the dark forests of Caliban to a ship that could unerringly track another through the warp but, like Fiana, the Lion did not trust anything to coincidence. There were forces at play – forces unleashed by Horus and his allies – that he did not fully understand, and until proven to the contrary the Lion was willing to believe his foes capable of anything.

'For the moment it is sensible to assume that our mysterious pursuer is a Night Lords ship,' the Lion said after a half-second of contemplation. 'Do you think it is possible to elude this enemy without undue risk or excessive delay to our journey? I would not have the foe learn of our destination and the secret held there.'

'I am not sure I would know what to do, lauded primarch,' said Fiana. 'It is not something a Navigator learns.'

'Surely you have experienced pursuit by other than a ship?' said the Lion. 'There are denizens of the warp that are known to chase vessels.'

'Of course,' said Fiana. 'I know a small repertoire of

evasive manoeuvres, but the usual response when facing such a crisis is an emergency translation into real space.'

'That will be our second option,' said the Lion. 'I would rather avoid the delay that would add to our journey. You have two days to shake our hunter. Report your progress directly to me, Lady Fiana.'

'As you command, lauded primarch,' said the Navigator, sweeping down into a long bow.

When Captain Stenius and Lady Fiana had departed, the Lion called to his seneschal to attend him.

'I am deeply suspicious of this craft that follows us, Cor,' the primarch said. 'Have the weapons crews sleeping beside their guns, and double the watch strength.'

'As you command, my liege,' said Corswain. 'If you have time, we should discuss the strategy you wish to employ when we arrive at Perditus. The last contact we have shows that the Iron Hands and Death Guard were just beginning hostilities. It is possible that one side or the other may have gained the upper hand since then.'

The Lion pushed aside thoughts of phantom ships and concentrated on the wider task.

'We treat Perditus as hostile,' he declared. 'It is impossible to say for which cause any other force fights. Death Guard, Mechanicum, Iron Hands: all are to be treated as enemy until I say otherwise.'

FOR TWO DAYS Fiana and the other three Navigators aboard the *Invincible Reason* performed several manoeuvres that would, in normal circumstances, separate them from the following ship. They frequently changed flows within the warp, shifting the battle-barge from the fast-moving stream of the Nhyarin Flow to the more sedate currents that drifted from its outer edges. They dived into swirling eddies, a risky proposition even before the recent tumults that had engulfed warp space. Twice they turned the ship fully about and forged into counter-flows, taking them away from the route to Perditus.

Always the other ship found them again, sometimes never breaking away, other times vanishing only to appear on the edge of detection an hour or two later, following unerringly in the battle-barge's wake.

After the two days allowed by the Lion, Fiana and Stenius convened again with the primarch to discuss the next course of action. With the Lion was Corswain, summoned by his master. It was Stenius who spoke first.

'Whatever force guides our pursuer, it is beyond our means to shake them loose, my liege,' announced the ship's captain.

'Not wholly beyond our means,' said Fiana, earning herself a sharp look from Stenius; enough to betray the existence of a previous argument between the two, though his partial facial paralysis prevented any more meaningful expression.

'I will not risk my ship,' Stenius said flatly.

'You have an alternative?' said the Lion, directing his gaze to Fiana.

'Three days ahead, perhaps four, there is a well-known anomaly, which we call the Morican Gulf. It corresponds roughly to the Morican star, a dead system. There is a region that is like a gap in the warp, a bottomless gulf surrounded by a turbulent maelstrom. It is possible to run the outer edges of this whirl, and the storm should mask our departure route.'

'And the risks?' asked Corswain.

'The null space, the void in the eye of the storm, can becalm a ship, leave it stranded for days, for weeks, sometimes forever,' said Stenius, shaking his head in disapproval. 'It should not be considered at the best of times, and our mission at Perditus is too important to risk delays or worse.'

The Lion considered this, weighing up the merits of losing the pursuer against potential calamity. He disregarded the Navigator's plan, but remembered the earlier conversation he had shared with Fiana.

'Lady Fiana, you suggested before that we might make an emergency jump to real space. Is it possible that we could do so whilst the other ship has been blinded by one of your manoeuvres?'

'Possible, yes, lauded primarch,' said Fiana.

'There is no guarantee that our phantom ship has not the means to detect such a thing,' said Corswain. 'We have no idea of their capabilities. As I understand it, any translating ship creates ripples, an echo along the warp currents. If the Night Lords have a psyker or some other means to track our normal movements, a translation would be as clear as a summer day to them.'

'An emergency jump even more so, lauded primarch,' added Fiana. 'The backwash would be like dropping a boulder into a lake; even an inexperienced Navigator could detect it.'

'There is also the danger that our warp engine rift will collide with the Geller field of the other ship,' said Stenius. 'Whatever means they have to follow us, they have to stay close to use it.'

'Interesting,' said the Lion, a chain of thought set in motion by the Captain's warning. He looked first at Corswain and then fixed his eyes on Stenius. 'Little brothers, have the ship secured for an emergency translation, but keep the gunnery crews at their stations. Lady Fiana, I want you to position the ship in a particular way. Find a swift-moving warp current from which you can quickly move to a contra-flowing one.'

'What is your intent, lauded primarch?' asked Fiana, a worried frown creasing her pale skin beneath the silver of her headband.

'Our enemy shadow our movements closely but not instantaneously,' explained the Lion. 'We will move in such a way as to draw them extremely close, and then we will activate the warp engines to jump back to real space. The other vessel should be caught in our exit wake and drawn from the warp after us. In real space our enemy will become vulnerable to attack.'

'If both ships are not torn apart, my liege!' said Captain Stenius. He was about to continue his objections, but the Lion cut him off with a sharp gesture.

'You know my intent. The plan is not a subject for discussion. Lady Fiana, it will be up to you to choose the optimum moment for translation. From everything I have heard of your skill previously, I expect success.'

'Of course, lauded primarch,' said the Navigator, her face set with determination. Her reputation had been placed on the line, and for a Navigator aspiring to be the next Matriarch of her House there was no commodity more valuable than the praise of a primarch.

The Lion looked at Stenius and leaned forwards, his voice dropping low.

'You understand my orders, captain?' asked the primarch.

'I do, my liege,' Stenius replied quietly.

'Then you are both dismissed,' said the Lion. He reached a hand out towards Corswain. 'Stay a moment longer, little brother.'

When the ship's captain and Navigator had departed, the Lion motioned for Corswain to approach the throne.

'I am worried about Stenius,' confessed the primarch. 'At first he delays bringing the fact of our pursuit to my attention, and now he seems reluctant to resolve our predicament.'

'I am sure there are no grounds for suspicion, my liege,' said Corswain, affecting a formal tone, disquieted by the subject of Stenius's loyalty.

'Sure, little brother? One hundred per cent certain? You would vouch for Stenius yourself?'

Corswain hesitated at the challenge in the Lion's voice. After a moment, he lowered to one knee and bowed his head.

'I have no doubt about Captain Stenius, my liege.

However, to allay any reservations you may harbour, I shall have Brother-Redemptor Nemiel report to you.'

'As you see fit, little brother,' the Lion said, offering a rare smile.

III

THE NARROW CHAMBER atop the navigational pilaster could barely hold all four of the Navigators. What the primarch had asked for required a very specific set of circumstances. Fiana and her fellow Navigators each surveyed a stretch of the warp, seeking the conjunction of flows needed to bring the *Invincible Reason* quickly back towards the phantom ship. All other preparations had been made; the ship's company were braced for the potentially devastating drop back into real space, while Fiana had warned her companions of the deleterious effect it could have on their minds.

'I have something,' said Ardal Aneis, Fiana's younger brother. 'A counter-nebulous promontory, on the port bow.'

Fiana directed her unnatural gaze in the direction Aneis had mentioned and saw what had caught his attention. Three warp streams, one very strong, the other two weaker but approaching each other at steep angles, came together to create a three-dimensional whirlpool. The outflow curved back over the battle-barge's path and intersected with a dead pool that slowly leached back into the Nhyarin Flow.

'Captain Stenius, please direct primary navigational control to my console.' The communications pick-up buzzed in Fiana's shaking hand and she resolutely avoided the concerned looks in the eyes of her fellow Navigators. She received the affirmative from Stenius and a few seconds later the screen below her left arm flickered into life. A diagnostic sub-routine scrolled quickly across the pale green glass and then the screen went blank.

Fiana's voice dropped to a whisper as she keyed in the manoeuvre required to plunge the ship into the heart of the promontory. 'Remember the pride of House Ne'iocene.'

There was no sound, in the warp. No real tidal pressures or inertia pulled at metal and ferrocrete, but even so Fiana could sense the tortured mass of the *Invincible Reason* as its Geller field realigned, shoving the battle-barge from one streaming eddy of warp energy into another. Fiana felt a moment of sickness as her othersense lurched and spun, while all around her, the clashing currents of the psychic promontory smashed together like the slavering jaws of an immense, immaterial beast.

Kiafan, youngest of her siblings, fell to his knees beside the chief Navigator, emptying the contents of his stomach upon the floor between snarled gasps of pain. Fiana ignored the distraction and keyed in another instruction on her runepad. The ship settled into a trough of psychic power for several seconds, before rising up, ejected from the promontory like a grain of sand caught in the spume of a breaching whale.

Fiana gritted her teeth and made a final adjustment to their course, forcing herself to peer along the unwinding threads of energy that unravelled before her. She anchored the Geller field onto the strongest and then pushed aside her companions to collapse into the only chair in the chamber.

'Captain, we are on our new heading,' she gasped over the comm. Steadying herself, she looked for the bobbing mote of energy that was the other ship's warp signature. She located it ahead, approaching quickly. There was no time to waste. Even from their prepared idling state, it would take several minutes for the warp engines to charge to full power. Any longer and they would be right on top of the phantom ship, their Geller fields merging. The effect of translating in such close proximity to another vessel would be certain destruction for both ships.

'Translate now, captain! Activate the warp engines!'

TRYING TO EMULATE the example set by his primarch, Corswain stood immobile on the gallery above the *Invincible Reason*'s strategium, just behind and to the left of the statuesque Lion. On the other side of the primarch was Brother-Redemptor Nemiel. The Chaplain wore a skull-faced helm, so that nothing could be seen of his expression, concerned or otherwise. Lady Fiana's snarled command had not helped settle Corswain's mood, and had set the command crew below into frenetic activity. The navigation aides moved quickly from station to station in the bright glow of their screens, monitoring power outputs and safety thresholds as the plasma reactors of the battle-barge went up above one hundred per cent output in preparation for the warp engine activation.

Corswain clenched his jaw as he felt an ill-defined pressure building in his skull. It was not like a concussive shockwave or the pull felt in a plunging drop-pod, but more like a container slowly being filled, reaching its capacity and yet not bursting. The ache was behind his eyes, mental not physical. Aside from the brain-juddering dislocation of teleportation, it was the most unpleasant sensation he had ever encountered in his long years of service to the Legion.

A glance at the Lion confirmed that if the primarch suffered the same discomforts as his little brothers, he showed no outward sign of it. The commander of the First Legion stood with legs braced apart, arms folded across his breastplate, eyes fixed on the multiple screens that made up the strategium's main display wall. The aides working below acted and interacted like organic parts of a complex machine, the hub of which was Captain Stenius in the command throne. Inquiry and reply, report and command all flowed through the ship's captain, who orchestrated the whole endeavour with curt responses and clipped orders.

Corswain could only imagine the thoughts occupying Stenius at the moment. Warp translation was difficult enough in perfect conditions, and the current conditions were far from perfect. Another glance at the Lion showed Corswain that the primarch's attention had moved, from the grey blankness of the screens to Stenius.

It was impossible to discern real meaning from the primarch's inscrutable glare, but that did not stop Corswain from speculating, occupying his mind with such idle thoughts in order to distract himself from the coming moment when reality and unreality would clash and they might all be wiped from existence.

The Lion's comments regarding Stenius concerned Corswain on two levels. At first hand, he wondered what he had missed that had been seen by the primarch's insight. Corswain was, for the moment at least until they were reunited with Luther and the rest of the Legion on Caliban, the right hand of the primarch. It was his duty to foresee his master's commands and act before they required the Lion's attention. If there was some facet of Stenius's manner that he had missed, Corswain felt he was not properly fulfilling his duties.

Contrary to this was the worry that there was nothing amiss in Stenius's behaviour, which did not bode well for the Lion's current state of mind. Since Tsagualsa the primarch had brooded, even more than Corswain had become accustomed to. His master had said nothing of what preoccupied his thoughts, speaking only of the ongoing campaign against the Night Lords, but even those conversations had been touched by a new determination, bordering on a hunger for victory that Corswain had not seen in the Lion since the earliest days of the Crusade. The seneschal's brush with death had forced Corswain to acknowledge his own shortcomings and apply himself to his duties with greater endeavour; perhaps the primarch felt the same.

'Warp translation in ten seconds.'

Stenius's monotone declaration cut through Corswain's meandering thoughts. He balled his hands into fists, knowing what was to come. The Lion stepped forwards, gripping the balcony rail in both hands as he stared down at Stenius, eyes narrowed. The primarch opened his mouth a little, as if he was about to speak. He said nothing and shook his head slightly, lips pursed.

'Beginning translation to real space.'

This was the part Corswain hated the most, in sensation most alike to the disembodied lurch of teleportation. For an endless moment the *Invincible Reason* was held between two dimensions, perched on the precipice between the material and immaterial like a wanderer standing at the crossroads of fate. A moment before, it had been adrift on the tides of the warp, cocooned within a bubble of reality kept intact by its Geller field. Now it was in the true universe, plucked from the unnatural currents, its Geller-borne reality imploding as real space engulfed the vessel.

Corswain's head reeled for several seconds, dizzied by a sense of unreality, his surroundings seeming out of step with him, disjointed and fragile.

The sensation passed, leaving a faint pulsing behind Corswain's eyes.

The Lion was already barking orders for the short-range scanners to be brought online, eager to see whether his plan had worked and the phantom ship had been dragged out of the warp by the risky manoeuvre.

'All power to local augurs and broad-band auspex sweeps,' said the primarch, striding towards the long sweep of stairs that led down into the main chamber of the strategium. 'Redirect long-range signalling and sensors to comm-net scans. Find me that ship!'

* * *

THE SYSTEMS OF the *Invincible Reason* scoured the surrounding space for seven minutes. Corswain and Nemiel had followed their primarch down to the main floor, and had been joined by Captain Stenius who had surrendered his position of direct command to the Lion. Nothing was said for those seven minutes, as the scanner technicians worked feverishly to determine whether the plan had succeeded.

'Legiones Astartes ident-contact, my liege,' announced one of the strategium attendants. 'Twenty-two thousand kilometres from starboard bow. Eclipse-class light cruiser. Night Lords. Broadcasting as the *Avenging Shadow*.'

'Monitoring warp field fluctuations, my liege,' said another. 'Transferring to main display.'

The largest of the strategium's screens blurred into life, filled with an expanse of stars. In the bottom right corner, a shifting corona of light silhouetted the enemy light cruiser, trapped in a vortex between real space and the warp.

'Hard starboard, thirty degrees, down-plane twelve degrees,' snapped the Lion, having made the navigational calculations in only a couple of seconds; even with the aid of a trigometric cogitator Stenius would have taken at least two minutes to get the exact heading required. 'Ready torpedoes, tubes three and four. Flight crews to Thunderhawks and Stormbirds.'

The primarch's orders rang across the strategium, setting teams of officers and functionaries into motion. As this new activity settled, the Lion crossed the floor to the weapons control consoles. Stenius took a step after him.

'My liege, a full torpedo salvo will have a much greater chance of destroying the enemy.'

'I do not wish to destroy them, captain. We will capture the ship and seize whatever technology they have employed to track us here. I am inputting the torpedo guidance codes; they will not miss.'

'Of course not, my liege,' said Stenius, stepping back, only the tone of his voice betraying his chagrin.

'I request permission to lead the boarding parties, my liege,' said Corswain.

'Denied, little brother.' The primarch did not look up, his fingers dancing across the rune keys of the main weapons console. 'We will cripple their ship and I will lead the attack myself.'

'I do not think that is a good idea, my liege,' said Corswain, daring his master's displeasure. 'The warp interference surrounding the enemy vessel is highly unstable. The ship could be dragged back into the warp while you are aboard.'

The Lion's fingers stopped their tapping for a moment and the primarch straightened. Corswain prepared himself for a rebuke.

'Denied, little brother,' said the Lion, resuming his work. 'I will need you to remain on board the *Invincible Reason*.'

Corswain automatically glanced at Stenius, guessing his primarch's intent. The Lion's distrust remained.

'Brother-Redemptor Ne–'

'Is not a command-level officer, little brother.' The Lion's words were curt but not harsh. He finished his task and turned towards Corswain, deep green eyes boring into the seneschal's skull. 'You will remain on board, Cor. Unless you have any other reason why that should not be the case?'

'Torpedoes bearing on target, my liege,' declared a weapons tech, stilling any reply that Corswain might utter; he had none. 'Firing solution has been plotted as per your calculations.'

'Launch when at optimum angle,' said the Lion. 'Engines all ahead full towards the enemy.'

'Aye, my liege,' replied Stenius. He activated the internal communication system and repeated the order to the Techmarines manning the reactor chambers.

'Tube three cycling. Tube three launching. Tube four cycling. Tube four launching.' The words were spat mechanically from the mouth grille of a half-human servitor enmeshed by a tangle of wires to the weapons bank. The haggard figure was little more than a torso and head protruding from a cylindrical console, his eyes stapled shut, ears replaced with antenna-jutting vocal receivers.

On the main screen, the beleaguered Night Lords ship was dead ahead, the streak of the two torpedoes racing from the battle-barge towards it.

'Twenty-three seconds to torpedo separation. Twenty-seven seconds to impact,' grated the weapons servitor. Already the blazing plasma drives of the torpedoes were just another glimmering pair of stars against the backdrop of the galaxy, gradually dwindling with distance.

'My liege, I have Lady Fiana requesting contact on the internal comm,' said an aide.

'Direct through speakers,' replied the Lion, long strides taking him back across the strategium to stand beside the command throne.

'The Night Lords ship is doing something strange with its warp engines,' the Navigator reported over the internal address system. Corswain saw his primarch frown at her imprecise language.

'Be more specific, Lady Fiana,' said the Lion. 'What can you see?'

'Forgive my vagueness, lauded primarch. It is hard to describe to one possessed of normal sight alone. There is something – some *things* – moving in the Geller field around the enemy ship. It looks like fragments of warp space are actually inside the ship, but that is impossible.'

'I have heard the word too often lately,' snarled the primarch. 'What is the significance of this to us?'

Before Fiana could reply, the Lion's attention was drawn elsewhere.

'My liege, the enemy ship is turning, trying to break

free from the warp breach. They are closing quickly with our position.'

'Detecting an incoming hail, my liege.'

The two reports came almost at the same moment and the Lion hesitated for the first time since coming to the strategium, unsure which piece of information to respond to first. The pause only lasted a fraction of a heartbeat before the decision was made.

'Adjust course by two points to port and ready starboard batteries,' ordered the primarch. 'Decrypt hail and transfer to main speakers.'

The air was filled with static hiss for several seconds while the automated decryption systems deciphered the incoming transmission. What came out of the speakers sounded like the garbled hissing of a snake, every syllable spat with derision. The Lion's face twisted in a lopsided smile and he looked at Corswain.

'I never cared much for Nostraman, Cor. You have studied it, I know. Tell me, what do they say? I cannot imagine that they are begging for mercy.'

'They praise you for the trick in dragging them into the light, but then there come the obtuse threats. They say that they will have a reckoning in Slathissin and we will all meet our doom.'

'I do not recall any system called Slathissin, in Thramas or elsewhere,' said the Lion.

'It is a reference to their barbaric past, my liege,' explained Corswain. 'It is the lowest hell, where the souls of the fallen exact vengeance on those that wronged them, reserved for traitors, patricides and worse.'

'There is no such place, their threats are empty,' said Nemiel, speaking for the first time since he had arrived at the strategium. He looked at Corswain through the lenses of his skull-shaped helm, his expression hidden. 'There is no hell, and there are no such things as souls.'

A few seconds later, laughter sounded over the transmission, edged with insanity.

'You are wrong, son of Caliban. So wrong. As you will find out very soon. Slathissin opens its gates for you all.'

'I gave no order to transmit,' said the Lion. 'Cut the feed now!'

'We have ears nonetheless, proud Lion.'

'We are not transmitting any signal,' confirmed one of the communications attendants.

'My blade waits for your throat, disbeliever. I am Nias Korvali, and at the last midnight I will have a bloody revenge.'

There was a shout from one of the technicians monitoring the scanning arrays, just a few seconds before an automated siren blared across the strategium.

'The enemy ship is activating its void shields and warp engines, my liege!' came the panicked cry.

'Madness,' muttered Nemiel. 'The feedback from the void shields will tear them apart.'

'Fire arrestors, full turn to port!' snarled the Lion. 'That same feedback will create a wave in the warp breach, ripping it apart. Activate Geller fields, prepare for unplanned translation!'

'Torpedoes separating.' The servitor's monotone declaration cut through the activity, and Corswain looked up at the main screen, as did the Lion, Stenius and several others.

There was a brief twinkling as thrusters fired and the torpedoes ejected their multiple warheads towards the Night Lords ship. As if in response, the multicoloured bruise on reality that surrounded the target vessel shimmered violently, waves of kaleidoscopic energy pouring from the warp breach in iridescent flares.

The light cruiser appeared to fold in upon itself, the implosion releasing another blast of warp power as its void shields tried to shunt raw psychic energy back into the warp itself, creating a loop that fed into the breach between universes. One moment Corswain was looking at the enemy vessel in the heart of an ever-moving circular rainbow, the next the whole screen was filled with rippling lines and coils of pulsing warp energy; and then he realised that the convocation of energy was not on the screen, but in the air around him.

IV

'STAY CALM.'

The Lion spoke without haste, pouring reassurance and strength into those two words as he felt the touch of panic settling upon the dozens of crew manning the strategium. There was not a man or woman aboard the ship that had not faced death more than once, but being engulfed in the warp breach was a test that none of them had faced before.

He activated the internal comms system with a flick of a finger.

'All captains and other officers maintain discipline in your sections. We are experiencing a temporary situation that will be resolved swiftly. You have your standing orders, obey them.'

The primarch felt his heart beating a little faster than normal, but it was just an expected response to an emergency. He took a moment to review the situation.

The *Invincible Reason* was caught betwixt the warp and real space, trapped in a rift caused by the Night Lords' detonation of their warp engines. The Lion could feel the energy of the warp pulsing through and around him, suffusing the material of the ship, the air, his body. Only a few seconds had passed since the warp tide had engulfed them and everything seemed slightly distorted, as if he was standing at an angle to normality, looking in from a slightly different place.

The lights on the display consoles winked strangely, fluttering to an aberrant rhythm that represented no system on the ship. The muted voices of the crew were dislocated, sounding as though they came from a great distance. The visual screens had gone blank, unable to replicate the vortex of power that was whirling about the ship. Captain Stenius stepped up beside the primarch, a faint afterglow left in his wake, trails of glimmering sparks falling from the edges of his armour as he moved.

'Status report,' said the Lion. 'Void shields. Geller field. Warp engines.'

'Aye, my liege,' replied Stenius, his voice echoing for a moment inside the Lion's head. More fiery trails danced in the air as the captain raised his fist to his chest in salute.

'We have reports of fighting!' This came from Corswain, who had moved to one of the main monitoring stations, his voice sounding like a distant shout though he was less than ten metres away. 'Starboard gun decks, levels eight and nine.'

'Enemy?' snapped the Lion. 'A Night Lords teleport attack?'

'No clear report, my liege,' said Corswain. 'It is very confusing.'

'Get down there and establish some order, little brother. Clear head, discipline and courage.'

Corswain nodded and headed towards the doors while the Lion turned his attention back to Stenius, one eyebrow raised in question.

'Warp interference prevents us raising void shields, my liege. We would suffer the fate of the Night Lords. The same is true of the Geller field; we've not fully translated and to activate it would risk a massive feedback loop. Warp engines are still cycling back to potential from our translation.' Though the captain's face was immobile, his shoulders sagged. 'We are trapped here for the moment, my liege.'

The Lion absorbed this without comment, the reality of the situation brought home by the captain's stark words. He formed a plan of action.

'We cannot break free from this storm, so we must ride it to the heart. Have the warp engines readied as soon as possible. We will make a full translation back into warp space and activate the Geller field to stabilise normality. Have Lady Fiana report to me immediately. Understood?'

'Yes, my liege.'

The main doors hissed open and fifteen Dark Angels in Terminator armour entered, combi-bolters and power fists at the ready. Their immense armour was black as pitch and trimmed with silver, broken only by the sigils of the Legion on their shoulder pads and the scarlet skull emblems on their huge chestplates; the personal blazon of Brother-Redemptor Nemiel who was there to meet them.

'Maintain order, brothers,' the Chaplain told his bodyguard. 'Be watchful and show no hesitation.'

STEPPING OFF THE conveyor at gun deck nine, his retinue of ten legionaries in close step behind him, Corswain still had no better idea what was happening or who had attacked the ship. The comm-feed was alive with reports of the unidentified assailants sweeping from bastion to bastion and he could hear bolter fire and heavier weapons echoing along the corridor from the gun platforms towards the prow. It was possible, though highly unlikely, that the Night Lords had managed some form of long-range teleport as a last-ditch act before their ship was destroyed; it would not be the most unbelievable act the Night Lords had performed recently.

The gun deck was composed of a main corridor nearly a kilometre long, with access passages every two hundred metres leading to each of the gun turrets, which in turn were self-contained keeps housing the macrocannons and missile pods used for close attack against enemy ships. They were designed to withstand boarding and Corswain could see that the defence bulkheads had been dropped on the closest platforms, isolating them from the rest of the ship. How any attacker had managed to breach several platforms at once in such a short space was beyond his reckoning.

Several dozen unarmed crew members wearing plain black livery came streaming past, heading to aft, fleeing the fighting. There was a wild look in their eyes and they paid him no heed as he called for them to stop and explain what was happening. Corswain had never seen such terror in the eyes of seasoned men before.

Another burst of furious gunfire sounded ahead as the seneschal and his bodyguard pounded down the corridor towards the fighting. Deck Captain Isaases was supposed to be in charge, but was not responding to Corswain's calls on the comm; probably already dead.

Amidst the detonation of grenades, a handful of Dark Angels backed into the main passage, bolters blazing into the turret doorway of Gun Keep Four fifty metres away, two flamers licking promethium fire into the opening.

Corswain's auto-senses dimmed his sight for an instant as a flare of bright energy erupted from the opening; pink and blue flames exploded into the passageway, carrying with them the burning bodies of two more Dark Angels. The seneschal had never seen any weapon like it, and broke into a sprint, readying his pistol and power sword as he closed with the group of legionaries. The two warriors who had been caught in the attack flailed around on the floor as multicoloured flames danced across their armour, melting through their suits like a plasma blast.

A demand for a report died on Corswain's lips as he came level with the turret doorway and saw what was within, all reason driven from his thoughts for a moment.

The interior of the gun keep was ablaze with multicoloured flames, and in the heart of the blinding inferno cavorted strange shapes. They were like nothing Corswain had seen before, and he had encountered many strange enemies in his years of service to the First

Legion. The alien creatures seemed to be composed of the fire itself; headless, legless bodies with faces in their chests and long gangling arms that spouted more fire from maw-like openings at their ends. Their torsos flared out to frilled edges where legs should have been, jumping to and fro with contorted twists. The creatures were setting everything ablaze with abandon, the crackling of the fires accompanied by inhuman screeching and cackling.

Corswain's pistol felt heavy in his hand as he raised it and for the first time since he had been old enough to hold a weapon his hand trembled as he took aim. Eyes that were made of pure white fire regarded him malignly from the heart of the inferno, burning into his psyche as surely as the flames had melted through the armour of the dead Dark Angels. It seemed as if Corswain looked into a bottomless abyss of flame, the sight searing into his memory like a brand.

He opened fire, but the explosive bolts detonated in the flames before they reached their targets.

The creatures were at the doorway, flames licking at the floor of the main passage. Corswain adjusted his aim and sent two bolts hammering into the emergency release controls. The bulkhead slammed down just in front of the maniacal aliens, cutting off the infernal fire, and eerie silence descended.

Trying to make sense of what he had seen, Corswain noticed that the bulkhead was starting to glow at its centre, the unnatural flames of the attackers now turned to the purpose of burning through the metres-thick portal. As he watched the glow spreading, droplets of molten material starting to stand out on the plasteel like the sweat on his brow, the seneschal judged that it would only be a matter of a few short minutes before the creatures escaped their temporary prison.

In the quiet that had descended, he looked at the other Dark Angels, but like them could think of nothing to say, no orders to give, numbed by the bizarreness of what they had encountered.

'Seneschal!' The warning came from Brother Alartes, one of his personal guard.

Turning to look aft, Corswain saw the air swirling with power, as it had done when the warp rift had first engulfed the ship. Shapes were forming in the miasma: monstrous red hounds with scaled flesh and fangs of iron, their tails tipped with venom-dripping barbs, heads surrounded by an armoured frill. The infernal hounds were almost fully formed now, their growls and snarls resounding along the passageway. In moments they would be upon him.

The apparitions reminded him of old tales from Caliban and a word sprang to mind, loaded with loathing and fear: *nephilla*. Corswain found himself speaking, issuing a command out of instinct that he thought he would never utter as a Dark Angel.

'Fall back! Retreat and seal the gun deck.'

He stepped back towards the closest conveyor, firing his pistol at the monstrous dogs, though he knew his bolts would have little effect. The other Dark Angels were with him, filling the corridor with the flicker of bolts.

The swish of the conveyor doors opening behind him flooded the seneschal with relief in a way he had never thought possible. He gratefully backed into the chamber as the enormous, incorporeal hounds bounded down the corridor towards him.

To stay would be to die.

THE WALLS OF the Navigator's lounge shimmered with pre-echoes of what was to come. Fiana could see before-images of monstrous creatures pawing at the substance of the ship, her third eye granting her a vision of what was to be. Coiden stood at the door, a laspistol dangling pointlessly in his left hand, his right on the frame of the open portal as he peered into the antechamber, looking not so much with his eyes as his othersense.

'It's clear,' said Coiden, turning to look at Fiana past the high collar of his long vermillion coat.

'Kiafan, follow Coiden; Aneis, stay with me.' Fiana ushered her siblings towards the door with a last look back to the spiralway that led up to the navigation pilaster. Something large and slug-like was heaving its bulk through the metal of the escalator steps, becoming more solid as it pushed through from the warp.

Fiana slid up the metal band blocking her third eye and opened the leathery eyelid covering the orb. She concentrated on the solidifying apparition, channelling the energy stream that allowed her to pierce the veils of the warp. Here, in real space, that stream erupted as a scourging beam of black light that struck the beast between the waving fronds surrounding its fanged maw. The thing withered under Fiana's psychic glare. Its insubstantial form scattered into tattered mist as the energy that bound it to the material plane was thrust back into warp space.

A cry from Kiafan alerted her to more creatures in the passageway outside and she joined the others at a run. Winged, hook-clawed spectres hung from the vents in the ceiling, having seized the hood of Kiafan's robe to drag him into the air. With her normal eyes, Fiana could see a smudge of movement above Kiafan as the desperate Navigator tried to turn his third eye on the two creatures who had seized him from behind; with her othersense she saw gargoyle-like creatures with long bony limbs and stone-like flesh.

Coiden and Aneis combined their third eyes to blast the hideous creatures back into their immaterial realm, causing Kiafan to fall heavily to the floor. He grasped his ankle and looked up at Fiana with tear-filled eyes.

'I think it's broken,' he moaned.

'They're coming through the walls,' said Aneis. Humanoid and other shapes were coalescing through the bare plasteel bulkheads around the Navigators; too many to destroy.

'Pick up your brother,' Fiana told Coiden. She grabbed Aneis by the shoulder and dragged her brother past the pair. She gave him a shove towards the door leading through the next bulkhead. Something pot-bellied and cyclopean was forming out of a dark pool of rust and slime spreading across the floor of the passage beyond.

'Clear a path,' Fiana said.

'Where to?' Aneis asked, his youthful face almost white with fear.

'The strategium,' replied Fiana. 'We must reach the protection of the Lion.'

HAVING RECOVERED SOME of his equilibrium, Corswain did all that he could to organise a defence of the gun decks, but the mysterious invaders were all but impossible to confront. From the scattered outbreaks across the *Invincible Reason*, it was clear that the attack was not confined to the gun batteries, or even the starboard decks. Pockets of foes were appearing across the vessel, with a large number seemingly intent on taking over the warp core chamber. With foes materialising behind defensive lines, making a mockery of any physical barrier that could be erected, Corswain had mobilised the ship's company into hundred-strong patrols.

Not far from the strategium, he and his bodyguard came across Lady Fiana and her family. They were being escorted by Sergeant Ammael and his squad and though the Navigators looked distraught and haggard none of them seemed to be seriously injured. The seneschal relieved Ammael of his obligation and sent him to the engine decks where the fighting was becoming protracted.

When the group reached the strategium, they were confronted by an unexpected sight. There were no signs of fighting here; the technicians went about their duties with crisp calmness, diligently ignoring the scene that was playing out in their midst.

The Lion stood at the centre of the main chamber, and before him knelt a Dark Angel, a white tabard over his black armour, head bowed in obeisance. Surrounded by his personal guard, Brother-Redemptor Nemiel stood over the kneeling legionary, his pistol and crozius in his hands.

'Wait here,' Corswain quietly told the Navigators, motioning for them to stand to one side. The Lion heard the whispered words and looked across at Corswain.

'Your timing is unintentionally impeccable, little brother,' said the primarch. 'I am faced with a dilemma.'

'My liege, I do not know what is happening here, but I am sure it can wait a while. We need your guidance. The ship is under sustained attack, from creatures that are almost impervious to our weapons.'

'The punishment of oath-breakers brooks no delay,' said Nemiel. As he approached, Corswain recognised the kneeling legionary. His helm was under his arm, his face half-hidden behind long waves of black hair. It was Brother Asmodeus, formerly of the Librarium.

'Oath-breaker?' said Corswain. 'I do not understand.'

'My little brother has transgressed,' said the Lion, though there seemed no anger in his voice. 'Upon being attacked, he broke the Edict of Nikaea and unleashed the powers of his mind.'

'He performed sorcery,' snarled Nemiel. 'The same vileness perpetrated by the Night Lords that now threatens our ship!'

'That is to be decided, Brother-Redemptor,' said the Lion. 'I have not yet delivered my verdict.'

'The Edict of Nikaea was absolute, my liege,' said Nemiel. 'Warriors of the Librarium were to curtail their powers. Asmodeus has breached the oath he swore.'

'Did it work?' said Corswain.

'What?' said Nemiel, turning his skull-faced helm in the direction of the seneschal.

'Asmodeus, did your powers destroy the enemy?'

The former Librarian said nothing, but looked up at the primarch and nodded.

'Interesting,' said the primarch, his green eyes fixing on Corswain as if to see into his thoughts.

'I have seen first-hand what these things can do. They are…' said the seneschal, hesitating to use the word. He took a breath and continued. 'We face nephilla, my liege, or something akin to them. They are not wholly physical and our weapons do little damage to their unnatural flesh.'

'They are creatures of the warp, lauded primarch.' The group of Dark Angels turned as Lady Fiana approached. 'They are made of warp-stuff, and the breach has allowed them to manifest in our world. They cannot be destroyed, only sent back. The gaze of our third eyes can harm them.'

'Is this true?' asked the Lion, stooping to lay a hand on the shoulder of Asmodeus. 'Were your powers capable of harming our attackers?'

'From the warp they come, and with the power of the warp they can be banished again,' said the Librarian. He stood as the Lion changed his grip and guided the legionary to his feet. He met the primarch's gaze for a moment and then looked away again. 'Brother-Redemptor Nemiel is right, my liege. I have broken the oath I swore.'

'A grave crime, and one that I will be sure to prosecute properly when the current situation has been resolved,' said the Lion. He looked at Nemiel. 'There are two others of the Librarium aboard: Hasfael and Alberein. Bring them here.'

'This is a mistake, my liege,' said Nemiel, shaking his head. 'The abominations that attack us, these nephilla, are a conjuration of sorceries. I swore an oath also, to uphold the Edict of Nikaea. To unleash further sorcery will endanger us even more. Think again, my liege!'

'I have issued an order, Brother-Redemptor,' said the Lion, drawing himself up to his full height.

'One that I cannot follow,' said Nemiel, his tone hard, though Corswain could see the Chaplain's hands were trembling with the effort of defying his primarch.

'My authority is absolute,' the Lion said, clenching his fists, his lips drawn back to reveal gleaming teeth.

'The Edict of Nikaea was issued by the Emperor, my liege,' said Nemiel. 'There is no higher authority.'

'Enough!' The Lion's roar was so loud it caused Corswain's auto-senses to dampen his hearing, as they would if he was caught in a potentially deafening detonation.

The seneschal was not entirely sure what happened next. The Lion moved and a split-second later a cracked skull-faced helm was spinning through the dull-glowing lights of the strategium, cutting a bloody arc through the air. Nemiel's headless corpse clattered to the floor as the Lion held up his hand, pieces of ceramite embedded in the fingertips of his gore-spattered gauntlet.

Corswain looked at the face of his primarch, horrified by what had happened. For a moment he saw a vision of satisfaction, the Lion's eyes gleaming as he stared at his handiwork. It passed in a second. The Lion seemed to realise what he had done and his face twisted with pain as he knelt beside the remains of the Brother-Redemptor.

'My liege?' Corswain was not sure what to say, but as seneschal he knew he had to act.

'We will mourn him later,' said the Lion. The primarch stood up, his gaze still on Nemiel's body. He broke his stare and looked at Lady Fiana, who flinched as if struck. There were three droplets of blood across the pale flesh of her right cheek. 'Tell the Librarians they are relieved of their Nikaean oaths. Lady Fiana, you and your family will each lead a company of my warriors. Cor, assemble eight counter-attack forces.'

'Eight, my liege? Three for the Librarians, and one each for the Navigators, I understand. Am I to lead the other?'

'I am,' said the Lion. 'No creature, nephilla or any
other, attacks my ship without retribution.'

V

WHILE HIS SENESCHAL organised the forces of the Dark
Angels, the Lion made his way to his personal arming
chamber. Five Legion serfs were awaiting him inside the
stone-clad room, dressed in dark green surplices, with
heavy boots and gloves. Each wore a pistol at his belt
too, though the Lion had encountered no enemy on his
way there and they appeared unmolested.

The reports of attacks were growing in frequency as the
nephilla – or whatever their immaterial assailants were
– seemed to be widening the breach from warp space to
allow more of their kind to manifest.

The walls of the chamber were covered with weapons of dazzling variety, either made for the primarch
or seized as spoils of conquest from the hundreds of
cultures he had encountered during the Great Crusade.
It had begun with his first Calibanite short sword, presented to him by Luther on acceptance into the knightly
order; that simple blade held pride of place at the centre
of the display.

It was the one affectation he allowed himself, this
collection of weaponry. He had spent long times here
contemplating the many ways mankind had devised to
kill an enemy, though of late his throne chamber had
been a more regular haunt. He paused for a moment
of thought, moving along the walls, touching a hand
to favourite pieces, running a gauntleted finger along
blades and spikes in appreciation of their craftsmanship.
In war, just as in other pursuits, mankind was creative,
showing insight and genius even with the most barbaric
level of technology.

Many of the weapons were too small for his fist and
were mounted for ornamentation only, while others served a different purpose in his hands: swords for

normal men wielded as knives by the Lion. Some were traditional, ancient designs, while others had monomolecular edges, power field generators, electro-fields and other technological improvements.

There were spatha, longswords, bastard swords, mortuary swords, flambards, rapiers, sabres, scimitars, khopeshes, colichmardes, tulwars, shotels, falchions, misericordes and cutlasses; myrmex, cestus and knuckle dusters; baselards, stilettos, dirks and daggers; cleavers, sickles and kopis; mattocks, clubs, picks, maces, flails, morning stars, mauls and war hammers; hatchets, tomahawks, hand axes, double-bladed axes, long-bearded axes and adzes; pikes, partisans, fauchards, sarissas, voulges, Lochaber axes, boarspears, tridents, halberds, scythes, half pikes and hastas.

He did not rush himself, but took the time to collect his thoughts, considering the enemy of the day. In his youth he had slain nephilla with his bare hands out of necessity, though they were all but impervious to most mortal weapons; another benefit of his primarch heritage. This day he would go armed, and he took up two blades, heavy hand-and-a-half broadswords by the reckoning of normal men but easily held in each fist by the giant primarch. They were superbly crafted, the product of a Calibanite artisan whose name had been lost to history. Their names were inscribed along the edge of each blade in florid lettering: *Hope* and *Despair*. Each had a long fuller to lighten the blade weight, and they were edged with a crystalline compound sharper than any metal, unbreakable and never needing to be sharpened. The Lion had found the pair of swords used as ceremonial pieces by one of the order masters, and becoming enchanted by their glittering edges had insisted on a trade, gaining them for the exchange of an unblemished sablesabre pelt the primarch had prepared by his own hand.

Armed with the twin blades, the Lion joined his

allotted company at the main gateway above the reactor rooms and warp core, where the fighting was fiercest. Several wounded legionaries were being dragged up the access ramp, suffering a variety of horrendous wounds: burns and slashes through their armour that had gouged down to the bone.

'Fight with pride, die with honour,' said the Lion, raising his swords in salute to his little brothers. They fell in behind their primarch, forming five lines each fifty strong.

The corridors were littered with the dead; unarmoured serfs and crew for the most part. Their ragged bodies were heaped in bloody piles and choked the doorways to side chambers. Some had heads or limbs missing, others were little more than blackened lumps of charred flesh. Some were arranged in lewd poses with each other, eliciting a growl of disgust from the primarch.

Here and there, flies and maggots were already crawling through the filth of the dead, burrowing beneath the skin of the fallen and feasting on lifeless eyes. The Lion heard muttered curses uttered by his company, but had no desire to silence them, for he felt like cursing also.

He stopped as he came across the form of two dead Dark Angels. He knelt beside them. Their armour was half-melted as if by acid, and their skin was pock-marked by blisters and buboes. Caliban had occasionally been wracked by strange plagues, and the clusters of triple pustules that corrupted the skin of the pair of dead Space Marines struck a chord in the memory of the Lion.

'We have to burn the dead, lest corruption spread,' he said solemnly as he straightened. A trail of slime, like that of a snail, only a metre wide, led away from the bodies and passed into one of the passages leading away from the main corridor. The primarch detailed a squad to hunt down the creature that had left the trail and pressed on towards the main engine rooms several hundred metres ahead.

From nowhere, eight nephilla sprang into being ahead of the primarch. The warp rift had become so strong that it took almost no time at all for the attackers to materialise. These creatures were vaguely humanoid in shape, with lean, hunched bodies and wiry arms. They had legs like those of a dog and their flesh was the colour of blood and faintly scaled. Their heads were elongated, with black horns running back along the sides. In clawed hands they held triangular swords of gleaming bronze. Eyes of pure white regarded the Lion for a moment while forked tongues licked needle-like teeth.

With snarling war cries the nephilla attacked as one, raising their swords as they rushed towards the Lion. He did not wait for the enemy to come to him, but sprang forwards to meet them. In his left hand, *Hope* parried two blades swinging towards his groin, while *Despair* hacked through the neck of one of the creatures, parting the immaterial tissue of its body without pause.

The Lion felt a shock of energy ripple through him from his hand as the creature exploded into a shower of blood, coating the floor and the Lion's armour with crimson. There was no pause to marvel at this strange death, for the remaining seven creatures were trying to encircle the primarch.

Bolt shells whined and cracked as the other Dark Angels did their best to help their commander. The detonations had little effect on the nephilla, but provided distraction. Sweeping *Hope* in a wide arc, the Lion sheared through an upraised blade and parted the bodies of two more attackers even as he stabbed *Despair* through the face of another. The blades of the nephilla bit at his black-and-gold armour, cutting deep into the enamelled plates in a way no mortal weapon had ever done, though the Lion's flesh remained unmarked.

Parrying another swing of an infernal blade, the Lion twisted and brought *Despair* down onto the head of a nephilla circling behind him, cleaving through black horn and red skin. There was no skull beneath the flesh, and the creature collapsed into a crimson pool like the others. In two more seconds and a flurry of blows, the Lion had despatched the rest of his assailants, and his armour was awash with sticky red fluid. It smelt like blood, but he knew it could not be; the creatures had possessed no veins or arteries or hearts to carry such a thing.

Perturbed by this discovery, the Lion continued on, calling for his guard to follow swiftly as he splashed through the slick of red. He signalled Stenius, who had remained in the strategium.

'How long until the warp drive is operational, captain?'

'Less than twenty minutes, my liege,' came the reply after a few seconds. 'We have a problem, though. The enemy have driven the engineers from the warp core and are attempting to break into the containment chamber. Lord Corswain and Lady Fiana are trying to break through from the aft decks, my liege.'

'I will meet them in the main core chamber, captain.' The Lion broke into a run, his long strides quickly leaving behind his company of Dark Angels.

CORSWAIN FELT ONLY a little better that he had Lady Fiana for company. The gaze of her third eye was devastating to the enemy, but she tired quickly and had to rest for several minutes between bursts. For those periods, it was up to him and the other Dark Angels to protect her with their mundane weapons. It was not impossible – the nephilla could be destroyed by weight of fire or a particularly powerful blast of a lascannon or such – but it was hard work and the force was expending ammunition and power packs at a prodigious rate. They had less than half the stores they had set out with by the time they reached the conveyors and stairwells that dropped down into the warp core chambers.

They had encountered all manner of horrifying foes

on the two-kilometre journey aftwards: soaring disc-like beasts ringed with razor-sharp claws and possessing mouths that could chew through a legionary's armour in a few seconds, six-limbed entities with giant lobster claws and lashing tongues coated with venom, ever-changing apparitions with leering faces in their torsos that cavorted and wheeled about whilst spitting sorcerous fire from their fingertips.

Corswain's original force of two hundred Dark Angels now numbered just over half that; twenty-eight had been slain or were in the apothecarion, the others had been left as rearguard to defend against the enemy who could materialise anywhere.

With his personal guard close by him, the seneschal descended the main stairway into the bowels of the engine decks while other squads split to clear out secondary access routes. The steps were littered with the bodies of dead crew. Amongst the decapitated and disembowelled corpses were a few legionaries, their black armour rent open, their flesh hideously corrupted and twisted. Corswain had no idea what could have caused such horrendous injuries, and agitation caused him to tighten his grip on his bolt pistol and power sword as they reached the deck below.

All was clear, save for the stench of death coming from the bloated corpses of engineers and serfs. The passages here were lined with power conduits, piping and cables, which all showed signs of decay and disrepair, marked by patches of corrosion and slicks of moss and algae. Knowing that Stenius would never allow such a poor state to exist on his ship, Corswain was forced to conclude that the decrepitude was somehow a side effect of the nephilla's presence.

The same was true on the next level down, and still no foe could be found. Meeting up with sixty of his Dark Angels, Corswain readied himself for the descent to the warp core deck. The corridor and stairwells thrummed with energy, but not just the power of the reactor that was being fed into the area; there was a tension in the air, an intangible shadow that clouded his thoughts.

'The warp presence is almost total here,' warned Fiana. Her face was screwed up with effort, sweat running down her brow and cheeks, her lip trembling. 'If it were not for the lack of alarms, I would think the warp core had been breached.'

'Everybody stay alert,' Corswain told his warriors; somewhat unnecessarily he realised, as everybody was on edge. 'No friendlies. Destroy everything that moves.'

He led the force down into the warp core sector. The walls were plated here, thick ferrocrete layered with adamantium. In layout, the deck was oval, a main corridor running around the core room itself, with branching passageways leading to monitoring stations and watch rooms.

The dead were everywhere, some of them so horrendously mutilated that it was hard to tell that they had once been men and women. In the first hundred metres, Corswain counted seven dead Dark Angels, two of them in the livery of Techmarines. The first door to the warp core was another hundred and fifty metres ahead and the piles of the deceased grew larger the closer they came to the gate.

Gunfire sounded from behind, and at the same time a wave of nephilla poured from the doorway leading to the main core chamber. They were of a type, all small creatures with faces in their chests, their unnatural flesh a glowing pink colour. Sparks and trickles of fire dripped from the open ends of their splayed fingers as they gambolled and cartwheeled along the corridor.

The Dark Angels opened fire, a hail of bolts meeting the nephilla fifty metres away. Corswain fired his pistol repeatedly, directing his shots against the same target until finally the creature ruptured, clouds of pink mist erupting from the wounds. Rather than fall, the nephilla started to shudder and spin crazily, a juddering shriek emitted from its lipless mouth.

Corswain stopped firing, shocked by what happened next.

The pink nephilla was mutating, growing an extra head, splitting into two other forms. Its pinkness turned purple and then into a deep blue as two smaller versions of its former shape snapped into existence with an audible popping noise. The blue creatures snarled and frowned at their attackers, fingers flexing menacingly. The same was happening to others, turning the pink tide into a wash of pink and blue as other nephilla were torn apart by gunfire only to re-emerge in their newer forms.

Firing on semi-automatic, Corswain plunged forwards, sword raised. He was just a few strides from the front of the blue mass when a black beam seared past him; the third eye of Lady Fiana. It tore a gouge through the mass of nephilla squeezed into the passageway, causing their bodies to disperse into blue and pink sparks where it touched them.

His pistol empty, Corswain swung his sword at the closest enemy, the power-field-edged blade hitting the outstretched arm of the creature. The impact felt strange, not at all like the slowing of a sword cutting into flesh, nor like the sudden jar of a strike against armour; it felt as though Corswain struck some fantastic rubber that bent under the strength of the blow before rebounding into its former shape.

Fiana's third eye blazed again, opening up a gap for the Dark Angels to plunge forwards into the midst of the foe, their bolters roaring, the sergeants' chainswords whirring and power fists crackling. Fire engulfed them, purple and red, crackling along the edges of their armour, seeping into the cracks and joins. Corswain's right greave was set alight, the paint peeling away to reveal the ceramite beneath, which started to slough away. As he chopped his sword into the leering face of a nephilla, he noticed in a detached way that the flame gave off no smoke, and that unsettled him even more than the fact that his leg was on fire.

The edge of the pelt hanging down his back caught fire, but before the flames spread, they dissipated, vanishing as swiftly as they had materialised. Turning his attention back to the enemy, he realised that they had all been destroyed. A multicoloured mist hung in the air, like droplets of dye in a zero-gravity environment.

As he reloaded his pistol, Corswain signalled his primarch on the direct command channel.

'My liege, we are about to enter the main core chamber,' he reported. 'How close are you?'

'Two decks down, little brother.' The Lion's voice betrayed no strain, though his next words were a testament to the ferocity of the opposition ranged against him. Corswain could hear feral howling and inhuman shrieking in the background, much of it cut abruptly short. 'I am facing several dozen enemies at the moment. It will take me some time to slay them all. My force is moving up, about three hundred metres behind me. Secure the core chamber and I will meet you there shortly.'

Acknowledging his primarch's reply, Corswain reloaded his pistol and gathered his warriors – seven fewer after the latest encounter – and headed towards the gateway to the core chamber. The gate itself was several metres high, the blast doors that had been brought down still in place but torn and melted through, leaving a hole large enough to step through.

Corswain expected the portal to be held against them, but no nephilla opposed the Dark Angels as they entered the portalway. High pitched shrieking and wailing sounded from the main chamber beyond, a sound impossible for humans to make. Stepping through the breached barrier, weapons at the ready, Corswain moved into the hall housing the warp core.

The core itself was in a heavily shielded octagonal

structure at the centre of the high-domed chamber, enclosed by layer after layer of protective sheaths. Mechanicum symbols were etched into the housing, forming an intricate web of lines and shapes filled with gleaming metal against the obsidian-like stone of the warp core.

Dozens of nephilla – the pink and blue creatures they had just fought – were frenziedly hurling themselves at the core, clawing at it with their hands, trying to burn their way through with jets of pink flame. Their screeches were utterances of rage and frustration. Other creatures swirled about the upper gantries surrounding the core, swooping and climbing like Gadian skysharks. The nephilla paid the Dark Angels no heed as they strode into the chamber, weapons levelled, intent as they were on breaching the warp core.

'Destroy them all!' barked Corswain, opening fire with his pistol.

The fusillade of the Dark Angels – bolters, heavy bolters, lascannons and missiles – ripped into the mass of creatures gathered around the core structure. Spreading out along the walkways, the legionaries kept up the murderous rain of fire, some turning their weapons towards the ceiling as the circling beasts above dived down with piercing screams, their tails lashing, the barbs and serrations that ringed their manta-like bodies undulating as they descended.

The chamber filled with a swirling miasma of dissipating energy as the Dark Angels let fly with their fury, billowing clouds of warp power streaming upwards. Through the mist, Corswain saw something else moving, coalescing from the floating fragments that drifted up like embers from a fire. Something larger than anything he had yet seen, towering above the Space Marines, even taller than the Lion yet not so bulky.

Red lightning flared from the mist, ripping through Sergeant Lennian's squad, cracking open armour and searing flesh in a long burst of raging energy. Their smoking bodies were flung through the air by the blast, smashing high up against the ferrocrete walls.

The thing that emerged from the swirling maelstrom of dying nephilla looked like a giant, nightmarish bird, at least four metres tall. It stood upright like a man, but its thin, twisted body was supported on legs like those of a hawk or eagle, taloned feet scarring the metal floor, leaving sparks in its wake as it advanced. Robes of fire hung from its torso, blown about by some unnatural wind. Its arms were long and sinewy, and in its clawed hands the creature held a staff made of solidified flame, ever-changing in colour. A pair of wings spread from the beast's back, almost reaching from one side of the chamber to the other, iridescent feathers trailing on the ground.

It had two heads on long scaled necks, one like some grotesque vulture, the other serpentine, both crested with long multi-coloured feathers that dripped red and blue droplets of fire. And its eyes... Corswain regretted meeting that abominable gaze in an instant, but was unable to look away. The nephilla's eyes were black: the black of the gulf between stars, the black of the darkest cave of Caliban. The seneschal saw himself reflected in those ebon orbs, a tiny figure against the huge expanse of the universe – a tiny, insignificant mote surrounded by the enormity of existence.

The nephilla lashed out with the tip of its staff and more lightning filled the chamber, ripping apart another half a dozen legionaries. Bolter rounds exploded without effect against its ever-shifting hide and lascannon beams reflected harmlessly from its wings.

Lady Fiana stepped past Corswain, her whole body shaking as she pulled free her headband to reveal her third eye. The seneschal ripped away his gaze from her just before that warp eye was opened, and watched the beam of darkness that sprang towards the nephilla. It struck the creature full in the chest, detonating with a flare of dark energy, rocking it back a step but doing no more.

With a horrified gasp, Fiana unleashed her warp sight again, but this time the nephilla released one hand from its staff and stopped the beam with its palm. The energy coalesced around its fingers, playing from fingertip to fingertip like a miniature storm, while its snake head arched down to examine the flashing cloud of power. Eyes narrowing, it looked up at Fiana and thrust its hand back towards her, releasing the energy.

The Navigator shrieked as her body was engulfed by blackness, veins and arteries pulsing under her skin, blood streaming from eyes, ears and nose. She fell, and lay unmoving.

Corswain turned his attention back to the nephilla, and raised his pistol. Both of the creature's pairs of eyes were scanning around the chamber, necks craning to take in all of the Dark Angels. With a sweeping gesture, it sent a wave of power surging across the hall, smashing the legionaries from their feet. Corswain was hurled back with the others, crashing to his back beside the portalway.

Stretching up to its full height, the nephilla turned both heads towards the seneschal. It seemed to relax, staff held out to one side in one hand, the other stroking through the fires of its robes.

As all four of those black eyes fixed upon him, Corswain felt something inside his head, like a warp translation but sharper, like a pinprick in the centre of his mind. He tried to block out the sensation of fingers pulling apart his thoughts and memories, examining them one by one, but could not stop the creature's mental assault.

Suddenly the seneschal's limbs went numb. He stood up, with no volition, but was otherwise immobile. Around him, the other Dark Angels were just recovering from the shockwave of the creature's last attack.

Corswain tried his best to resign himself to his death, but it was hard. He never had thought his life would end like this, as helpless as a newborn, facing an enemy that he could not even begin to comprehend. He wanted to spit a curse, or dedicate his last breaths to his primarch and Emperor, but he was denied even this honour. His body was not his to control.

The nephilla reached out a bony finger and beckoned him forwards.

LASHING OUT WITH an armoured boot, the Lion sent the hound-like beast tumbling down the corridor. Taking half a dozen strides, the primarch brought both of his swords down across its back as it tried to right itself, carving it into three pieces that spattered into gore across the decking.

He stopped for a moment to assess the situation. The flight of stairs down to the main core chamber was only fifty metres ahead, and the passageway was free of enemies. He could hear his company fighting behind him, the retort of bolters echoing up from the stairwell he had just left. Though he knew his little brothers were in a dire situation, he had to focus on his objective: regaining control of the core so that the warp engines and Geller field could be engaged.

The comm buzzed as he stepped forwards, and he heard Corswain's voice. The seneschal sounded strained, as if speaking through gritted teeth.

'My liege, the way is clear to the warp core. You must come at once. There is something else here, something we cannot destroy.' The comm-link hissed for a few seconds. 'It... It wants to speak with you.'

THE LION ENTERED the warp core chamber at a full run, taking in the scene in a few moments. Several dozen Dark Angels were stood around the perimeter, their weapons directed at a monstrous bird-like nephilla but not firing. In front of the creature was Corswain, standing immobile just a few metres from it, arms hanging limply by his sides.

Cease your attack or this one will be destroyed.

The words came to the Lion's thoughts directly, bypassing his ears. Their tone was soft and melodic, in contrast to the haggard, harsh-looking creature that had undoubtedly sent them. The nephilla's intent was immediately clear and he skidded to a halt, coming to a stop with his swords held ready to defend himself. There was no reaction from his warriors, and he guessed that the words were directed to him alone. He did not know whether their passivity was voluntary or enforced, but it was clear they were in grave danger.

'It is not I that launched an attack,' said the Lion, taking a step closer to the apparition. 'Leave now.'

And make a waste of all the effort that it took to reach this place? I have been searching for you a long time, Lion of Caliban.

There was something familiar about the creature's voice, like a half-remembered dream. The Lion could not place from where, but it was not the first time he had heard this. His mind stirred with vague recollections, of pleading and entreaty.

Yes, that is true. I have come to you before.

'Get out of my thoughts.' The Lion stepped to his left and focused on blocking the creature from his mind, mentally bringing up a shield as though he were defending himself against a physical attack. It was a trick he had learnt as he had stalked nephilla on Caliban. One of the bird-beast's heads followed him with its inscrutable gaze, the other stayed fixed upon Corswain.

That might work in the real universe, but not here. You are in my realm now, or at least teetering upon the brink of it. You cannot ignore me this time.

'I do not treat with aliens,' said the Lion, taking a few

more steps to his left, closing the gap between himself and the nephilla.

Alien? Alien? There was despair in the voice. *I am more than some simple creature of your universe. I am the giver and the receiver, the crux of fate, the master of the parallels. The past and the future are laid before me. Do not mistake me for some petty foe to be vanquished by mere might of arms.*

'You have nothing to offer that I will accept.' The Lion was directly behind the creature now, its snake head still regarding him with an unblinking stare while the vulture transfixed Corswain.

That is not true. However, you do not desire power, that much is plain. Your ambition is woefully stunted for one of your abilities. You are happy to let your brothers dwell in the light of your father's adoration. You even sacrifice your own to stay true to the memory of what once was.

The two necks were starting to cross each other as the Lion continued his circling. He resisted the lure of the accusation in the creature's words, which echoed with the taunt made by the Night Haunter.

Freedom, Lion of Caliban. I can give you freedom. You know that you do not really care for these lesser beings. They are a distraction to you. Their frailties, their petty squabbles, are unnecessary trifles to be avoided. Even this war that you fight, it is without consequence.

'Horus cannot be allowed victory.'

Horus's victory is not your concern. All things are fleeting, even the lives of great Warmasters. I have witnessed the rise and fall of every civilisation in the universe. None of them can endure, Chaos always consumes them in the end.

That word – Chaos – resonated through the Lion's thoughts. He had a fleeting glimpse of eternity, of the entropy of the universe, ever-changing, new lives born out of death, of stars decaying to create worlds and worlds dying to form new stars, all in constant flux.

'The Emperor has shown us a new way. The Imperial Truth will endure for eternity.'

Laughter resounded inside the primarch's skull.

Foolish! Your Emperor is nothing more than a fraudster with grand ambitions. His empire is no greater than any other edifice of Mankind, and it will tumble just as easily.

The words were spoken with scorn yet they lit a spark of hope in the Lion's breast – the creature spoke of the Emperor in the present tense. It thought that the Master of Mankind still lived.

The nephilla could not follow the Lion's progress any further with its snake eyes, and for a moment it broke its gaze from Corswain, serpentine head swinging towards the seneschal while its vulture-like visage fixed on the primarch.

It was only a split second but it was all the Lion needed.

Before its gaze was on Corswain again, the Lion launched himself at the nephilla, sword outstretched. With astounding speed it reacted, twisting its whole body in his direction, staff coming up to spew forth a sheet of forking energy.

'Kill it, Cor!' snarled the Lion as wreaths of crackling energy enveloped him, sending pain coursing through every limb, surging into his chest and pounding in his head.

With a roar, the primarch broke free from the net of lightning that surrounded him, still lancing his sword towards the nephilla's body. A hail of fire hammered into the creature from the encircling Dark Angels as Corswain leapt away, the seneschal's bolt pistol spitting rounds.

Predictable fool.

The nephilla's staff swept out, turning aside the Lion's first blow. Twisting, wings furling, the creature sidestepped the Lion's charge, its serpent head lashing out towards his throat with bared fangs.

The Lion turned mid-stride, dropping *Hope* which had been deflected by the nephilla's parry. His gauntleted fingers curled around the slender serpentine neck as the primarch allowed himself to fall to the ground. His grasp unbreakable, the Lion dragged the nephilla down with him, its chest plunging onto the waiting point of *Despair*.

Harmed but not slain, the nephilla reared up, taking the sword from the primarch's grasp, wings spreading once more, now bat-like and shimmering gold. Its vulture's beak rammed into the side of the Lion's helm as it sought to pull its other head free from his grip. Wings beating fiercely, it tried to lift away, but the Lion's grasp held firm as he was pulled back to his feet.

'Did you see this coming?' snarled the Lion, hammering his fist into the pommel of the half-buried sword, driving the blade fully into the nephilla. The primarch felt a moment of contact, something deep within him connecting with the substance of the nephilla. His anger raged, finding conduit through his arm, into his fist, given vent along the blade of the buried sword like white fire pulsing from the Lion's heart.

The creature's piercing shrieks ripped through the Lion's mind. Its body burst into a globe of power, filling the chamber with expanding flame that sent the primarch reeling, droplets of the molten sword pattering against his armour.

Silence descended. The black of his armour was covered with a patina of roasted gore and his mind was still throbbing with the death-scream of the nephilla. The primarch picked himself up, retrieved *Hope* from where it lay on the deck and made his way over to the warp core control panel. Much of it was scorched and broken, and he started to pull away cracked panels to expose the circuitry beneath. He made a quick assessment of the damage and activated the comm.

'Captain Stenius, I will have the warp engines operational in seven minutes. Ready the Geller field and prepare for translation.'

* * *

VI

ONCE THE INVINCIBLE REASON had translated fully into the warp, protected from the maelstrom of energy by its Geller field, the Dark Angels took the offensive. As had been proposed by Lady Fiana, the nephilla were much weakened, unable to draw on the power of their realm, making them vulnerable to the weapons of the Dark Angels. With the newly-restored Librarians and the Lion leading the purge, every part of the battle-barge was scoured, the remnants of the attackers driven out of hiding to be gunned down. For two days the scourging continued, passageways and gun decks, engine rooms and mess halls, dormitories and drill ranges resounding to the roar of bolters and the vengeful battle cries of the First Legion.

Nearly three hundred Dark Angels had fallen during the fighting, many of them within the first hours of the assault. More than twice that number of Legion serfs and crew had also been slain. The apothecarion was filled with those legionaries who had survived, some of them with hideous, grotesque wounds that festered with unnatural decay or continued to blister and bleed despite the best efforts of the Apothecaries.

Amongst those being treated was Fiana, who had survived the backlash of her third eye, but only barely. She looked to be a wizened, aged crone as she lay in her bunk, her body otherwise undamaged but her mind dislocated by the psychic assault suffered at the whim of the nephilla. Despite this, she and her fellow Navigators did all they could to assist the legionaries. Cut off from the warp by the Geller field, the nephilla's presence was easily discernable by their othersight, and they guided the Dark Angels kill squads unerringly to their targets, no matter how dark and isolated their hiding places. On top of this, the Navigators had to guide the *Invincible Reason* to Perditus, pressed to find the utmost speed by the urging of the Dark Angels' primarch.

IT WAS EIGHT more days of travel before the Navigators announced that they were in the vicinity of Perditus. Lady Fiana had recovered a little more from her ordeal, and was able to take her place in the rota of Navigators steering the ship. On reaching their destination, she requested an audience with the Lion before she would allow the *Invincible Reason* to translate back to real space. As before, the Lion met with her in his throne chamber, attended to by Stenius and Corswain. Fiana had noticed the seneschal check on her condition several times when she had been in the apothecarion, but she had not had the opportunity to discuss what they had encountered. Now was not the time, the Lion was clearly impatient with the delay in translation.

'There is something amiss, lauded primarch,' Fiana explained when the primarch demanded to know the cause of her hesitation. She was forced to lean heavily on a cane that one of the Techmarines had constructed for her from a length of ribbed piping, its finial fashioned from a piece of jet-black stone, the ferrule made from a carefully cut section of the material used in the joints of power armour. Her voice had become a wheezing whisper, her words punctuated by heavy gasps. 'By all calculation and observation, we have reached Perditus, yet for the last three hours we have been unable to sight any warp beacon to confirm this categorically.'

'The storms?' suggested Corswain.

'On the contrary, the warp is incredibly placid in this locale, disturbingly so. There is almost no movement whatsoever, as if the currents have been flattened, stretched into non-existence. It is this dampening effect that I believe obstructs the beacon signals.'

'It is no mystery,' said the Lion, his expression easing into a less agitated state. 'We observed the same when we first came here. This pooling phenomenon is, I was led to believe by the Mechanicum, a side effect of the work they are performing at Perditus. It confirms that we have arrived. Make arrangements for translation as soon as possible, Captain Stenius.'

'There is something in the warp causing this oddity, lauded primarch,' insisted Fiana, taking a laboured step towards the primarch. 'I and the others can feel its presence, sense the pressure it is placing on the warp. The stability here is hiding a far more turbulent undercurrent.'

'Your observations have been noted, Lady Fiana,' said the primarch. He stood up, ending the conversation. 'Please continue to make your reports on the matter to Captain Stenius.'

Fiana railed against this casual dismissal, unable to shake the disquiet she had felt at this sinister discovery, but knew better than to debate the matter with the primarch. He was already turning his attention to Corswain. She dipped her head in acquiescence, understanding that the mystery would have to be solved another day.

SEVERAL DARK ANGELS ships had already made transition to the Perditus system when the *Invincible Reason* broke through into real space and established contact, though nearly a dozen vessels were still in transit in the warp. Fleet movements had never been easy through the warp, and the storms had exacerbated the problem considerably. It was one of the main reasons the Dark Angels had been unable to force a decisive encounter with the Night Lords in Thramas; by the time sufficient vessels arrived in a system to confront the enemy the elusive Night Lords had time to escape direct conflict.

The Lion weighed up his options: to wait for more of his flotilla to arrive or to press on towards the Mechanicum station on Perditus Ultima. Surmising that the Iron Hands and the Death Guard would both be aware of their arrival, the primarch saw no cause for delay and directed the five ships present in his fleet to advance in-system at full speed.

Passing the uninhabitable gas giants at the edge of the system, the Dark Angels picked up sensor readings of two fleets engaged in a protracted manoeuvre for position around Perditus Ultima, the closest planet to the star, on the very edge of the habitable zone. Ident-codes and intrafleet signals marked out the vessels as Iron Hands and Death Guard ships, each flotilla numbering no more than half a dozen ships; even combined they would be no match for the might of the Dark Angels that would be arriving. Despite hails, communications could not be established with either fleet, or the ground station on Ultima.

Crossing the orbit of Perditus Secundus, just five days from their destination, the warriors of the First Legion were in range to detect forces deployed onto the surface of Perditus Ultima. Comm-intercepts indicated that a stalemate persisted there as well as in space. The ships of both the Iron Hands and Death Guard were conducting an extra-orbital ballet, each trying to gain position over the world to support their troops on an offensive action, but neither was able to gain the upper hand without risking a decisive, and potentially devastating, space-borne engagement; thus the two sides were locked together at arm's length, neither prepared to wager possible defeat against a push for victory.

Summoning a council of his captains, the Lion determined a course of action for the Dark Angels.

'We will position our fleet directly between the Iron Hands and Death Guard, and announce that all hostilities are to cease,' he told the assembly of officers gathered in his throne room aboard the *Invincible Reason*. 'If neither side is willing to risk an engagement with each other, for certain they will not be keen to take on a fresh foe.'

'A risky proposition, my liege,' said Captain Masurbael, commanding the frigate *Intervention*. 'What is to be gained by placing ourselves in harm's way? Our arrival and numbers will be known to both sides already, there is no reason to expose ourselves to the danger of direct attack.'

'Purpose and threat,' replied the Lion, smiling coldly. 'We are to make our intent and determination crystal clear from the outset, lest our adversaries think we issue idle demands. Perditus is under the aegis of the Dark Angels and the sooner we establish the fact, the swifter we will conclude our business here and return to the battle with the Night Lords.'

'What of the Death Guard, my liege?' asked Corswain. 'Should we not simply attack, with the aid of the Iron Hands? They are known to have declared with Horus from the earliest days of the rebellion.'

'Until we can establish the loyalty of both factions here, and that of the Mechanicum as well, we should not suppose any aid from either side. The Iron Hands have been leaderless since Manus was slain at Isstvan. Who can say what their current agenda is or where their true loyalties lie? Similarly, it has been reported that those Legions that sided with Horus did not do so wholly. Whole companies and fleets have been spread far across the galaxy, and with the warp storms isolating many sectors we must not hastily pre-judge any situation, little brother. It may be the case that in Perditus, it is the Death Guard who are loyal and the Iron Hands who have turned from the Emperor's cause.'

Corswain absorbed his primarch's wisdom with a nod, while Captain Stenius took up the conversation.

'Is it your intent that we also gain position to place troops on Perditus Ultima, my liege?' said Stenius. 'Are we to break through the Iron Hands and Death Guard cordons for low orbit?'

'That is exactly my intent, Captain Stenius,' replied the Lion. 'The *Invincible Reason* will spearhead the thrust to Perditus Ultima, passing between the lead elements of the two enemy fleets. We shall broadcast warnings that any hostile action will be met immediately and decisively with overwhelming force. I will issue fleet instructions when we have concluded here. Are there any more questions?'

The tone of the Lion indicated that he did not expect any further debate and the assembled captains lowered to their knees to accept their primarch's command. When the others were dismissed Corswain loitered in the audience chamber, wishing to speak with his lord in private. The Lion waved for him to speak his mind.

'It is possible that what you say is true, my liege, but the likelihood of the situation is that the Iron Hands are loyal to Terra and the Death Guard are sworn to Horus,' said the seneschal. 'We should arrange our advance to favour defence against attack from the Death Guard.'

'As you say, little brother,' said the Lion. 'Yet do not be so sure in the loyalties of the Iron Hands. We are living in complex times, Cor, and there is no easy division between those who fight on our side and those who fight against us. Antagonism towards Horus and his Legions no longer guarantees fealty to the Emperor. There are other powers exercising their right to dominion.'

'I don't understand, my liege,' confessed Corswain. 'Who else would one swear loyalty to, other than Horus or the Emperor?'

'Whom do you serve?' the Lion asked in reply to the question.

'Terra, my liege, and the cause of the Emperor,' Corswain replied immediately, drawing himself up straight as if accused.

'What of your oaths to me, little brother?' The Lion's voice was quiet, contemplative. 'Are you not loyal to the Dark Angels?'

'Of course, my liege!' Corswain was taken aback by the suggestion that he might think otherwise.

'And so there are other forces whose foremost concern is their primarch and Legion, and for some perhaps not even that,' the Lion explained. 'If I told you we would abandon any pretence of defending Terra, what would you say?'

'Please do not joke about such things,' said Corswain, shaking his head. 'We cannot allow Horus to prevail in this war.'

'Who mentioned Horus?' said the primarch. He closed his eyes and rubbed his brow for a few moments and then looked at Corswain, gauging his mettle. 'It is not for you to concern yourself, little brother. Prepare the task force for the attack, and let wider burdens sit upon my shoulders alone.'

FROM HIS VANTAGE point behind the armoured windows that pierced the central tower of Magellix station, Captain Lasko Midoa had an uninterrupted view of the whole Mechanicum complex. His attention was directed to the south and east, towards outposts Seven, Eight and Nine, currently occupied by his Death Guard adversaries. Behind the low octagonal structures spread the mirrored screens that ran the circumference of the entire facility, creating a micro-climate of thermal updrafts that assisted in keeping down the temperature at Magellix, making it inhabitable if not tolerable. Beyond were the upthrusts of Perditus Ultima's mountains, their bases hidden behind a blanket of dense greenish fog a thousand kilometres across, their summits many kilometres above the plain glistening from golden refractive materials that coated the rock.

The ever-present mist layer distorted the distances, so that although the outer stretches of the facility were several kilometres away, their bulk was magnified to make them seem almost within bolter range. Heat shimmer from the mirror wall compounded the problem. It did not help the captain's sense of perspective to know that his foes were inside the stubby keeps, ready and able to launch an attack at any moment.

With Midoa stood Captain Casalir Lorramech, commander of the Ninety-Eighth Company. The two Iron Hands officers had their helms removed, making the most of the processed atmosphere inside Magellix; for the bulk of the thirty-eight days since they had arrived on Perditus Ultima they had been in full battle gear. The pair were almost identical, with close-cropped silvery hair, broad faces and leathery skin. Only two features separated them. Lorramech had natural blue eyes while Midoa had silver-lensed inserts. Midoa also had a tracheal respirator replacing his lower jaw and throat, which hissed rhythmically with his breathing. When he spoke, his voice issued from a small speaker-comm unit set into the bone of his right cheek. The speech device transmitted Midoa's words in a sing-song cadence that was quite at odds with his mechanical appearance.

'And you are sure that they are heading directly for orbit?' Midoa asked, responding to Lorramech's report that the Dark Angels had continued towards Ultima at full speed.

'Yes, Iron Father,' said Lorramech, whose voice was deep and gravelly, each word uttered with gritted teeth and barely moving lips. Midoa was incapable of smiling at the use of the ancient honorific, but it was a source of pride that his fellow captains had chosen to raise him up to command of this expedition. 'Course and speed are consistent with an orbital heading. They will be in high orbit in less than three hours.'

'But they still have not breached the comm-dampening shell?'

'We have not yet been able to directly communicate with the Dark Angels.'

'And what of them?' said Midoa, pointing out through the window at the Death Guard positions. 'What are they doing?'

'The enemy seem intent on an intercept course,' replied Lorramech. 'With your permission, I will signal the fleet to counter-manoeuvre. We will engage the Death Guard ships and provide a screen for the arriving Dark Angels. They have two battle-barges amongst their flotilla, which would be valuable orbital support.'

'You have my permission,' said Midoa. 'We have an unforeseen and fortuitous opportunity, Casalir. Have all but one in ten squads drawn down from their patrols and garrisons and mustered in the main vehicle pool. It is my intent to launch an attack.'

'It will be as you say, Iron Father,' said Lorramech. 'With the aid of the Dark Angels, we will drive the Death Guard from Perditus and secure the Tuchulcha engine.'

It took most of the next hour for Midoa to gather together the forces he required for the counter-offensive. Squads and companies were drawn in from their positions across Magellix and the surrounding rocky plateau, moving in secret along underground highways that had been dug beneath the surface of Perditus Ultima long before the Emperor's compliance fleet had arrived.

The Iron Hands sallied forth from the main gateway of Tower Two, Predator battle tanks and Land Raider armoured carriers spearheading the thrust, while the force's Rhinos and the larger Mastodon transports followed behind the more heavily armed screen.

Almost immediately, defensive fire from Tower Eight punched through the gloom of Perditus's atmosphere: stabs of laser and the flare of heavy cannon fire. The vanguard of the column spread out into covering positions, the tanks taking up stations behind enormous scattered boulders, jagged escarpments and the shallow ferrocrete blocks that housed the station's atmosphere filtration fans. Soon the return fire of the Iron Hands was lancing into the slab walls of the outer towers, ripping trails through ferrocrete and cracking massive glassite observation decks.

Behind the storm of fire, the next wave charged onwards in their Rhinos, hatches and doors battened down as the transports roared across the undulating rocky ground at full speed. Midoa was in the lead vehicle, keen to set an example for his warriors to follow. The slower, bulkier Mastodons, each quadruple-tracked and towering above the Land Raiders, powered through the dust and fog as quickly as they could, their heavy tracks carving fresh ruts in the baked surface of Perditus Ultima.

Before they reached Tower Eight, the Iron Hands came into range of the guns at Tower Nine. Midoa had known this and speed was the best defence against the strengthening crossfire. There were three hundred metres of ground to cover where both towers could fire at full intensity, before the bulk of Tower Eight obscured the arcs of fire of its neighbours.

Being first across the killing zone had its advantages. The gunners were unable to adjust their aim quickly enough to target Midoa's Rhino, but ten metres behind him Sergeant Haultiz's transport was struck full-on by a lascannon beam. Engine boiling smoke, the breached Rhino skidded to a halt, the black-and-silver armoured warriors within spilling out onto the dusty rock while more transports poured past them. Midoa's orders had been simple: stop for nothing. The Iron Hands in the other transports barrelled past their stranded brethren, knowing that the surest way to protect their fellow legionaries was to mount an assault on the gun positions manned by the Death Guard.

The fifteen seconds it took to dash through the blazing kill zone was the longest fifteen seconds Midoa had felt in his life. He was crouched in the rear compartment with his command squad, all of them tensed and ready to extract if a hit forced them to bail from their transport even while it was moving. Over the comm, Midoa learnt of a second Rhino being hit, and then a third, but by the time the lead transports were within a hundred metres of Tower Eight's secondary gate, seven of the Rhinos and three Land Raiders had pierced the cordon of fire. A further eight Mastodons followed behind, each carrying forty Iron Hands warriors, their power fields soaking up autocannon shells and lascannon blasts with actinic flashes of energy.

As the Rhinos slewed to a halt beneath the guns of Tower Eight, Captain Tadurig and his squad disembarked swiftly, approaching the wall of the tower ahead. With them they had brought a phase field generator; a device Midoa had overseen the creation of since arriving, with the aid of his Mechanicum allies. It took only a few seconds for the Iron Hands legionaries to assemble the four-legged platform and install the phase field generator, the bulk of the machine taken up with an energy distillation dish at the centre of which were thousands of wire coils to transmit the phase field into place.

Joining his warriors, Midoa made a last few adjustments to the machine which he had painstakingly assembled and rigged from old tunnel-delvers and other pieces of warp-tech machinery left over by Perditus's previous inhabitants. They had used the channelled power of the warp as freely as the Imperium employed plasma and electricity, much to the amazement of Midoa.

With a thrum of magnetic actuators sliding into position, Midoa pulled the activation lever and stepped back. He had not yet had time to test the device – he had been planning on using it during a subterranean assault on Tower Nine in a few days' time – but he knew that in theory it would work. Muttering an old Medusan proverb, he waited for the power capacitors to reach full potential and then switched on the conductor coils.

The phase field sprang into life, looking like a cone of pearlescent energy. Everything within the field disappeared, including a circle of the Tower Eight wall some three metres in diameter. After a few seconds, Midoa signalled for the machine to be shut down and with his squad on his heels, stepped through the newly-made gap.

Inside, the phase field had displaced a swathe of the room within the tower, along with another interior wall and the ceiling twenty metres further on, exposing the floor above and a basement level below. Neatly severed cables sparked while sliced atmosphere recycling pipes dribbled contaminant-laden steam into the air. Their suit lamps piercing the darkness inside the tower, the Iron Hands pushed on with weapons ready.

'WHAT DO YOU mean, Tower Eight has been breached?' Calas Typhon, First Captain of the Death Guard Legion, Commander of the Grave Wardens, was in a foul mood already, and the news of the Iron Hands' success did not improve his humour.

'A phase field generator, commander,' replied his second, Captain Vioss, who was forced to take a step back as his senior turned; Typhon and his subordinate's massive suits of Terminator armour almost filled the command blister on the top of Tower Seven. Vioss's voice was a low, slurred hiss, his speech impaired by an ugly suppurating wound in the right side of his jaw. 'Sarrin had too much focus on the gateways and the breach through the wall has him outflanked.'

'Why now?' demanded Typhon, his top-knot of dark hair flicking like a horse's tail as he twitched his head in annoyance. 'Have they received some signal from the Dark Angels?'

'Impossible, commander,' said Vioss. 'The *Terminus Est*'s deathfield is still functioning, no communication is able to pass from surface to outer orbit.'

'And the Dark Angels continue on their course directly towards Perditus Ultima?'

Vioss nodded, his sallow face deeply creased by a scowl.

'They will have orbit in less than two hours, commander.'

'Then we have less than two hours to punish our idiot foe for his foolhardiness. He should have waited until orbital supremacy was guaranteed. Signal the fleet and tell them to stave off engagement as long as possible. That should afford us an extra hour at least while the Dark Angels are forced to consider their options.'

'You plan to bring forward the next attack, commander?'

'Yes, right now, may the Father take your eyes!' Typhon crashed his fist into Vioss's shoulder, sending him reeling into the wall of the glassite-domed cupola. Motes of rust drifted in the air from the impact, shed from the corroded edges of Vioss's armour. 'We must free Tuchulcha while we have the chance. A lot depends on our success here. Tell Ghrusul to assault from Tower Nine, we will trap our enemy between us and drive onwards to the central facility.'

'For the Father,' said Vioss, bowing his head. 'The Grave Wardens will not fail.'

THE SUBTERRANEAN PASSAGEWAY was five metres high and twice as broad, lit by thin, dust-covered yellow strips in the floor and ceiling. The rails of an ancient locomotive system rusted at the centre of the tunnel and raised platforms ran along the walls to either side. Normally it was a gloomy place, but the arrival of the Iron Hands and Death Guard had turned it into a place of pyrotechnic brilliance.

Bolter fire echoed along the five-hundred-metre length of the interchange, the shells expelled by the exchange hurtling in both directions in a criss-cross of bright flares. Now and then the miniature blue star of a plasma shot shrieked across the gap or the red flare of a missile trail illuminated the murkiness. Blossoms of frag missile detonations appeared amongst the line of twenty Death Guard Terminators advancing on Tower Eight.

At their head, Commander Typhon roared his men onwards. Like his warriors, he was protected by the massive bulk of his modified cataphractii armour, painted white in the colours of the Death Guard.

Rounded plates that heaped up higher than the top of his knightly helm protected his shoulders, his chest and gut encased in segmented slabs of ceramite, arms and legs sheathed in thick greaves and vambraces. Adamantium mail hung in sheets across the joints of his armour. The left arm of his suit was incorporated into the bulk of a reaper autocannon, its twin barrels spitting a rapid-fire hail of shells towards the Iron Hands, chewing through the ammunition belt like a starving dog devouring a strip of sinew. In his right Typhon held a manreaper, a wickedly-bladed power scythe, symbol of his rank, and a smaller copy of the weapon wielded by his primarch, Mortarion. The glow of its power field shone a sickly yellow light on the white Terminators around him.

Heavy support Terminators backed up the twenty warriors of the spearhead, their cyclone launchers sending showers of missiles over the heads of their companions, detonations cracking the plastite sheathing of the tunnel walls and tossing silver-and-black armoured legionaries into the air. Combi-bolters spat rapid-fire rounds as the Grave Wardens continued to close, marching unharmed into the teeth of the enemies' fire.

The Iron Hands fell back, unable to match the Grave Wardens with their heavier armour and weaponry, but progress was slow. Ghrusul had reported entering Tower Eight twenty minutes earlier, yet Typhon was still two interchanges from breaching the tower from below. He was expecting word from Vioss at any moment, telling him that the Dark Angels were in orbit, but until then he was determined to press on with the attack.

The leading squads of the Grave Wardens were within fifty metres of the end of the interchange held by the Iron Hands when Typhon's helm crackled with the signal of an incoming comm-link. Rather than the sibilant whisper of Vioss, he heard a deep voice filled with authority that caused him to involuntarily stop in his tracks. Around him, the rest of the Death Guard were similarly immobilised and the fire from the Iron Hands died away within seconds.

'The world of Perditus Ultima is under the protection of Lion El'Jonson of the First Legion,' boomed the message. 'You are to immediately cease all warring and quit this planet. Any resistance will be met with ultimate force and there will be no prisoners taken. Failure to comply with my demands will result in your immediate destruction.'

As if breaking from a trance, Typhon staggered forwards a step, almost losing his footing. Only in the presence of Mortarion had he ever experienced anything like the reaction he had just felt and he quickly realised that it was not just the Dark Angels that had arrived: their primarch was with them. He could sense the unease of his warriors as they came to the same conclusion, and the advance that had shuffled to a halt was slowly turning into a withdrawal. Ahead, the Iron Hands were backing away from their positions too, cowed by the same tone of authority that had pierced the minds of the Death Guard.

Typhon gritted his teeth and shook his head to rid himself of the fugue that had descended on him following the Lion's proclamation. He knew that there was something else at work here, not just the innate command of a primarch. Typhon opened up his mind to the warp, sensing the waves of energy that were part of, yet separated from, everything in the material universe. When he had been a member of the Librarius his powers had been considerable. Mortarion's hatred of warpcraft had finished Typhon's exploration of his other nature when the Dusk Raiders became Death Guard, and so he had committed himself to becoming First Captain. Now, with the encouragement of darker sponsors, Typhon had once again embraced the warp-born side of his powers, learning far more about the universe and its mysterious ways than he had ever thought possible.

It was this that had first brought him in contact with the Father, and it was his warp-self that now detected the gentle interplay of energies being directed at the surface of Perditus Ultima. It seemed the Lion was no longer impressed by the Council of Nikaea's decision either and had allowed his Librarians to reclaim their birthright.

With this knowledge, Typhon was able to extend a little of his will, seeking a means to block the resolve-weakening presence of the Dark Angels Librarians. Despite his personal prowess, he was up against several trained minds, and so he turned to that shadowy force that had accompanied him these past years. He asked the Father for help, and help was granted.

With a surge of psychic energy buzzing through him, its touch like the tread of a thousand tiny insects in his mind, Typhon cast a pall of shadow over his Grave Wardens, shielding them from the assault of the Dark Angels psykers. Almost immediately they ceased their withdrawal and turned to him, expecting orders.

'Fools!' he rasped, pointing his manreaper at the retreating Iron Hands. 'Now is not the time to step back, now is the time to attack! Slay them all.'

IN A DARKENED chamber in the bowels of the *Invincible Reason*, the Lion stood between four of his Librarians, listening to their murmuring voices. All of the psykers had donned their old ceremonial robes of blue, their faces hidden by the shadows of the cowls pulled over their heads. It was better that this was kept from the sight of the ordinary battle-brethren. Confusion and hearsay could breed superstition faster than any explanation could thwart it.

Corswain stood to one side, his agitation audible as he shifted his weight from one foot to the other and back again, his armour creaking with each movement. The Lion ignored his seneschal's discomfort. This way was better, cleaner. If the Death Guard and Iron Hands could be forced to parley without fighting, it would be in the best interests of the Dark Angels.

The Lion sensed Corswain straighten and he turned his gaze upon the seneschal.

'It's not working, my liege,' said Corswain, sounding relieved by the fact. 'Sensors show that the Iron Hands are retreating from a renewed Death Guard assault. They are being pushed back into the main facility.'

'I warned them,' snarled the Lion. 'None will doubt my authority.'

'Shall I signal Captain Stenius, my liege?'

'Yes. If the Death Guard do not comply with my wishes, Magellix station will be obliterated. Tell Stenius to launch the torpedo.'

VII

SLASHING THE YELLOW-GLEAMING blade of his manreaper across the chest of an Iron Hands sergeant, Typhon shouldered his way through the doorway leading out onto the courtyard in front of Tower Eight. He was swathed by the shadow of the eight great Mastodons, their gun sponsons silenced and their canopied driver's cabins emptied by the boarding actions of his Grave Wardens, who were now pressing on towards Tower Three. From there the main gate of Magellix would be within reach.

'Commander, we have received a signal from the fleet.' Vioss's tone was urgent.

'Why have they not yet attacked the Dark Angels?' snapped Typhon as he lumbered up the gentle slope of the courtyard not far behind the line of his advancing warriors.

'The Dark Angels have positioned themselves between our ships and the enemy. Any attack against them will allow the Iron Hands to move around the flank of the flotilla. We have more urgent concerns, commander. The Lion's battle-barge has launched a torpedo towards Magellix.'

'A bluff,' Typhon replied instantly. 'The Lion will not destroy Magellix any sooner than I or my counterpart in the Iron Hands. The contents of that facility are too precious to risk destruction. Continue the attack.'

'Are you sure, commander? We have detected a cyclotronic warhead. It will obliterate everything at Magellix and a hundred kilometres around. It will destroy Tuchulcha as well as us. The fleet also reports detection of seven more Dark Angels vessels heading in-system.'

Typhon paused, a thought occurring to him. He voiced his doubt to Vioss.

'What if the Lion does not desire Tuchulcha, but merely wants to prevent us from gaining possession?'

'Commander, we cannot risk *guessing* the Lion's intent. We must pull back. We can achieve nothing if we are annihilated.'

Growling to himself, Typhon activated the company-wide comm-stream. He snapped out a series of commands, pulling back his warriors from their final assault on the main gate. Instead, he established them in positions overlooking the central tower of Magellix and guarding the tunnel network beneath. When he was finished issuing orders, he switched his comm-unit to a general broadcast.

'Happy now, Lion of the First?' he snarled. 'I will respect any ceasefire observed by the enemy. Know now that you intrude upon the business of the Death Guard Legion, and it will go poorly for you.'

Surprising Typhon – he had expected no reply to his invective – the comm crackled with a return signal. It was the same resonant voice as before – the Dark Angels primarch. It was too late to reconsider his scornful words, and his disdain would not allow him to offer any apology for them even if the Lion demanded it.

'Look to the western skies.'

Typhon turned his gaze as instructed. He saw a flash of light in the upper atmosphere, and what appeared to be a suddenly-spreading electrical storm set the jade clouds roiling. Seconds ticked past before the crack of the torpedo's detonation reached the commander's audio pick-ups.

'You are to pull back all forces from Magellix station. I will grant you safe passage back to your vessels. You, Captain Typhon, will remain at Magellix with a body-guard of no more than one hundred warriors to attend a parley under my aegis. The rest of your force will remove themselves to two hundred thousand kilometres from orbit. Failure to comply will result in your destruction. The same conditions have been transmitted to Captain Midoa of the Iron Hands.'

The link cut before Typhon could respond, not that he had anything to say in the face of such a bald ultimatum. He watched the dark clouds of super-heated gases expanding like a blue stain across the western sky and realised that the Lion did not make empty threats. For the moment, his mission was compromised, but that did not mean he had to abandon his objective entirely; he had means unknown to the Dark Angels.

'Vioss, one hundred of the Grave Wardens to form an honour guard. All other forces are to return to orbit. Have the remaining Grave Wardens embark on *Terminus Est* and I want you to take personal charge of the dearth-field. We shall allow the Lion to believe he is master of Perditus for the time being.'

'I understand, commander. The Grave Wardens will re-arm and repair in preparation for the next offensive. We will not suffer defeat here.'

THE FOG COVERING the inner courtyard of Magellix station was dispersed by the plasma and steam of a descending Stormbird. The eagle-like craft put down, its landing struts taking the weight as the dust settled around it and the mists began to seep back between the perimeter towers.

There were already a thousand Dark Angels arranged by company between the arriving ship and the main gate of Magellix. To one side of the force waited the Death Guard while the Iron Hands were guarded behind a cordon on the opposite side of the open space. Only Typhon and Midoa had been permitted to approach the Lion's landing craft, two armoured giants amongst a gaggle of a dozen Mechanicum acolytes dressed in red robes, the heads of all but two encased within breathing domes; those other two had rebreather attachments inserted into their faces and chests and required no further assistance in the thick Perditus atmosphere.

The Lion stepped out on the descending ramp of the Stormbird with Corswain to his right and the recently-arrived Captain Tragan to his left. Behind came a number of banner bearers and other attendants carrying such articles of Caliban as usually accompanied the primarch; plaques, goblets, crowns, shields and other items associated with the Lion's multitude of ranks and duties. Behind them came the cabal of Librarians, now numbering six from the fleet mustering in orbit, their blue robes flapping in the slow but strong breeze – the higher-pressure air of Perditus turned even a sluggish gust into a wind that could bowl over a normal man. As one the Dark Angels silently lifted bolters, heavy weapons or swords in salute to their commander-in-chief.

The Lion needed no helm, though the air was acrid in his throat and made his lungs feel stretched by its weight. He wanted to impress upon all present that he was a primarch, with the force of an entire Legion to command, and not just any Legion; the Dark Angels, the First Legion. His standard bearers took up station on either side of the route to the main gate, the Lion's many titles shouted through their external address systems.

The Lion's armour had been polished to a gleam, the black enamel as glossy as midnight oil alloyed with diamond, the gold shining like the heart of a star. A scarlet cloak draped from his shoulders, its train five metres long, kept aloft by the artifices of Caliban; ten suspensor-floating devices wrought in the shape of short blades etched with the names of the Knightly Orders of his homeworld. On his left hip the Lion wore his greatsword, *Adamant*, its ruby-encrusted pommels and gold-chased hilt and crosspiece glittering as brightly as his armour. Below the right side of his breastplate the Lion's belt was hung with six cylinders each the size of a man's forearm, bound with platinum, the dull red leather cases containing the Proclamations of Caliban; the first laws decreed by the Lion after his ascendancy to command of the Dark Angels, swearing Caliban to the service of the Emperor for eternity.

Sweeping down the ramp with his entourage keeping step as best they could, the Lion advanced on the waiting Mechanicum dignitaries. They introduced themselves in ascending order of rank, so that the Lion instantly dismissed the first eleven shrivelled, half-machine men and women and focused all of his considerably intimidating attention on the last: High Magos Khir Doth Iaxis, Overseer of Magellix and Custodian of Tuchulcha, as his heralds attested.

Iaxis was a tiny man, perhaps no more than a metre tall, taken to be a child attendant by the Lion until the magos had pulled back his hood to reveal a near-conical head and ageing, pinched face. The back of the magos's skull was extended by a series of segmented plates that came to a rounded point and moved strangely of their own accord, contracting and expanding slightly, perhaps as mood or effort occupied the Mechanicum priest. Thin bony fingers jutting from veined hands rubbed and entwined together, almost hidden in the cuffs of Iaxis's heavy sleeves, and his slight shoulders were no wider than the Lion's greave. If the diminutive tech-priest felt at all threatened by the giant looming above him – and the Lion could have easily crushed him with his foot like a titan of myth – the magos did not show any hesitation. His thin, reedy voice was almost muted by the bubble of the breather dome encompassing his small head, but the words were spoken with authority and precision.

'We are pleased to welcome you again to Perditus Ultima, Lion of Caliban,' said Iaxis, nodding his head inside the breather dome. 'Please follow me.'

The Lion felt a moment of impatience, expecting to be forced to check his stride in the company of the minuscule Iaxis, but his fears were misplaced. As the magos's entourage dispersed, they revealed a set of mechanical legs, which Iaxis ascended quickly by means of a narrow ladder at their rear. Placing his own legs inside the struts of the machine's pelvic arrangement, his robe rucking up briefly to reveal pale, wiry legs interlaced with reinforcing struts, Iaxis settled into the ambulator. With a hiss of actuators, the legs straightened, bringing Iaxis almost to the height of the Lion's shoulder. In the presence of his minions, Iaxis would have been above them all, but the primarch still stood taller than the mechanically-bolstered magos.

As they walked to the main gate the Lion became aware of a silver-and-black shadow hovering close to Corswain's shoulder: Captain Midoa. Glancing to his left, the Lion saw Typhon walking shoulder-to-shoulder with Tragan. The Lion ignored the other captains until they were all inside the entrance chamber behind the main gate. Once inside, the Lion turned and addressed his 'guests'.

'Captain Typhon, Captain Midoa…' The Lion was not sure what he was going to say to them. They were an inconvenience at the moment, but as he had explained to Corswain aboard the *Invincible Reason*, it did not suit to make hasty or arbitrary judgements about the loyalty and agenda of others. He instead addressed Iaxis. 'Magos, please convey the two captains to a suitable part of the facility where they may await my return. Little brothers, you will watch them for me. Captains, I remind you that all of Magellix is under the protection of my aegis. Do not think for a moment to dishonour me.'

With that matter perfunctorily dealt with, the Lion turned his back on the two captains and continued across the gate hall. The chamber sloped downwards slightly, the far end broken by three archways, each leading to a set of moving steps that descended further into the bowels of Magellix.

'The door on the right, primarch,' prompted Iaxis: 'Let me show you what all of this fuss is about.'

MOST OF THE Mechanicum facility had not existed the last time the Lion had been on Perditus Ultima, but the tunnels beneath were familiar to the primarch. Though they were now sheathed in plasteel struts and plastite board, the meandering passageways were etched into the Lion's memories, so that once they disembarked from the fourth internal conveyor, some half a kilometre below the surface, he was able to find the path unerringly towards the cavernous chamber where the machine was kept.

The last time he had walked these tunnels, frenzied machine-cultists had been dying by his hand. The people of Perditus had been enslaved to the machine and died in droves to the guns of the Dark Angels and the newly-renamed Death Guard. The Lion's first encounter with Mortarion, a tense affair that had ended with neither primarch liking the other, had taken place only three months earlier, and the two Legions had been fighting side-by-side as a display of unity for the Emperor. The Perditians had howled praise to their inanimate overlord even as they perished. Now the tunnels rang only with the boots of the primarch and the thud of Iaxis's walking apparatus.

Coming to the central cavern, the Lion found further passage barred by an immense doorway, emblazoned with the symbol of the Mechanicum. Iaxis stalked forwards on his artificial legs and pushed a hand towards a reader-plate set into the metal beside the portal. The Lion's sharp eyes glimpsed a design on the wrist of the tech-priest as he extended his arm; a faint outline almost indiscernible from the rest of the overlying skin. The primarch knew it for what it was immediately: an electoo, a hidden mark that could be realised into being by a pulse of bio-electricity. The Mechanicum made wide use of them – as did some of the more secretive orders on Caliban and many other societies throughout the Imperium – but the Lion had never before seen the design concealed on Iaxis's arm. It was of a stylised dragon, wings furled, coiled tightly about itself so that its neck merged with its body and its head lay alongside its tail.

'Your electoo, what is its significance?' the Lion asked as door locks rumbled into the walls and a heavy clanging sounded from within the door itself. 'I thought myself learned in the customs of the Mechanicum, but it is a device I do not know.'

Iaxis inhaled sharply and glared at his wrist as if in accusation. His expression mellowed after a moment, becoming one of embarrassment rather than shock as he regarded the primarch with yellowing eyes.

'A childish totem, Lion, nothing more,' said Iaxis. He paused and a moment later the dragon appeared prominently on his withered flesh, glowing a deep red. 'The Order of the Dragon, something of a defunct sect now, I am pleased to say. It is remarkable that you could see that pigmentation beneath my skin, I had quite forgotten it.'

The door opened with a hiss of venting gases, swinging inwards to reveal the cavern etched into the Lion's memories. Much had changed, but it was unmistakably the same place. The vaulted ceiling, nearly seventy metres high and banded with rock strata of many colours, was pierced now by rings bearing heavy chains from which hung guttering gaslights. The walls, nearly two hundred metres apart at their widest, were obscured behind panels of Mechanicum machinery and devices, so that the bare stone was hidden behind banks of dials and levers, flashing lights and coils of cabling and pipelines.

Gantries and walkways, steps and ladders were arranged around the device itself, with sensor probes, monitoring dishes and scaffolding further enmeshing the centre of the warp device. The thing itself was still there; the sentience, or at least semi-sentience that had enslaved a whole star system hanging in mid-air like a world in the firmament. It was a perfect sphere of marbled black and dark grey, with flecks of gold that moved slowly across its surface. Ten point six-seven metres in diameter – the Lion remembered the Mechanicum's first measurements exactly – it was made of an unknown material, impenetrable to every sensor, drill and device the Mechanicum had brought with them.

The Lion knew that the thing was regarding him with some alien sense. He was not sure how he could tell, nor how the warp device could sense him in return, but the fact remained that he was convinced it saw him this time as much as he had been convinced the first time he had entered this hall. On that occasion several hundred rag-clad Perditians had died in the next few minutes, unwilling or unable to lay down their primitive weapons, forced to defend their demigod to the last breath and drop of blood.

There was something else different, at first unnoticed amongst the rest of the Mechanicum clutter. Two protuberances now extended from the sphere, one at each pole, each only a few centimetres long. The rounded nodules touched against circuit-covered plates stationed above and below the device, which in turn were linked by a dizzying web of wires and cables to the surrounding machines. On a mat in front of the orb lay a small boy, aged perhaps no more than seven or eight Terran years.

He lay immobile on his side, eyes unblinking, as stiff as a corpse, which he might have been were it not for the gentle rise and fall of his chest; the Lion could hear the boy's heart beating ever so slowly, and could smell sweat and urine on the air.

A pipe extended from the boy's back, and another from the base of his skull, joining him with the mechanical array surrounding the warp engine. As soon as the Lion's eyes fell upon the boy, he sat up, moving jerkily like a badly-controlled marionette. The eyes were glassy, the limbs moving stiffly. With a glance at the alien orb, the primarch saw the golden motes were moving more swiftly than before, forming brief patterns in the dark swirl.

'You have returned.' The boy's voice was flat and devoid of emotion, his face featureless. A hand raised and waved erratically.

'It talks now?' said the Lion, the words half-snarled as he turned on Iaxis. The tech-priest shrugged.

'We could not discern anything of its construction or workings, but it seemed likely that it had some means to communicate with the Perditians before we were forced to wipe out their society. It took us nearly thirty years simply to devise this crude interface. We have learnt a lot from Tuchulcha. It is very cooperative, if a little enigmatic and, well, alien.'

'I hear too,' said the boy. 'You seem displeased.'

'You remember me,' said the Lion, before he could stop himself. He glared at Iaxis. 'Why the boy? We fought to rid Perditus of slaves and you have given it another.'

'Oh, that,' said Iaxis with a dismissive wave of the hand. 'It's just a servitor, Lion. We tried all manner of computational, logarithmic and cipher-based languages, but none of them worked. When presented with a servitor, though, it was able to tap into the established neural interface in only a few days.'

'What a coincidence,' said the Lion.

'There is no coincidence. I was designed to assimilate with the human form, Lion. May I call you Lion? I overheard the magos use it. Is that the correct form of address for one such as yourself?'

The primarch wanted to ignore the device's questions, but the boy's voice lingered in his thoughts.

'What are you?' said the Lion, stepping forwards until he was within arm's reach of the puppet-servitor.

'I am Tuchulcha, Lion. I am the everything. I believe the magos and I are friends, though he sometimes grows angry with me. I try to remain patient with his outbursts.'

'I asked what you are, not who you are. Curse you, what am I saying? You are a machine, a sophisticated machine and nothing more.'

'I am everything, Lion. Everywhere. I was once Servant of the Deadly Seas. Now I am the Friend of the Mechanicum.'

'You are dangerous,' said the Lion. 'A war is being waged for possession of you. I should destroy you and save much turmoil and bloodshed.'

'You cannot destroy me, Lion. Not physically, nor do you desire it. All things desire to possess me. The one they call Typhon dreams much about me. The mind of the other, Midoa, is closed to me. It contains too much iron for my liking. You... You are neither open nor closed. You scare me, Lion. It was not until you came that I knew what fear was. Your return scares me, Lion. I do not wish to be destroyed.'

It was hard not to imagine the words being uttered were from the boy, but the Lion forced himself to focus on the glistening orb rather than its animated avatar.

'Iaxis, my puppet needs more nutrients.' As Tuchulcha said this, the boy's bladder emptied, sending a watery stream down his leg to puddle on the plasteel floor. 'My apologies, Lion. I have not yet mastered the basic functions of this form. Its pathways were underdeveloped.'

'It is the third servitor we have had to attach,' explained

the tech-priest. 'The previous ones aged unnaturally, hence the youth of this specimen. We are hoping it will survive for a few years longer than the previous interfaces.'

'You seem to know a lot about what is happening on the surface,' said the Lion, suppressing the distaste he felt at Iaxis's uncaring attitude to the expenditure of human lives, even if they were unthinking servitors.

'They pass through me, and I come to know them,' said Tuchulcha. 'Their minds touch upon mine. Yours does too, but it is far too heavy to carry. How do you cope with such a burden?'

'My intellect?' said the Lion.

'Your guilt.'

The Lion did not answer straight away, not trusting himself to reveal something in front of Iaxis that he would rather remained inside his own thoughts.

'What use is it?' he demanded of Iaxis, turning away from the boy-puppet. 'It was agreed with the Mechanicum that Perditus Ultima and the device were spared only because you thought it might have some purpose we could harness for the Imperium.'

'And it does, it does!' Iaxis seemed quite animated at this. 'Tuchulcha, will you please show the primarch what you are capable of.'

Before the Lion could offer any protest, he felt his mind and body lurch, the sensation somewhere between that of a warp translation and a rapid teleportation. Darkness clouded his vision for an instant, and when his eyes were clear, he found himself no longer in the cavern beneath Perditus Ultima.

They were unmistakably in his throne room aboard the *Invincible Reason*. Tuchulcha and his avatar, minus most of the monitoring equipment, floated behind the throne, while Iaxis stood where he had been, a couple of metres to the primarch's right. Sirens were blaring and the voice of Captain Stenius was bellowing over the internal speakers.

'Battle stations! All crew report to battle stations. Geller field is being raised. Five minutes to full enclosure. Repeat, we have unexpectedly translated to the warp, Geller field is being raised, be prepared for attack.'

The Lion was dumbfounded, unable to comprehend what had happened for several seconds. He eventually realised that Tuchulcha must have moved the battle-barge into the warp and displaced itself, the primarch and tech-priest onto the vessel an instant later. Part of the Lion was appalled by the dangerous situation and Iaxis's naiveté in allowing this to happen; a greater part of him marvelled at the unprecedented power on display.

'Tuchulcha,' the Lion said slowly, thinking it would be wise to be 'friends' with the unpredictable machine, 'where are we now?'

'We are adjoined to the place you call Perditus, Lion.'

The primarch turned to Iaxis, brow furrowed.

'Adjoined? We are in the warp. How is this possible? We were far too close to the world, to the star, for a translation.'

'Tuchulcha does not have to worry about that sort of thing, Lion,' the tech-priest said with a toothless grin. 'It is able to burrow directly from real space to warp space, without any backwash or graviometric displacement.'

'Why have I not learnt of this before?' demanded the Lion.

'Our studies are far from complete,' replied Iaxis. 'At the moment, we are at the whim of Tuchulcha, and as you see it is a little, well, temperamental.'

'Tuchulcha, I wish you to return us and the ship to Perditus Ultima.' The Lion kept his tone calm and friendly, suddenly aware of how precarious his position had become.

'Of course, Lion.' The boy's thin, blood-starved lips twisted into an abhorrent approximation of a smile. 'What do you wish me to do with the rest of your ships?'

* * *

VIII

THE LION'S AUDIENCE chamber was quiet, occupied only by the primarch and his seneschal. The Lion was seated in his throne, betraying no sign of his thoughts or mood, as impassive as a statue. Corswain stood at the primarch's right, trying his best to conceal his own misgivings at the emerging situation. As time silently ticked past, he could no longer hold his tongue.

'My liege, I do not question your judgement in this matter, but I must admit to my own ignorance. We have secured Perditus Ultima and possess enough force to destroy the Death Guard outright, yet you invite their commander to a parley? I have an ill feeling about this. And to have the Iron Hands' captain present at the same time seems counter-productive.'

The Lion turned his head and regarded Corswain for a moment, his expression stern.

'You are right not to question my judgement, Cor.' The primarch's lips formed a thin smile, lightening his demeanour, if only a little. 'However, my reason for this meeting is straightforward. Before I decide on our following course of action, I must ascertain for myself the extent to which the knowledge of Perditus's secret has spread. Though he probably does not realise it, I remember that Captain Typhon took part in our original expedition here. He was just a company captain, I recall. That he knows of Tuchulcha's existence is unsurprising, but I sense that his agenda is not as transparent as it would first appear.'

'And Captain Midoa, my liege?'

'His presence here is an oddity, little brother. It might be chance that he intercepted the Death Guard attack, but coincidence does not sit well with me as an explanation. I must know why he came to Perditus, and on whose authority he claims to act. The Iron Hands are leaderless, my brother Ferrus slain at Isstvan, and I thought his Legion rendered inconsequential. It appears that I am wrong, and so I must have answers to questions that nag at me.'

The comm-piece in Corswain's ear chimed and he listened for a moment to the communiqué from Captain Tragan.

'Our guests will be here imminently, my liege,' Corswain said.

'Good,' replied the Lion, directing his gaze back to the double doors. A few seconds later, those doors hissed open, revealing Tragan and a guard of thirty Dark Angels. In their midst were Captains Typhon and Midoa; the first easily seen in his huge suit of Terminator armour, a head taller than the surrounding warriors. At first glance, Typhon's armour appeared in poor repair, much patched and stained, the white of the Death Guard mottled in places with oil and battle damage. A moment's further inspection, however, revealed to Corswain that the Terminator suit was poorly maintained only on a cosmetic level; Typhon moved freely, every step accompanied by a wheeze of servos and hiss of fibre bundles. A short blade hung at his belt and in his hands he held his scythe-like manreaper.

Midoa followed behind the Death Guard commander, his black-and-silver armour showing signs of fresh paint and polish. His black cloak was tattered at the edges and a fresh scar was healing on his brow. Corswain had expected someone older, Midoa's fresh features a counterpoint to the seals and marks of honour that adorned the chestplate and shoulder guards of his suit. Like Typhon, he was still armed, with a power sword at his waist and a twin-barrelled combi-bolter slung on a strap over his shoulder.

'Thank you, Captain Tragan,' said the Lion. 'You may leave us.'

Corswain turned in surprise, but his primarch's attention was fixed on the two newcomers.

'My liege?' Tragan could not stop the question before he spoke it.

'Please return to your duties, captain,' said the Lion, keeping his tone affable. 'I am certain that our guests refused to surrender their weapons on principle only. I would expect no less from officers of the Legiones Astartes. They would not be so foolish as to test me on my own ship.'

With a glance at Typhon, Tragan nodded. The Dark Angels fell in behind their commander as he departed. The Lion gestured for Typhon and Midoa to approach.

'Am I to be your prisoner?' snapped Typhon, his voice echoing from the external speakers of his suit. 'If you are to execute me out of hand, then do so and be done with it.'

'You will address me properly, commander,' the Lion replied, showing no anger at the Death Guard's accusation. 'I have yet to decide your fate. Do not give me cause for upset.'

Typhon said nothing for a few seconds, subjected to an unblinking stare from the primarch. Under the force of that gaze he eventually nodded and slowly lowered to one knee.

'Lord Jonson, Primarch of the First,' said Typhon. 'Forgive my impertinence.'

'Perhaps,' said the Lion. He waved a hand for Typhon to stand. 'What is your purpose in coming to Perditus, commander?'

'I'm sure you already know it, Lord Jonson,' said Typhon.

'And still I wish it heard in your own words.'

'The warp device, Lord Jonson,' Typhon said, glancing at Captain Midoa. 'I came to Perditus to claim possession of it.'

'Interesting.'

'The Warmaster desires this device, for reasons that you should know well. It is inopportune that you should seek to thwart his plans in this way. He will take it badly.'

'Horus will take it badly?' snarled Corswain, stepping

forwards. 'The Dark Angels do not answer to Horus.'

'In time they will, I am sure,' Typhon replied smoothly, looking briefly at the seneschal before returning his attention to the Lion. 'Your opposition to the Night Lords is expected, but unnecessary. It is an irrelevance, made personal by mutual antagonism. What is Thramas to the Dark Angels?'

'They are the Emperor's worlds, and we will protect them,' said Corswain, laying a hand on the hilt of his sword. 'Treachery does not go unpunished.'

'Be quiet, little brother,' said the Lion, shifting in his throne to rest an elbow on the sculpted arm, chin lowered onto his closed fist, eyes still fixed upon Typhon. 'Let the commander speak freely.'

'I have nothing more to say, Lord Jonson,' said the Death Guard.

'Your threat is meaningless, commander. What you say is irrelevant, but what you do not say is so loud that it deafens me.'

Typhon started to speak but the primarch silenced him with a raised hand.

'You make no mention of my brother, Mortarion, your primarch. Do you still fight for the Death Guard, commander? Or do you pursue an ambition at odds with your lord? If Mortarion desired the device you mention, he has the resources of an entire Legion at his disposal. Why would he send such a small flotilla to claim such a precious prize? No, Mortarion is not the hand that guided you here, commander.'

Straightening, the Lion rested his hands on his knees and leaned forwards.

'Similarly, you invoke the name of the Warmaster, but it is not Horus's will that despatched you to Perditus. Perhaps as you say, I am an irrelevance to my traitorous brother, but that does not mean Horus would wish to pit his sons against mine in open conflict. He destroyed three Legions at Isstvan, but my Dark Angels were not amongst them. Curze, Mortarion, Horus; none of them desire full scale war with my Legion, and for good reason.'

In reply Typhon was silent, perhaps regretting his words, or fearing that further argument would only serve to betray him more deeply. The Lion moved his dark gaze to the Iron Hands commander.

'And you, Captain Midoa, what purpose brought you here?'

'To secure Perditus Ultima against the traitors, Lord Jonson,' replied the captain, looking across to Typhon. 'We arrived just in time, it appears.'

'And who set you upon this purpose, captain?'

'We were part of the four-hundred-and-sixth expeditionary fleet, lord, far from Isstvan when the muster was called. When we learnt of the tragedy that had befallen our Legion, we did what we could, securing such worlds as we had newly brought to compliance, fighting those traitorous forces that we encountered. Six months ago we were intercepted by an Ultramarines fleet near Ojanus, and received summons that Lord Guilliman was gathering all loyal forces at Ultramar. We answered the call, and later the primarch despatched us to Perditus, fearing the traitors might attempt to seize the device held by the Mechanicum.'

The Lion accepted this with a slow nod, deep in thought.

'And now that you have learnt of Perditus's secret, what is your intent?' asked the primarch.

'It is not safe to leave the warp engine here, lord. It is too powerful to risk its misuse, and so I believe the best course of action is to relocate it to the safety of Macragge.'

'Indeed,' said the Lion, eyebrows arching high. 'You took that decision upon yourself?'

'Lord Guilliman had intimated that such a course might be necessary, lord.'

Fingers drumming quickly on the arm of his throne,

the Lion moved his gaze from one commander to the other and back again, before looking at Corswain.

'When we have concluded this parley, send word to the captains, little brother. The fleet is to assume formation for the bombardment of Perditus Ultima.'

There were outbursts from Typhon and Midoa, which fell on deaf ears.

'As you command, my liege,' said Corswain.

'You cannot destroy the warp engine!' said Midoa, taking a step forwards. 'If its power can be harnessed, it could be the weapon that enables us to turn the tide on the traitors.'

'You suppose too much, captain,' the Lion replied sharply. 'I too received Guilliman's summons. I do not concur with his plans, and I would no more trust him with this engine than any servant of Horus. I consider Ultramar no safer place for this device than Perditus, and even if Guilliman does not use it for his own purposes I cannot allow it to fall into the hands of the Emperor's enemies.'

Typhon's laugh rang around the chamber as Midoa made further protest.

'Your good humour is misplaced, commander,' snapped the Lion, silencing Typhon's mirth and Midoa's arguments. 'I am of a mind to let you depart Perditus without the engine, so that you might take word of its destruction to whatever masters you wish to claim. However, slight me again or dishonour my audience and I will be content to allow your lieutenants to perform that errand in your stead.'

Silence greeted this proclamation and the Lion stood up, signalling that the audience was at an end.

'Perditus Ultima and its prize will be destroyed within hours. Tell my brothers that there is nothing for them here.'

* * *

IX

ON THE MAIN display, the tiny speck of light that was Captain Midoa's shuttle disappeared behind the shadow of his heavy cruiser, the *Fastidious Prosecutor*. Looking at a sub-screen, the Lion saw the *Terminus Est* of the Death Guard powering away, its plasma engines almost lost against the light reflecting from Perditus Ultima's surface. The primarch was about to turn away, with both Typhon and Midoa now returned to their respective ships, when he overhead a message from Lady Fiana coming through to one of the communications attendants.

'Relay that connection to speakers,' the Lion demanded, pointing a finger at the Legion serf, who complied immediately, eyes wide with surprise.

'Lauded primarch, my family and I are detecting a distortion in the warp around Perditus Ultima,' Fiana repeated, her voice coming through the address grilles all around the strategium.

'Tuchulcha?' asked the primarch.

'No, this is something different. It is like a miniature vortex, a hole burrowing through the warp.'

'Burrowing from where? To what does this hole lead?'

'Give us a moment, lauded primarch. Ardal is ascending the pilaster for a better fix on the location of the disturbance.'

'Raise void shields,' snapped Captain Stenius. 'Arm weapons batteries and sound the call to battle order.'

The Lion was content to let his subordinate take the appropriate defensive measures. He waited with arms crossed, gaze moving between the main screen, the sub-display of the *Terminus Est* and the speaker located to the right of the display array, as if he could see Lady Fiana beyond.

'Detecting a power surge from the *Terminus Est*, captain,' announced one of the serfs at the scanner consoles.

'Just raising void shields, captain,' said another almost immediately after.

'The warp disturbance is local, very small.' Navigator Ardal's voice was reedy over the internal comm. 'I do not know how, but it seems to be originating from the Death Guard flagship.'

'Where to?' snarled the Lion. 'Where is it directed?'

'Perditus Ultima, lauded primarch. It's some kind of warp tunnel, straight into the heart of the facility. I've never seen anything like it.'

'Corswain!' The Lion's use of the seneschal's name automatically switched the battle-barge's systems to a direct address channel. Almost unnoticed, a tiny icon blinked on a sub-screen, indicating on a schematic of the *Invincible Reason* that Corswain was in the transit corridor outside the starboard launch bays, having seen off Midoa and Typhon.

'Yes, my liege?'

'Assemble your guard, and the Librarians, at teleporter chamber two. I will meet you there.'

'Where are we going?'

'Lay in coordinates for the Magellix facility. The Death Guard are trying to steal the warp engine.'

TYPHON'S MANREAPER PARTED the tech-adept from pelvis to throat, the scythe's power field fizzing and cracking with vaporising blood. The ragged remains of the tech-adept flopped to the bare stone of the floor as a squad of skitarii burst from the doors ahead. The Mechanicum's bionically-augmented warriors sported a variety of laser weapons and rocket launchers. As red las-blasts seared down the tunnel and the corkscrew contrails of guided rockets followed, the Grave Wardens opened fire. Typhon's autocannon thundered in his fist while a counter-barrage of missiles and bolts hammered into the half-machine defenders of Perditus Ultima.

The Terminators continued their implacable advance, stepping over the sparking, bloodied remnants of the skitarii, passing into the corridor that led to Tuchulcha's

prison. More skitarii appeared and were cut down, the
Grave Wardens all but impervious to the weapons carried by their foes.

At the head of the column, Typhon was still trying to
push aside the side effects of the warp-teleportation he
had employed to bring his warriors inside the facility.
The Father had not been so generous in his gifts this
time, and Typhon's skin felt heavy beneath his armour.
His whole body itched and his head occasionally swam
with the effort he had expended to punch a hole through
reality.

'Why did we not do this when we first arrived?' rasped
Vioss, striding alongside Typhon to the left. 'We would
have retrieved the device long before the arrival of the
Dark Angels.'

'I did not know that Tuchulcha was awake,' replied
Typhon. 'It will have to transport itself back to *Terminus
Est*, for I do not have the power. It is of a far greater mass
than it looks, the bulk of its construction existing only
in warp space.'

'A feat of engineering,' said Vioss, his sarcasm plain
to hear.

'A miracle of the Father,' Typhon corrected him as
they came to the chamber of Tuchulcha. The Death
Guard commander stopped, seized by a sudden pain in
his abdomen. He gritted his teeth as he felt something
squirming through his insides; or at least a sensation he
considered similar to having his intestines burrowed out
by some hellish rodent. In a few seconds the pain had
passed and he barrelled forwards through the next set
of doors.

The globe of Tuchulcha hung in the centre of the room,
surrounded by the entrapments and delving devices of
the Mechanicum. Typhon was struck by the beauty of
the patterns that flowed across the device's surface. A
melange of oily colours merged and split, creating a hyp-
notic effect. With some effort, the Death Guard leader

broke his gaze from the floating orb, seeing a red-robed figure kneeling before the device, hood covering head and face.

Typhon aimed his reaper autocannon at the kneeling figure, but his finger did not squeeze the trigger as a child's voice broke the quiet.

'Stop! Do not harm him!'

A youth had stepped out of the tangle of cables surrounding Tuchulcha, sallow-skinned, connected to the apparatus imprisoning the device. It took a moment for Typhon to realise that the servitor-body was being manipulated by the machine.

'He is of no consequence,' said the commander. 'He has been your jailer, and should be punished.'

A liquid-filled gasping emanated from the servitor-youth, which Typhon realised was laughter.

'I cannot be imprisoned, not by the likes of this creature,' said Tuchulcha.

'Good, then you will be able to come with us.'

The boy did not reply, but looked away, head tilted back as if he was gazing through the rocky ceiling of the hall.

'You do not have long, Typhon of the Dusk Raiders,' he said. 'The Lion comes, seeking your head. Your warriors are being slain.'

As if in confirmation, the first reports crackled across the comm-net. The rearguard of three squads of Grave Wardens were under attack. Their report was short-lived, talking of the blazing sword of the Dark Angels' primarch, and of nightmare hooded creatures by his side that had eyes of flame and claws of iron. Ten seconds passed and Typhon heard no more from his men.

'He has brought his psykers with him,' Typhon told Vioss. 'I cannot contend with their combined abilities. Warn Charthun and the second line, they must fall back towards this position.'

'As you wish, commander,' said Vioss.

'We are the Death Guard now,' Typhon corrected Tuchulcha. 'I cannot take you back to my ship by my own hand. You must come with me if you want to be free.'

'Free?' Again there was the strangled gurgling of laughter from the animated boy. 'I have been waiting a long time for the Lion to return. I saw him, the first time he came, and knew that my saviour had been delivered to me. The Perditians trapped me here, but with the aid of Iaxis I have been able to loose my bonds. I have remained solely because I knew the Lion would return to me.'

'He seeks to destroy you,' said Typhon.

'He seeks to possess me, as all others have before,' replied Tuchulcha. 'Fear not for me, brave Typhon. You must fulfil your own destiny. Your primarch awaits you. It would be such a waste for you to be slain here. Here, let me help you.'

Typhon's protest died in his throat as he felt the surge of translocation. A moment later, he was on the strategium of the *Terminus Est*, his remaining Grave Wardens around him.

'What was that about?' said Vioss, shaking his head. The captain turned to the surprised attendants at the bridge controls. 'Set course for the nearest translation point. The Dark Angels will be after us soon enough.'

'No need,' said Typhon, feeling a pressure in the back of his mind that he recognised well. 'Tuchulcha has already put us well out of harm's way.'

DISMISSING HIS SERFS, Typhon was left alone in his chambers, the bare metal bulkheads spotted with rust, lit by the unfettered glare of the light strips in the ceiling. He peeled off the last layer of his undersuit, tossing the sodden mesh aside to reveal his pallid flesh. He could not understand what had happened. The Father had sent him to Perditus to rescue Tuchulcha from the clutches of the Mechanicum, but he had failed.

The ache in his gut was still there, and the Death Guard commander looked down at his stomach. Beneath his flesh could be seen the rigid plates of his black carapace. There was something else, pocking his skin just below his breast plate. He could not see so clearly past the curve of his muscled chest, so Typhon turned and looked at himself in the polished bronze of his mirror.

Just beneath his solar plexus were three blisters, each as large as his thumbtip, arranged in a triangle, touching each other. They were dark red, surrounded by a black ring, weeping clear fluid. He felt no pain as he gently prodded one of the buboes with his finger. In fact, the sensation sent a thrill of pleasure through his body.

Typhon had a moment of realisation. He *had* freed Tuchulcha. By travelling to Perditus, he had turned the Lion's eye towards the world, setting in motion a course of events that led somewhere Typhon did not know, but was to the grand design of the Father. The trio of blisters on his flesh was a reward; a sign from the Father that Typhon's loyalty had been noted. He was marked now and forever, marked by the love of the Father.

It was just the beginning, of course. The Grave Wardens were only the first. The Father wanted them all. The Father wanted the love and loyalty of every Death Guard; the love and loyalty of Mortarion above anything else.

'ARE YOU SURE that was all the message said?' Captain Lorramech shook his head, eyes fixed on Midoa. The two of them walked back to the strategium, heading from the conveyor that had brought them up from the docking bay.

'That was all the Lion said I was to say,' confirmed Midoa. 'He was very specific. "Tell Guilliman I have a reply for him," the Lion told me. "Tell him to wait for me. I am coming." That was it.'

* * *

THE LORD OF the First Legion sat as he so often sat these nights, leaning back in his ornate throne of ivory and obsidian. His elbows rested upon the throne's sculpted arms, while his fingers were steepled before his face, just barely touching his lips. Unblinking eyes, the brutal green of Caliban's forests, stared dead ahead, watching the flickering hololith of embattled stars.

Iaxis and his device were safely stowed in the deepest holds of the *Invincible Reason*. Magellix station had been turned to molten slag and rubble in a few hours; nothing was left for any other Legion to claim.

The Lion's lips moved, so slightly that perhaps a casual observer would not have noticed. Also none but those with the superhuman hearing of a primarch would have heard the words that came from his near-unmoving lips.

'I have Curze now,' the Lion said, speaking only to shadows. His monologue stopped every few moments, as though to allow someone else to speak. 'With Tuchulcha, we will be able to trap the Night Haunter. We have to be careful not to act too swiftly. Yes, when the time is right, but not before. If Curze notices a drastic change in our strategy he will respond, perhaps abandoning Thramas altogether. You are right, that would not be helpful.'

The Lion paused and wiped a fingertip across his brow.

'Guilliman is a misguided fool at best, and a traitorous dog at worst.' He took a deep breath. 'I know that, but I would no sooner bend my knee to him than to Horus. Curze has the truth of it, but I was blinded by my anger. It has fallen to me to be the scale upon which history will be balanced. Every event has its counter, every brother his equal. Curze seeks to sap my morale and the strength of my Legion with unending war. Such shall be the duty of the Dark Angels. Yes, they will be ready for the task. There will be no new Emperor, only a lifetime of war. My brothers will bleed each other dry, contesting for eternity until there can be no victor. No, not even him. There is only the Emperor, none is worthy of inheriting that mantle. I will ensure the Legiones Astartes destroy themselves before another matches the power upon Terra. That is true. Faced with the prospect of mutual annihilation, my brothers may come to terms. Horus will be forced to acknowledge the Emperor again, and Guilliman and the others will not usurp their true master.'

Again the Lion stopped, with a slight shake of the head. He turned his gaze to his left, and out of the shadows appeared a diminutive figure. It was no taller than the height of a man's knee, clad in an ebon robe, tiny and nimble black-gloved hands visible, but the rest of its body and face hidden in shadow. The diminutive creature looked up at the Lion and two coal-like glows briefly lit the inside of its hood.

'No, it is too important,' said the primarch. 'Even if what you say is true, I cannot return to Caliban yet. Come what may, I have to stop Horus and Guilliman.'

The small figure bowed its head, and the Lion did the same, his whisper full of sorrow.

'Yes, even if it costs me my Legion.'

THE SERPENT
BENEATH

Rob Sanders

~ DRAMATIS PERSONAE ~

The XX Legion 'Alpha Legion'

ALPHARIUS/OMEGON	Twin Primarchs
SHEED RANKO	Captain, Lernaean Terminator Squad
URSINUS ECHION	Librarian
ARVAS JANIC	Commander, Tenebrae 9-50 Installation
GORAN SETEBOS	Sergeant, 3rd Company Squad 'Sigma'
ISIDOR	Legionnaire
ARKAN	Legionnaire
KRAIT	Legionnaire
VOLION	Legionnaire
BRAXUS	Legionnaire
ZANTINE	Legionnaire
CHARMIAN	Legionnaire
VERMES	Legionnaire
TARQUISS	Legionnaire

Imperial Personae

VOLKERN AUGURAMUS	Mechanicum Artisan Empyr
GRESSELDA VYM	Witchseeker Pursuivant, Brazen Sabre Cadre
MANDROCLIDAS	Strategarch, Geno Seven-Sixty Spartocid

Non-Imperial Personae

XALMAGUNDI	'Calamity', Soulfuel, Witchbreed

ALPHA

'EVERYTHING PROCEEDS IN accordance with the primarch's wishes, my lord.'

'And yet, I am uneasy,' replied Omegon. The mighty warrior wandered the darkened oratorium, his attention moving slickly between schematics on the walls and data-slates on the round table at its centre. Ursinus Echion stood before him only as a hololithic ghost. 'The Tenebrae 9-50 array is a tactical priority, brother. Much relies upon the technology's continued operation.'

He seated himself in one of the chamber's thrones. He rested his elbows on the armrests, and steepled his fingers pensively. 'You understand my concerns?'

'Of course, Lord Omegon,' the pellucid Echion replied.

Omegon remained thoughtful. Echion no longer wore the robes of the Librarius, instead opting for the plain attire of a company legionnaire. As one of the Legion's senior psykers, he had been an obvious choice to oversee the operation of the new empyreal technology, even if his status as a Librarian had remained a secret.

'You understand my concerns,' Omegon repeated, 'but do you share them?'

329

He watched a shimmer of doubt cross the Librarian's hololithic face. The temptation to lie. The decision not to.

'The Pylon Array was constructed precisely to specification,' Echion admitted. 'It is operating satisfactorily.'

'Speak your mind,' Omegon told him, 'as all of our calling are encouraged to do.'

'This technology is as ancient as it is alien,' Echion said, at length. 'If the designs for its construction and the orders to realise the project had not come from Alpharius himself, I would have thought the endeavour... misguided.'

'Your vigilance and mistrust serve your Legion well,' Omegon assured him. 'I have as much distaste for the xenos and their despicable ways as you, brother. But the hydra strikes with many heads, and we must indulge variety over prejudice, however natural such aversion might be. You know this, Echion.'

'Of course, Lord Omegon.'

'And as you said, it is the primarch's wish.'

'Yes.'

'Yet you are right to be cautious. Are you experiencing any difficulties?' he asked.

Again, Echion balanced honesty against prudence, against the prudence of honesty.

'From time to time we experience problems acquiring psyker slave-stock – on occasion this has brought us into conflict with the Sisters of Silence and their Black Ships. Nothing my legionnaires can't handle, of course.'

'Does it trouble you, brother? Trading in your own kind, thus?'

Echion considered his answer. 'The technology is... demanding. We all have our part to play. My kind, as you call them, must play theirs just as the Legion plays its own.'

'Quite,' Omegon agreed. 'Anything else? What of our allies?'

'The Geno Seven-Sixty Spartocid make restless sentinels but they carry out their duties peerlessly. The Mechanicum...' The Librarian paused. 'Artisan Empyr Auguramus is a *difficult* man. I monitor the Pylon Array's operation but he is responsible for its maintenance. He is unnecessarily harsh with the slave-stock and interprets his directives – how might one say? – creatively. I suspect he knows more about the technology's workings than he or his people let on.'

'That sounds like a problem.'

'He knows he is essential to the Tenebrae operation, so he takes liberties. It's probably me. I just don't like him.'

'A man would be ill-advised to take liberties with the Alpha Legion,' Omegon said coolly. He was out of the throne and back to pacing the oratorium. 'Master Echion, your work on Tenebrae has been outstanding but I want it to remain that way. I feel you would benefit from a fresh pair of eyes, to look to your interests.'

'If you feel that is necessary, my lord,' Echion replied. 'Do you have intelligence placing the operation in any jeopardy?'

'Not directly, but our allies and enemies alike have learned much from us. We do not only have to guard against the Emperor's spies in our midst; the Warmaster, too, has his fiendish ways. We should *never* underestimate the threat of the xenos and then, of course, we must keep our own friends faithful. Operatives can be bought, but those that share our path can also lose their way.'

'Of course.'

'That is why I must ask you to send me encrypted specifications for the Tenebrae base's security and defences,' Omegon continued.

Echion raised an eyebrow. 'Commander Janic is in charge of base security–'

'Then I'll need them from him. Schematics for the installation, the full designation of troops at your disposal and details of garrison rotations. That should get us started.'

Echion nodded. 'What do you intend to do with such information, my lord, if you don't mind my asking?'

'It will guide me in the best ways to serve you, Master Echion. It will help me decide where the vulnerabilities lie, and what other resources I can put at your disposal to ensure the continued, smooth operation of this most important of Legion projects.'

'I thank you for your concern and attentions, Lord Omegon.'

The primarch was standing by the thick transpari-steel of the lancet port. He stared out at the void – cold, empty and eternal.

'And yet I feel there is something else,' he said, absently. 'Something you have yet to confide, brother. Something beyond these mortal concerns.' He turned, noting Echion's look of uncertainty. 'Perhaps your gift has given you some special insight, something that brings you unhappiness.'

The Librarian lowered his head slightly.

'Might I have permission to speak freely, sir?'

Omegon continued to stare out into deep space. 'Always.'

'About the Pylon Array. The aether is in a state of calmness that I have never known. I reach out across it with my mind and my thoughts travel far, like a stone bounced across the glassy surface of a still pool.'

'Continue, brother.'

'I have always suffered a touch of the sight. What the Chief Librarian used to call a "foreboding". Useful in the chaos of battle – momentary glimpses of blades before they strike and las-bolts before they are sent my way.'

'You have prognostic abilities,' Omegon confirmed tightly.

'Yes, my lord,' Echion said.

'Enhanced in the presence of this xenos abomination?'

Echion was careful with his words: 'Flowing more freely, from a becalmed source.'

'And what do you see?'

'The future, my lord. Terrible and true.'

'Your own?' Omegon asked.

'The Legion's.'

'And...?'

'I fear we have taken a wrong turn, my lord,' the Librarian said with a pained expression. 'Or that we soon will. Our current path takes us to a dark place.'

Omegon nodded. He understood all too well what Echion was saying.

'Have you spoken of this to anyone else?' Omegon asked.

'Of course not,' Echion replied. 'The Librarius was formally disbanded, but for the requirements of specific missions and assignments. The legionnaires under my command are not aware of my gift.'

'What about your former master, the Chief Librarian?'

'No. I confide only in you, Lord Omegon.'

'And I am listening, brother. I do not doubt your capabilities, enhanced under these special circumstances. I fear, however, that you glimpse the journey and know not the destination. Trust in this: there are many futures, many eventualities, many paths that the Alpha Legion might take. It is our enemies' failing to see only what is presented to them in plain terms. Their undoing is to be blind to our myriad methods. Let us not make the same mistake. You can rest assured that Alpharius knows the darkness you have witnessed and has seen the light beyond. If we stay true to one another, to the purpose for which we were all created and to the principles upon which our Legion was founded – we will find the light together. We will achieve enlightenment. We will secure the ultimate victory.'

Echion bowed his head. 'I thank you for your confidences, my lord.'

'And yours, Master Echion. I shall expect Commander Janic's triple-coded transmission shortly. Now, if you'll excuse me, I have matters of equal gravity to attend to.'

'Of course. Hydra Dominatus, Lord Omegon.'

'Hydra Dominatus.'

The hololithic display crackled to a static miasma and then blinked into nothingness above the display tablet. Omegon stood framed by the deep darkness of the lancet port.

A voice came from the shadows. 'He's going to be a problem.'

Sheed Ranko emerged from the rear of the chamber, and strode around the breadth of the table. He was a hulking warrior – almost as big as Omegon himself – and captain of the Lernaean Terminator squad, and master of the strike cruiser *Upsilon*. An honoured veteran and gifted tactician, he had been at the twin primarchs' collective side since the Legion's first irregular conquests of the Great Crusade. 'I mean it,' he said again. 'Echion's going to be a problem.'

'Or the solution to one,' Omegon mused. Ranko joined him by the viewing port.

'As much as I enjoy sitting in on your status reports,' the captain said, 'I presume you grace the *Upsilon* with your presence because you need something.'

Omegon gave him a thin smile. 'A favour. The advice of an old friend. Nothing you haven't done for me a thousand times before.'

'I serve your interests,' Ranko told him, taking a throne at the obsidian table and indicating for the primarch to do the same.

'And I the Legion's, captain.'

'Where's Alpharius?'

'Returning from council with the Warmaster,' Omegon told him honestly. 'He's assembling the fleet. I expect the *Upsilon* will receive her orders soon.'

'You are here on his behalf?' Ranko asked.

'In his interests, yes.'

'Then what can I do for you both, and the Legion?'

'Before I tell you, I need you to understand something, Sheed,' Omegon said, fixing the veteran's gaze. 'Legion operations always require a certain degree of secrecy and discretion.'

'Yes.'

'This goes far beyond that,' Omegon said simply.

'Fair enough,' Ranko replied, intrigued. 'Want to tell an old friend why?'

'I'm mounting a sensitive operation.'

'All Alpha Legion operations are sensitive.'

'And none more so,' Omegon spoke in hushed tones, 'than when you are infiltrating *your own* Legion.'

Ranko stared grimly at him.

'No one knows the Legion like you,' the primarch continued. 'No one has operational experience across as many theatres. You've seen many of them prosecute their duty under fire. All Alpha Legionnaires are exceptional, but I need legionnaires not only of singular talent but also of a very specific disposition. It's going to get... *confusing*.'

'You want recommendations.' Ranko said, matter-of-factly. Gone was the warrior wit and the pleasure of seeing an old friend. This was something else entirely. 'It would help if I knew a few details of the operation, so I can gauge exactly what it is you need.'

'I'll have them shortly,' Omegon replied.

Ranko looked from the primarch to the hololithic tablet, and back to Omegon again.

'You're going to hit the Tenebrae installation?'

Omegon nodded. 'My informants and astrotelepathic intercepts have detected a leak.'

'Within the Legion?'

'Yes. Sensitive data and information relating to the placement of Alpha Legionnaires and operatives, on both sides of the conflict.'

'I don't believe it,' Ranko said. 'I mean, I do, obviously. But how is this possible?'

'This is a civil war,' Omegon reminded him. 'There are those placed among the Legions loyal to the Emperor who secretly supply the Warmaster with intelligence and appropriated materiel. Why not the other way round?'

Ranko continued to marvel in disappointment and disbelief. 'Because this is the Alpha Legion, lord.'

'A fact of which I am painfully aware,' the primarch sighed. 'I have been monitoring the situation, of course, in the hope that the leak could be identified and neutralised. That was until Alpharius's own safety was almost compromised.'

'Alpharius?'

'A rendezvous from which he had to promptly withdraw,' Omegon said. 'Whoever they were, whether they fought for the Emperor or the Warmaster... they could have taken my brother right then and there.'

'And you traced it back to Tenebrae?'

'A partially decrypted astrotelepathic message, originating from the base,' Omegon confirmed. 'Times and movements. They knew exactly where and when to strike.'

'Echion, then.'

'Possibly. The Octiss System. It's one of the few outlying regions uncompromised by warp storms. You heard him yourself – the Pylon Array calms the immaterium. An astrotelepathic message might reach Ancient Terra from there.'

'How is Alpharius taking it?' Ranko asked.

'Spitting venom, as you might expect. We have no time to investigate. The war moves apace. We do not have the luxury of tracking this back to an enemy sponsor, not when even our attempt to do is likely to be reported. Tenebrae is compromised. It must be destroyed – leak and all – before knowledge of the array or even the installation itself falls into the hands of another Legion.

Ranko placed a hand upon the table. 'You need legion-naires, then, who can infiltrate an Alpha Legion base and will not question the order to kill their brothers. Many of whom they will know to be innocent.'

'Yes.'

The captain paused for a moment, soaking up the enormity of the task.

'Then you need Goran Setebos – Sigma Squad, 3rd Company. His team were responsible for hitting the matrix outpost on Oblonski's World. Setebos is pretty cold, even for the Legion, but if it's victory over every-thing else, then he will do what needs to be done.'

'Where is he currently deployed?'

'Running interference on the 915th Expeditionary Fleet, I believe.'

'Thank you, Sheed,' Omegon said.

'You're also going to need a psyker,' the captain con-tinued, 'and you can't just pull one from the Legion – in all likelihood, Ursinus Echion will have had some role in their training.'

'An operative then?'

Ranko shrugged. 'The question is, who? To go up against Echion, you are going to need someone really special. The problem is, the more special they are, the more dangerous they are to everyone else.'

'You don't always have to fight fire with fire,' Omegon muttered, then seemed to reconsider. 'No readers. No tele-paths. There's problem enough with leaked information.'

'Agreed.'

'You have a suggestion?' the primarch asked.

'Perhaps,' Ranko said. 'We've been decoding trans-missions from the Black Ships that Echion mentioned. The same name keeps cropping up. Successive Sisters of Silence cadres have failed to capture a witchbreed called Xalmagundi on the hive world of Drusilla.'

Omegon nodded. 'Sounds promising. Any other advice?'

'Echion and Commander Janic are going to have that installation wrapped up tight,' the captain insisted. 'You're going to need someone on the inside.'

'I already have a candidate in mind,' the primarch assured him.

Ranko nodded.

'Has it really come to this? Our own Legion?'

'With treachery in our midst, we cannot falter,' Omegon said. 'Traitors, wherever they are found, must be dealt with decisively. Sacrifices must be made.'

Omegon crossed the oratorium and took a pair of chalices from a tray. He offered one to Ranko. 'Thank you for your assistance with this, old friend. There are few to whom I could turn with this.'

'At your service, always,' the captain said, raising the chalice for a toast. 'To mission success, and to necessary sacrifices.'

The pair drank. Ranko pulled the rim from his lips thoughtfully. He found himself looking down into the depths of the chalice.

'You know what that is?' Omegon asked.

'Yes, my lord,' the captain answered after a moment.

'Then you know what it is that I ask of you.'

Ranko downed the rest. 'What you ask of us all,' the captain said. 'Everything.'

BETA

THE PLANET WAS slowly turning itself inside out, though
Phemus IV had been quietly raging for millennia. A
crepuscular ball of igneous rock and soot storms, it was
covered in a rash of volcanic eruptions. Cracked through
with glowing fractures, it resembled a celestial bauble
that had been dropped and was about to shatter.

The only creatures to make their homes in the Phemu-
sian nightmare were migrant tribes of greenskins that
routinely roamed the lava-dashed landscape in order
to avoid seasonal eruptions. Sergeant Goran Setebos
only knew these tribes by the banners they carried and
the crude symbols painted on their corrugated hovels.
Squad Sigma had ascribed names to the tribes based
upon the scrawled iconography: the Spumers; the Green
Devils; the Scorchers; the Magmatusks; the Fireball Clan.

For the past month, the Alpha Legionnaires had been
engaged in a war by proxy. They had not killed a single
greenskin or even discharged a single round from their
soot-smeared bolters. They were shadowing a far more
dangerous prey across the volcanic highlands, razorb-
lade canyons and dismal basalt plains.

The V Legion.

The Khan's swift savages. The infamous White Scars.

Black rock crumbled in Setebos's grasp. If his palm hadn't been protected by the ceramite of his gauntlet, the remaining shard of glassy rock would have pierced straight through. The sergeant was clinging to a rockface, punching handholds and toe-picking his way up the midnight crag. Beneath him, the nine other members of Squad Sigma followed up through his improvised purchase points. Glooping beside them was a sluggish lava fall, a slow-moving torrent of molten rock that bathed the armoured legionnaires in the perpetual heat of a furnace.

At the top of the escarpment, Setebos unlocked his bolter from his belt and crunched through the gravel of a volcanic crater. Magma had eaten through the rim to create the falls and Setebos chose his footing carefully around the bubbling margins. One by one, the Alpha Legionnaires made their way over to the far side of the crater, their grimy plate glinting in the fiery glow.

'This looks good,' he said. 'Isidor.'

Legionnaire Isidor consulted a scuffed and scorched data-slate, turning it and his armoured form around to match their most recent relief maps with the surrounding topography. He gestured east with an outstretched gauntlet.

'If the Fireballs haven't started moving by now,' he announced, 'this should light a fire under their monstrous arses.' He handed the slate to Vermes, who counter-checked his cartography.

'This channel should then join with the one from this morning,' Setebos murmured.

'Affirmative.'

The whole squad remembered all too well the channel they had crossed with some difficulty a few hours before. Braxus had almost pitched into the hellish river of molten rock.

Behind them, Krait had started to prepare a cache of seismic charges, which the legionnaire punched into the crater wall with his gauntlet. 'The greenskins in Quadrant Seven-Seventeen should be funnelled through to this gorge here, with little choice but to join the Magmatusks.'

'Unless they just attack them like the last lot did,' Braxus murmured.

'Always a possibility with orks,' Setebos agreed. 'Krait, are we ready?'

'Two more charges; ten more seconds.'

'Legionnaires, over the edge,' Setebos ordered.

Squad Sigma hauled themselves over the lip of the crater before skidding down through the grit and scree of the volcanic slope. The Alpha Legionnaires had been doing this for weeks, trekking across the infernal landscape and strategically setting their demolitions. Remaining an unseen and undetected presence, various covert teams like Sigma had frustrated the White Scars' hopes of a swift xenos extermination in the local systems, by manoeuvring the greenskin warrior tribes on Phemus IV into tactically superior strategic formations. By forcing the groups together and concentrating the greenskins in larger numbers, Setebos and his squad had succeeded in bogging the Khan's warriors down in countless meat-grinding engagements. The White Scars themselves could now only dream of racing over the open plateaus, fragmenting the tribes and cutting the orks to pieces, as was their wont.

'Sergeant!' Isidor hissed across the vox-link. 'Contacts!'

Making their ungainly way down the gorge at the foot of the slope was a ragged string of orks. They bore the crude iconography of the Fireball Clan and carried an assortment of mismatched weaponry. Some were wounded, suggesting that they were only a splinter group of a larger tribe that had been caught in some kind of ambush.

'Take cover,' Setebos ordered over the vox-link, 'and do not engage. I repeat, do not engage.'

As the legionnaires scrambled into less than desirable cover on the scree slope, the orks continued their wretched stomp up the ravine. Taking positions behind crags and boulders, the thick coating of ash on their plate went some way to disguise the Space Marines from the xenos barbarians. Remaining completely still, Setebos – who was closest to the ravine floor – watched the monsters lope past, oblivious.

The rumble of distant eruptions was suddenly cut through by the high-pitched whine of engines, and looking back down the gorge, Setebos caught sight of three Imperial jetbikes rounding the volcano's flank. He had no idea how the White Scars kept their plate and vehicles so clean and white in the rain of ash and soot clouds.

The Scars tracked in on the column of orks – they had probably already been searching for them, Setebos reasoned. The Khan's hunters were not known for allowing their prey to escape. They leaned into the handlebars of their mounts and gunned the wailing engines, tearing up the gorge, trailing a cloud of soot in their wake.

Bolt-fire ripped up through the greenskins at the rear of the column, bringing the rest of the monsters into sudden and savage life, their brute weapons ready. The White Scars hammered through fully half of the beasts before accelerating overhead.

One patchwork monster swung its axe at one of the oncoming vehicles. The White Scar rider simply leaned out to one side, allowing the butcher's blade to pass harmlessly over his helmet.

Setebos watched the riders rocket away around the volcano base. It was classic V Legion tactics: the greenskins – normally so formidable as a sea of crude blades and blazing gunfire – were now scattered and grunting furiously with their weapons held high. Within moments the jetbikes were back, strafing the mindless creatures with more streams of bolt-fire.

Their fellows dropping about them in ragged heaps, the final two brutes roared at the swarthy sky. The first jetbike passed between them at high speed, prompting both to take optimistic swings. Predictably the second and third White Scars glided in after them, curved chainswords screaming as they cut the monsters down. With one greenskin's head hanging from his body by only a thread and the other clutching its spilling innards, the White Scars' work was done.

Turning and idling back up to the site of the massacre, the Scars dismounted. Slipping their heads out of their helmets, the Khan's warriors allowed the luxurious length of their hair and moustaches to fall freely, before drawing their short curved blades and stabbing at the fallen orks to ensure the monsters were truly dead.

Only one of the three, an eagle-eyed warrior indeed, caught sight of something amiss on the volcanoside. A shape that seemed out of place, perhaps? Stepping back to his bike he slipped a pair of magnoculars from the saddlebag and brought them up to his dark, piercing eyes. The White Scar would have called out, either to the armoured Alpha Legionnaire hiding on the rubble-strewn slope or more likely to avert his own brethren, but he could do neither with Setebos's blade at his throat and the Alpha Legion sergeant holding him by his hair.

Suddenly aware that they were under attack, the two remaining White Scars made for their jetbikes. The first saw Braxus coming for him – he snatched the length of his serrated chainblade from a sheath that ran the length of the mount, and with a harsh battle cry swung it back around in a whirling arc. Braxus was forced to abandon his tackle and slide down through the grit and onto his side, but the White Scar was swift to recover. Even so, Arkan and Charmian cannoned into him, one slamming into the Space Marine with his domed pauldron while the other went for the weapon.

Isidor was nowhere near the third White Scar by the time he reached his jetbike. Instead of going for his weapon, the Scar leapt and mounted the vehicle. The manoeuvre was accomplished with the grace and confidence of one born in the saddle, and before the Alpha Legionnaires could do anything the White Scar had leaned around and banked the accelerating vehicle back up the craggy gorge.

Setebos's blade slipped through his struggling prisoner's throat with ease.

'Isidor, jam his transmissions,' the sergeant barked, pointing with the bloodied tip of the knife. Isidor skidded around the two legionnaires still wrestling with their foe on the basalt and scrambled for the jetbike's comms.

'Got it!' he called.

Setebos watched the escaping jetbike streak for freedom. Zantine brought his bolter up, but the sergeant placed his ceramite palm on the weapon's barrel. There would be no convenient but cacophonous firefights, with the distinctive sound of reciprocal bolter fire betraying the presence of another Space Marine force on Phemus IV. As always, the Alpha Legion would remain unheard, unseen and unknown.

'Krait!'

'Yes, sergeant.'

'Now.'

The detonators fired. The seismic charges set in the crater wall blasted the igneous rock into glassy splinters. Rubble crashed down the volcanoside, bouncing and shattering as it rolled its way down into the ravine. The fleeing biker saw the danger. He tried to turn but there simply wasn't enough room. The Space Marine tucked to the side and slipped from his saddle, skidding and clattering through the volcanic shale in his armour plate. The jetbike struck the growing wall of shattered rock and tumbling debris, and became a brief nova of light, sound and twisted shrapnel.

Setebos saw the White Scar scrambling though the black gravel before getting to his feet. He ran with powered, determined steps, pulverising the grit under his boots.

The spilled magma was coming.

The explosion – designed to sound like any other violently erupting volcano – had opened the molten floodgates. A torrent of radiant death flowed down the slope towards the White Scar. The Alpha Legionnaires watched the lava swell eat up the incline and then flood the gorge, just as Krait and Isidor had intended.

The flow swamped the stricken Space Marine, knocking him from his feet and plunging him, shoulder and then face first, beneath the surface. The White Scar flailed only for a moment, his immaculate ceramite scorching, before sinking – backpack and all – beneath the slurping surface with a flare of powered discharge.

Charmian looked to his sergeant. 'Sir?'

There were three of them now, pinning the remaining White Scar face down against the ravine floor.

'Make it quick,' Setebos hissed, before directing the rest of the squad up a slightly more forgiving incline on the opposite slope.

The White Scar screamed furious insults at his captors but they did not last long; Charmian took the sides of the Space Marine's head in his powered gauntlets and twisted it violently to the side. There was a splintering crack, and the White Scar's resistance became a limp slump before the legionnaires released him.

As Squad Sigma made their way up the craggy slope, the gully behind them glowed. The disgorged river of molten destruction had replaced the site of the brief battle, scouring any evidence of the Alpha Legion's presence from the face of the planet.

'Hold.'

Setebos suddenly halted. The legionnaires held their positions, scanning the charred landscape for more greenskins.

'More Scars?' Isidor put to the sergeant, but Setebos was holding the side of his helmet with his gauntlet against the rumble of volcanic eruptions rolling across the tortured land.

After a moment, he turned to them once more.

'We're being recalled. Something special. I've been given extraction coordinates.'

Isidor nodded with approval, but the rest of them gave their sergeant only the blank optics of their helmets.

'Let's move. With any good fortune, we'll be off this rock within the hour.'

Operatus Five-Hydra: Elapsed Time Ω3/-633.19//DRU Drusilla Hive World – Hive Chorona

HER MOTHER HAD called her Xalmagundi. The undercaste called her Calamity, for the disasters she had brought down upon her people. The bitch off-worlders that came for her called Xalmagundi 'soulfuel' and 'witch-breed'. Her unnatural gift had killed them all.

Death had driven her topside. She had left the under-hive behind with the rubble and the bodies. As a young girl she had little idea how to control her deviant abilities; objects would move about her, seemingly of their own accord. Violently, if she was so disposed.

What started out as a trick to amaze the caste urchins soon carved horror into underhiver faces. Even amongst her own people in the Delve – where skin was ashen and untouched by the sun, where eyes were large and black, where the wretched eked an outcast's existence – she was an aberration. When her teenage tantrums brought quakes to the underworld, even her cavern-kin rejected her.

They drove her out with stories of her past. They told Xalmagundi of her horrific birth, and how as a screaming newborn she had broken her mother from within, shattering bones and rupturing organs. All with the cursed power of her unreasoning, infant mind.

Driven from cavern community to cavern community, Xalmagundi was a freak among freaks. Again the tears came to quench the loneliness but with them came anger and hatred. The benighted realm about her became a quake-stricken nightmare, and it seemed then that even the darkness shook. With tremors rippling through the fragile foundations of the hive, the world above came crashing down onto the world below.

That night, the Delve – home to the undercaste for longer than anyone could remember – became just another pulverised strata in the hive's long history.

She was hunted as she migrated spireward. The hive-quakes had been felt throughout the city and there were those who made it their business to know their unnatural origin. Xalmagundi learned to control her emotions and the telekinetic horror that sometimes came flooding with them. Her appearance, which many hivers found unsettling and horrid, still brought her to the attention of the authorities, but when they failed to bring her in and enough people had witnessed the devastating power of her gift, the off-worlders came.

Off-worlders with gifts of their own: a silent sisterhood, in whose mere presence Xalmagundi's more extreme abilities were nothing and under whose gaze it was agony to exist. She had heard that the Sisters had been sent by the Emperor himself, which their fine armour and weaponry indeed seemed to confirm. Xalmagundi could not conceive what the Emperor of Mankind would want with her. Having sent his mutes armed to the teeth, she could not think it was for any good reason.

The killing continued. Squad after squad of the Sisters hounded her through the hab-quarters and industri-scape of mill stacks, but all had failed to acquire their prey.

Xalmagundi stared into the fire. She watched the tongues of flame flicker and dance. Her camp had been some kind of villa once, the mansion-hab of an Imperial Army officer or palace official. The wind whistled through the dilapidated stonework and around crumbling furniture. The psyker pulled her ragged cloak tighter – she was used to the subterranean warmth of the underhive and the furnace-heated mills. The further spireward she travelled, the more biting the cold felt upon her thin, pale skin.

She had come to Spire Pentapolis precisely *because* it had been long abandoned. The Chorona Hive was so named because of the five minor spires that had grown up about the primary apex like a crown, but it had been decimated by a virulent contagion hundreds of years before. Every attempt to re-colonise the spire had resulted in a resurgence of the disease, and new measures required to quarantine and cleanse Pentapolis of its plagued inhabitants. So, the ghostspire now remained as a cautionary tale on the skyline – too large to demolish, too recent in the memory to embark upon the next inevitable attempt to repopulate and appropriate the precious space.

Xalmagundi rubbed at her temple. She had a headache. Perhaps she had been staring at the fire for too long…

No. Realisation shivered through her. The pain in her head had been subtle at first but had steadily grown: it felt like a knife, slowly slipping its way into her brain. She had felt that before.

There was no time to lose.

Xalmagundi leapt over the fire and sprinted through the derelict villa. She was light and lithe, but a short lifetime of being hunted had also made her fast and strong. She was not alone in the building – she was sure of that. This was confirmed a moment later when explosive lines of daylight shot through the thin walls of the villa, bolt-rounds spraying rockcrete fragments across the room. Xalmagundi willed herself on.

Her hunters had surrounded the building, moving up behind the villa walls. It now felt as though she had *six* knives embedded in her brain. The pain was excruciating, and through the crippling agony she couldn't find her way to the part of herself she usually relied upon in such circumstances. The part of her mind in which fear and frustration translated seamlessly into spontaneous, telekinetic destruction. All she could think to do was put one foot in front of another. She needed to get away. Not only to escape being blasted apart by boltfire, but also to get out of the sisters' overlapping influence.

The walls on either side of Xalmagundi erupted as two more hidden attackers unleashed their weapons at her. The villa had become a deathtrap, a nexus of criss-crossing gunfire – even as she ran, she felt the tug of stray rounds snatching at her trailing cloak.

As ruined masonry began to tumble to the floor, Xalmagundi's hunters were revealed: aurulent visions in plumed helmets, picked out in white and scarlet. They clutched their furious boltguns and chased Xalmagundi up the length of the villa.

She burst from the shadows and onto the stilted terrace beyond, and was blinded by the sudden daylight – as an underworlder, her large black eyes were hypersensitive to even Drusilla's meagre sun. She skidded to a stop, putting her slender hand out in front of her hooded face, and it dawned on her that this might have been the Sisters' plan all along. She was fast and agile but she couldn't outrun a bolt-round in the open. In the midst of battle, with masonry and gunfire searing through the air, her instinct had been to flee. Not a single projectile had managed to find her in the chaos and now she had hit the terrace, the bolter fire had ceased altogether. Xalmagundi couldn't help feeling that she had been corralled, in the same way the underhivers would beat their way through the tunnels, driving verminipedes into the waiting nets of their companions.

The sky roared above her. It was difficult to peer into the brightness-blotched heavens, but a carrier or shuttle of some kind hovered above the roof of the villa. As her vision cleared and acclimatised to the Drusillian day, she shielded her brow with the palm of one hand and saw the armed carrier bank for another pass. A silent Sister sat harnessed into an open doorway in the side of the shuttle – she wore a targeting helmet, and in her grip Xalmagundi could see the long barrel of some exotic rifle.

The psyker's lip wrinkled with fury. The Sisters of Silence would kill her if they had to, but would much rather tranquilise her like a dangerous animal, for the trip to their precious Emperor. Xalmagundi would not be bagged like some prize for a spireborn's wall.

Once again she was running, her bare feet thudding into the weathered stone of the terrace. She felt the other sisters behind her, encumbered by their armour but desperate to succeed where previous cadres had failed. The carrier had completed its turn and was bearing down on her – Xalmagundi could see the silhouette of the helmeted sniper, hanging out of the side of the shuttle. The fleeing psyker peeled off suddenly to the right, allowing several rifle shots to snap off the stone and putting the sniper on the wrong side of the carrier to take another.

Xalmagundi ran an assault course of decaying architecture; she hurdled a decorative wall, before diving through the gap left by several smashed and missing balusters. The mouldering architecture provided her with cover, but more importantly it slowed the armoured Sisters of Silence who had to clamber over the obstacles with their heavier wargear. Rolling, she pushed herself back up onto her feet and sprinted for the terrace edge.

The carrier dropped to one side, bringing it level with the stilted platform, and Xalmagundi could feel the sniper lining up her shot. She could also feel something else – the relief of knives being retracted, bit by bit and one by one from her stinging mind. She was drawing away from the Sisters. Xalmagundi didn't want to risk looking back.

Every moment counted. Every step counted. The last step counted the most.

Xalmagundi launched herself from the edge of the stilted terrace and out into the nothingness beyond. Her hood fell back and her cloak began to flap about her, and she felt the sniper's rushed shot slice past her ear. Xalmagundi's arms started to swing and her legs worked the air as the psyker's slender body hurtled downwards, past the haphazard architecture of Spire Pentapolis. Below her was the mountainous accretion of Hive Chorona, the smog-cloaked industrial powerhouse from which the crown of minor spires sprang. It was coming up fast to meet her.

Looking up, Xalmagundi watched the carrier dive after her. The Sisters stood on the precipice of the terrace, watching in silence as the psyker fell to her death. As she tumbled away from them she felt something return within her, as though an amputated limb had been restored to her in full working order.

She closed her eyes and willed disaster.

The south face of the spire trembled. The agglomerate architecture shuddered from top to bottom, blasting a shower of rockcrete, torn girders and gargoylesque masonry chunks into the open air. Like a pressure building down the shaft of the spire, the ripple of destruction vaulted debris and colossal rafts of architecture out across the sky with the force of a titanic explosion. Far above her now, the terrace buckled and fell.

Xalmagundi angled her descent and hit the first spinning chunk like a cat, only to slip from its smooth surface moments later and tumble away. Clawing her way onto another she was frustrated by a third colossal brace of rubble striking her temporary platform, smashing it into pieces beneath her and forcing Xalmagundi to shear it in two with her mind.

Snatching her way onto the warped length of a structural column, the psyker allowed herself a moment to focus on the retreating carrier and the flailing bodies of Sisters tumbling to their deaths amongst the collapsed architecture. The psyker fell with the destruction for a few moments before latching onto the busy flourishes of a passing wall section, and held on for her life. She had been fortunate – her gift gave her extraordinary telekinetic power. It did not, however, lend her any extraordinary reflexes, and any one of the crashing shards of rock and metal could crush her instantly, or cave in her fragile skull in a moment of inattention.

Below, Xalmagundi could see the havoc she had unleashed. The base of the ghostspire was being buried in the shattered remains of the collapsed south face, and a cloud of dust was billowing up to meet her. As she plummeted down through the haze, the psyker focused her mind, concentrating on slowing the runaway mass of the great object. Her face twisted into an ugly snarl as she willed the beast into a gentler descent. Other colossal blocks of stone thundered past, only to shatter against the growing rubble-mountain at the foot of the spire.

The psyker's mind ached with the effort.

Despite Xalmagundi's unnatural influence, the gigantic fragment still struck with unimaginable force, catapulting the psyker down onto the rockcrete platform protruding from the side of a dormant smokestack. Incredibly, she landed on her feet but immediately felt something give in her leg, shot through with white-hot pain.

She tumbled into a roll that took her down the platform's steps and the world became a sickening kaleidoscope. Beyond that, all she knew was the thunderous white noise of falling masonry.

The world suddenly stopped turning; a rusted metal landing had brought her to an abrupt halt. Her head was gashed in several places and her arm hung numbly at her side. All she wanted to do was stay down and die.

Looking back up the steps she saw an enormous shard of buckled rockcrete crash through the platform as though it were paper, followed by a whipping tangle of support cables that tore at the staircase. She forced herself up, but immediately slipped back onto her rump with a cry of pain – her leg was shattered, and bone was protruding from the flesh in several places. Trying her best to focus on the leg and ignore the various other agonies competing for her attention, she gritted her teeth and straightened the bones, providing a telekinetic splint for the smashed limb. Sharp fragments retracted back within the torn muscle, making it at least possible to struggle to her feet.

Half hobbling, half tumbling, she made her way downwards through the thick, choking dust as the last of the southern spireface found its way to earth. Soon she reached the murk of a manufactorum dragway, though she could see barely a metre in front of her face.

Limping horribly through the miasma, the psyker began hacking and coughing. The air was thick with powdered stone and several times Xalmagundi had to stop to choke up stringy spittle laced with grit. Her face was pasted with clots of fresh blood.

The post-catastrophic silence was suddenly broken by the rhythmic crash of rotor-cannons, and the murk swirled as something unseen passed overhead. The cannonfire hammered up the street, creating two parallel troughs of mangled rockcrete.

Xalmagundi half-fell into a littered alcove, allowing the churning gunfire to continue up the dragway towards the smokestack. The remaining Sisters were clearly no longer interested in taking her alive. She stared up through the swirling dust, searching for the armed carrier; if she could spot it then she could use her power to fling the winged menace into the ruined face of the Chorona Spire. But the sky was just a blanket of shadow, and she saw nothing.

As the cannons ceased, Xalmagundi thought it best to change her position and hobbled out onto the ploughed-up dragway, but froze as she encountered a wall of dark silhouettes blocking her path.

She squinted and tensed, ready to bring the adjoining manufactorum down upon the shadowy forms. Their outlines radiated violent intent; they were hulking and armoured, and like the sisterhood cadre they carried boltguns. They fixed on the psyker with the haunted lenses of their helmets.

An unarmed giant stepped forward from the imposing ranks.

'Xalmagundi?'

The psyker was stunned to hear her name come from the huge warrior. As the dust began to clear between them she recognised them as a host of the Emperor's Angels. Like everyone else on Drusilla, she had only seen such legends crafted in stone, but the plate and the weaponry were unmistakable.

The leader halted. His ceramite creaked. She knew he had sensed her influence, the loose telekinetic embrace in which she now held his armoured form. The Emperor could send who he wanted! Xalmagundi would not be taken! She would crush the legendary warriors inside their battle plate like an invisible fist around an empty rations can.

'How do you know me?' she spat.

'Xalmagundi, my name is Sheed Ranko,' the voice came again, deep and measured. 'I assure you, we mean you no harm,'

'Ratcrap,' she returned, watching him for any signs of movement. She ran her gaze down the motionless line of Angels. Each held himself and his weapon casually, as i waiting for something. Not a single barrel was aimed at the psyker. Xalmagundi narrowed her grit-flecked eyes – this oddness only served to stoke her suspicions further.

'Allow me to demonstrate,' the giant announced. 'Sergeant, her pursuers?'

Behind the leader, another Angel brought up his weapon's scope to further enhance his optics, and sighted into the murky sky.

'The Sisters of Silence,' the sergeant hissed. 'Brazen Sabre Cadre, out of the Black Ship *Somnus*. Pursuivant Gresselda Vym. Inbound.'

'Bring them down,' Ranko commanded.

Another Angel broke ranks and brought up the bulk of a missile launcher onto his armoured shoulder. He pointed the weapon up into the sky and stared through a targeter of his own.

'Acquisition?' Ranko asked. 'Do you have the shot?'

'I have it.'

'Then take it, brother.'

Xalmagundi flinched as the missile blazed up into the sky and disappeared, before the flash of an unseen explosion ripped through the obscurity like sheet lightning. Within moments the wreck of the carrier fell from the heavens, belching a trail of black smoke and falling debris. The pilot was desperately trying to regain some control but the craft was a smashed ruin – it cut through a tall metal chimney before passing over their heads and crashing into the facade of the manufactorum. Its disappearance in the dust-choked distance was swiftly followed by a further explosion, and the sounds of hull shrapnel ringing off the rockcrete walls.

Xalmagundi almost faltered and had to reach out to steady herself. She brought her attention back to the Angel who called himself Sheed Ranko.

'Sergeant,' he said, not taking his glowering optics from the psyker. 'Take two legionnaires and finish off any remaining Sisters.'

The Angel left the wall of shadow with two of his hulk-ing comrades, but Ranko addressed her again. 'Aren't you tired of being hunted?'

'I can take care of myself,' the psyker shot back, savagely.

'Prove it,' Ranko challenged her.

Xalmagundi's lip curled. She turned and looked up at the pinnacle of the Chorona Spire, just beginning to emerge from the great bank of dust.

Her eyes narrowed. Her pupils became stabbing points of darkness.

The derelict spire gave a thundercrack of internal agony. The pinnacle began to shake as a deep rumble built from within the accreted nightmare of the ghost-spire's already weakened foundations, and loose chips of stone shook around their feet.

Xalmagundi's jaw became taut with destructive desire.

The pinnacle suddenly disappeared; like an unfor-tunate underworlder in a sinkhole, the spire dropped down below the haze.

Every living soul within fifty kilometres would have heard the pulverising boom of successive floors and con-structs falling in on themselves. The spire was collapsing straight down – like a black hole, some irresistible gravi-tational force was dragging an avalanche of girders, buttresses and crumbling stone downwards through the guts of the structure. As it fell inwards upon itself, the colossal city-spire sent a cloud of dust and debris into the sky. The sound was excruciating: shearing metal; ancient stone cracked asunder; the ear-bleeding roar of the spire's sheer mass crashing down into the hive below.

Xalmagundi stood with the Emperor's Angels as the collapsing agglomeration drove a blizzard of ancient dust and grit down the narrow dragway. Ranko asked for the magnoculars. He brought them up to survey the new mountain of scrap and rubble Xalmagundi had created from the ancient spire, just with the power of her mind.

'My word, it seems you *can* take care of yourself,' Ranko said to her, obviously impressed. 'Can you also take care of other things for other people, I wonder?'

Operatus Five-Hydra: Elapsed Time Ω2/-417.85//SSA San Sabrinus – De Sota City

OMEGON WAS ONE amongst many.

The primarch stood in the hustle and bustle of common humanity. Sweaty faces leered, shoulders barged past. Strangers manhandled him in an attempt to get by on the crowded esplanade, but they could not and would not know that they were in the presence of a galactic prince – a son of the Emperor, a lord amongst Angels.

He would have cut an imposing figure on the crowded thoroughfare. Instead the citizens of De Sota City saw one of their own, a miserable specimen of unimportance: a trademonger or cartelier, presented in hololithic semblance. The amulet field generator concealed upon his person disguised the perfection of his true form, cloaking him in the vague impression of mortal mediocrity.

Casting a casual glance across the teeming esplanade, Omegon spotted several more examples of unexceptional humanity: a slavedrover here, a merchantman's purser there, and a trafficker keeping a low profile. They were all his Alpha Legionnaires, members of Effrit stealth squad in a similar disguise to his own, with others further up and down the thoroughfare.

It wasn't difficult to blend in. De Sota City was like a swarming emporium, where everything was for sale and everyone was selling something. Some, it seemed, had come to sell their souls, and it was one such individual that had brought Omegon to San Sabrinus.

The esplanade was one of many that served the crowded galleria. Dirty tapestries hung from the buildings like decorative sashes; stained sheet roofing gave the avenue the feeling of being inside a tent, while tattered drapery rippled gently in the breeze. It housed the shabby offices of various off-world brokers, including many illegal and unlicensed operations, but that did not stop hordes of street vendors from choking up the thoroughfare with their wares and constant calling. Omegon had been feigning interest in one such parasite for the last few minutes, offering the gabbling vendor a little local currency to keep him interested, despite the fact that he had no idea what the pitcher was selling – the man was draped in small cages and carried a rod and reel of some kind.

Over the vendor's bobbing shoulder and between excitable hands that thrust the tiny cages at Omegon's face for inspection, he spotted their mark – moving with self-importance up the thoroughfare was a Mechanicum artisan. His robes were broad, the deep red of the Martian priesthood, and his ample shoulders supported a busy cogitator bank. The illuminated hood hid a fat face that was flesh-plugged with dirty lines and needles. His lips had long since been sewn together, but a vox-unit hung around his almost non-existent neck; from this he would routinely snatch a trailing microvox and place it against one of his many chins.

This was the infamous Volkern Auguramus: Artisan Empyr, and secret Alpha Legion operative.

Keeping him in sight, Omegon tracked the artisan up the esplanade. Very few vendors bothered Auguramus, since he was flanked by four demi-clawed combat servitors. Grabbing the cage vendor by the face and pushing him out of his path, the primarch slipped into the crowd. Omegon watched as two of his disguised legionnaires made a pass through the throng from the opposite direction.

Auguramus stopped outside an off-world broker's office. Omegon walked past as his quarry looked furtively about before entering, accompanied by one of his dead-eyed drones.

Taking positions a little way up the esplanade and making rotating passes, the Alpha Legionnaires waited for him to re-emerge. When he eventually did he was in an apparent hurry, his cybernetic thugs clearing a path for him through the throng.

'Effrit Seven – the broker,' Omegon said quietly into his vox-bead.

Leaving his subordinate to investigate the artisan's dealings, Omegon and the rest stuck with Auguramus through the lower galleria.

'Looks like he's heading for the starport.' That was Effrit Two. 'We're going to have to take him soon. It's all gallerias from here on in. Very public.'

'Effrit Seven,' Omegon said in a low voice. 'What have you got?'

'A consignment for twenty thousand decatonnes of stone from a dead-world quarry in the Beta Ghastri system, to be transported by talon brig to Parabellus. That's Quall sub-sector.'

'What kind of stone?' Omegon asked surreptitiously.

'Serebite. Inert feldsparic silica. Sparse and precious, according to the consignment slate. A lot of coin must have changed hands.'

Omegon recognised the name and, by extension, its purpose.

'Let's take him,' Omegon announced over an open channel.

Auguramus continued his determined march, his clawed servitors never leaving his side, always maintaining the same equidistant four-point configuration around him. Omegon's legionnaires began to make increasingly regular passes, with the primarch himself maintaining a deliberately less than artful tail. Before long the artisan started to notice the same faces in the crowd. His gaze began to dart around as he scanned the masses for suspicious activity – he doubled as an operative for the Alpha Legion, and so understood the dynamics and principle of a tail. What Auguramus didn't understand was that in this case his Alpha Legion tail was making its presence painfully obvious.

As the artisan hurried across the galleria, Omegon initiated the second stage of the operation: Alpha Legionnaires in their amulet-field disguises began making crossing passes at the target. Auguramus had the measure of those following him now and recognised many of their faces, but by moving across the galleria to avoid them against the flow of the multitude, his servitors soon found it difficult to clear their master's path.

As members of Effrit approached each other in the crowd, the legionnaires brushed shoulders and exchanged their hololithic semblances. With their amulets changing hands in choreographed patterns, it would be far more difficult for the mark to keep track of his pursuers.

Auguramus stared into the crowds, probably on the lookout for assassins or grab-teams. His eyes routinely returned to Omegon, who was maintaining a steady pace and swiftly convincing the man that he was about to be intercepted.

'We have a boulemart coming up,' Effrit Four hissed over the open channel.

'Move in,' Omegon said. This time he was not careful about how he spoke, and Auguramus – who had been peering above the heads of the crowd at him – saw the stranger's lips give the order.

Panicked, the artisan moved with his servitor guard over to the side of the galleria. Omegon watched him sidle over to the boulemarts leading off the main esplanade, and felt his prey's temptation to run building into irresistible paranoia.

Four members of Effrit closed in on Auguramus from different directions, in plain sight, but Omegon saw the surprise evident on the artisan's face as one by one his pursuers disappeared. Each one had inexplicably vanished in the crowd.

Spinning around, Auguramus's surprise was replaced by horror as he found himself alone. His servitors were no longer there to protect him.

In their place were the four strangers who had been approaching, now staring silently. Auguramus cast about for any chance of escape. He found only more faces that he had come to recognise in the crowd, and Omegon swiftly bringing up the rear. It was too much for the poor man.

'Stay away from me!' he blurted before bolting for the boulemart – a narrow arcade lined with stalls and porch bazaars. Omegon watched him blunder straight through a rag curtain and past a handful of bewildered onlookers.

The servitors stood, silently obeying their master's last command. Omegon had simply arranged for the closing legionnaires to plant their field generators on the bodyguards as they passed, before disappearing back into the multitude. Auguramus believed that they had abandoned him and had been replaced by members of a grab-team when, unwittingly, he had dismissed and mindlocked them.

Tearing aside the curtain, Omegon found two disguised Effrit squad members holding the artisan in a porchway. They stood either side of the heavyset man, their short blades nestling in his folds of neckflesh, and one also held the microvox to Auguramus's throat.

Omegon approached with predatory composure. Auguramus instantly recognised him as the shadow that had been following him through the mercantile world masses.

'You're making a big mistake,' he yelled at Omegon. 'I have influence with the feared and the powerful. You couldn't even imagine…'

Omegon took the field generator from his belt and dialled down through the hololithic frequencies. The image of a De Sotan nobody shimmered and warped

until it finally fizzled away to the reality it concealed –
an armed Alpha Legionnaire, the Legion insignia upon
his chest. The other two warriors did the same.

Auguramus stared wide-eyed at his sponsors. He had
no words or pleas for such a turn of events.

'Oh, I think I *might* be able to imagine, Artisan Empyr,'
Omegon said. 'I too have influence with the feared and
the powerful. They trust you with their secrets: they wish
to know why you are trading them with the rest of the
Imperium.'

Auguramus found it difficult to catch his breath. Omegon's reveal had been shocking enough, but he struggled
to speak with two blades resting at his throat like a pair
of shears.

'I'm not… selling anything…' Auguramus managed.

'I know, Artisan Empyr,' Omegon told him. 'You're
buying. And you're doing what you do best – you are
building. Except you're not building for us. You're building for yourself.'

'Did Master Echion send you?'

'Master Echion had his suspicions, but no.'

'What do you want?' Auguramus gasped.

'I want you to restrict your talents to the wishes of your
sponsors.'

'But the technology is… remarkable. Potentially even
superior to the devices on Perditus.'

'I know,' Omegon replied. 'It was I who supplied you
with the specifications and the original materials.'

'It is clearly xenos in origin. Ancient. Where did you–'

'Where I acquire my information is my concern. Now,
if you test my patience again with another ill-advised
question, I'll take your head from your shoulders and
leave your fat carcass dumped in an alley.'

Auguramus restricted his response to a fearful nod.

'You are gifted among even your kind,' the primarch
admitted. 'That is why we came to you. That is why we
took you into our trust. Do not make the mistake of

thinking you were the only prospect. There are others who can still deliver what we need.'

Again, a nod of pale-faced dread.

'Artisan Empyr,' Omegon said, 'why are you building a replica of the Tenebrae Pylon Array on the agri-world of Parabellus?'

'The technology,' Auguramus told him delicately, '– alien though it may be – could revolutionise the Imperium. It could secure our astrotelepathic network and the immeteorology of our trade routes.'

'Open your eyes. The galaxy doesn't need revolution,' Omegon told him. 'It suffers a little too much from that already. You're securing the Warmaster's Imperium before he has even won it. I don't care if your intentions were noble – an operative of the Alpha Legion cannot expect to betray his masters and live long afterwards.'

'D-d-don't kill me, please...' Auguramus begged. 'I can still be useful...'

Omegon leant in with an ominous intimacy. 'We are the Alpha Legion, Volkern. Whether they know it or not, we always find a use for *everyone*.'

GAMMA

THE BOARDING TORPEDO *Argolid* drifted through the void
of the Octiss system. Like a bullet through the black,
the torpedo sliced through the frozen absence, iInertial
velocity maintained, course unwavering.

Octiss was like a forgotten corner of the galaxy. A debris
field of rock and ice circled in the silence, begirdling the
bright but bleary 66-Zeta Octiss; it was a shattered realm,
a sea of cosmic offal in which pockmarked planetoids
and lighter-than-air giants scudded.

Inside the *Argolid*, everything was a frosty darkness.
Squad Sigma stood to attention in their boarding cages.
Legionnaire Arkan sat strapped into the pilot's throne in
front of a set of rudimentary controls. Omegon stood
at the narrow strip of armourglas that could only chari-
tably be described as a viewport. Wiping the rime from
the surface, he allowed a brighter shaft of light to cut
through the gloom of the torpedo compartment. 66-Zeta
Octiss was close, then. Rune banks and decking twinkled
and glistened with an icy sheen.

A few hours earlier, Omegon had had Arkan shut down
everything with a power signature within the torpedo

– heat, gravity, life support. The legionnaires were all decked out in full plate and helmets, and had engaged the maglocks on their boots. The *Argolid* had fired its final burn before going dark and hurtling between the mute fury of two gas giants. The serene deep-ocean green of their smooth surfaces belied the true nature of the planets: unimaginable depth and pressure, winds thousands of kilometres in speed, eternal storms and cyclonic pits, intense radioactive fields and a comet-trap gravitational influence.

Arkan held a simple astrolabe to his helmet optics and made measurements through the cleared section. The shaft of sunlight suddenly disappeared, indicating that something of size had moved between the *Argolid* and the uncomfortably close Octiss star.

'Well?' Omegon looked to the legionnaire.

'On target, my lord,' Arkan replied. 'As long as we don't hit anything.'

'We cannot afford the attention that a correctional burn might attract,' Omegon told him, but there was little they could do about the fragments of metal and rock spinning serenely through deep space about them.

Before the reinforced nose-cone of the boarding torpedo rolled the stately magnitude of Tenebrae 9-50. Like a mountain range plummeting through the void at colossal speed, the asteroid was rugged and irregular, scarred by craters, impact sites and chasmic fractures. Arkan pointed out a deep cleavage in the asteroid rockface, a natural feature designated as the 61° 39' Ecliptic, or colloquially to the base personnel as 'Vacuity's Bosom'. The deep fissure had been chosen as the Alpha Legion's point of entry.

Omegon watched the colossal asteroid tumble towards them, rotating around its bulbous centre of gravity. The primarch was silently impressed with Arkan's calculations. The boarding torpedo was not only closing on their target solely under the power of inertia, but it was being almost effortlessly targeted towards a jagged pit gaping in the asteroid's midriff, all while the gargantuan rock itself slowly spun in the void.

Dropping down through the chasm, the boarding torpedo pierced the silky darkness of the asteroid's interior. Here there was no light at all, not even the pinpricks of distant stars for company. Omegon looked to Arkan – he was monitoring a handheld chronometer.

The boarding torpedo was designed to breach the armour of enemy vessels and the amalgamate hull sections of abominate space hulks, but Omegon believed that Tenebrae 9-50 would prove more of a challenge and so had planned for alternative disembarkation protocols. Once again wiping the film of ice from the viewport, he put his faceplate to the surface. Even with his more-than-human eyesight, the primarch could see absolutely nothing.

'Legionnaire–' he cautioned, but Arkan's chronometer completed its countdown with a single click.

'Launching counterhook,' Arkan announced, pulling on a pair of pneumatic paddles set in the runebank above. A loud pressure snap reverberated through the torpedo as a harpoon launched from the rear of the craft, trailing an adamantium alloy line. Satisfied that the harpoon had embedded itself deep within the bedrock, Arkan reported: 'Firing grapnels; engaging resistance.'

Rather than tearing the rear out of the torpedo with a dead stop, the legionnaire brought the craft to a disciplined halt through the increasing drag offered by a heavy-duty gear assembly. Omegon could feel the hull trembling, and the assembly began to emit an grinding screech. He put out his arms to steady himself. The boarding torpedo was clearly decelerating but it was difficult to tell in the absolute darkness of the rocky trench whether or not it would be fast enough.

The *Argolid* suddenly lurched; the counterhook had run its line. The legionnaires were secure in their boarding cages, while Arkan was strapped into the pilot's throne. Omegon was thrown forward, but with his powered gauntlets fixed around the rail the primarch didn't travel far. Yanked back a little on its tether, the torpedo proceeded to float through the darkness, scraping against the irregular wall of the shaft before bumping to rest against the cold rock. Omegon nodded, to the legionnaires and to himself.

'Squad disembark. Vox silence until we reach the airlock.'

Firing the starboard bulkhead, Sergeant Setebos kicked off into the lightless gap. The asteroid had next to no natural gravity and the legionnaire drifted through the blackness, bolter clutched in one gauntlet. He activated his suit lamps with the other.

The halo of light around the sergeant glinted off the bottom of the shaft, showing the Alpha Legionnaires just how close they had come to a terminal impact. Floating one by one in the gloom, Squad Sigma joined him by a narrow cave entrance.

Lead on, sergeant, Omegon signed, prompting Setebos in turn to put Zantine on point. The Legion's battle-signals were a fluid exchange of deft hand movements, delivered and received with ease born from decades of use.

Flipping their own suit lamps on, the squad leapt across the open space in a disciplined column. Snagging outcrops and pillars of rock with ceramite fingertips, the legionnaires pushed off using their legs and coasted across to each new foothold. Zantine held his bolter out in front of him, stabbing the barrel at the receding darkness of branching tunnels and hollows. It was a labyrinth of labyrinths – dark, with zagging passages leading off in every direction, including shafts thrusting both up and down into the depths. It was universally rough, rocky and thoroughly unrecognisable.

Zantine swiftly established a general heading and

despite deviations demanded by serpentine crawlways, choke points and bottlenecks, he kept Squad Sigma moving with purpose through the asteroid's fractured innards. Legionnaire Vermes brought up the rear, routinely sweeping the muzzle of his bolter across the inky blackness which followed in their wake.

Vaulting across the deep darkness of a crevasse, the Alpha Legionnaires soon found themselves confronted by a sheer wall of rock. Climbing up the precipice, their armoured legs dangling behind them, they gathered about Zantine. The Space Marine was hanging next to the narrow aperture of a tunnel entrance. Omegon watched as Sergeant Setebos wordlessly assisted the legionnaire in disconnecting his power cables and stabilisers, and stripping the pack from Zantine's back.

Passing it through the narrow gap, Setebos helped Zantine in the deadweight of his ceramite suit through the opening. Squad Sigma repeated this procedure until each legionnaire had negotiated the entrance and silently re-established power, life support and sensory feeds to their battle plate.

A long crawl awaited the legionnaires on the other side. Punting their armoured forms along with their gauntlets, they increasingly encountered shattered rock and regolith hanging in the tapering space. The grit and stones tip-tapped against the legionnaires' helmets and pauldrons, and Omegon found himself pushing clusters of small rocks ahead of him so that he did not get wedged against the low roof.

The tunnel emptied out into a larger cavern and Omegon had opportunity to scatter the floating rubble out of his path, though Zantine seemed to have found a collection of much larger boulders and zero-gravity erratics, great shards of rock hung in the dark, gently bumping each other with crushing force in the crowded space.

A sudden hand signal from Zantine swiftly brought the Alpha Legionnaires to halt. Like the thunder of a closing storm, a dull rumble swept through the rocky chamber. The cavern walls began to shudder and shake, while grit and regolith that had been dislodged by the quake drifted before the Space Marines and started to clot the darkness. The great stones began to clash with the walls and each other, smashing and splintering.

Auguramus had warned Omegon and the squad about the tidal quakes. The installation itself benefited from its own gravity and structural dampeners, but the rumble of powerful tidal tectonics was still an occasional hazard, especially where the Pylon Array was concerned. The conflicting gravitational forces of the Octissian gas giants pulling at the asteroid provided them with a fractured internal structure through which to infiltrate, but it also presented a serious danger to the squad as long as they remained within it.

Grasping a trembling ledge, Isidor reached inside the tunnel opening. Legionnaires were still exiting the tight confines of the crawlspace. It was clear from the clashing crags in the cavern that rock was moving against rock – without gravity the movements were unpredictable. The crawlspace was collapsing from below, and bedrock was rising against the legionnaires' chestplates, seemingly intent on crushing them against the rough ceiling.

Kicking away and swimming through the throbbing gloom, Omegon joined Isidor in grabbing his brothers and hauling them out into the cavern. Assisted in this way, Tarquiss and Krait scrambled clear, but Vermes was struggling – already, fragments of rubble were packing the legionnaire into a crawlspace grave. The closing rock drove chisel-tipped crags and spurs at the Space Marine's body that scored lines into the indigo of his plate.

Omegon reached back into the closing tunnel. He gestured for the legionnaire to take his gauntlet but the only response he received was a few grunts of exertion over the vox.

Setebos was suddenly beside him, and he jammed

the length of his bolter between the closing sides of
the shuddering outlet. The weapon immediately began
to bend and buckle and the sergeant instead thrust his
grasping hand towards Vermes as well.

They all heard the legionnaire growl in frustration
before his gauntlet gripped the primarch's own. Omegon heaved at the legionnaire, bracing himself against
the rockface. Isidor and Setebos reached further in, looking for purchase on Vermes's pack and plate. Between
them, Omegon and the legionnaires pulled with all of
their powered might, but the asteroid had Vermes firmly
in its rocky jaws. They hauled at the doomed warrior for
as long as they could before the collapse threatened to
claim them too.

Vermes's vox-link crackled to a deathly static, then
went silent.

Squad Sigma held there for a moment, in the cold and
the dark. The legionnaires stared at the press of compacted rock – a stone cold reminder that the galaxy still
had surprises in store for them, and that even with the
Legion's meticulous planning, they could not always be
anticipated or avoided.

Keep moving, Setebos signed, slapping the pauldron of
the legionnaire floating next to him. Drawing his bolt
pistol and screwing the squat barrel of a silencer in place,
the sergeant urged the squad on through the crowded
chamber of butting rocks.

They scrambled up, around and over the smashing obstacles, with shards and fragments raining in all
directions, several of them suffering scrapes and dents
in their plate. As one boulder drifted at Omegon with
the threat of pasting him into the cavern wall, the primarch braced himself hard against the rock face. With
his gauntlets held out in front of him, he tried to slow
the hefty progress of the object, before shoving back and
sending it drifting away through the crowded cavern in a
tumble of smaller debris.

As Squad Sigma climbed up through a twisted shaft in the cavern's roof, the craggy walls shivered to stillness once more. The legionnaires held their position for a moment, with Sergeant Setebos swimming up between different members of the team and checking for injuries.

The price we pay for unannounced entry, Omegon told him. Setebos nodded in agreement, and directed Zantine to continue, prompting the legionnaire to drag himself further up the corkscrewing passage.

Within moments he had returned. *Light ahead*, he announced.

The Alpha Legion fell to priming their weapons, while Omegon and Setebos joined the point-legionnaire in his climb. As they twisted up the shaft, the primarch saw that Zantine was right – the tunnels opened out into a much larger chamber ahead, the rocky ceiling of which was airbrushed in a brazen light.

Go dark, Omegon ordered, and the three of them killed their suits' illumination.

Setebos propelled himself up off a jagged ledge and floated up past Zantine and the primarch with his silenced bolt pistol leading the way. He stopped at the rim of the opening, his plate highlighted in the metallic glow. He looked down at Omegon, questioningly.

Proceed, sergeant.

Operatus Five-Hydra: Elapsed Time $\Omega 1/$-216.82$//XXU$ XX Legion Strike Cruiser Upsilon

THE PLANNING CHAMBER was a sea of copper faces. The large obsidian table at its centre was round, and as such none had any claim to status – all who were seated there were equal. There were no strategems handed down from on high. No rituals or protocols. Only problems, and the keen minds that together would provide solutions. A Legion's wisdom.

Omegon rested his elbow on the arm of his throne, and his chin upon his fist. Sitting there, amongst solidarity in skin and bone, Omegon might have been peering at himself through a prism. Around the table sat a full squad, crafted in their twin primarchs' image, each gene-blessed with Alpharius-Omegon's many gifts and each surgically sanctified with the tautness of a noble jaw and eyes of glacial depth – eyes that burned blue with intensity, intelligence and acceptance. In turn, the obsidian surface reflected back twice their silent number in shadow.

This unanimity of the flesh made the other members of the gathering, dwarfed by their Alpha Legion comrades, seem somewhat out of place, though the psyker Xalmagundi needed little help with that. Her pallid skin and dark lips marked her out as an underworlder, though she was at least out of the rags in which Squad Sigma had found her. Her big, black eyes were partially hidden behind tinted goggles and a lho-stick drooped absently from the corner of her mouth, its sweet smoke curling into the air. Her arm was in a foil sling and bore the signs of recent surgery.

Around her neck hung a thick metal collar, an inhibitor that checked the witchbreed's devastating telekinetic talents. Xalmagundi had objected at first, but Sheed Ranko had insisted on the precaution while the psyker was on board the *Upsilon*. Rather than finding it painful, like the presence of the silent Sisters, Xalmagundi had admitted that the dampener was in fact quite soothing and imposed upon her a state of not unpleasant calm and docility. This was a feature Omegon himself had insisted upon. He had seen no reason to torture his guest unnecessarily, and Volkern Auguramus had made the adjustment himself.

The Artisan Empyr meanwhile sat busying himself with the continual exchange of needles and feedlines between the flesh-sockets in his face: Omegon assumed it was a nervous tic. Auguramus had taken every opportunity to prove his usefulness and renewed loyalty, from constructing Xalmagundi's collar to enhancing the received Tenebrae security schemata with his own more technical details. The artisan turned his illuminated hood to one side as his internal logic engine updated itself.

'There seems little point in introductions,' Omegon said. 'We all know who we are.'

Auguramus seemed vaguely amused. 'I thought you all called yourselves "Alpharius",' he said, his microvox held to his throat.

'Times change,' Omegon replied coldly. No one made any further comment.

'Tenebrae 9-50,' he continued, depressing a stud on his throne to conjure a hololithic representation of the asteroid. 'Class-C planetesimal housing the Tenebrae installation. Tenebrae is an Alpha Legion base, clearance level Vermillion, and Tenebrae is our target. Does anyone need a moment to consider that implication?'

Setebos and the other members of his squad took their icy gaze off the hololithic asteroid. If they were going to object to the nature their target, now was the time. Setebos gave a slight shake of his shaven head.

'Intelligence leads us to believe that Tenebrae and the Vermillion-clearance projects developed there have been compromised,' the primarch continued. 'A confirmed leak.'

'An operative?' Isidor asked, looking to the Artisan Empyr.

'A member of the Legion,' Omegon replied. He observed with interest the ripple of surprise that passed through the gathering, and the immediate efforts that all made to mask it.

'Recipient?' Setebos asked.

'It could be anyone,' Omegon told them gravely. 'The Emperor's spies, the Warmaster's dogs of war, xenos infiltrators. It's unimportant now. This matter must be handled decisively. The Tenebrae installation *cannot* fall into the hands of an enemy. We are to scratch the base, scratch the technologies operating there and scratch all base personnel.'

Omegon let the order sink in. This time the legionnaires didn't flinch.

'Why not destroy it directly, using the *Beta*?' Krait ventured.

'The *Beta* is deployed elsewhere,' Omegon replied. 'Besides, I have the morale of the Legion to consider. This would be better handled in secret.'

'Personnel compliment of the base?' asked Setebos.

'Tenebrae houses a garrison of fifty legionnaires,' Omegon told them.

'Fifty?'

'Clearance Vermillion,' Isidor reminded him.

'And an Imperial Army sentry force, a one-quarter battalion of the Geno Seven-Sixty Spartocid,' the primarch added.

'The Seven-Sixty are a well drilled regiment,' Legionnaire Braxus offered. 'I had opportunity to observe them during the compliance of the Ferinus Worlds. They won't easily spook.'

'They've never had to face the Alpha Legion,' Setebos grinned.

'The Spartocid will keep,' Omegon assured the squad. 'Our first problem is gaining entry to an installation garrisoned by our own Legion.'

'If their training and experience are a given, then it's reasonable to expect that they will anticipate whatever we propose here, now,' Volion muttered.

'Why not stage an inspection?' Charmian suggested, settling back into his seat.

'That leaves an astropathic trail,' Omegon reminded him. 'Our arrival would need to be reported and verified.'

'Plus a Vermillion-clearance inspection will need setting up, which in turn leaves its own trail,' Isidor said.

'I need this station to go out like a light, as if it were

never there,' the primarch said. 'If our enemies come looking, I don't want them to find even a grain of dust. I want them to question the validity of all the previously leaked information.'

'What about the installation's imports?' Tarquiss asked. 'Cargo crates. Ammunition drums. I got aboard the III Legion's flagship in a bombardment shell case before Isstvan.'

'Commander Janic is responsible for base security,' Omegon replied. 'I suspect he has more rigorous protocols and procedures than Fulgrim's... *distracted disciples*.'

Auguramus brought the microvox to his throat again. 'Triple checks. Different officers. It's impossible to get anything in or out of the installation without rune certification from Janic himself. Everything and everyone is searched, documented and augur-scanned for good measure. Believe me, I've tried.'

'Let's not waste time trying to second guess Janic,' Setebos suggested. 'He's Alpha Legion: he's going to have secured the installation as well as any of us. We need something outside of his jurisdiction, and therefore outside of his control.'

'What about the asteroid itself?' Arkan offered. Omegon found himself nodding. Once again he turned to the Artisan Empyr.

'Why was Tenebrae 9-50 selected for the array?'

'Alpharius entrusted Master Echion with the actual selection,' Auguramus said. 'My calculations merely specified the Octiss system and the surrounding regions as counterclonically related, in terms of its dynamic immeteorology, to Chondax.'

'Speak plainly, Volkern,' Omegon said. 'Tell us about the rock.'

'That's the genius of it really,' Auguramus went on, unperturbed. The Artisan Empyr's admiration came through loud and clear. 'Tenebrae 9-50 is the site of existing clandestine operations, unknown to the rest of the Imperium.'

'Xenos?' Isidor enquired.

'Indeed. The *demiurg* are a spacefaring race that rarely enters Imperium territory.'

'That at least explains why I have never heard of them,' Setebos murmured. 'Hostile?'

'They are technologically advanced but seem to enjoy cordial relationships with other xenos cultures, several of which were eradicated during the Great Crusade,' the artisan told them. 'Principally they are miners and traders.'

'The demiurg are mining the asteroid,' said Omegon.

'Yes. The interior cave systems and caverns of the asteroid house a small host of automated mining machines, harvesting rare and precious metals.'

'What about the demiurg themselves?' Isidor asked.

'Initial surveys showed that Tenebrae 9-50 has no established orbit,' Auguramus replied. 'The demiurg operate a hidden "shunt network" across our space. They use unmanned electromagnetic conveyer stations to propel resource-rich asteroids from prospecting fields to their xenos clients' homeworlds. It takes hundreds of years, but by the time the asteroid arrives in-system, the automated mining machines have excavated and processed the arranged shipment.'

'And no one has yet detected this?' Volion put to him. 'Throughout the two hundred years that we stormed across the galaxy?'

'We may be the first,' Auguramus confirmed. 'Imperial forces can't investigate every chunk of rock floating through the void between star systems.'

'This could work for us,' Omegon said, bringing up the hololithic network of known shafts, hollows and excavations in the asteroid. 'The xenos explorations do run close to the installation foundations in sectors Seventeen through Twenty-two.'

Zantine pointed to the surface. 'What about long-range auspectra and listening nodes?'

'The base has considerable coverage,' Auguramus said with some regret. 'Approach by gunship or Stormbird will be detected.'

'Captain Ranko will oversee our extraction by Thunderhawk upon completion of our mission, and bring us back to the waiting *Upsilon*,' Omegon informed them. 'Our entrance, however, will be less straightforward than our exit.'

Arkan stood, sighting down his arm through the hololith. 'What about a torpedo shot? Powered down and launched out of auspex range, obviously.'

Omegon smiled. They were trying to impress him.

'No propulsion, no flight control, no course corrections,' the primarch said. 'That would be one hell of a shot, legionnaire.'

'Yes, my lord,' Arkan assured him with a grin. 'It *would* be.'

Omegon considered the plan, as it was taking shape. 'Volkern, tell me: will these automated abominations provide any resistance?'

'I cannot know the alien intentions of such technologies,' the Artisan Empyr cautioned, 'but my impression is that they are armed only to defend their xenos masters' prospecting rites. If attacked, I have no doubt they would assume their shipment was in danger and respond in kind. They strike me as having a territorial logic. They present no danger to the Tenebrae installation because the base isn't built on anything the automated machines want, or need to defend.'

'Let us hope you're right,' the primarch said.

Operatus Five-Hydra: Elapsed Time $\Omega 2/003.53$//TEN Tenebrae 9-50 – Trojan Asteroid

Omegon clawed his way across the ceiling of the cavern. The sergeant and Zantine had led the way out of the shaft. Squad Sigma followed in a column, hauling themselves up on crags and rocky ledges, their armoured legs drifting behind. Setebos had taken them all the way to the roof, and as Omegon pulled himself along, he allowed his gaze to fall upon the reason for their circuitous route.

Below them, giant machines were tearing into the rocky bowels of the asteroid in the silence of the void. Bulbous and brazen, they reminded Omegon of pregnant arachnids, stabbing into the cave floor with the stiletto points of their many legs. Set in their bellies were rotating maws of pulverising metal teeth that bored into the rock like a drill, and from their tapering abdomens dribbled a thread of molten, metallic ore which was carried away along an electromagnetically guided path. It was this web of glowing issue seeping from the monster machines that lit the cavern, though every few moments the bronze shimmer was overwhelmed by the flash of a fat beam of light; it was with these cutting beams that the automatons were taking the cavern apart.

Beams that could cut a careless Space Marine clean in half.

As Squad Sigma moved through the network of caves, it became apparent what a large scale operation the automated mineworks were. The giant mechanical mites were the backbone of the endeavour, tearing away tirelessly at the guts of the asteroid, shredding regolith and ion-bleeding source elements. But they were not the only automated machines to haunt the caves: an array of smaller, clinker-shell drones seemed to hover methodically from one mining monster to the other, monitoring production lines and administering continuous maintenance.

After a while the Alpha Legionnaires were forced to return to the cave floor, since the wall and ceiling of the chamber were dominated by the crawling lith-consuming automatons. With bolters trained upon their thick brazen armour, Squad Sigma waited as – at Setebos's command – Krait proceeded to plant seismic demolition charges. Cave by cave, chamber by chamber this continued, with Krait wiring the caverns in sequence and the rest of them silently ducking drones and giving the larger xenos creations a wide berth.

Following a growing number of molten streams, Setebos took the squad into what appeared to be some kind of storage chamber. Being careful not to disrupt the fields guiding the liquid metal, and with his pistol held upright, the sergeant grabbed at the rough wall and brought himself to a halt. Omegon joined him at the cavern entrance.

Before them was a floating lake. Streams of liquid ore had been guided to a containment vessel: a reservoir of molten metal, hanging in the weightlessness of the great cavern and held in check by crackling brassy orbs which drifted lazily around it. It was remarkable – no trace of the heat or energy field showed up on any sensor sweep, even at close range. Little wonder, then, that the demiurg shunt-network had remained hidden from the Imperium for so long. Omegon could well imagine chambers like this throughout the asteroid, where the extracted ore of rare and precious metals was stored ready for trade, once the asteroid reached its distant destination.

Giving orders not to interfere with the pooled metal reservoir, Omegon directed Setebos and Zantine to lead the squad around the chamber. Auguramus had informed the Alpha Legion that any interference with the mining operation would likely be interpreted by the xenos machines as a hostile action. As they crawled below the drifting lake, the primarch ordered Krait to plant a double cache of hidden charges at the heart of the cavern.

Activating their suit lamps once more the Alpha Legionnaires pushed on through the darkness beyond into a tight labyrinth of smaller tunnels, with their weapons at the ready. Zantine in particular didn't want to run into a mechanical beast in the confines of the passage without the means to defend himself.

As Omegon and Setebos extracted themselves from the disorientating network of passages, they found Charmian scrambling up and across the wall of a natural dead end cave – a chamber seemingly untouched by the xenos mining machines. Slipping an auspex from his belt, he began to sweep the wall.

What do you have? Omegon signed. Zantine brought the auspex up to his faceplate and double-checked his measurements.

The base, Zantine responded. *Through that wall.*

Operatus Five-Hydra: Elapsed Time Ω1/-215.65//XXÙ
XX Legion Strike Cruiser Upsilon

'I THINK THAT a cluster of meltabombs should handle it,' Krait told Omegon and the gathered Alpha Legionnaires. 'We want to burn an access way in, not bring the base foundations down on top of our helmets with a seismic charge.'

'That still doesn't solve a whole host of other problems,' Setebos interjected. He turned to Omegon. 'My lord, as soon as we breach the base perimeter then their atmospheric pressure will drop and vent into the vacuum. Life support will seal the affected section and lock off the bulkheads, leaving us stuck outside.'

'The sergeant's right,' Isidor agreed. 'Even if there weren't alarms – which there will be – everyone on the base will know the perimeter has been penetrated. The atmospheres of their own sections will go rushing by them.'

Omegon rested his elbows on the arms of his throne. Bringing his palms together he made a pyramid from his fingers.

'Artisan Empyr,' the primarch said after a moment. 'How deep do the foundations of the Pylon Array – and therefore, those of the base as well – sink into the rock?'

Auguramus nestled his microvox and narrowed his eyes.

'As deep as you *need* them to go,' the Artisan Empyr replied, with a hint of mirth. 'They could probably benefit from being deeper, if you take my meaning. Especially with the greater frequency of quakes, caused by the proximity of the gas giants. As soon as I return, I shall set engineering crews to blasting out chambers for new seismic dampeners. Janic will not oppose me.'

'Those crews'll need an airlock, of course,' Isidor joined in, chuckling. 'To facilitate the movement of workers between the base and the excavation, as it were.'

'Of course,' Auguramus nodded.

Omegon allowed himself a smile. Focusing past the hololithic representation of the asteroid and onto the base itself, he zeroed in on the foundations of a tall, square structure around which the many floors of the installation were constructed.

Like a stake thrust through the heart of the base, the Pylon Array dominated the schemata.

'What's this here?' the primarch asked, indicating a section just above the foundations.

'The generatorum,' Auguramus replied. 'Power for basic operations: light, heat, life support and artificial gravity.'

'What about the Pylon Array?' asked Vermes.

'It uses an *alternative* source of energy,' the Artisan Empyr told the legionnaire. 'The generatorum will mostly be my people: enginseers, servitors and the like. Do with them as you will. There are, of course, Imperial Army sentry posts and pict-surveillance.'

'The sentries and enginseers, leave to us,' Omegon said, 'but we'll need you to knock out surveillance and the gun positions though. Not a problem for one of the Mechanicum, I presume.'

'Of course not, my lord,' Auguramus said. 'But won't

shutting down the pict feeds alert the sentries in the security nexus?'

'They won't be in the security nexus,' Omegon told him. Auguramus looked relieved.

'And why not?'

'Because, artisan,' the primarch replied, '*you* will be in the security nexus, monitoring our progress through the base and advising us of incoming threats.'

'But the sentries...'

'Time to get your hands dirty,' Setebos said, slapping him on the back.

'Don't worry, I'm not expecting you to personally tangle with a pair of officers from the Geno Seven-Sixty Spartocid,' Omegon said.

'Poison,' Braxus suggested. 'Or electrocution.'

'Be creative,' Omegon finished.

Auguramus nodded slowly, wobbling his chins.

'Sir,' Isidor said, turning to Omegon. 'The Geno troops aside, sooner or later we are going to have to exchange fire with our Alpha Legion brothers. They outnumber us five to one.'

'Just because we are facing our own kind,' Omegon replied, 'doesn't mean that we should abandon the principles of the Hydra – they have served our Legion well, and will continue to do so in future.'

'So, we need to hit Janic and his garrison from all sides,' Setebos agreed.

'They won't fall apart like the Night Lords did at Ceti-Quorum,' Charmian warned.

'Or the Angels at the Thunderhead,' Braxus added.

'Which in itself is predictable,' Omegon said. 'When we deal with our own we deal in the known unknowns. We need distractions for our brother legionnaires. Equalisers to level the field.'

'Your plan, my lord?' Setebos asked.

The primarch leaned in on the hololithic display. He considered their options.

'The Artisan Empyr's own skitarii forces could be brought into play,' Omegon said, nodding at Auguramus. He then pointed out a secured block on the schemata. 'The psi-penitorium offers possibilities too. Also, our route of entry could be wired with detonators, so as to rattle our xenos neighbours into action at an appropriate time.'

Krait nodded in appreciation.

'What about Master Echion?' Auguramus put to the primarch. 'He's formerly of your Librarius–'

'What do you know of such matters?' Omegon shot back.

The Artisan Empyr put up a hand defensively. 'My lord, he has an intimate understanding of the immaterium. An obvious choice for this installation's purpose. Is he the leak?'

'It's possible,' Omegon nodded.

'Is he... powerful?'

'Why? Do you yearn to bleed him on your unholy edifice?'

'My point is that he's going to be more than a match for your young lady here,' Auguramus replied, nodding towards Xalmagundi. She was almost asleep at the table, the collar lulling her into a blissful slumber.

'Don't underestimate our guest,' the primarch told him. 'She has a crucial role to play. A conflict avoided is a conflict won without loss.'

Through the slits of her eyes, Xalmagundi looked at Omegon and then back into the deep, reflective darkness of the table.

Operatus Five-Hydra: Elapsed Time Ω2/004.21//TEN Tenebrae Installation

THE OPTICS ON Omegon's helmet compensated for the searing flash of the melta bombs. The rock around the flash glowed before starting to bubble and spit, and dribbling away in slurps of magma before cooling into spirals of blackened rock. As it sloughed away, shafts of light began to stream through from the cavern beyond, illuminated by construction lamps. Led by Sergeant Setebos, one by one the squad crawled through the rapidly cooling opening.

They were now within the peripheral influence of the installation's artificial gravity – their plate no longer drifted across open spaces, and the weight of the ceramite brought them down to the floor and kept their feet firmly rooted there. Omegon enjoyed the reassuring crunch of grit under his armoured boots.

Their movements became swift and certain. No longer hampered by the asteroid's internal disorientation, Squad Sigma fell into a long-practiced and familiar two-by-two stealth pattern. One of the advantages of being a beast with ten heads was having twenty eyes, constantly alert for potential ambushes and the chance of discovery. Moving up through the silent drilling equipment and unspent demolitions, the Space Marines moved between dangling cables and toppled construction lamps. Using every crag and outcrop for cover and tracking their partners as they went, the column of legionnaires swept up the freshly-bored tunnel.

Omegon fell into place opposite the lumbering Braxus – the primarch required no special treatment. He was not a dignitary to be escorted, or an officer leading the way.

He was one of many, who in turn were *legion*.

As Setebos reached a recently installed airlock at the end of the tunnel, the squad scattered into the nooks and crevices along the roughly excavated walls. The sergeant held up three fingers to Volion, prompting the legionnaire to back up beside the bulkhead.

Two fingers. One.

The sergeant cranked the lock and opened the thick door. Volion's bolter immediately pushed its way into the widening gap, with the legionnaire's shoulder close

behind it. With his optic sighting down the length of
the weapon, Volion went in, scanning the pressurisation
chamber for threats.

Clear.

Squad Sigma fell in swiftly behind him. Tarquiss
pulled the heavy door closed, and Isidor fell to working the lock controls, repressurising the chamber with a
breathable atmosphere.

The inner portal opened, and Volion's bolter thrust
out once more. His weapon sight darted from a low
bench, to another bench, to an empty void-suit, to a battered tool locker.

Setebos's voice seemed deafeningly loud over the vox,
after what had seemed like hours of enforced silence.
'Let's move.'

Dropping down onto the mesh flooring, the legionnaire led the way with Setebos close behind. Filing down
the narrow locker berth in pairs, their weapons tracking
the pair in front in synchronised sweeps, Squad Sigma
stalked through the storage area.

At a corner, Volion fell to a crouch and held up his
closed fist.

The squad froze. They could hear voices.

Resting the curve of his pauldron against the wall, Volion
rounded the corner – his bolter found two transmechan-
ics changing out of their robes and into void-suits. As the
first saw Volion's weapon on him, he dropped his bulbous helmet in surprise. Sergeant Setebos and Charmian
moved up past Volion and strode towards them.

'My lords?' the second transmechanic asked, assuming
the Alpha Legionnaires to belong to the base but clearly
unnerved by their presented weaponry.

Holding his bolter under the breech, Charmian enveloped the Mechanicum underling's entire face in his
gauntlet. The little man's hands clawed at the ceramite
as Charmian crushed his skull, and his companion's
protest died on his lips.

With a sudden glint, Setebos's gauntlet came up. The sergeant's combat blade slashed across the other trans-mechanic's throat, and he crashed to the floor.

Volion padded forward between the bodies, leading the way once again with his bolter, and with Setebos and Charmian falling back into position behind him.

Changing vox frequencies and checking his belt chronometer, Omegon hissed.

'Auguramus, you miserable sack of bolts – where are you?'

A few moments later, the artisan's voice chirped across the connection.

'A thousand apologies, my lord. I had a few problems with the Geno officers in the security nexus. There's blood... There's a lot of blood... on the... uhh...'

'Volkern, I need you to focus,' Omegon said, calmly. 'We're about to enter the generatorum. Monitor the vox-channels and pict feeds for security patrols.'

'Yes, my lord.'

Squad Sigma left the rough chambers of the base foundations and moved up through a set of maintenance stairwells. Before them stood a pressure-sealed bulkhead.

'Auguramus,' Omegon called. 'We're at M72c.'

The locking mechanism clunked, and with a gust of air the bulkhead chugged aside.

The generatorum was swathed in dirty steam. Thick cabling covered the decking like a carpet of serpents, and draped from ports in the ceiling. Thermo-crystal magna-reactors boomed their supercharged energy output and occasional arcs of lightning seared between them, roasting the air. The silhouettes of grimy servitors stood obediently at their posts, while enginseers prowled the machinery, monitoring and administering sacred oils.

One such hooded priest was shocked from his catechism by the sudden appearance of the legion-naires. Volion pressed on impassively with his bolter up.

388   ROB SANDERS

Before the enginseer could quiz the legionnaires about
their presence in the generatorum, Setebos stepped out
from behind a heat exchanger, placed the muzzle of his
silenced bolt pistol to the priest's plated temple, and
pushed his hood against the burning metal of the reactor
vent as the squad moved silently past. The priest went
to gabble his apologies but Setebos put a muffled bolt-
round through his skull. Prodding the fallen body with
the toe of his boot, the sergeant rejoined the rear of the
column.

Moving like phantoms through the swirling clouds
of oily steam and coolant, Squad Sigma ended all who
had observed their entrance. Under the stagnant gaze
of their servitors, seven more enginseers and the three
lex-mechanics manning the generatorum runebanks
died with economic efficiency. Building a murderous
momentum through the rows of reactor vents, it didn't
take the Alpha Legionnaires long to work up to the sentry post at the engineering section blast door.

Five soldiers of the Geno Seven-Sixty Spartocid stood
at their post, beneath the surveillance pict-mounted barrel of a multi-laser sentry gun that hung silently on its
ceiling rail.

The Spartocid were muscular but humourless warriors. Their helmets covered their faces – bar two grim slits
for their eyes – and each sported a miserable crest, the
length of which being some indicator of rank. Thread-
bare cloaks hung from the carapace of their shoulders,
their armour being a collection of mismatched plates
patched with inferior metals. They carried stubby broadburn lascarbines with fat barrels and chunky powerpacks.

The Seven-Sixty had an illustrious history but the Great
Crusade had eventually run the Geno regiment into the
ground. A long forgotten and inglorious war with the
abhumans on Dycenae plunged the proud warriors into
obscurity. Cut off, poorly supplied and never reinforced
– the Alpha Legion had found them surprisingly easy

converts, promising greater glories in the war to come.

'Auguramus,' Omegon hissed down the vox-link.

'I'm tracking your progress through the generatorum, lord,' the artisan replied.

'Jam vox-communications on the engineering level,' Omegon told him. 'Then take control of the generatorum sentry gun and run it down to the reactors.'

At the sudden awakening of the sentry gun, the Spartocid warriors stared up at the ceiling. They heard the whir of the multi-laser's movement, but more importantly the charging whine of the weapon's bulky power pack. As the weapon left them and trundled along its rail towards the steam-swathed heat exchangers, the soldiers broke into two groups – three of the warriors marched under the itinerant gun, their own carbines snug at their shoulders, while two remained on the door.

Within the oily clouds of steam, amongst the crackling reactors, Squad Sigma waited. As one of the Spartocid passed a copse of dangling cables, his helmet came in line with the silenced muzzle of Sergeant Setebos's pistol. A muffled bark sent him sprawling into his blood-splattered comrades, and they turned and brought their carbines to bear on the nest of pipes and powerlines. Arkan and Braxus stepped from the shadows and grabbed the distracted soldiers from behind, slipping plated arms around their necks and twisting their heads clean off.

As the sentry gun returned to the blast door, without the accompanying soldiers, the remaining Spartocid watched it with nervous anticipation. The post officer went for the wall-mounted vox-bank, in the hope of making contact with his missing sentries, and neither he nor his comrade noticed the wall of shadow appear and intensify in the steam bank.

The shadow became a silhouette, and the silhouette resolved into a transhuman nightmare.

Taking long, unstoppable strides, Omegon approached

the blast door. He was halfway towards the Spartocid by
the time they understood what was happening.

'Identify yourself,' the officer called out in his thick
accent.

Omegon did not answer.

'Legionnaire!' the Geno officer insisted. 'Observe security protocols.'

As the broad muzzle of the soldier's carbine met the
primarch's chestplate, Omegon snatched the barrel away
in a flash and grabbed the Geno officer's throat with his
other hand. As the Spartocid officer swatted uselessly at
the ceramite of the primarch's forearm, Omegon slowly
crushed the bones in his neck.

The soldier went for a ceremonial blade, but Omegon backhanded it from his grasp and launched him
upwards, smashing his helmet into the bulky frame of
the sentry gun. Something snagged, and the dead man
hung suspended from it like a marionette.

Stepping over the officer, Omegon activated the blast
door. As the thick bulkhead slid aside, Squad Sigma
emerged from the shadows of the generatorum. With the
sentry gun and its grim puppet humming along the rail
ahead of them, the legionnaires moved on.

'Across the antechamber,' Auguramus advised them
over the vox-link, 'you'll find the auxiliary stairwell leading to the upper levels of the installation.'

'Auxiliary?' Omegon questioned.

'Most of the tech-adepts and sentries use the lifters,' the
artisan explained. 'The stairwell less so. It winds around
the base of the Pylon Array. Some of the Imperial Army
garrison are uncomfortable around the artefact.'

Passing the doors of the bulk lifter, Volion led the
squad across an antechamber towards the stairwell access.
Without warning, the doors of the lifter began to part,
and Zantine and Tarquiss parted and slammed their backs
into the wall either side of the bulk elevator. The rest of
the squad moved towards the wall and out of sight.

Within, the legionnaires could hear a pair of engin-seers moving heavy equipment. The mesh gate rose, and Zantine and Tarquiss were suddenly there in front of them, the butts of their bolters aimed at the priests' hooded faces. With an awful crack of bone and spray of blood, Zantine's went down immediately. The second was thicker set and had a metallic mask of a face, and so the impact from Tarquiss's bolter stunned but failed to drop him. Stumbling back against a load-lift servitor, he barely had time to recover before a Space Marine combat blade was plunged into his chest.

Grabbing the legs of the bodies, the legionnaires dragged them across the gateway, preventing the lifter from closing and bringing anyone else down from the upper levels.

'Auguramus,' Omegon called out. 'Lock off all access-ways to the stairwell.'

'Affirmative, my lord. The psi-penitorium is two floors up from you,' the Artisan Empyr told him. 'I have already authorised the prisoner transfer under my coding, as you requested. My skitarii will be expecting us, although there are twenty more stationed on the same level for emergencies.'

'Like the one we are about to create?'

'Yes, my lord.'

'Send a personal vox-message to Master Echion, informing him you have a situation in the penitoria and require his immediate assistance,' Omegon said.

'But–'

'Do it now, then lock off the vox-channels on the whole level.'

The legionnaires bounded up the stairwell, tightly hugging the wall as they rounded each successive cor-ner with their bolters always trained up the next flight of stairs.

Beyond them lay the breadth of the Pylon Array. Through the mesh of the inside wall, the Alpha

Legionnaires could see the glossy black stone of the constructed xenos artefact, and feel the low hum of aethereal energies. The stone Pylon thrust up through the base's superstructure, with entire installation floors and sections built around it.

Sidling along the mesh-covered stone, Volion signalled. *Footsteps.*

'Auguramus?' Omegon growled.

'Only a tech-priest, lord,' he replied. 'Ahh, it's my assistant and her bodyguard.'

Squad Sigma held their positions, each legionnaire silent and ready. Volion slid along the wall on his pauldron and held there on a small landing. An aged female Mechanicum priest appeared around the corner – around her head, keeping sparse lengths of straggled grey hair in check, was a metal band. A third cybernetic eye was set in the band, and the tech-priest was using it to read a data-slate, while carrying several others in her free arm.

Grabbing the priest in his vice-like grip, Volion pulled the woman past him and hurled her off the landing and down the flight of stairs. Her servitor bodyguard reacted immediately, bringing a chainblade arm attachment to roaring life and swinging it at Volion, but the legionnaire batted the drone back. He followed up with a sudden charge, crushing the servitor into the wall with his armoured shoulder.

The chainblade bleated to a stuttering stop and the legionnaire pulled back, allowing the guard's broken body to slump to the floor.

Omegon watched Arkan check the crumpled body of the priest. It had been a long fall. She was dead; her neck was broken.

'Auguramus. Open accessway DT367b.'

In answer, the clunk of a locking mechanism cleared and Setebos looked through the gap between the auxiliary opening and the wall. Joining him on the penitorium level landing, Omegon peered through the crack as well.

The accessway opened out onto a broad deck serviced by the locked lifter, and several passages and stairwells ran off the deck, leading to other sections of the installation. Opposite was the formidable black gate of the psi-penitorium. Two skitarii sentinels stood either side of the bulkhead in their rust-coloured robes, each bearing a bionic weapon replacement instead of a right arm. Their faces were ghoulish rebreather masks with clicking telescopic opti-sockets.

The gate opened and Omegon could hear the screams of madness and the moans of distress echoing down the wide passageway beyond. Two further skitarii gaolers pushed a tall cage on rails down the passage and out through the gate. The black metal of the cage sizzled with energy; within was an emaciated woman, naked and pale. She was curled up foetus-like in the cage bottom, rocking and groaning in pain. One of the skitarii slashed the side of the cage with the length of his electro-flail, drawing a yelp of agony from the psyker prisoner.

'Sergeant,' Omegon said. 'Take your men up the lifter shaft. Master Echion is about to call for support from the Legion dormitories. Ensure it never reaches him.'

Setebos nodded his understanding and had Braxus remove the port cover of a devotional maintenance duct. One by one the Alpha Legionnaires disappeared into the wall.

'Volion. Charmian. You're with me,' Omegon said.

He took Charmian's bolter and fell into step with Volion behind him, as they left the stairwell and made their way across the broad deck. As they approached the psi-penitorium gate, the two impassive skitarii guards stepped forward to bar their way.

Charmian played his part well. Not slowing, and with Omegon and Volion flanking him like an officer escort, the legionnaire walked straight at them.

'Prisoner inspection,' Charmian told them. 'You

already have your clearance from the Artisan Empyr. Don't waste my time.'

After a moment's hesitation, the Mechanicum warriors parted and the gate rumbled open. Charmian didn't break his stride. With Omegon and Volion, the legionnaire marched down the wide, dismal passage beyond, being careful not to stumble on the floor rails. After passing through two more gates and between two more pairs of sentinels, the Alpha Legionnaires entered the main penitorium.

At the centre of a runebank hub the trio encountered a crew of lex-mechanics, skitarii guards and a heavily augmented skitarii tribune, who sat wired directly into an observation throne with a spread of optics and motion-tracking matrices sprouting from his grisly head. Around the hub chamber, a series of railed passages led off into darkness. Each echoed with the collective moans of imprisoned psyker slaves.

'Where is my prisoner?' Charmian demanded as he entered. The tribune gave the approaching legionnaires a gaze of blank confusion. 'Not prepped. Not caged?' Charmian growled. 'I was assured full cooperation by the Artisan Empyr.'

A skitarii sentinel with a flamer for an arm stepped out from one of the adjoining passages. Staring at Charmian with his whirring mask optics, he silently indicated that the Space Marines should follow him.

With the pilot flame from the skitarii warrior's weapon lighting the way like a flickering candle, Omegon marched past the dreadful cries of tormented witch-kin in the psi-shielded cells. The black shielding of the cells sapped the witchbreeds of their potency, and afflicted them with a soul-draining agony.

At the bottom of the passage, the skitarii came to a halt. Two of his fellow sentinels were standing outside an open cell. They had positioned one of their rail cages at the entrance, and were manipulating a set of controls mounted on the wall. They increased the energy flow running through the psi-shielding and the prisoner threw herself from the cell and into the cage with a pained screech.

Like an animal, Omegon thought.

Out of the unbearable field, the psyker was clearly relieved. She collapsed in a heap, breathing heavily. Stripped naked by her captors, Omegon could see her ribs and the bumps of her spine through her pallid skin. The crackling cage, although made of the same draining material and visiting a similar form of debilitation on the prisoner, couldn't deliver the same intensity as the cell. This gave each prisoner a moment or two of respite and a motive to transfer voluntarily from one to the other – it was a smooth operation and, although sickened by what he saw, Omegon was impressed by the system's economy.

Sealing the cage, the skitarii began pushing it along the rail towards the hub. The Alpha Legionnaires remained close to the sentinels and their cybernetic guide, until they crossed the third intersection.

Stepping up behind the guide, Volion silently slipped the tip of his combat blade under the skitarii's forearm fuel line. With the weapon's promethium supply cut off, the legionnaire seized the sentinel in an arm lock and plunged the full length of his blade through the rust-red hood and down into the warrior's brain. However, Charmian wasn't as delicate or precise as his brother legionnaire; grabbing one of the two gaolers from behind, he hefted the flailing deadweight of flesh and machinery into the air and slammed it down on the passage floor, expecting the cybernetic warrior's neck to snap across the rail.

But it did not. Surprised but fully functional, the sentinel brought its stubby volkite arm attachment up to meet the hulking Space Marine standing over it. Charmian's helmet – opened up by the shot – dashed the ceiling with broken ceramite and fragments of skull.

Volion cursed and brought his boot down savagely on the sentinel's mask, and this time its reinforced alloy neck gave a satisfying snap over the rail and the weapon slumped back to the floor.

Omegon wasted no time in dispatching the third warrior. Thrusting his gauntlet forward, the primarch plunged his armoured fingertips through the sentinel's flesh and augmented organs, and allowed the dying wretch to sink to the floor.

With her gaolers dead about the cage, the prisoner hauled her weakened body up the crackling bars. She rested her forehead against the dark metal and gave Omegon her big, underworlder eyes.

'Xalmagundi. You look unwell.'

'Get me out... of this bloody cage...' she hissed.

Smashing the lock mechanism with his bloodied ceramite fist, Omegon freed the psyker and helped her from the draining influence of its confinement.

Down the passage, they heard the grumble of the hub security gate opening. Peering up through the gloom, the primarch could make out the unmistakable forms of Alpha Legionnaires stood before the skitarii tribune and his runebanks.

It was Ursinus Echion, and a two-man escort.

The Librarian seemed to be berating the tribune, Omegon guessed, for being summoned to the penitorium unnecessarily. Then, in mid-sentence, he stopped. Turning slowly, he peered down the dark passage. The Librarian had clearly sensed something: in all likelihood, Xalmagundi's presence – raw, potent and unchecked. He took several cautious steps towards the passage opening. His copper face creased with fury.

Omegon and the psyker melted into the shadows, followed swiftly by Volion.

'Summon the rest of your skitarii,' Echion called back at the tribune. 'You have an escaped prisoner. Sound the alarm!' As deep klaxons rang through the hub, Echion turned to his Alpha Legion escorts.

'Call a squad down here. Now.'

DELTA

UNSLIPPING HIS BOLT pistol from its belt holster, Echion strode up the passage. The tribune had hit the general alarm and the hub became a wash of bloodshot light and ear-splitting noise. The psyker slaves screamed and shrieked in their cells, banging on the thick, black metal of the doors and howling like agitated animals.

As he and his escort reached the bodies of Legionnaire Charmian and the skitarri surrounding the breached cage, Echion scanned the gloom with his pistol. The cell door at the bottom of the passage was wide open...

Moments passed. The Librarian seemed unsure.

'Where's that squad-'

Before he could finish, the Space Marine nearest to him dropped his bolter and began clawing at his own battle helm. Echion grabbed his arm to steady him, but the ceramite began to crumple under his gauntlets. Some terrible force was crushing the legionnaire inside his armour like a great invisible vice, his pauldrons and chestplate buckling with a metallic groan.

Echion turned to find his other escort pinned against the wall, gurgling and choking.

Both of the stricken warriors screamed, and then fell slackly to the floor in a crushed, bloody heap. Echion whirled around, his pistol ready.

'Show yourself!'

Echion was suddenly struck by an incredible force, with such ferocity that his armour caved in across the plastron. He crashed through the cage and became entangled in the crackling bars, which proceeded to creak and contort around him. Another invisible blow sent him spinning boots-over-shoulders through the darkness.

He cracked off a succession of blind shots from the floor, but the dreadful unseen force smashed into him again and again, hurling both him and the misshapen cage down the passage and cracking them against the ceiling.

A final burst of automatic bolt-fire ran the pistol dry, but before the Librarian could reload the weapon he was torn from the wreckage of the cage by an impact that split his already crumpled chestplate. The invisible blow sent him through the air and into the deep darkness offered by the open cell door.

'I'm here, Alpha.' A slender silhouette presented itself in front of the opening, before willing the cell door to slam shut with a metallic boom.

Ursinus Echion pushed himself painfully to his feet.

'Janic, respond,' the Librarian coughed into his vox-link before spitting blood at the filthy cell floor. 'Code Crimson. Repeat, Code Crimson.' He changed channels. 'Strategarch Mandroclidas, respond.'

No answer came. He switched again. 'Artisan Empyr? Does anyone read me?'

He glanced about in the absolute darkness of the cell, sweat beginning to bead his brow. He shuffled over to the door. Closing his gauntleted fist, he began to pound on the dark metal. The psi-shielding was crippling the Librarian. There was no response to his vox-calls. He was alone in the dark.

Or at least, he thought he was.

Omegon had seen enough. Given time, he was sure that the psyker would find a way out of even this prison...

'It seems my concerns were warranted, Master Echion.'

The primarch watched the Librarian's face change rapidly from the shock of realising that he was not alone in the cell, to alarm as he recognised the voice addressing him. Through his helmet's augmented vision Omegon observed the psyker's shift in demeanour.

Echion put his back against the withering wall of the cell. Without the advantage of his own helmet optics he could not make out the primarch in the nullifying darkness.

'My lord,' Echion said, trying to remain calm and keep the anger and frustration out of his voice. 'I do not understand. A dangerous psyker is loose. The Pylon Array is under threat, exactly as you predicted.'

'Not our finest hour, is it Echion?' Omegon told him honestly. 'The only consolation you might take from this is that you were infiltrated by your own.'

'Infiltrated...' the Librarian repeated, 'by the Alpha Legion?'

'Yes, Echion. By the Legion.'

'Is the base compromised, then?' Echion asked, his eyes darting in the blackness.

'In every way imaginable.'

Echion's shoulders sagged. The Librarian was beginning to understand.

'I'm deeply sorry if I failed you in this, my lord,' Echion said. 'Our enemies-'

'Our enemies are no longer your concern,' Omegon interrupted him. 'No one will ever find a single shred of evidence that this installation ever existed.'

'You're going to scratch the base?'

'The base, the xenos technology, and all who could speak of its existence. Many will suffer the ultimate price for this failure.'

The Librarian nodded. 'I understand. Might I ask-'

The darkness lit up with the bark of bolter fire.

The bolts tore into Ursinus Echion, spraying blood and ceramite fragments across the walls. Only when the Librarian's body hit the floor did the fusillade cease, leaving Omegon and Volion in the darkness of the cell, the crash of automatic fire still ringing in the enclosed space.

'Xalmagundi,' Omegon called. 'Get us out of this bloody cell.'

The cell door gave a tormented creak before being ripped from its hinges and spinning off down the passageway towards the chaos of the penitoria hub, where Omegon could make out ranks of alarm-rallied skitarii attempting to secure the block. He stepped out of the cell, flanked by Volion.

Emerging from a side passage, the naked Xalmagundi – all pallid skin and bone – joined them. As an underworlder she seemed quite at home in the darkness. She gestured up the corridor towards the waiting tech guard.

'You wish me to destroy them?'

'Of course,' Omegon said, rolling a dead sentinel out of its tattered robe. 'But first, put some clothes on.'

Operatus Five-Hydra: Elapsed Time Ω1/-214.77//XXU XX Legion Strike Cruiser Upsilon

'And then we fire the detonators,' Krait said with confidence across the midnight sheen of the table.

'No,' the primarch corrected him. He tapped a series of studs on the arm of his throne, and the obsidian surface blinked to become a document of glyphs and symbols flashing by. Letter by letter, numeral by numeral, the document was being decrypted.

'Don't underestimate Janic. Echion's *specialisation* gives him primary responsibility for the array, but he'll leave security to Arvas Janic.'

The gathered legionnaires examined the commander's service chronicles as they spooled past.

'Know the mission, know the man,' Omegon instructed. 'And he's led a host of them himself. As you can see, this was always the history of a legionnaire destined for captaincy: several awards from previous commanding officers, including Thias Herzog and Ving Neriton; commendations for both innovation and constancy under fire. Veteran's crux. The Ouroboron. Victories at Ignatorium and Five-Twenty Nine. Had some bad luck with the K'nib at Selator Secundus, but didn't we all, and lost three legionnaires during the eradication of the Thorium Abominiplex – which is unsurprising given how many troops were lost by Lord Mortarion. Still, these are the service annals of a ruthlessly efficient and inventive commander. A record of which the Legion is justifiably proud. It's almost a shame we are going to have to ruin it.'

'Only three of these were garrison duties, though,' Isidor indicated, running his finger across the glassy surface. 'A submerged "halting site" – whatever that is – on the ocean world of Bythos...'

'Tactical outpost 'Epsilon/Loco', masquerading as a giga-container, routinely exchanged between bulk lifters over Isstvan IV,' Setebos interjected.

'And a Class-3 listening post in the ruined Gardens of Ptolemy on Prandium,' Isidor continued.

'None of which were compromised,' Omegon reminded them. 'His security logs for Tenebrae confirm a mix of sentry points and alternating patrols that he has implemented for the Geno troops at his disposal. He will not trust these alone, however, and will have a contingency strategy established between his own legionnaires for a perimeter breach – he will not rely upon allies or operatives, if things get out of hand. With his own squads he favours staged fallbacks, tactical demolitions, promethium cleansing, gauntlet approaches, mined cutroutes, wired bulkheads and blackouts.'

'As soon as Janic knows the base is under attack,'

Setebos extrapolated, 'his legionnaires will likely be drilled to lock it down and restrict the penetrating force to non-essential sections.'

'Aye,' the primarch admitted. 'He'll trap us, and send for Legion support. There'll be an arranged protocol.'

'Probably our intercept annex on the Belis-Aquarii Telepathica relay,' Isidor suggested.

'The *Phi*, possibly even the *Gamma*,' Arkan added. 'Neither vessel is stationed far off.'

'Either way, we've got to hit both the astropathic choir in the chantry and everything in the surface hangar,' Omegon told them, 'before Janic enforces his lock down. There is some good news, however. The logs show a heavy reliance on strategic simulation and statistical estimations run through the base cogitators. Both of which we have.'

'What do the numbers say?' Isidor asked.

'That an attack on the Tenebrae installation would be largely futile. It does not factor in, however, detailed previous knowledge of the base, familiarity with Alpha Legion tactics or possession of the simulation data itself.'

'Meaning, unsurprisingly, Janic has never considered infiltration by his own Legion,' Setebos said, raising his brow. 'You have re-run the cogitations, my lord?'

'Yes,' Omegon told them. 'Tenebrae is no different from any other target. Standard Legion tactics apply. Probabilities of success increase in line with multiple approaches and avenues of attack. We have to hit Janic's garrison from every angle – keep our brethren busy while we complete the operation.'

'Sir, if I may,' Isidor said. 'It is likely that there are operational elements that Commander Janic has withheld from the logs. Definitely from operational personnel, like the Artisan Empyr, and possibly even from his own legionnaires. He's Alpha legion, my lord. He will have some surprises waiting for us. Something we haven't anticipated.'

'Indeed,' the primarch agreed, nodding his head thoughtfully.

Operatus Five-Hydra: Elapsed Time $\Omega2/004.89//TPA$ Tenebrae Installation

'Sergeant Setebos reports heavy resistance on the dormitory level,' Volion reported from his vox-link. 'Tarquiss is down.'

Omegon was about to reply but the order stuck in this throat.

There was something wrong. Something out of place.

Striding up the penitorium passageway towards the hub with Xalmagundi and Volion, the primarch's focus was on the skitarii forces sealing off their exit. But as they passed a side passage it became apparent that they were not alone in the corridor – he caught the briefest impression of movement and the dull glint of ceramite.

Time seemed to slow. The flash of muzzles lit up the dungeon gloom. The crash of boltfire was everywhere, like thunder rolling up the passageway.

'Suppressing fire!' Omegon ordered as he grabbed Xalmagundi and tore her out of the crossfire. Volion responded with a withering hail from his bolter, directed down the side passage – Alpha Legionnaires were moving up towards them, using the recessed cell doorways for cover.

Emerging low, the primarch gunned down the nearest three legionnaires before disappearing back around the corner. Almost immediately, Volion's suppression fire resumed, giving Omegon precious moments to think. He adjusted the channel on his vox-link.

'Sergeant,' he called. 'Report!'

Across the vox he could hear the incessant bark of exchanged bolt-fire.

'We've been outmanoeuvred on the dormitory level, sir,' Setebos admitted. 'Taking casualties. Exits blocked.' The sergeant was drowned out by his own pistol for a moment. 'The dormitories don't exist on this level. The schemata misled us. We walked straight into a firefight.'

Omegon felt his lips curl into an involuntary snarl.

Also missing from the base schemata had been the secret entrance to the psi-penitorium through a dummy cell at the bottom of the side passage. Presumably to facilitate the retaking of the level in the event of a containment breach, garrison legionnaires had used the hidden portal to answer Ursinus Echion's initial calls for reinforcement in the penitoria hub. Now the ambush Omegon had planned for the requested legionnaires had been thwarted by a counter-ambush – mixed in with feelings of anger and frustration, the primarch couldn't help but feel a sting of pride at Janic's tactical prowess.

Explosive bolts tore up the walls and floor around Omegon and Xalmagundi. The skitarii forces flooding the hub had started working their way down the main passage, leading the way with optimistic blasts from their weapon-limbs. Once again, the primarch had to pull the delicate psyker out of harm's way, shielding her with his ceramite bulk.

'Reload!' Volion called. Instead of offering covering fire with his bolt pistol, Omegon unclipped a pair of grenades from his belt and tossed them down the side passage.

The twin blasts rocked the corridor, killing two more garrison legionnaires outright and knocking several more from cover and into Volion's deadly sights.

This could not continue. With Space Marines closing on the junction from one direction and skitarri sentinels from the other, the only fallback position was Xalmagundi's open cell, but Omegon had no intention of returning to the soul-sapping darkness. He was battling his own Legion: surprises were to be expected. It was time, however, to wrestle back the advantage.

'Xalmagundi!' he shouted, loosing a flurry of bolts. 'Time to rattle some cages!'

The psyker understood.

Lowering her head and closing her big, black eyes, Xalmagundi concentrated on her immediate environment. A new sound joined the din of gunfire: the shriek of metal contorting; locks shredding and hinges warping.

A thick cell door close to the junction blasted out of its reinforced frame and struck the opposite wall with crushing, unstoppable force, followed by another, and another. It was as though pressure was building in each successive cell down the passage, reaching an explosive crescendo which burst the psi-plate shielding from the walls. As the booming force worked its way through the penitorium, ripping doors from containment cells on both sides of the corridor, the advancing troops halted. The doorways that had provided them with much-needed cover were now like horrible pressurised deathtraps.

Garrison legionnaires were crushed against the walls, or knocked from their feet by the impacts. Those fortunate enough to be between doorways were now caught out in the open, and more fell to Volion and Omegon's renewed fire.

As the final cell door smashed into the wall, they worked their way up through the carnage, stepping over the armoured bodies of crushed legionnaires. Where their brethren had survived the explosive telekinetic assault, Volion and the primarch kicked weapons out of reach and put their blades through smashed helmets with deadly precision.

In the cells, the prisoners began to stir.

The building insanity of the tormented echoed in the darkness of ruptured doorways. Witchbreeds were hissing, cackling, sobbing and speaking to themselves in dark tongues. They knew they were free, but seemed suspicious of their sudden freedom.

Omegon saw emaciated men, women and mutants emerging from the supposed safety of the shadows.

Ducking into the only cell whose door was open rather than missing, he almost trampled a waif of a young girl, who had a grotesquely enlarged skull and misty eyes.

'Go!' Xalmagundi urged him, motioning the primarch past the child-witch and into the open cell. At first Omegon thought the she was going to embrace the child out of some kind of maternal instinct or mutant solidarity, but instead Xalmagundi threw her out and slammed the cell door shut, and put her back against the draining black metal.

Volion activated his suit lamps and made for the caged ladder that led both up through the ceiling and down through the floor of the dummy cell. The primarch shook his head in irritation – the shaft seemed to run through all levels of the Tenebrae base, but hadn't been part of the original schemata. Infiltration would have been a great deal easier with knowledge of that, he mused.

As Volion pointed his bolter up the ladder and began to ascend, they heard the sound of gunfire beyond the cell door. The skitarii sentinels had evidently worked their way down to the abandoned junction and opened fire on the emerging witch-kin. However, the sound of tech-guard weaponry was soon replaced with the harrowing shrieks of deviant psykers unleashing their fury and myriad talents upon their attackers.

Omegon couldn't even imagine what the witchbreeds were doing; the various ways in which their terrible vengeance might manifest. Something particularly vile was happening right outside the door, he was certain of that. It sounded like bones breaking... or *stretching*.

'Sergeant, are you still with me?' Omegon called across the vox as he and Xalmagundi climbed up after Volion.

Setebos crackled back through the din of combat at his end. 'Receiving you.'

'Status, sergeant?'

'We're another legionnaire down, my lord,' Setebos

reported. 'Janic misrepresented the schemata. There was no dormitory, only a Legion ambush.' Again the sergeant's voice was drowned out. 'Krait has used the last of his melta bombs to break through the walls to the assimularum and the refectory. This level is flooded with garrison troops. Janic is throwing everything he has at us.'

Omegon listened grimly to the sergeant's report. Arvas Janic had been more than equal to the task of securing the base. The commander had withheld information even from his closest allies. He had had dummy tactical objectives constructed and had organised reactionary gauntlets and ambushes, in order to stall any attempt to conquer the Tenebrae installation.

The game wasn't over, however. The primarch had not played his trump card.

'Sergeant,' Omegon returned down the fragmenting vox-link. 'I appreciate your difficulties. Rest assured that we have encountered a few of our own. Your orders are to extricate your squad by any means necessary and return to the lifter shaft. Make your way to the surface. We'll meet you there. Commander Janic might be throwing everything he has at us. We, however, have barely begun.'

'Yes, my lord,' Setebos replied with cold assurance.

'And, sergeant – tell Krait it's time to fire the detonators.'

'Received. He'll be pleased about that, at least.'

As they climbed, Omegon felt a string of deep, shuddering vibrations in the rungs of the ladder. Beyond the shaft he could hear the havoc that they had unleashed throughout the base: Space Marines were engaged in desperate firefights, using the base like a giant tactical training ground, Alpha Legionnaire against Alpha Legionnaire. The corridors and stairwells echoed with the footfalls of the Geno Seven-Sixty, bolstering sentries and creating hold points. Witchbreeds were out of their cells and tearing through the penitoria, using the full extent of their devastating powers upon their Mechanicum gaolers.

The installation superstructure itself was trembling.

He switched vox frequencies.

'Artisan Empyr...'

'My lord, thank the Omnissiah,' Auguramus replied over the channel. 'You must assist me. I've been discovered.'

'You are not the only one, Volkern,' Omegon replied coldly.

'The Seven-Sixty are trying to gain entry to the security nexus,' Auguramus babbled.

'Are you secure?'

'For now. I see from the pict feeds that they are bringing in cutting equipment for the bulkhead.'

'Listen to me carefully, Auguramus,' Omegon said.

'I'm trapped in-'

'Artisan!' the primarch roared. 'We are working our way to you. I need you to stay focused.'

'Yes, lord,' Auguramus replied miserably.

'Re-route all sentry guns on the dormitory level to support Squad Sigma,' Omegon told him.

'I don't know if I can do that from here,' Auguramus told him, panic creeping back into his voice. 'I fear that they have locked out some of the-'

'You will find a way, Artisan Empyr,' Omegon assured him as he climbed.

'The penitoria hub reports being overrun.'

'And I want that chaos to spread. Contact Strategarch Mandroclidas and your senior skitarii tribune, and inform them that the witchbreeds have escaped containment and used their powers to enslave the Alpha Legion.'

'They won't believe that.'

'Auguramus,' Omegon told him with an adamantium edge to his voice. 'You will *make* them believe it. There is little the unknowing won't believe about the unnatural. Play on their prejudice and fear. Besides, the base is in danger and the Legiones Astartes have been compromised. You are the ranking operative. The commanders will, of course, check in with each other – the skitarii will independently confirm the containment breach. Strategarch Mandroclidas will report Alpha Legionnaire hostilities.'

'Yes, my lord.' Omegon could almost hear the artisan's mind working through the possibilities.

'Do this, Auguramus. We will be with you directly. Omegon out.'

Above him, Volion stopped climbing without warning.

'What is it?' the primarch enquired.

'High-tier operations level,' the legionnaire said. 'Security nexus, base command, and the Astropath chantry.'

'If the schemata are to be trusted,' Omegon cautioned.

Turning a pressure wheel in the wall of the shaft, the primarch opened a duct hatch and peered through. The corridor onto which it opened was empty.

'Legionnaire, take this ladder straight to the surface hangar. The mission continues according to plan. It is imperative that no legionnaire escapes Tenebrae 9-50 to tell of our intervention here. Take out the hangar sentries, and provide covering fire for Xalmagundi – she can use her gift on the Stormbirds, shuttles and Mechanicum lighters.' He turned down to the psyker. 'I mean it, Xalmagundi. Take no chances. When I get up there I want to find nothing but scrap.'

'You can count on it,' she assured him.

Omegon checked his chronometer. 'How soon could you start working on velocity and trajectory?'

'As soon as I can see what I'm manipulating and where it's going,' the psyker reminded him.

'Both will be hard to miss once you're up there,' the primarch said.

'I told you, I've never handled anything of this size before.'

'I have faith in you, Xalmagundi,' Omegon said. 'Now go, both of you. Time is against us.'

'What about you, my lord?' Volion asked.

'The chantry falls to me.'

'That was Vermes's responsibility.'

'Aye, it was,' Omegon replied.

'Let me accompany you, my lord,' the legionnaire insisted.

The primarch climbed up and out of the portal. 'No. Get Xalmagundi to the surface. Only she can complete the mission. You have your orders, legionnaire.'

Closing the hatch on the Space Marine's impassive optics and Xalmagundi's underworlder eyes, the primarch slipped back into the Tenebrae base.

Operatus Five-Hydra: Elapsed Time Ω1/-214.12//XXU
XX Legion Strike Cruiser Upsilon

'So XALMAGUNDI WRECKS the hangar and Vermes's blade silences the choir of Astropaths,' Sergeant Setebos confirmed.

Omegon nodded. 'The Tenebrae installation must disappear like the light from a snuffed candle. We cannot risk survivors. We cannot risk craft fleeing the base. We cannot risk astrotelepathic reports of our operation.'

'With any luck, the garrison won't know *what* to report,' Arkan offered, 'and they'll certainly think twice before reporting that the base is being hit by their own Legion.'

'We can hope,' the primarch said.

'Assuming we can infiltrate the installation and confound the garrison,' Isidor put to him through the spectral shimmer of the hololithic display, 'how do we actually scratch the base?'

'Demolitions,' Krait volunteered immediately. 'Clean. Simple.'

'Or we could overload the generatorum magnareactors,' Tarquiss offered. 'That worked well enough aboard the *Carnassial*.'

'Or, instead of confounding the garrison,' said Volion,

'we could slit their throats one by one and then destroy the installation at our leisure.'

'I think you underestimate what you're dealing with,' Auguramus suddenly piped up, his voice a metallic echo through the micro-vox.

'Explain,' Setebos hissed.

The Artisan Empyr looked to Omegon, who nodded slowly.

'You talk of detonations and overloads,' Auguramus went on. 'This isn't a rockcrete bunker or ammunition dump. The Pylon Array is a colossal artefact of ancient xenos design, built to exact specifications and using materials the properties of which we are only now just beginning to appreciate-'

'What was this abomination constructed to achieve?' Isidor interrupted.

Omegon adjusted the focus of the hololithic display. Pulling out, Squad Sigma was treated to a phantasmal representation of the asteroid, which the primarch turned about its ungainly axis. The rock was a pock-marked vision, dominated on one side by a deep and well defined crater, the result of some ancient collision in which Tenebrae 9-50 had come off as the victor. Closing in, Omegon revealed phase field generators constructed about the hollow's circumference, and the sheen of an energy barrier cutting off the space within the crater from the void. Within the crater wall, a surface hangar had been excavated, and the rocky regolith of the crater floor was dominated by smaller security structures.

These were centred around the colossal reach of the Pylon Array.

It was like a great needle or obelisk, reaching for the stars but blacker than the void itself. The broader base of the abominate construction was fussy with scaffolding, but its tall, tapering pinnacle pierced the environmental containment field and reached out from the crater like an antenna sprouting from a parabolic reception dish.

'Imagine, for a moment that you understood anything about empyreal immetereology,' the Artisan Empyr continued. 'We consider the warp a reality alternate to our own and consisting wholly of raw energy. An ocean immeasurable. Powerful. Unpredictable. Deadly.' Auguramus cast his gaze down the line of identical faces. 'But also, useful. Mankind has sought to brave the dangers of the warp in order to build an empire and embark upon a crusade of galactic conquest.'

'You remind us of a history of which we are a part,' warned Braxus.

'A crusade mounted and an Imperium held together by the promise of communication and cooperation. Our thoughts and our vessels traverse this tumultuous realm. When storms wrack the warp, then the immetereology becomes unstable – both destructive and obstructive. Astrotelepathic communication and navigation become impossible.'

'Get to the point.'

'Within an ordinary meteorological system,' Auguramus went on, 'like an atmospheric weather system, there are areas of high and low pressure. Storms form in response to the extreme pressure differences in these areas.'

'And?' Charmian prompted, refusing to get caught up in the artisan's growing excitement.

'The immetereology of the warp is not dissimilar. The unfathomable workings of the Pylon Array produce an area of unprecedented calm within the warp. The range of astropathic communication is extended.'

'But this creates storm fronts and immetereological disturbances in the regions beyond,' Isidor said.

'Exactly!' Auguramus almost shrieked. 'An unintentional consequence of the xenos technology's operation. Far more useful than anything possessed by the other Legions.'

'A consequence that Alpharius has used to further the

Warmaster's aims,' Omegon informed the gathering.
'Upon building this technology in the Octiss System,
and charging it with immaterial energies sapped from
the Mechanicum's psyker slave-stock, we have succeeded
in enveloping bordering regions in a communications
blackout: Draconi, Tiamath, Chondax and the Scellis-
Trevelya straits. We have not only restricted the White
Scars Legion to the Chondax system, which was Alpharius's promise to Horus, but we have kept Jaghatai Khan
veiled in ignorance. He is blind to the atrocities of civil
war and deaf to Dorn's commands to return. Without
the Scars and the Great Khan at the Emperor's side, the
Warmaster's victory will be assured.'

A murmur ran through the group. Omegon waited a
moment before continuing.

'The loyalists have also been denied reinforcement
from the Regnault Thorns, the Seventh-Suckle Parthenari
Shieldmaidens, and the Uzuran Sabreteurs: seventy-two
thousand fighting souls, all delayed at Draconi. The Legio
Cybernetica Maniple Theta-Iota and the Legio Gigantes
Titan Legion were also lost, presumed destroyed, while
in transit through Scellis-Trevelya.'

'A powerful weapon indeed, my lord,' Isidor said.

'You see then, that this technology cannot be allowed
to fall into the hands of the enemy,' Omegon insisted.
'That is why, powerful as it is, it must be destroyed.
Utterly.'

'Seismic charges and super-critical magnareactors cannot
provide the kind of assurance we need,' Auguramus added.
'The very material from which the Pylon Array is constructed – remaining in certain configurations – is likely to
maintain a residual immaterial presence. My calculations
show that a blanket orbital bombardment could provide
the coverage required, but even with the *Beta* at your disposal, or one of the Mechanicum vessels, Tenebrae 9-50
would simply disintegrate and spread recoverable evidence
of the Pylon Array's existence all over the system.'

'There has to be a way,' Setebos said, to which several Squad Sigma legionnaires nodded in agreement.

'There is,' the primarch told them. 'We need to destroy the entire asteroid.'

Isidor frowned. 'I thought we just agreed that was unwise.'

'The demiurg shunt these asteroids inertially between conveyer stations,' Omegon said, 'but if another force could be applied to the rock mid-voyage, a small deviation would soon make a large difference. Especially if the asteroid's velocity could be increased.'

The primarch and the Alpha Legionnaires turned their heads in unison to look at the dozing psyker.

'Enough force to change the rock's trajectory and put it – base, Pylon Array and all – into a nearby star.'

Too numbed by the psi-dampening collar to mount any objection, Xalmagundi gave them all a lazy, cynical glance through the ghostly representation of the asteroid.

'I've never... manipulated... anything... that size... before,' she mumbled.

'Then the true extent of your powers has never been tested, but from what I've heard already, I'm impressed. And that was working against gravity and atmospheric friction.'

'What is our exit strategy?' Setebos put to Omegon.

'Yes,' Vermes agreed. 'Rolling the asteroid into 66-Zeta Octiss does seem an elegant solution to our problem, but that means we need a tightly scheduled evacuation.'

'The *Upsilon* will be stationed just out of sensor range,' the primarch said. 'I've put Captain Ranko personally in charge of our extraction. He will leave with the finest from his Lernaean squad as soon as our mission is underway, and evacuate us from the Tenebrae surface in the Thunderhawk *Chimerica*.'

Isidor nodded before looking over at his sergeant. They both seemed satisfied.

Omegon checked his chronometer and stood. As the gathered Alpha Legionnaires and operatives did likewise, the hololith flickered and evaporated.

'We have preparations to make and little time to make them,' he said. 'Before we go, let me say this: I understand the conflict in your hearts, how one may beat for duty while the other bleeds for your Legion brothers who will be sacrificed. But this is civil war. It is a time of confusion, and realigned loyalty. We have many heads but we act as one – one Legion with a single will. We are a union of the alike and the like-minded. We will not tolerate treachery. We will not allow our compact to fracture. We will not suffer the short-sightedness of our brother Legions, nor the averted gaze of the wider Imperium. We are Alpha Legion and we take the long view.'

The assembled legionnaires thumped their fists on the table in salute.

'As Alpha Legion, however, you are expected to think for yourselves. If anyone here today wishes to absolve himself of this responsibility; if he finds that under these most unique of circumstances he cannot imitate the action of the hydra; if he chooses not to be the whetstone upon which his Legion is sharpened, then he shall suffer no censure or judgement. He can walk away knowing that there are others who would be his brother's keeper, and he can wait out this mission in the brig of the *Upsilon* before returning to duty.

Omegon looked down the line of identical faces, searching for any seed of doubt or misgiving. He saw only cold-blooded determination in their arctic eyes.

'Brothers. Hydra Dominatus.'

'Hydra Dominatus,' Setebos returned, followed by the rest of the squad.

'Then let our enemies see the fallen fruit, sitting warm and inviting in the afternoon sun,' the primarch said. 'And let us be the serpent beneath, hidden and waiting to strike.'

* * *

*Operatus Five-Hydra: Elapsed Time Ω2/005.17//TEN
Tenebrae Installation*

OMEGON MOVED LIKE a ghost through the unfolding catastrophe. Leading with his bolt pistol, but clutching his combat blade at his side like a hooked talon, he slipped through unnoticed.

The installation passageways, sections and stairwells were bathed in the bloody light of warning lamps, and the spinning emergency beacons that added a sickly amber urgency to the base's interior. The primarch's movements were swift and his footfalls light, and lost beneath the insistent wail of klaxons. This had meant that those who had been unfortunate enough find themselves in his path had not heard Omegon's caving of skulls, breaking of necks and slashing of throats as he approached.

Near the armoury, a three-quarter squad of Spartocid soldiers rounded a corner ahead of Omegon. They were clutching their las-carbines to their chests and running with their faded cloaks rippling behind them, and a Geno subalterix clutched a vox-unit to the side of his plumed helmet, trying to get clarification over gunfire crowded channels. Upon sighting Omegon, in his Legion plate, the group slowed and angled the broadburn muzzles of their stubby weapons at him. They had clearly heard the equally unbelievable reports either of Alpha Legion infiltrators compromising the base, or warp-possessed garrison legionnaires running amok on the penitorium level.

He had to think fast. Aiming his bolt pistol down the adjacent empty corridor, Omegon repeatedly squeezed the trigger, emptying the magazine at some unseen target. The primarch then feigned alarm and began furiously reloading.

'Get down here!' he roared at the hesitant Spartocid.

More a conditioned response than a strategic assessment of the situation, the subaltrix and his men rushed on, their carbines presented and ready. As they burst around the junction corner they opened fire, slashing the empty darkness beyond, scanning for an enemy but blinded by the blurred flash of their own weaponry.

Omegon allowed them to take a few more steps before he moved. Bringing up his freshly loaded pistol he blew gaping holes through the backs of their skulls. Even as the squad began to drop around him, the subaltrix urged his soldiers to keep firing in the mistaken belief that they were still being engaged from the corridor.

Moving on from the massacre, Omegon reached the thick doors of the lifter shaft – through the metal he could hear the exchange of gunfire. Stabbing the tip of his combat blade between the edges and twisting it, he managed to prise the doors open and claw the mesh gate upwards. Omegon peered down the shaft and then up into its gloomy heights.

Aside from the cacophony of battle on multiple levels, the most distinctive sound rising up from the installation depths was the haunting madness of liberated witchbreeds, shrieking and howling in the darkness. They were unleashing hell throughout the base and indiscriminately venting their fury and unnatural powers upon skitarri sentinels, genic Spartocids and Legion forces alike. A sudden eruption of directed soulfire ripped through the lifter doors several floors below, lighting up the darkness and blasting a garrison legionnaire into the shaft wall opposite. Omegon watched him fall, writhing in spectral flame, before smashing straight through the roof of the lifter car.

The primarch felt a tremor through his gauntlets. Moving across to the rocky passageway wall, he put the side of his helmet to the stone. A series of grinding rumbles came from the base superstructure.

He was running out of time.

Reloading his bolt pistol with the last magazine, the primarch set off once again through the installation's ear-splitting, labyrinthine murk.

The chantry was a small block cut off from the rest of the operations level by bulkheads and a series of sombre archways. Each displayed the symbol of the Adeptus Astra Telepathica, a single eye looking down upon Omegon as he slipped past.

Pushing the muzzle of his pistol through the green velvet drapes, the primarch found the Astropaths within the sanctuary. There were tarot wafers spread on the polished floor of the chamber.

They were on their knees before him. All men. All hooded. All terrified. They looked pleadingly up at him with their grisly, empty eye sockets. At first this confused Omegon, until he realised – looking down at the abandoned wafers – that they had already seen what was to happen next. They bowed their heads and pulled back their hoods.

Omegon was not one to prolong suffering unless it served a purpose. He fell to doing what was necessary: hovering his bolt pistol at the back of the Astropath's heads, he executed each in turn, quickly and efficiently.

Turning to withdraw through the blood speckled velvet, Omegon stopped. There were three Astropaths, and yet there were four sub-sanctuaries leading from the chamber. Only one of the chambers had its drapes drawn.

Storming forward, he swept the drapes aside and came face to face with the chief chorister – a lean, elderly Astropath – standing before a lectern. The floor about her was of polished metal into which hexagrammatic wardings and seals of safeguarding had been carved. She was clutching a thick staff bearing the icon of the all-seeing-eye, and mumbling the encryption rites of astrotelecommunication.

'Desist,' Omegon growled at her, bringing the pistol up.

Suddenly there were arms everywhere, thick and armoured in heavy plate.

Two garrison legionnaires lunged from hiding, inside the sub-sanctuary entrance. They reached for the primarch's pistol with grasping hands, hauling it off to one side as the weapon spat a trio of rounds that narrowly missed the mediating Astropath and mauled the lectern. Two more legionnaires cannoned into him from behind, sending the wrestling throng crashing into the sub-sanctuary wall. Another shot went into the panelling before the pistol was out of his grip.

'Remember,' the sibilant voice of an officer cut through the violence, 'I want him alive.'

This was all Omegon needed to hear. Reaching for the legionnaires' sheathed combat blades hanging at their belts, Omegon spun and buried the first blade in its owner's neck. He knew there was a weak spot between the gorget casing and the helmet seals: he knew this because his own Alpha Legion plate sported the same weakness. He stabbed at two more of his assailants with the second blade, and pierced through the eye lens of the last.

Momentarily shrugging off the attentions of the wounded Space Marines, the primarch threw the knife point-over-pommel down the length of the sub-sanctuary. The weighty blade thudded into the side of the Astropath's hood, and the chorister collapsed against the lectern before tumbling to the ward-inscribed floor.

With her message silenced, Omegon heaved himself and his assailants into the other wall, running the huddle of power armoured legionnaires one into another. Slamming an articulated elbow joint into a faceplate before following with a gauntleted fist to another, Omegon took a shoulderplate in the gut. Slammed into the far wall and cracking the panelling, he brought his knee up savagely, again and again, buckling the warrior's ceramite. Pushing him away, Omegon readied himself as another legionnaire came at him with his fists, and the pair of them dissolved into a graceful blur of half-parried pummelling and powerful counter strikes.

As the legionnaire lunged, Omegon stepped aside. Allowing the Space Marine follow his path of momentum, the primarch got his gauntlets around and under his backpack. He fingered the release clasps and tore the apparatus from the legionnaire's suit before smashing him down into the floor with the dead weight of it.

He turned just in time to smack aside an oncoming combat knife – the legionnaire wielding it had been the one Omegon had first stabbed, and the Space Marine's gorget and plastron were slick with blood where he had extracted the blade. Omegon smashed the pack across the legionnaire's helmet before planting it in the midriff cabling of another, bending him double.

The graceless brawl continued and the sub-sanctuary rang with the crash of armour plate. Fibre bundles crackled and contracted. Ceramite buckled beneath superhuman blows. The primarch moved from opponent to opponent, checking the lethality of oncoming attacks and following up with as much lethality as he himself could spare before being forced to engage the next.

The bloodied knife was back. It slashed and thrust, and he snatched the wrist and gauntlet of the wielder in an attempt to wrest it back again. Omegon wrenched the offending arm towards the ceiling and turned beneath it, hearing the seals crack and cabling snap. With one fluid movement he twisted the legionnaire's arm to breaking, before ramming him helmet first into the wall panelling with a crunch of vertebrae. The combat knife, Omegon had pried from the grip of the Space Marine's broken hand and kept for himself.

Clutched like a dagger, Omegon brought it around in a searing arc and drove the blade tip through the half-blinded warrior's intact optic and into his brain. With a sickening squeal of tortured ceramite, the primarch tore the weapon free again and allowed him to drop to the floor.

Only one of his four opponents was still on his feet – the legionnaire struck down with one outstretched gauntlet and knocked the slippery blade from the primarch's grip. Omegon shoved him up against the wall panelling, and brought his ceramite knuckles in again and again, each economic strike followed swiftly and pneumatically by the next.

The faceplate crunched. An optic cracked.

Again the legionnaire's grasping gauntlets reached for Omegon, but again the primarch beat them back, and grabbed the dazed warrior by both sides of his ruined helmet. He fired the pressure seals and ripped it from the Space Marine's head.

He looked down upon copper skin and harsh blue eyes that were like unto his own. That didn't stop him clutching the helmet by its piping and smashing the crest and bonding studs savagely into the legionnaire's unprotected face over and over until he dropped to the metal floor.

Heaving with exertion, he stood with his back to the curtained doorway. 'Commander Janic, I presume,' he muttered between breaths. He turned, the bloody helmet still in his hand. 'I have to commend you on-'

Janic's bolter barked. Omegon felt the mass-reactive shells punch into his armour, and detonate within his flesh. White hot agony flared, though his superhuman body fought to resist it.

Omegon's legs went out from under him.

Dropping the legionnaire's ruined helmet, he stumbled and crashed back into the wall. With his pack sliding down the panelling, the primarch slipped down onto the metal floor, his spilled blood beginning to flood the hexagrammatic carvings.

He saw Arvas Janic standing over him in the subsanctuary doorway, amongst the green velvet drapes. The commander's face was a taut mask of bitter intent, his helmet maglocked to his belt.

'You were saying?' the commander said, venturing forward.

Omegon reached down his armour and found three fat, ragged punctures in the lower cuirass. He explored each opening with a fingertip and checked the position of each wound. To the side of the navel. Above the hip. Omegon nodded to himself. They had all missed the spine. He knew his body had gone into overdrive, with different organs, suprahormones and engineered processes interacting to reduce the severity of the wounds.

Placing his gauntlets and boots flat on the floor, Omegon pushed his backpack a little farther up the wall. Through the superstructure he felt a distinctive rumble. Something more than a distant quake.

'You were saying?' Janic repeated.

'Warning shots?' Omegon asked.

The commander nodded.

Omegon coughed blood inside his visor. 'I was saying that you should be commended for the first class security and counter measures employed on this base.'

'Don't patronise me,' Janic warned with a snarl. 'If it were truly first class, you wouldn't be here.'

'I see your point,' Omegon told him. 'Yet particular highlights were your ambushes here and on the dormitory level. You knew we'd try and silence the chantry – a priority target –and you even left the dummy dormitory on the schemata. Very clever.'

'Enough of this,' Arvas Janic said. 'Remove your helmet. You will identify yourself and your designs on this installation. You will reveal how you came to know of its location. You will admit to your true Legion and deliver the name of the commanding officer foolish enough to despatch you here on a suicide mission.'

'You sound confident of that, commander,' Omegon muttered with grim humour.

'Now. Later. It matters not,' Janic promised. 'We are renowned for our patience, and our methods of persuasion. While my legionnaires comb this base for evidence, my superiors will hunt your sponsors back along the trail you have undoubtedly left in coming here. Meanwhile, I'll have my Apothecary take you apart, piece by piece – starting with your feet and working up – harvesting your organs one by one until you feel like volunteering the information I wish to know.'

'I don't suppose you would believe that I am an Alpha Legion officer and that this base is under inspection?' Omegon asked the commander.

'No,' Janic returned with a sneer.

'Or that this is a simulation designed to test your suitability for promotion?'

'No, sir, I would not. As I'm sure you're aware, this is a Vermillion-clearance operation. Our orders here come directly from the very highest authority: the primarch himself. So too would authorisation for the inspection or simulation to which you allude. A lot of my men are dead. What kind of an inspection involves brother legionnaires spilling each other's blood?'

'A very serious one, commander,' Omegon said, wedging his backpack into the gap between the lectern and the wall. 'Now, let me tell you what I really know, and why I agree with you that it matters not.'

Below them both the base superstructure trembled again, more fiercely this time. Omegon motioned the commander in closer. Bringing the bolter up between them, Janic leaned in.

'Hydra Dominatus, brother,' the primarch whispered.

Janic's brow furrowed. He straightened. His face screwed up in fury and frustration.

'What?'

He backed away, and then his eyes fell upon the helmet clasped in Omegon's hand.

His helmet, unlocked from his belt.

The sub-sanctuary suddenly became a maelstrom of howling, wind churned debris. Escaping air screamed through the wide vents in the wall above Omegon's head, and every loose object in the chamber was dragged towards the open bulkheads outside. Drapes, discarded weapons, and the bodies that littered the chamber all whipped past the primarch in a few seconds of shrieking turbulence, dragged through the narrow doorway by the irresistible expulsion of artificial atmosphere. One moment Arvas Janic was before the primarch with his bolter in hand, and the next he was being smashed through the doorways and corridors of the section and whipped along a roaring path of least resistance to the yawning lifter shaft beyond.

Alone in the evacuating sub-sanctuary, Omegon's backpack held him wedged in place against the wall, and he was further anchored by the maglocks of his boots, freshly activated at the rumble of the demiurg mining machines cutting up through the foundations of the base.

As they had done so – jarred into action by Krait's territory-threatening trail of planted demolitions – the xenos monstrosities had smashed up through the same pressurised system of locks that Squad Sigma had been careful to use upon infiltrating the installation. The mining machines' entrance had been less discrete, however, and as a result of the automatons cutting and tearing their way in, the base had been depressurised, breached and had lost its artificial atmosphere to the void.

Suddenly there was silence.

As predicted, the cogitator banks governing the installation's environmental controls had sealed off the breached lower levels. It had all been over in moments.

Deactivating the maglocks, Omegon hauled himself up and scrambled for the exit. With one gauntlet over his wounded stomach, the primarch threw himself around corners and through the crooked layout of the operations level.

Half running, half stumbling through the command

section, he found the chambers devoid of Alpha Legion officers or the Geno Seven-Sixty Strategarch. Only servitors wired into their thrones remained – sitting there with their jaundiced, lidless eyeballs and rot-retracted lips. A large runescreen flashed through a sequence of levels, with most blocks and sections blinking crimson. It wouldn't take long for the demiurg mining machines to crash through an emergency bulkhead, or to cut their way up and through to the upper levels.

Stomping past the vox listening posts and long range auspex stations, Omegon came across a security bulkhead that had a rough hole burned through the thick metal. He recognised it immediately: the security nexus.

Clutching his abdomen, the primarch risked a moment to peer through the plasma-torched opening. Inside, the chamber was dark and lit only by banks of pict-screens. Strapped into an observation throne that moved between the rows of screens on a rotating gimbal, Omegon found the fat carcass of Volkern Auguramus. The Artisan Empyr had indeed been discovered by Spartocid soldiers, and his robed body was riddled with merciless las-fire. The screens told of more murderous desolation across the base.

Omegon saw Alpha Legionnaires exchanging fire with skitarii sentinels and rallied contingents of the Spartocid. The screens glowed ghoulishly with flash of las-carbines, flamers and boltguns. Witchbreeds in all their wretched variety pounced on their victims, tearing them apart with supernatural strength, or vomiting forth warp-flame and arcs of green lightning. One of the witches – a gangling, twisted creature – had dislocated her jaw like some kind of snake and was screeching at soldiers and sentinels with deadly effect.

The garrison legionnaires had been faring better in the lower levels with their well-practiced formations and tactics, but the appearance of great brazen xenos machines bursting up through the decking had proved more of a challenge. The bulbous, arachnoid monstrosities buzzed through the Alpha Legionnaires' armour with their heavy cutting lasers.

The confusion and carnage had a terrible beauty to it. An admirable chaos, that was a true reflection of the doctrine of the hydra – its multiple heads striking in disparate but co-ordinated devastation.

Leaving behind the corpse of the Artisan Empyr, Omegon ducked back out of the nexus and stumbled down the adjoining passage. The lumen strips overhead fizzed and went out, only for the darkness to be abruptly interrupted by the searing flash of intense cutter beams searing up through the metal decking. He skidded to a stop to avoid a pair of the beams, sizzling with alien energy and slicing their way across his path, before ducking through a mangled bulkhead.

Beyond a decimated scriptorium and around an agonising succession of corners, Omegon found his way to the lifter shaft. The lifter doors and mesh gate remained open, though the lifter car was lost to the vacuum ravaged depths. Heaving himself onto a maintenance ladder with some difficulty, he began the torturous climb to the surface.

Each rung was a new and singular torment. His abdomen felt as though burning stakes were being hammered through it. Blood slicked his grip, and dripped from his wounds down into the yawning shaft below.

He was approaching the top when he realised that he wasn't the only one climbing the shaft – the gloom echoed with the approaching clatter of a many-legged colossus. Looking down, Omegon could see the brassy glint of a xenos machine making its way unimpeded up the sheer vertical; the stabbing motion of its legs chewed up the metal walls and propelled the monster with ease.

The ladder lurched from its mountings and then began to rock back and forth as the abomination started to chew, its rotating maw of pulverising teeth grinding at the metal. As the ladder twisted, buckled and came away from the shaft wall entirely, Omegon made a desperate leap across the shaft for the hangar level doorway.

With a single gauntlet he managed to reach the ledge, hooking onto it like a grapnel and ignoring the agony in his belly. Reaching up with his other hand too, he hauled himself upwards only to find that the doors were still closed.

Chewed up within the rotating maw of the demiurg machine, the ladder whipped about the open space, slicing through the blackness and thrashing against the walls. The primarch let go of the ledge with one hand and hammered on the closed doors before letting the arm fall again. His gaze fell to the xenos arachnoid looming up beneath his flailing legs. The rotating maw of metal teeth roared its mechanised intention to devour him alive.

Sparks suddenly lit up the gloom as boltfire rippled off the machine's thick brazen armour and interlocking teeth. The mining machine continued unperturbed, the grinding mouth still gaping open, but two braces of Legiones Astartes grenades clunked down from above and disappeared into the belly of the beast.

Many pairs of gauntlets grabbed at his arm and backpack, and heaved him up into the light. The cacophonous din of the grenades detonating within the brazen belly of the beast was suddenly silenced by the forced closing of the lifter doors.

As Omegon was dragged away he could see nothing but blotchy brightness – his plate's autosenses had been momentarily overloaded. As they re-calibrated from the darkness of the shaft to the relative light of the asteroid surface, he could hear legionnaires about him calling for Sergeant Setebos. Gunfire still rattled in the distance.

'He's wounded,' came Isidor's unmistakeable voice.

'I'm fine,' Omegon grunted. 'Status report.'

Goran Setebos appeared, and helped him to his feet.

'But my lor-'

'There's no time, sergeant,' the primarch warned.

The hangar deck was a vision of telekinetic destruction. Omegon could make out a wrecked Thunderhawk, and a mountain of scrap that might once have been a flight of Mechanicum lighters, humpshuttles and Imperial Army transports. Xalmagundi had been thorough, as instructed.

The deck was also littered with bodies: Spartocid sentries, whose responsibility it had been to guard the hangar.

'Stay down, sir,' Isidor said as a las-bolt round seared the air above their heads. Falling to a pained crouch behind the shattered remains of an engine column, the primarch surveyed the scene. The hangar opened out onto the crater that Squad Sigma had observed in hololithic representation. At its centre, thrusting out of the crater like an accusatory finger was the black shaft of the Pylon Array.

'We lost Zantine,' Setebos reported, indicating the armoured body laid out nearby. The legionnaire had a neat bolt hole in the side of his helmet.

'Janic has at least two squads of legionnaire snipers stationed in hides about the crater wall. Those positions weren't on the plans either.'

'What about Xalmagundi?' Omegon asked.

'She's with Volion and Braxus,' Krait told him. 'Out in the crater.'

'There's something else, my lord,' Isidor announced.

'Speak,' Omegon said.

'Captain Ranko and the *Chimerica* are overdue. Long overdue. No vox contact, either.'

'Take me to Xalmagundi,' the primarch ordered.

Leading the way with his blade drawn, Setebos stepped between the larger rocks and regolithic rubble. Omegon followed nearby, still holding a gauntlet across his bolt-chewed abdomen, with Krait and Isidor offering suppression fire close by.

Overhead, Omegon saw the reason that his auto-senses had struggled to adjust outside of the lifter shaft: above the crater, there was not a scrap of void. The raging surface of the Octiss star reigned above them, filling the firmament with an overwhelming, golden radiance. The phase field generators were the only shield standing between Squad Sigma and the intense radiation of the star.

Two more las-bolts rocketed past Omegon, and he gave silent thanks for the star's blinding glare, without which Janic's sniper legionnaires would have had a far easier job of picking them off.

Dropping down into a hollow, Omegon and the legionnaires found Xalmagundi. Volion crouched near the psyker with his boltgun aimed over her shoulder, whilst Braxus complained to himself behind a boulder that was receiving more than its fair share of attention from the legionnaire snipers.

Xalmagundi was knelt in the regolith, with her outstretched fingers in the deep grit and dust. She had been given back her tinted goggles, through which she stared up into the blinding heavens. Her pale skin was streaked with sweat, from her ongoing efforts to shift the trajectory of the great asteroid and send Tenebrae 9-50 into the embrace of 66-Zeta Octiss.

The witchbreed did not look well at all. Black tears rolled down the sides of her face from her large, underworlder eyes.

'Volion?' Omegon said as he skidded down into the boltfire-molested hollow. 'Projection?'

'Both trajectory and velocity are good, my lord,' the legionnaire reported. 'Tenebrae 9-50 and the Pylon Array are destined for the surface of that star.'

'Omegon?' Xalmagundi croaked. 'Is that you?'

The primarch crossed the hollow and knelt down beside the psyker.

'It's me.'

'I can't see a damn thing,' the underworlder told him. Her words were accompanied by a further cascade of midnight tears down her porcelain cheeks. 'I'm blinded.'

'You have done well, Xalmagundi,' the primarch told her. 'Very well.'

'Can your people fix me?' the psyker asked. 'Can they fix my eyes?'

Omegon held out a hand towards Setebos. The sergeant glared at him for a moment before turning over his bolt pistol.

'They can fix you, Xalmagundi,' Omegon promised.

The shot echoed around the crater. The psyker's fragile body fell across the grit and rubble. What was left of Squad Sigma stared at Omegon.

'Permission to speak freely, my lord,' Setebos said.

Omegon settled down in the hollow, his armoured knees deep in the dust.

'Granted, sergeant.'

'That strikes me as a waste,' Setebos told him. 'She could have been of further use to the Legion.'

'That strikes me as sentimental,' Omegon replied. 'Which truly *is* a waste. That's not your reputation, sergeant. It was my impression that there is little you wouldn't do for your Legion. Little you wouldn't sacrifice for victory.'

'And nothing in my conduct on this mission suggests otherwise,' the sergeant returned. 'It's just there seemed no reason to execute the girl.'

'She was expendable, sergeant,' Omegon told him. 'As are we all. Regicide pawns in a greater game.'

'Where is the *Chimerica*?' Isidor asked warily. 'Where's Captain Ranko?'

After a pause, Omegon reached for the clasps on his helmet. The seals disengaged and he tossed it into the dust.

Sheed Ranko regarded Setebos and Squad Sigma with his own eyes. The legionnaires stared at the captain in mute disbelief.

'A greater game,' Ranko repeated.

The captain could still taste his primarch's blood. Omegon had mixed a little of his shed vitality with the wine the pair had taken on the *Upsilon* – an offering of the primarch's thanks, and much more. He had tasted remembrance and come to know the secrets of his gene-sire: early days spent by the twins on their distant homeworld, scheming their way to supremacy; the paradoxical horror of the alien Acuity; the gradual realisation of what would be required of each of them in the years still to come…

Ranko had borne the burden of this offering and had done what his primarch had asked of him a thousand times before. He had taken his place. He had acted like, spoken like, all thought like his primarch.

He had *been* Omegon.

Braxus scrambled down from his position and through the grit of the hollow.

'What's happening?' the legionnaire rumbled.

'Some details of the mission have been withheld from us,' Setebos explained without taking his gaze off Ranko. 'The captain is going to explain them to us now.'

Ranko gazed back at Setebos. Then allowed his eyes to wander among the gathered legionnaires.

'What does your primarch ask of you?' he put to them.

'The *Chimerica* isn't coming, is it sir?' Isidor asked. When Ranko didn't answer, the legionnaire said, 'There is no Thunderhawk extraction. Lord Omegon isn't coming for us.'

'No,' the captain said finally.

'Options?' Setebos said, turning to the squad.

'The garrison Stormbird and other craft have been destroyed,' Krait told him.

'There is only one way off this rock,' Volion told them. 'The boarding torpedo. We have to return to the *Argolid*.'

Setebos grunted. There was little time to discuss alternatives.

'Fastest route?' he asked.

'Temperature's too hot on the unshielded surface,' the legionnaire replied. 'Even in our plate. We have to go back through the base and the mineworks.'

'There's not much chance of that,' Braxus said, checking the ammunition left in his bolter's magazine.

'Better than the chance we have against *that*,' Isidor countered, thrusting a ceramite thumb up at the raging heavens.

'Then we're decided,' Setebos said, rising to his feet.

'You won't make it,' Ranko told them. 'You don't have even one tenth of the time you'd need to make that return journey, even without hostilities.'

'You would ask us to just sit here on this rock and die?' Setebos spat back.

'I ask nothing of you,' Ranko told them honestly. Then he repeated, 'What does your primarch ask of you?'

Setebos and the legionnaires looked at one another. The sergeant nodded.

'Everything.'

EPSILON

Operatus Five-Hydra: Elapsed Time Ω1/138.11//XXB
XX Legion Battle-barge **Beta**

THE COMMAND DECK of the *Beta* was quiet. Officers and retainers went about their business calmly and professionally. There was little indication that the Alpha Legion battle-barge had just launched a massive orbital bombardment and that a crater-dashed mountain range on the planet below was about to be levelled.

Alpharius stood in his ceremonial plate to one side of the bridge, gazing out through the great viewports at the unfolding apocalypse. The agri-moon of Parabellus was an unremarkable planetoid – a red dustball streaked with dark ranges of crop-yielding ziggurat mountains. Even from orbit, the angular terraces were visible, giving the moon the appearance of an abstract map complete with lines and contours.

The primarch watched the largest of the black smears disappear beneath the flare of the first cataclysmic detonation. Down on the surface, entire mountains were collapsing and terrace-farming communities were being annihilated by the heaven-dropped fires of armageddon.

On the other side of the command deck and clad in an identical plate, his twin primarch Omegon regarded the

435

growing armada of Alpha Legion vessels following in the *Beta*'s ponderous wake.

'Something vexes you, brother,' Alpharius called out across the deck.

'No,' Omegon replied.

'It was not a question.'

Omegon turned and crossed the bridge, finding his twin enjoying the spectacle of the moon's destruction. 'If you must know, I was thinking about trust.'

'A valuable commodity,' Alpharius replied, 'that can be both bought *and* misplaced.'

'It was misplaced in Volkern Auguramus, certainly,' Omegon said. Now millions of people have to die as a result.'

'It is most precious – and strongest – when is occurs naturally. Like between brothers,' Alpharius said.

'Tell that to Horus,' Omegon muttered.

Alpharius turned from the destruction and narrowed his eyes at his twin.

'Fair point,' he conceded. 'Trust can be hard to come by, even amongst the closest of kin.' Alpharius let the point hang between them before moving on. 'Volkern Auguramus was a gifted artisan. An operative in whom we placed great trust. He took the gift the Cabal had bequeathed us to aid the Warmaster, and perverted it for his own gain. That is why this unfinished Pylon Array on Parabellus must be destroyed, why the Parabellan farmers must now die with their crops in a nuclear winter. It is also why you left one of the galaxy's foremost Artisan Empyrs gutted like a common thief, in a back alley on San Sabrinus, I presume.'

A legionnaire approached them from the rear of the command deck.

'My lords,' he interrupted, 'the captain wishes you to know that the strike cruisers *Lambda* and *Zeta* are inbound, as well as the *Alpha*.'

'Very good,' Alpharius nodded.

'At least that's the end of the matter, then,' Omegon said, returning to their conversation.

'Perhaps,' Alpharius replied. 'You believe the Tenebrae installation to be in jeopardy?'

'I'm still trying to confirm that.'

'We shall have to do better than that, brother,' Alpharius insisted.

'I interrogated Auguramus myself.'

'No leaks?' Alpharius raised an eyebrow. 'No sponsors? No collaborators? He didn't even sell the designs for the Pylon Array.'

'Parabellus was a personal project, it seems,' Omegon maintained. 'The trail is dead. There are no leads taking us anywhere else. I told you, I handled this myself.'

Alpharius turned to the waiting legionnaire. 'Tell the captain that as soon as the *Alpha* has joined us, to set a secondary course for the Chondax system.'

'Chondax?' Omegon asked, a little surprised. 'The Khan? But what of the original plan?'

'Somebody's interested in Tenebrae, I'm sure of that,' Alpharius muttered. 'Our Navigators tell us the immetereology in that region is calming; our Astropaths believe that messages might get through once more. Our operatives report that the White Scars Expeditionary Fleet has almost completed its compliance and that the Khan could soon make preparations for warp transit.'

'We don't know–'

'We do,' Alpharius said. 'Perhaps it's Malcador, or the Angels of Caliban – *somebody* has gotten to the Tenebrae installation. We must accept that and move on. We must read the moves ahead of time, and position the fleet to the greatest advantage. Dorn will recall the White Scars, and the Khan's loyalty is still firm. If the Warmaster is to succeed then we cannot allow the V Legion to reach Terra. Are we in agreement, brother?'

'Of course,' said Omegon, nodding slowly. 'Aren't we always?'

OMEGA

OMEGON STEPPED INSIDE the confines of his chamber. Like his brother, he did not keep stately rooms or quarters of rank distinction and significance. His dormitory cell was small and sparse, and apart from its temporary nature it was no different from that of any Alpha Legionnaire.

He stood there in the darkness, his ceremonial plate resting against the cell door, and breathed deeply. Whenever he closed his eyes he found the horror of inevitablility waiting for him – the scalding truths that the Acuity had presented to him and Alpharius.

The Third Paradox…

He rubbed his eyes with a finger and thumb; his mind ached with responsibility. He thought on the tortuous network of contacts and relationships, secrets and lies, betrayals and bought allegiances. They were spread out across the galaxy and closing like a net. Omegon saw himself at the knotted heart of the entanglement. He would tug on various threads and exert his influence however he might, but he also felt drawn between the increasing demand of their concerns.

The primarch activated the chamber's floating lumen

orbs. His arming cabinet was open, and his operational plate – a suit indistinguishable from that of any other Alpha Legionnaire – sat on its reinforced frame. His boltgun, blade and pistol were displayed also, as well as his helmet, which seemed to fix him with the dead gaze of its blank optics.

Beside it, covered by a loose shroud, was his *other* suit of armour.

To the casual eye, it was plain and unadorned.

'Let him see the fallen fruit, sitting warm and inviting in the afternoon sun,' Omegon whispered to the empty battle plate. 'And let me be the serpent beneath. Hidden and waiting to strike.'

ABOUT THE AUTHORS

Hailing from Scotland, **Graham McNeill** worked for over six years as a Games Developer in Games Workshop's Design Studio before taking the plunge to become a full-time writer. Graham's written a host of SF and Fantasy novels and comics, as well as a number of side projects that keep him busy and (mostly) out of trouble. His Horus Heresy novel, *A Thousand Sons*, was a New York Times bestseller and his Time of Legends novel, *Empire*, won the 2010 David Gemmell Legend Award. Graham lives and works in Nottingham and you can keep up to date with where he'll be and what he's working on by visiting his website.

Join the ranks of the 4th Company at *www.graham-mcneill.com*

Nick Kyme is a writer and editor. He lives in Nottingham where he began a career at Games Workshop on *White Dwarf* magazine. Nick's writing credits include the Warhammer 40,000 Tome of Fire trilogy featuring the Salamanders, *Fall of Damnos*, the Space Marine Battles novel, his Warhammer Fantasy-based dwarf novels and several short stories.

Read his blog at *www.nickkyme.com*

Gav Thorpe has been rampaging across the worlds of Warhammer and Warhammer 40,000 for many years as both an author and games developer. He hails from the den of scurvy outlaws called Nottingham and makes regular sorties to unleash bloodshed and mayhem. He shares his hideout with Dennis, a mechanical hamster sworn to enslave mankind. At the moment Dennis is under house arrest for attempting to use Skype to hack the world's nuclear arsenals. Gav's previous Black Library novels include fan-favourite *Angels of Darkness* and the epic Sundering trilogy, amongst many others. You can find his website at *www.gavthorpe.co.uk*

Rob Sanders is a freelance writer, who spends his nights creating dark visions for regular visitors to the 41st millennium to relive in the privacy of their own nightmares, including the novels *Atlas Infernal* and *Legion of the Damned*.

By contrast, as Head of English at a local secondary school, he spends his days beating (not literally) the same creativity out of the next generation in order to cripple any chance of future competition. He lives in the small city of Lincoln, UK.

An extract from

Shadows of Treachery

edited by C.Z. Dunn
Available October 2012

One hundred and forty-one days before the Battle of Phall
The Phall System

MY SCREAM WOKE me from the dream.

My eyes snapped open. For a moment I thought I was blind, that I was still on Inwit and that the cold had stolen my sight. Then the chill touch of my armour cut the long-distant past from the present. I was not blind, and my brother had fallen from my hand long ago. I felt cold, as if the dream had reached into reality to wrap me in a memory of Inwit's chill. Ice covered my helmet's eye lenses, turning the view into a frosted haze of slowly shifting light. The ice was pink, the colour of snow melted to slush by blood. Warning runes pulsed at the corner of my eyes, slow, dim red.

Hard vacuum warning...
Armour integrity warning...
Gravity condition zero...
Injury assessment...
Armour power low...

I could not remember where I had been, or how I had come to be freezing while my armour died around me. I blinked, tried to focus my thoughts. Sensations began to creep across my body: a numbed echo of pain from my right leg, a black absence of all feeling from my left hand, a metallic taste on my tongue. *I am alive,* I thought, *and that is enough for now.* I tried to move my right arm, but the armour resisted no matter how hard I strained. I tried to close my left hand. Nothing. I could not even feel my fingers.

I looked back to the weakening pulse of the warning runes. The armour had cycled down to minimum power, turning it into little more than a lifeless shell of metal. It was keeping me alive, but it must have taken severe damage.

I closed my eyes, steadied my pulse. I knew where I was. I was floating free in the vacuum of space. The armour was keeping my body warm, but it was failing. Its power would fade, and I would begin to bleed more heat into the void. My enhanced flesh would last for longer than that of an ordinary human, but the cold would eventually reach my hearts and still their twin beats to silence. It was only a matter of time.

For a second my control almost broke. I wanted to scream, to thrash against the iron embrace of the armour. It was the instinct of a creature trapped beneath the water, its last breath burning in its lungs, the blackness of inevitability closing around its life. I let out a slow breath, forcing the instinct to stillness. I was alive, and while I lived I had a choice.

'Re-power all systems,' I said. A pulse of electric sensation ran through my body as the armour obeyed.

Almost as soon as the armour powered up it began to scream. Sympathetic pain stabbed into my spine. Overlapping warning chimes filled my ears. Angry runes pulsed across my helmet display. I blinked the warnings away and the chimes faded. There were at most a few minutes of power left before the armour became a tomb. I brought my right hand up and scraped the melting ice from the helmet lenses.

Light poured into my eyes, raw and white-edged. I was floating in a vast chamber lit by sunlight that came from a source somewhere behind me. A layer of pink frost covered everything, glittering in the stark light like a sugar glaze on a sweet cake. Small crystals floated all around me, turning slowly with the last of their fading momentum. Irregular shapes coated in rose-coloured rime hung in mid-air across the chamber.

I blink-clicked a faint marker on my helmet display. The vox system activated with a moan of static. I set it to a full spectrum broadcast.

'This is Alexis Polux of the VII Legion.' My voice sounded hollow inside my helmet, and only more static answered me. I set the broadcast to a looped cycle that would last until the power faded. *Perhaps someone will hear. Perhaps there is someone that can hear.*

Something bumped against my shoulder and spun lazily into view: a frozen lump a little wider than my hand. It spun lazily end-over-end. I reached out to knock it away, and it turned over and looked at me with lifeless eyes.

Memory flashed through me: *the hull splitting with an iron roar as the ship spilled from the warp storm's grasp, blood arcing across the deck as debris sliced through the air; a human officer shouting, his eyes wide with terror.* I had been on a ship. I remembered the deck shaking under my feet and the screams of the storm outside the hull.

I jerked my hand back from the severed head, and the sudden movement sent me spinning through the frozen blood spray. The chamber rotated around me. I saw the ice-clogged servitor niches, and mangled banks of instruments. A tiered auspex dais pointed down at me from the floor, its screens and holo-projectors looking like the branches of a tree under winter snow. I tried to steady my momentum but I just spun faster. Warnings began to shriek in my ears.

Power failing…

Power failing…

Power failing…

Sights flicked past me, suffused in the warning rune's ruddy light. There were bodies fused to the walls by layers of blood ice. Sections of splintered yellow armour drifted amongst limbs and shattered bone. Severed bundles of cabling hung from the walls like strings of intestine. Streamers of data-parchment floated beside the foetal shapes of frozen servitors. I spun on and saw the source of the light: a bright white sun shining through a wide tear in the hull. I could see the glittering blue sphere of a planet hung against the star-dotted darkness. Between me and that starlight was a sight that made me stare as my view turned over.

Dead warships lay spread across the void. There were hundreds of them, their golden hulls chewed and split like worried carcasses. Vast strips of armour had peeled back from cold metal guts to show the lattice of chambers and passages within. Mountain-sized hulls had been portioned into ragged chunks. It was like looking at the jumbled remains of a slaughterhouse.

All my brothers are gone, I thought, and felt colder than I had for decades. I remembered Helias, my true brother, my twin, falling into darkness from the end of my fingertips.

Power failing… the warning runes chimed.

Final memories clicked into place. I knew where we had been going: where all of us had been going. I stared at the graveyard and knew one more thing with certainty.

Power failing…

'We have failed,' I said to the silence.

'…respond…' The mechanical voice filled my helmet, broken and raw with static. It took me a heartbeat to reply.

'This is Captain Polux of the VII Legion,' I said as my helmet display dimmed. Bursts of static filled my ears. I could feel the armour stiffening around me, its power finally drained. A quiet numbness began to spread across my body. The helmet display faded to black. I felt something bump into my chest and then fasten around me with a grind of metal. In the prison of my dying armour I could feel myself falling into darkness, falling beyond sight and pain, falling like my brothers. *I am alone in the darkness and cold, and I always will be.*

'We have you, brother,' said a voice that was a machine whisper. It seemed to carry out of a night filled with dreams of the ice and dead ships glittering in starlight.

From 'The Crimson Fist' by John French

THE HORUS HERESY

SHADOWS OF TREACHERY

Edited by Christian Dunn
and Nick Kyme

The *New York Times* bestselling series

Featuring stories from Dan Abnett,
Aaron Dembski-Bowden and Graham McNeill

October 2012 from
www.blacklibrary.com